It was worse than ripping off Fort Knox. The target was a politician. What a worldwide blow-up that would make. The American people were sick of assassinations, and they were not likely to believe any damned committee that tried to lay it in the lap of one crackpot.

MacInnes took a deep breath. "Well, he'll be no great loss to the country." If he didn't appear totally committed, he would never get out of there alive.

Harp relaxed. "Right you are, Mate. Think of how many millions of lives would have been saved if some dedicated German had managed to get Hitler."

MacInnes smiled. "Sure. Whoever knocks off this guy will be doing the country a big service."

MacInnes decided to play it straight . . . Better let them get organized and then nip it in the bud. The nipping depressed him. Before it was done, either he or Harp would be dead.

In collaboration with Lt. Col. C. R. McQuiston, co-inventor of the Dektor Psychological Stress Evaluator, whose years in Army Intelligence provide authentic background for this work of fiction.

decent
and
deadly lies

by
Franklin Bandy

CHARTER
NEW YORK

DISTRIBUTED BY ACE BOOKS
A DIVISION OF CHARTER COMMUNICATIONS INC.
A GROSSET & DUNLAP COMPANY

DECEIT & DEADLY LIES

ISBN: 0-441-06517-1
Charter Books
A Division of Charter Communications, Inc.
A Grosset & Dunlap Company
360 Park Avenue South
New York, New York 10010

Manufactured in the United States.

Dedicated with love to my wife, Beth, whose understanding and help made this book possible, and to my sons, Frank and John, whose achievements are a continuing source of pride.

deceit
and
deadly
lies

CHAPTER ONE

PASSENGERS ENTERING one of the arrival lounges at Kennedy Airport suspected they had a celebrity in their midst. The young woman, with her long, glistening straw-colored hair, her regal bearing, and the upward tilt of her beautiful nose, might have been a famous actress or an heiress secure in the knowledge of at least a billion dollars in the family trust.

Kevin MacInnes, her escort, was tall and slender, with wide shoulders and a trace of military stiffness in his carriage. His glance was alert, skipping quickly around the room, taking in everything and everyone. He was ten or fifteen years older than the young woman. At a glance he might have been a security man hired to protect her.

In contrast with her jet-set Halston suit of cotton poplin and Ferragamo shoes, MacInnes was dressed casually in gray flannels, a darker herringbone sport jacket, and an open-neck shirt of glen plaid. His modishly long light brown hair stopped at his collar in the back; in the front it was styled to cover part of his high forehead. His face was tanned and rugged, with a beak of a nose that jutted like a tomahawk, gray eyes, and a large mouth that seemed to be half-smiling even in repose.

There was no need for his alert watchfulness. Blame it on sixteen years of army intelligence. It was true that the contents of the black attaché case he carried were worth about five thousand dollars, but there was little likelihood that anyone would try to steal it. Nor was the heiress in any danger of being bombed, kidnapped, or otherwise harmed. Her name was Vanessa Peckham, and he had acquired her from a Venezuelan cabinet minister.

MacInnes wasn't sure whether the Venezuelan had tired of Vanessa or Vanessa had tired of Venezuela, but the transfer had occurred without any eruptions of pain or anger on either side. She was twenty-five and one of the most beautiful women he had ever seen. He was forty, and he wanted no more deep emotional attachments. The relationship with Vanessa was perfect. She was expensive, but she was highly intelligent, a good companion, and an incredibly dedicated bedmate.

A cab took them quickly to one of the airport's huge luxury hotels. Their mounds of luggage—

hers Mark Cross and Vuiton, his battered cases from Sam's Army and Navy Store—were quickly stacked on a wheeled luggage carrier by a miniskirted bellgirl who, after a brief stop at the desk for registration, escorted them to a large suite on the eighth floor. MacInnes carried the black attaché case.

It was seven-thirty in the morning and raining. Vanessa yawned, covering her mouth daintily. She took a quick look around the spacious living room, with its fresh flowers, its bucket of ice holding a bottle of champagne, and then she wandered into the large bedroom with its two queen-sized beds.

"How long do we have to stay here?" she asked, yawning again.

MacInnes, following her into the bedroom, said, "Not long. If everything goes well, we can be on the six-fifteen flight back to Palm Beach."

She glanced at the luggage. "Not even overnight?"

He smiled. "On the other hand, we might be here several days—if things do not go well."

She shrugged, then went to the large bed nearest the rain-streaked floor-to-ceiling windows. Pulling down the covers she said, "Well, I'm going back to bed. This is a hell of a time in the morning for a night person to be awake."

He watched idly as she stripped off her clothes. After she gracefully peeled off the last item, her panty hose, she tucked herself between the sheets, pulled the covers up, and lay watching him with a half smile, her big brown eyes wide, waiting to see whether he would join her or leave her to sink back into the slumber that had been so annoyingly interrupted at 3:00 a.m.

Momentarily tempted, he resisted. They were both night people. Sex in the morning was pleasant, but too relaxed and mild, a pale, sputtering little flame compared to the gaudy fireworks of night.

He bent over and kissed her. "Sleep for a couple of hours," he said. "I'll wake you at nine-thirty." He reached into his jacket and pulled out his Mark Cross billfold, a present from Vanessa, and extracted ten new one-hundred-dollar bills. He put them on the night table, tucking one end of the thin pile under the lamp base. "At nine-thirty I want you to get dressed and cab into New York. Go to Bergdorf Goodman or Tiffany's and buy yourself some little thing. Meet me back here for lunch at one o'clock."

She stared at him, unsmiling. "You don't have to do that," she said, looking quickly at the money. "I can prowl the Museum of Modern Art or do any number of things besides shop."

He sat on the edge of the bed. "You love to shop."

"That's true."

"So shop."

She looked at him for a few seconds sleepily, then said, "So okay." Her long lashes descended, and she was asleep before he left the bedroom. He closed the door slowly and quietly.

He ordered coffee sent up, then lit a cigarette and stood at one of the windowed walls staring at the bleak, rain-swept landscape with its runways in the distance, watching the constant rise and descent of the big jets.

MacInnes rarely mixed business with pleasure. At ten o'clock, business would arrive, and at five minutes of ten pleasure would walk out the door on a shopping expedition. Product of a redheaded Irish mother and a dour Scots Presbyterian father, MacInnes was frequently amused at the conflict of these heritages, one tugging him on to wild extravagance, the other pulling toward canny economy. He could easily have booked two suites, one for Vanessa and one for business, and thereby saved about nine hundred dollars. On the other hand, sending her shopping pleased him greatly.

MacInnes could claim two titles. Colonel, for one, as the culmination and termination of his army career. The second was odd. Among his jealous peers in his current business, he was known as the Lie King, a grudging, tongue-in-cheek admission that he was at the top of his particular heap.

Sixteen years a soldier, and now three years into a second career, he was quietly amazed to find himself suddenly at the top. He was the Lie King, without a doubt the most talented, the most sought-after in the entire world. To maintain his position he was unrelenting in the pursuit of truth. If the MacInnes escutcheon were brought up to date, it would bear the motto "The truth shall make you rich." His pursuit of truth had made him rich beyond his wildest fantasies, and he was growing richer every day. His services were sought by heads of state, cabinet ministers, tycoons of industry, governors, famous lawyers, oil millionaires, police commissioners, and sometimes even poor people in trouble. At forty he liked being rich. His fees were extremely high. Being rich could buy you a Vanessa Peckham to provide a fairly satisfying imitation of love.

Money, he told himself, was not his most important objective. Flight from boredom, that was it. The strongest conscious motivating force he could identify. As for his unconscious motives, well, to hell with them. He had no time for analysis. His penance for not delving too deeply was tithing, an ironic tipping of his hat to his upright but now silent Presbyterian father. MacInnes scrupulously gave ten percent of his time to those who deserved, but could not afford, his services.

The coffee arrived. He shrugged off the blank apathy that had settled on him while he stared at the rain and the perpetually soaring and descending jets.

He tipped the waiter, then sat down to enjoy the coffee and another cigarette. He wasn't sure what this morning's assignment involved. There would be a big fee, because the problem was big money. That much he had learned from the sparse, inhibited telephone conversation with Jason Hawthorne, a new and cryptic client. Many of his clients were inclined to be cryptic.

The coffee woke him enough to clear away his apathy. He crushed out his cagarette and busied himself connecting and setting up his equipment. First the black attaché case, which he opened and checked carefully. Then the large reel-to-reel tape recorder. Selecting a few items from his small tool kit, he made some simple changes and connections to the telephone, in the process adding an extension handset to the outlet.

A small dog started barking in the room across the hall. The high-pitched yapping continued, on and on. MacInnes ignored it for a while, but after ten minutes it began to annoy him. He reached into one of his suitcases and dug out his small portable Sony cassette recorder. He put it on a table near the door and switched it to Record.

He went back to the window table and poured a second cup of coffee. The shrill barking continued, MacInnes marveling at the unremitting outpouring. Didn't the little bugger ever have to stop to take a breath? He lit another cigarette and tried to ignore it.

Another ten minutes passed while the dog kept up his performance. Surely he would become exhausted soon? Probably the owner had left him without even water, and the poor beast would stop long enough, at least, to trot to the bathroom and drink from the toilet. Barking was thirsty work.

The dog had amazing powers of endurance. MacInnes finally jumped up, strode to the door, snatching up the Sony recorder enroute, and headed for the elevators.

At the desk in the lobby he placed the recorder gently on the plastic counter. As the clerk sauntered over, MacInnes said, "I want you to hear the kind of obscene things going on in the room across from mine."

The clerk, who had a tiny moustache and bushy hair, looked at the tape recorder and licked his lips nervously. Several guests moved closer, ears at the ready.

"Yes, sir?" asked the clerk.

MacInnes turned the volume dial as high as it would go and punched the key for Play. The high-pitched yapping filled the lobby.

The guests laughed and moved away.

"You expect me to have a business meeting in my suite with *that* going on across the hall?" Amplified, it sounded as though the dog were rehearsing for Carnegie Hall.

The clerk reached to shut off the recorder. "We'll change your room immediately, sir," he said.

MacInnes grabbed the man's wrist before he could touch the Sony. "You'll change the dog's room, not mine." The piercing barks, amplified, bounced off the farthest walls of the lobby, even bringing waitresses in from one of the restaurants to watch and laugh.

"But sir, those people have gone into the city for the day. It would be simpler to move you. Would you mind turning that thing off, sir?"

MacInnes held the clerk's wrist. "I don't give a damn whether they've gone to Alaska. You move that dog. Then when they get back, you move *them*. And you'd better move them a hell of a long way from me. Is that clear?"

The clerk swallowed hard. "Yes, sir. I guess we can do that, sir."

MacInnes released his wrist and turned off the tape recorder. "You really have a lot of nerve, expecting to inconvenience *me*, when those inconsiderate bastards have left an untrained dog to bark his head off all day. You can inconvenience *them*, understand?"

"Yes, sir. I think you're right. I hadn't thought of it that way."

"And get that dog out of there immediately. Within the next ten minutes."

The clerk grinned shakily. "Right away. You can depend on it—we'll do it right away."

MacInnes gave him one last indignant stare, then picked up the tape recorder and headed back to the elevators.

At nine-thirty MacInnes went in the bedroom to wake Vanessa. He sat on the edge of the bed and stroked her golden hair gently, intrigued at its fineness.

She opened her eyes. "Kevin, I have this overpowering urge to sleep." She turned and buried her face in the pillow. "Sleep is the only therapy that will cure me," came out in a muffled mutter.

He pulled the covers back and scooped her from the bed and stood her on reluctant feet, glancing with amused affection at her black triangle. Her hair was dyed so beautifully, by the most expensive hair dressers one would find in Rome, Paris, London, or New York, that even another woman would never guess the color was not natural—unless her big brown eyes gave it away. Did natural blondes ever have big brown eyes? A genetic question he was not prepared to answer, since it really didn't matter.

"Colonel, you are a complete and utter

stinkpot, sir," she said, stalking off to the bathroom. Military men were brutes in Vanessa's book. Lie kings were kind.

Jason Hawthorne arrived just as Vanessa was leaving. She gave him a brilliant smile and continued on down the corridor. Hawthorne stared for a few seconds at her long, gleaming hair, which bounced a little as she walked away.

"My secretary," said MacInnes, ushering him in.

Hawthorne was a ruddy-faced man with a gray, neatly trimmed moustache. Yale, class of '29, probably, but then MacInnes was mildly prejudiced, having gone to a state university.

"Lucky man," said Hawthorne, shaking hands.

MacInnes smiled. "Just toss your coat anywhere and make yourself comfortable," he said.

Hawthorne struggled out of his wet Brooks raincoat and handed it to MacInnes to hang up. "I don't know why we couldn't have met in my office. How long will it take?"

The coat disposed of, MacInnes settled into one of the comfortable lounge chairs. "It's easier this way." Easier for MacInnes. "As for how long, I can't answer that until I know the problem."

"My chauffeur is waiting in the lobby."

MacInnes stared at him blankly. The chauffeur was his problem.

Hawthorne selected the end of the sofa, inspected it for cleanliness, and then sat down. "Well, I suppose we should get down to business. As you know, Josh Rothstein recommended you to me."

MacInnes reached for his cigarettes. "How is Josh?"

Hawthorne fumbled in his coat pocket for a leather case and selected a long, thin cigar. "Fine. I think we'll be referring to him shortly as Judge Rothstein."

MacInnes smiled. "I'm delighted to hear it." A good choice for the New York bench. Josh was not only highly qualified, but incorruptible. MacInnes tried to avoid forming hasty opinions, but he intuitively disliked Hawthorne and wondered why Josh Rothstein would be his friend. Perhaps they were merely acquaintances and Josh was trying to do MacInnes a favor.

Hawthorne clipped the end of his cigar with a small gold instrument. "The problem I have is quite serious. I'm wondering if you have the capability of solving it."

MacInnes stared at him, tongue in cheek. "Well, if I fail, you can always consult a Ouija board."

Hawthorne frowned. "I'm not joking. This is an extremely important, and an extremely confidential, matter."

Hawthorne, MacInnes decided, was a pompous ass. "I'm sorry if I seemed flippant. However, if I can't help you, there'll be little left for you but clairvoyance. My black box stops short of that."

Hawthorne glanced over at the equipment MacInnes had set up. "So that's the famous black box. Maybe I should buy one myself. Save a lot of money."

"That you can do," MacInnes said. "However, the skill of the operator has a great deal to do with the correct interpretation of the results.'' Why was he being so damned modest? The fact was, he was a genius. For a hundred dollars, Hawthorne could hire a tolerably good psychological-stress evaluator operator. If the case was at all tricky, the answer would be ''Results are inconclusive.'' In his first years in the army, MacInnes's career had almost been ruined by an inept polygraph operator, a man who did not have the courage to say ''The results are inconclusive'' but settled for a bad guess.

''Your minimum fee of ten thousand dollars seems a bit steep,'' said Hawthorne.

MacInnes frowned. ''It can go much higher, depending on the job.''

Hawthorne lit the cigar he had been holding, using (of course) a gold Dunhill lighter. ''I suppose we had better get down to the case.''

''When you're ready,'' said MacInnes. For ten thousand dollars he could have the whole morning.

''Here's the situation. My partners and I are building what is, in effect, a small city. A vast area of condominiums, town houses, two massive shopping centers, and so on. There is a five-hundred-acre tract we simply must have to complete this project.'' He puffed on his cigar, sending a couple of nicely formed rings in MacInnes's direction. ''We must buy this five-hundred-acre tract. It has on it the lake we need, and it has the right terrain for the golf course. It already has a number of units of garden apartments on it. The fair market price would be about four million. The owner knows we want it, and we therefore expected to pay six million. He is standing firm on ten million.''

MacInnes nodded, crushing out his cigarette.

''We've tried to dicker him down without success. He's giving us a royal shafting. However, time is getting short. The deal must be consummated. We are prepared, I must say with great reluctance, to pay the ten million.''

''Hmmm,'' said MacInnes, rubbing his chin.

''Now we've heard, and this is completely unsubstantiated, that Bill Edmunds, the owner, has a cash-flow problem. It may be that he *has* to sell. For reasons too involved and irrelevant to explain, our deadline is tomorrow. We must make a final offer and stand firm on it.''

''I see.''

Hawthorne gestured with his cigar. ''It is our considered opinion, an opinion reached after much discussion, that Edmunds will take less than ten million. The question is, how much less?''

''Hmmm.''

''We can't afford to blow the deal. If we have to buy that five hundred acres in another contiguous area, it's going to cost us twice ten million.''

''Hmmm.''

Hawthorne puffed his cigar vigorously. ''Is that all you can say 'Hmmm'?''

MacInnes laughed. ''I'm thinking.'' It would be easy enough to find out whether Edmunds would take less. To find out exactly how much less, that was a tough one. But then he was paid to solve tough ones.

"Your job is to find out how low we can go in our final offer. Nine million, eight million? Seven million?" He glanced hopefully at MacInnes when he mentioned the last figure. Hopeful, but with a smile that said, "It would be nice, but we're approaching the impossible now."

MacInnes stood up. "I understand." He strolled to the windows and stared at the drizzle still streaking the glass. "This is a tough one. I can guarantee to find out whether he will take less. Pinpointing the exact amount is another story."

"Josh said you could do it."

"Tell him thanks."

MacInnes jammed his hands into his pockets and turned to face Hawthorne. "I think we'll handle this one entirely on a contingency basis. Forget the ten thousand. If I fail, you owe me nothing. If I succeed, you'll pay me ten percent of what I save you."

"Ten percent!"

MacInnes stared at him blandly.

"Why, man, we fully expect to get him down to nine million. That would make your fee *a hundred thousand dollars*!"

MacInnes shrugged. "So why don't you offer him that and save yourself a hundred thousand? Of course, you may miss out on saving another million or two."

Hawthorne stroked his moustache thoughtfully with his forefinger. "I don't like it."

The two men stared at each other, silent for a moment, eyes locked. Hawthorne shifted his glance first.

"Tell you what," said MacInnes. "I'll try to be fair about this. If he won't go below nine million, I'll accept the ten-thousand-dollar minimum. If he goes below nine million, I want ten percent of the entire amount saved. Ten percent of the difference between ten million and the selling price."

Hawthorne smiled. "You're not going to make me offer him eight million, nine hundred and ninety-nine thousand?"

MacInnes laughed. "No. We'll say it must be at least a hundred thousand under nine million. That way you'll be covered, right?"

Hawthorne thought about it, again stroking his moustache, this time with his little finger. Forefinger, rejection, up yours, MacInnes; little finger, acceptance, we'll sit down and have a cup of tea, old buddy. MacInnes, amateur psychiatrist, at work predicting. Actually, in college he had thought of becoming a psychiatrist, but he had given up the idea. It required more years than he could afford to be in school.

"I think I'll go with that," said Hawthorne.

"Ten percent."

"Agreed. Under the conditions we mentioned."

MacInnes strolled over to the rather elaborate imitation Florentine desk provided by the hotel and sat down. He uncapped his fountain pen and found some stationery in the first drawer. "All right, let's get down to work. How well do you know this Edmunds?"

"Quite well. We belong to the same yacht club. Used to play tennis together before my legs gave out. Play golf occasionally."

"Good." MacInnes scribbled a few words. "How did he make all his money? Real estate?"

Hawthorne shook his head. "Not really. He inherited a lot, and he has managed to expand the family fortune greatly in many different ventures. For instance, he owns a string of auto dealerships in about ten states."

"Hates Ralph Nader, I would imagine?"

"Vehemently."

MacInnes wrote some more, this time more slowly. "Drink?"

"Moderately."

"Women?"

"What do you mean?"

MacInnes smiled. "I mean, does he have a mistress, play the field, or is he strictly a homebody?"

Hawthorne shook his head. "My dear fellow, Edmunds is my age, sixty-eight. He's a widower, and if he has any energy left for erotic activities, I am not aware of it. Of course, I wouldn't rule it out. Those sex professors out in Indiana claim . . ." He paused. "But that's neither here nor there."

"How about food? Gourmet or ordinary?"

Hawthorne gestured impatiently. "Gourmet, I suppose, though he doesn't make a thing of it. How in the devil's name does all this relate to the question at hand?"

MacInnes scraped his chair around slightly to face Hawthorne. "I need to have a good picture of this man's personality. The conversation I am going to prepare for you must be delicately structured. It has to seem perfectly natural, but it has to also give me clear indications of various levels of stress."

Hawthorne put his cigar in the ashtray and left it to burn out. It was down to about two inches. "In other words, you're going to have me telephone him, converse with him in a way you have prepared, then put this conversation through your black box, and out will come the answer?"

If it were only that simple, thought MacInnes.

"Mr. Hawthorne—"

"Call me Jase."

He was being accepted as one of the elite. He nodded. "All right, Jase, as I was about to explain, I'll put your telephone conversation through the black box. The pen in the box will make a lot of confusing marks on a roll of graph paper. I will then study those marks. I will suffer the tortures of the damned trying to figure out exactly what they mean." *Tortures of the damned,* one of his father's favorite phrases. "You can call me Mac if you wish."

Hawthorne cocked his head to one side. "Good. No need to be so formal."

"I might also explain that this black box is a Dektor PSE, for psychological-stress evaluator. It measures the muscle microtremors in the voice. Your voice may sound perfectly natural when you're under stress, but there are subtle physiological changes. This very sensitive electronic device picks them up."

"I see," said Hawthorne, looking puzzled. "But all sorts of things cause stress. Anger, fear . . ."

This, of course, was the real problem. No machine on its own was a true lie detector; it became one only through the man who asked the questions and interpreted the answers. MacInnes said, "That's where the professional ability of the operator comes in. Sometimes it is easy to spot deception on the graph; at other times, very difficult. What it boils down to is the ability to spot subtle differences in stress, weigh them carefully, compare them, and so on."

"I see."

MacInnes smiled. "I happen to be the best."

Hawthorne raised one of his thin gray eyebrows. "I like your modesty."

MacInnes cocked his head, smiling. "Only by way of explaining why my fees are so high." He reached for a cigarette. "After all, the Shah of Iran asked me to come to Tehran today. I had to put him off to take care of your problem. I try to honor prior commitments." A white lie, but he *had* solved a problem for the Shah only last month.

Both of Hawthorne's gray eyebrows rose. "Is that so!"

MacInnes tried to look modest. It was not easy. The pause lengthened, and he finally said, "Well, let's get back to work."

Hawthorne nodded.

"Just how close are you to Edmunds?"

Hawthorne said, "Good friends." He shrugged. "Of course, when it comes to business . . ." He paused for a few seconds. "You might say all's fair in love and war."

"Business is war?"

Hawthorne smiled. "I'm speaking of love. I think we both love money—or rather, the making of money."

MacInnes picked up his pen, amused. Hawthorne was refreshingly honest. "Well, let me explain what I am going to do. This conversation I'm attempting to structure, I'll write down the subjects I want you to cover. Certain sentences and phrases will be underlined. These you must use exactly as I have written them. The other material you'll cover in your own way, in your own words. Just try to stick to the subject."

Hawthorne fished out another cigar. "I understand."

"It will take me a while to work this out. Say a half hour. If you'd care to have coffee, or"—MacInnes glanced at the champagne—"if champagne in the morning suits your taste, help yourself."

Hawthorne laughed. "Heavens, no!" He stood up. "I'll take a stroll in the lobby." He glanced at his watch. "I suppose we'll be at least another hour. I'll send Peter on a couple of errands."

MacInnes was already busy writing when Hawthorne left, closing the door quietly. He wrote quickly, in a loose scrawl, crossing out frequently. After finishing several pages he lit a cigarette and carefully read what he had written. Then he tore the pages up and started again.

The coffee was now lukewarm, but he poured another cup and sipped it, this time writing more slowly.

Finally, after a number of alterations, he was

satisfied. He recopied what he had written, writing in large, well-formed letters so that Hawthorne could read it without difficulty. He glanced at his watch. Exactly a half hour had passed since Hawthorne left.

There was a fast rapping. They might have coordinated their watches. He stood up and went to the door.

Hawthorne came in jauntily, smiling. "Are we ready?"

MacInnes said, "You're practically on stage." He handed Hawthorne the script. "Read this over and see if there is anything you can't handle naturally."

Hawthorne settled into his original position on the sofa and read the material carefully. When he finished he thought for a few seconds. "No, this seems clear enough. No problem."

MacInnes said, "Good. When you finish a page, lift it off and put it to one side carefully. I'd like to avoid any paper-rustling noises."

Hawthorne stood up. "I'll try to remember. Shall I call him now? Is your equipment ready?"

MacInnes moved to the table where he had set up the tape recorder and the PSE. He had also placed the extension handset there. "Yep, all set. I'll be listening in. If I signal you by tapping the plastic with my fingernail, make some excuse to ask Edmunds to hold a minute. Tell him your cigar has set the ashtray on fire or something. Then cover the mouthpiece tightly with your palm. I may have additional instructions."

Hawthorne licked his lower lip nervously.

"God, this is complicated."

MacInnes said, "Don't worry. I probably won't stop you."

Hawthorne nodded, dialing the operator. He got through to Edmunds quickly.

"Bill, how are you?" he said, his eyes fastened on MacInnes's script.

"All right. How are you, Jase?" The voice was subdued.

"How's your golf game? Still breaking a hundred and fifty?"

"That's all I need to beat you, you old fart." The voice picked up animation.

Hawthorne laughed. "I've just figured out how you developed that swing of yours."

"Yeah, how?"

"Watching an old lady trying to dodge a taxi."

There was the sound of a faint snort. "My twelve-year-old grandson writes better comedy material than that. I'll send him over to see you."

Hawthorne laughed nervously, glancing at the papers before him. "Yes, well, joking aside, I just called to see whether you'd like to have lunch with me one day next week."

There was another pause. "Sure, why not?"

"Good. I'll have my girl call your girl Monday and set a definite date. Incidentally, have you heard what Nader is up to now?"

"That son of a bitch!"

"I hear he's lobbying for a bill to make rear windshield wipers mandatory on every car, plus three built-in roll bars."

A moan that resembled the sad wail of a tomcat

chasing a female in heat came over the wire. "That goddamned son of a bitch! He's going to wreck the whole goddamned industry! Pretty soon nobody will be able to buy cars but the damned Arabs."

"Hold it, you'll blow a gasket!" said Hawthorne.

"That son of a bitch!"

Hawthorne was silent for a few seconds. "Bill, I probably shouldn't mention this, but, ah, well, we've been friends for a long time. I've been hearing some very disturbing rumors about you."

"What? What rumors?"

"I've been hearing that your cash position is very weak. Now Bill, if there is anything I can do, I want you to know—"

Hawthorne was interrupted by a yell. "What lousy bastard is spreading that kind of crap about me! Who? I demand to know!"

Hawthorne cleared his throat gently. "Bill, you know I can't divulge . . . All I can say is, it comes from a very reliable source."

"Reliable source, hell!" Edmunds yelled. "That's a goddamned lie. And when you see your reliable source, tell him that when I find out who he is, and *I will,* that I'm going to haul him into court."

Hawthorne idly scratched his ear, glancing at MacInnes with a smile. "Well, fine," he said finally. "Calm down. I'm glad to hear you're in good shape. No problems, eh?"

"Absolutely none. Things couldn't be better."

There was another pause. "Bill," said Hawthorne, "about this Blue Sea Village thing . . ."

"I was wondering when we'd get to that."

"My partners still think your price of ten is the biggest ripoff since the Great Train Robbery."

Edmunds chuckled. "You'll pay it."

Hawthorne's voice became sharp. "Don't depend on it. We're having new plans drawn. We're seriously considering eliminating that whole section."

Edmunds was silent for a few seconds. "The attorney general won't care for that." His voice was again subdued.

Hawthorne said, "That's the least of our worries. We can always prepare a new prospectus for the attorney general and offer refunds on the sales we've already made."

"Be a pretty messy situation though."

Hawthorne winked at MacInnes. "Of course, we'd prefer not doing it. But there's a matter of principle involved. We damned well don't want to pay ten million for property that's worth four."

"Horseshit."

"My partners believe you'd be *very* happy to get six million."

Another tomcat wail erupted. "Tell your partners to go fornicate with themselves. Jase, I want to make one thing perfectly clear. I will not take six million for that property. I will not take seven million. I will not take eight. I will not take nine. I will not take nine-five. I will not even take nine-nine." Edmunds paused, out of breath. "I will take ten. Is that clear?"

MacInnes tapped the mouthpiece with his fingernail.

Hawthorne said, "Excuse me a second, Bill. I dropped my cigar on the carpet." He covered the mouthpiece and looked at MacInnes. Covering his own mouthpiece, MacInnes said, "Break it off now. Don't discuss the property any more."

Hawthorne removed his palm. "Okay, Bill, found it. Well, what can I say? I've got to trot off to a board meeting. We'll be in touch about lunch next week, right?"

Edmunds seemed confused. He had expected more argument. He said, "Well, ah, okay, I suppose." There was a brief pause. "Okay, see you for lunch."

Hanging up, Hawthorne breathed a big sigh. "Thank God that's over. I'm afraid I wasn't cut out to be an actor."

MacInnes lit a cigarette. "You did exceptionally well. We had a bit of luck, too."

"How so?"

"His enumerating the various amounts he won't take."

Hawthorne nodded. "Ah, yes, of course. I can see how that would help."

MacInnes stood up and stretched. Last night had been very short on sleep. "Now I'll need an hour or so to analyze my charts. I hate for you to have to sit around and twiddle your thumbs. Why don't you take off and come back after lunch— say, two o'clock?" He stifled a yawn. "At that time I'll be able to advise you on the amount of your final offer."

Hawthorne groaned softly. "Back to the city and all the way out here again? Can't you call me or come to my office?"

MacInnes shook his head. "My equipment is all hooked up here. And it's just possible that we may have to call him again before making a final decision." He smiled. "Besides, I intend to monitor your offer and his answer. My fee is involved."

Hawthorne stared at him, lips tight. "Trusting fellow."

MacInnes said, "Why should I trust you, Jase? I've never done business with you before. I hardly know you. Would you trust me in similar circumstances?"

Hawthorne stood up. "Yes, I would. I'm very intuitive about character."

MacInnes walked him to the door. "Thank you. Nevertheless, we may really have to call Edmunds again. Think of the money I'm going to save you, and the inconvenience won't seem so great."

After Hawthorne left, MacInnes paced the big living room, sleepy and reluctant to work on the charts. Heavy eyed and yawning, he finally cleared the large table and prepared to attack the ten feet of chart paper the PSE had rolled out into a billowing pile on the floor. He set the tape recorder on Rewind, and when it clicked off, he began replaying the conversation, stopping the tape frequently to make abbreviated notes under the key areas of the chart markings.

"That son of a bitch!" and other remarks about Ralph Nader gave him a good sampling of normal stress. Then the conversation proceeded to rumors about Edmunds's cash position. "What? What rumors?" blocked out with heavy stress. Fear. It continued through Edmunds's threats to haul the bastard into court.

Hawthorne's "I'm glad to hear you're in good shape. No problems, eh?" brought an answer that showed even heavier stress: "Absolutely none. Things couldn't be better." Very heavy. Deception indicated, definitely! Edmunds was in trouble, no doubt about it.

MacInnes poured himself a glass of water and moved on to "We're seriously considering eliminating that whole section." Edmunds's answer, "The attorney general won't care for that," showed lighter stress, normal anxiety.

So far, it was too easy. Settling the amount to offer would be the tough part.

"My partners believe you'd be *very* happy to get six million."

"I will not take six million." Stress, definitely. "I will not take seven million." More stress. "I will not take eight." Stress continued to rise. It went up with each figure, blocking heavier with nine, nine-five, nine-nine, and "I will take ten. Is that clear?"

MacInnes crushed out his cigarette, disgusted. The damned thing was no challenge at all. Any reasonably bright recent graduate from Dektor's PSE school could have handled this one.

Still, he had structured a damned perfect conversation. The subject had snapped at every piece of bait offered and, in the final instance, had jumped right out of the water into the boat and said, "I'm Patsy, fry me."

He glanced at his watch. A quarter till twelve. Time for a quick nap before Vanessa returned. He strolled into the bedroom, kicked off his loafers, and collapsed on Vanessa's bed. In seconds he drifted off to sleep, her faint perfume pleasant in his nostrils.

The phone woke him at one o'clock.

"Kevin, guess who I ran into at Bergdorf! Tony and Ceci! We're having lunch at Côte Basque. Can you join us?"

Yawning, MacInnes said, "No, I'm sorry, I can't, love. My client will be back here at two o'clock. Have fun."

"Oh, please. Can't you call him and make the appointment later?"

MacInnes yawned again. "I think not, dear. I want to get this thing cleaned up this afternoon. Give my regards to Tony and Ceci." Regards, hell. A couple of worthless twits with too much money and nothing to do but trot around the world being beautiful people. So *in*. Bores unlimited. He wouldn't travel a half block to see either of them, much less twenty miles into the city. And was Ceci really there, or was it a tête-á-tête with Tony—or some other handsome, feckless, beautiful fellow? Vanessa could be sure he wouldn't come when she mentioned Tony and Ceci. Jealousy, jealousy. Not allowed. *Verboten. Prohibido. Defendu. Vietato.* He didn't own her. It was only a lease with a one-minute cancellation clause.

One thing about being in army intelligence for sixteen years, he had acquired four languages. If she should leave him, sorrow would follow. *Dolor, chagrin, kummer, dolore.*

She sighed, made kiss-kiss sounds, and hung up.

He dozed for another half hour and then sleepily called room service for a club sandwich and a bottle of Beck's beer.

At two-fifteen Hawthorne arrived, redolent of good Scotch and a fine lunch. He removed his raincoat, draped it over the back of a chair, and resumed his seat at the end of the sofa.

"Well, what's the good word?"

MacInnes yawned and collapsed into a comfortable chair. "Your final offer is six million. Make sure he understands that the offer is irrevocable. That there will be no more bargaining."

"Six million!"

MacInnes nodded.

"Are you certain? This is a very important decision." Hawthorne shifted uncomfortably on the sofa. "My God, I wouldn't want to kill this deal. Would it be safer to . . .?" His voice trailed off.

MacInnes smiled. "I know it's important to you. I wouldn't advise you to act on a wild-assed guess. If there was any doubt in my mind, I'd suggest you play it safe with a higher offer."

This time Hawthorne stroked his moustache nervously with two fingers. MacInnes decided he'd like to be in a high-stakes poker game with Hawthorne. The moustache stroking offered splendid possibilities.

"How can you be so sure?"

MacInnes rubbed his chin. "For one thing, he's definitely in trouble. Second, he started lying at six, and his stress signals went up with every figure."

Hawthorne shook his head. "I don't know. I really wonder how much we can depend on this, this instrument."

MacInnes said, "You're depending on me, not

28

the instrument. I didn't get the reputation I have by giving poor advice." He shook a cigarette out and held it unlighted. "If the charts were inconclusive, I'd tell you so. Once in a while they are, and I don't carry around any damned crystal ball. I'd say to you, 'This is only an educated guess. Act on it at your own risk.'"

Hawthorne stood up, as though wondering whether he should go to the bathroom or go home. Then he sat down again. "Six million . . ."

MacInnes lit the cigarette. Hawthorne's lack of confidence was beginning to irritate him. "Pick your own number if you're afraid," he said.

"You're sure it's six?"

"Definitely."

Hawthorne pulled himself to his feet reluctantly and walked to the phone, hesitating, eyes averted, as though the instrument were some obscene thing a right-minded chap wouldn't look at closely.

He picked up the phone and again got through to Edmunds quickly. MacInnes picked up the extension. Hawthorne wasted no time with badinage. They both knew the purpose of the call.

"Bill, I've had a long meeting with my partners. We're prepared to make a final offer. This is a take-it-or-leave-it offer. Plan A, you accept it; Plan B, you reject it and we take alternative steps."

Edmunds broke in. "Jase, for Christ's sake, what the hell are you trying to say to me?"

Hawthorne cleared his throat. "What I'm trying to tell you is that Plan B won't wait. I hate to press you, but we'll have to have your answer immediately."

Edmunds was silent for a few seconds. "All right, so what's your offer?"

"Six million. Not one penny more."

There was a crash, then silence. Edmunds came back on the line. "Sorry, the phone slipped out of my hand. Fell on the table." He sighed gustily. "Jase, if you weren't an old friend I'd hang up on you. Your offer is ridiculous; it's insulting. Tell your partners to get busy on Plan B." There was a loud click as Edmunds hung up.

CHAPTER TWO

HAWTHORNE REPLACED THE handset slowly, then turned to face MacInnes. His ruddy cheeks had paled around the edges. "*Now* see what you've done."

MacInnes expelled smoke toward Hawthorne, smiling. "He dropped the phone, didn't he?"

"What the devil difference does that make? You've put me in a very embarrassing and a very costly situation." He almost raised his voice, he was so angry.

MacInnes said, "Your office knows where you are, I suppose?"

"Of course they know where I am."

"I suggest you telephone and make sure that when Edmunds calls back he is given this number, plus room 867. Not my name. It's just possible he's heard of me."

"He won't call back."

MacInnes glanced at him impatiently. "He *will* call back." How could Hawthorne be so stupid? "He's frightened and angry. Give him five or ten minutes to face up to reality."

Hawthorne stood up. "He won't call back. I know Bill Edmunds."

"Get in touch with your office, dammit."

With a sour grimace, Hawthorne called his office and gave instructions.

MacInnes strolled over to the champagne bucket and after some nervous fiddling, managed to pop the cork. He poured a glass.

"Have some champagne and relax," he said, offering it to Hawthorne.

"Don't care for any, thank you." The *thank you* was definitely hostile.

MacInnes sipped his own champagne. "Give him ten minutes. He won't wait too long. If he waits too long, he's putting himself into a position of being offered five million, five."

Hawthorne walked stiffly to the sofa. "The *position* is that we are now going to have to pay him the full ten, or possibly even more. Also my partners are going to have to call him and say that I had no authority to cut off negotiations." He sat down, holding his back ramrod straight. "In short, I've been made a thorough fool of." He looked pointedly at his watch. "I'll give it ten minutes, no more."

MacInnes carried his champagne to the glass

walls overlooking the runways. The rain had stopped, though the sky was still overcast, leaden, depressing. Could he possibly have been wrong? The PSE didn't lie, but could his interpretation have been wrong? Edmunds's cash position could be bad without being *that* bad. But why lie about the amounts he would accept? There had been no gray area. Deception had been indicated with startling clarity.

If MacInnes was wrong, there was only one possible answer. Sometime between 10:50 A.M. and 2:20 P.M., Edmunds had had another offer for the property—an offer equal to or better than the six million. He shrugged. It would be a highly unlikely coincidence. But these things did happen.

Hawthorne stood up. "Ten minutes. I have no more time for this nonsense." He went to the chair and picked up his raincoat.

MacInnes strolled over to the door and stood blocking it. "Give it another ten minutes, Mr. Hawthorne. My fee is involved in this matter, and I'm entitled to a reasonable time to resolve it."

"Your fee!" yelled Hawthorne. "Man, you've cost us millions, and you have the nerve to talk about a fee!" He approached to within two feet of MacInnes. "Stand aside, dammit! I'm leaving!"

MacInnes remained solidly in his path.

"Stand aside, man!"

MacInnes said, "Before you leave, I have a few things to say to you." He held up his forefinger. "One, Edmunds *will* call within the next ten or fifteen minutes." He extended the middle finger, thrusting them both close to Hawthorne's face.

"Two, when he does call, I'll tell him that the six-million offer was a big bluff, that you're terribly sorry you tried to con him—and that you'll undoubtedly go to ten if he holds out until tomorrow."

There was an extended silence as the two men glared at each other. MacInnes could almost hear the wheels whirring in Hawthorne's mind. He would go to the lobby, of course, and divert any call to room 867 from Edmunds—not that it would be necessary.

MacInnes said, "I find your whole attitude highly suspicious. I think you're trying to cut me out of my commission. You want to leave here and make your own deal." He loomed threateningly over Hawthorne. "If you were not sixty-eight years old, I would be powerfully tempted to punch you right in the nose."

"Are you threatening me with physical violence?"

"No, I'm explaining why you are being *spared* physical violence."

The phone rang. MacInnes stepped aside and whipped the door open. "Go, Mr. Hawthorne. Get the hell out of my suite."

Hawthorne danced off toward the phone, weaving and bobbing, half-convinced that this maniac would catch him and actually throw him out of the room.

He snatched the handset off its cradle. "Hawthorne speaking."

MacInnes picked up the extension, smiling.

"Jase, this is Bill Edmunds. About your offer . . ."

"Yes, Bill?" Hawthorne's voice was coolly un-enthusiastic.

"You guys are trying to crucify me."

Hawthorne said, "It's a fair price, Bill, and there's a hell of a good profit in it for you."

"Make it six-five and you've got a deal."

Hawthorne coughed apologetically. "Sorry, Bill. When we say 'final offer,' it means just that."

The silence at the other end stretched out so long that MacInnes wondered if Edmunds had fainted. Finally, Edmunds said, "All right. I suppose it'll have to be six."

MacInnes leaned back, relaxed, while they discussed the details of closing the deal.

The call completed, Hawthorne turned to MacInnes with a big smile. "It seems that I owe you an apology."

MacInnes nodded, unsmiling.

"I should have had more confidence. You did a fine job." Two fingers on the moustache again. Nervous, decided MacInnes. "You'll have your check for one hundred and ten thousand dollars first thing tomorrow." He laughed lightly. "What a fee for a day's work!"

MacInnes bit his lower lip. Steady there. Keep calm. "The check will be for four hundred thousand dollars, Mr. Hawthorne."

"Four hundred thousand! For one day's work?"

"That was our agreement."

Hawthorne shook his head. "My understanding is that it was to be ten percent up to one hundred and ten thousand."

MacInnes stared at him long and hard. "Was that really your understanding, Mr. Hawthorne?"

Hawthorne shifted his eyes. "Absolutely."

MacInnes went over to the Uher tape recorder and rewound the tape to the approximate location he wanted. Hawthorne's voice came up loud and clear. "Josh Rothstein recommended you." He ran it forward fractionally until he reached his own voice saying, "If he goes below nine million, I want ten percent of the difference between ten million and the selling price." He allowed the conversation to continue until Hawthorne said, "Agreed. Under the conditions we mentioned."

Hawthorne had been staring, his mouth open. "You taped *our* conversation. Isn't that against the law?"

Without replying, MacInnes changed the recorder's speed, slowing it to fifteen-sixteenths inch per second, and switched the machine to put the conversation through the Dektor. He watched the chart as Hawthorne said, "Agreed. Under the conditions you mentioned." Heavy blocking. He ripped the chart paper off and turned to Hawthorne.

"No, it is not against the law. If it were against the law, you'd be in it up to your neck for doing it to Bill Edmunds."

MacInnes turned back and ran the tape forward at the regular speed until he came to "Was that really your understanding, Mr. Hawthorne?" He again slowed the speed and put Hawthorne's answer, "Absolutely," through the PSE. Heavy blocking.

He turned to Hawthorne. "Hawthorne, you're a cheat and a liar." He shoved the charts under

Hawthorne's nose. "You were lying when you said you agreed to the terms I specified. You were lying when you said you understood the maximum was to be one hundred and ten thousand. I'm surprised. I thought you were an honorable man."

"I *am* an honorable man," said Hawthorne, clawing his moustache with all five fingers.

MacInnes said, "It would appear not. I'm thoroughly disgusted with you."

Hawthorne jammed his hands into his jacket pockets. "My partners would think I was out of my cotton-picking mind paying you *four* hundred thousand dollars. Even a hundred thousand—"

MacInnes said, "I've saved you three million, six hundred thousand dollars—*after* you pay me the four hundred thousand."

"I know, but still, it's exorbitant. I might get them to agree to two hundred thousand."

MacInnes lit a cigarette. "You're not paying me two hundred thousand. In fact, you're not paying me four hundred thousand. You're not paying me anything."

Hawthorne's eyebrows went up. "I'm not?"

"No. I don't do business with crooks."

"Now, see here—"

"I'm sure that both Bill Edmunds *and* the attorney general will be happy to know what sort of slippery characters are involved in this Blue Sea Village thing."

"Now, just a minute—"

MacInnes turned his back on Hawthorne. "Goodbye Mr. Hawthorne. Our meeting is over. I must remember to tell Josh to be more careful of the people he associates with. Especially since he's going to be a judge."

"Now, look—"

"Goodbye!"

"Listen to me. You can't call a man a crook because he wants to bargain a little."

MacInnes pivoted to face Hawthorne. "Oh, it's just bargaining we're doing? Well now, that's different. I didn't understand it was bargaining we were doing." His mother's Irish lilt was showing through.

"Sure. You can't blame a man for trying to deal a little?"

MacInnes smiled. "Since we're bargaining, I'll say my fee is now five hundred thousand."

Hawthorne swayed dizzily. High blood pressure, probably, MacInnes thought. "Listen, let's cut out all this nonsense. I'll give you the four we agreed on."

"Five. Apparently we had no agreement."

"Oh for God's sake!"

"In exactly one minute it goes up to six hundred thousand." MacInnes glanced at the sweep hand of his watch.

Hawthorne collapsed into a chair.

"Thirty seconds left," said MacInnes.

Hawthorne held up his hand weakly. "Please. We'll make it five." He stood up shakily. "You'll have a certified check from us in the morning."

MacInnes said, "Sit down, Mr. Hawthorne. I'll have a notarized statement of the debt from you this afternoon, accompanied by your personal check for five hundred thousand dollars. Tomorrow morning you'll give me the certified check, and I'll return your personal check.''

Hawthorne sat down, holding his head. ''You don't have to go through all this nonsense. My word is my bond. Anybody will tell you that.''

MacInnes glanced at the PSE charts, chuckling. ''Your word, Mr. Hawthorne, is a pile of excrement. I wouldn't trust you with a crippled child's piggy bank.''

MacInnes telephoned the desk. The public stenographer was available, and she was also a notary public.

MacInnes sat down, rubbing his chin. It was the first time he had ever had to fight for his fee. Usually his clients were shocked at the size of his fees but paid up without a murmur. You had to pay for quality. True, this was the largest fee he had ever charged, but Hawthorne, the son of a bitch, should have been as happy as a kid in his first revolving door. Even paying his fee, he had saved the bastards three and a half *million* dollars. The world was full of ingratitude.

The public stenographer, an elderly woman with motherly assurance, arrived quickly and, using Vanessa's portable, soon had the necessary document typed, signed, and notarized. She even typed up Hawthorne's check. MacInnes tried to give her a ten-dollar tip, which she first refused, saying that the charge for her services would appear on his hotel bill. MacInnes tucked the bill into the pocket of her smock, and she left, smiling.

At the door, Hawthorne held out his hand. ''No hard feelings?''

MacInnes hesitated, then reluctantly shook hands. ''If you ever need my services again,'' he said, smiling, "don't hesitate to call someone else."

MacInnes closed the door, glancing at his watch. Only three o'clock. The session with Hawthorne had seemed interminable. It had left a sour taste in his mouth. Or was it the champagne? He put the glass down, called room service, and ordered a fifth of Dewar's White Label. The occasion called for stronger joy—or medicine.

He wasn't sure why, but he somehow felt guilty about the five hundred thousand dollars. It seemed exorbitant, putting him in the same ethical league with Hawthorne. At least the hundred thousand extra he had blackmailed helped him qualify. Of course, Hawthorne deserved it . . .

And think of the pleasure it would give Uncle Sam, who would collect seventy percent. Better Uncle than Hawthorne. And his own share, one hundred and fifty thousand, was a reasonable fee, considering his genius.

After Hawthorne thought it over he would realize what a potential gold mine the MacInnes talents offered. There'd be a fawning, friendly telephone call to "Kevin." MacInnes would ooze good fellowship. He would then plead pressure of other business and turn down the job, recommending the most inept PSE specialist he could think of.

The waiter rapped on the door, calling, "Room service."

MacInnes threw his jacket over the extension telephone and closed the Dektor case, then opened the door.

He signed the check, gave the waiter a dollar

bill, and sat down to pour a light Scotch on the rocks. Later he would have to take Vanessa in for an evening on the town. Dinner at Lutèce, a good play or musical comedy, finishing up at one of the "in" hangouts, the latter for Vanessa's benefit, because it would be a bore for him. There'd be Tonys and Cecis all over the joint.

He lit a cigarette and sipped the drink. Jobs with people like Hawthorne were not what he really wanted. The money was great, and without it he would not be in the seventy-percent bracket. On the other hand, he was plagued by a feeling of banditry, of financial pimping, of playing poker with marked cards.

The psychological-stress evaluator was awesome enough in its implications without using it for such tawdry purposes. It opened a window into the mind, invading privacy in a frightening, Orwellian way. It was Big Brother's tool, and it could be a tremendous weapon of evil as well as good. Whether the evil outweighed the good was academic. The instrument was here to stay, along with the computer, the electric light, and the atom bomb. It could be used to save the innocent and punish the guilty. In a future, better world, perhaps it would put the guilty where they could be rehabilitated. In the meantime, society had to be protected from those who menaced them, particularly with crimes of violence.

Early in his climb to Lie King status, MacInnes had traveled to a number of Latin American countries to train police officers in using the Dektor PSE. A step forward in civilization. It replaced lie-detection procedures that included pulling out a suspect's fingernails, holding lighted matches to his bare instep, electric shock applied to the genitalia, and a variety of other methods highly successful in obtaining confessions from the innocent as well as the guilty. But 1984 was still a long way off in Latin America. Many of the law-enforcement officers still believed in the good old methods. Their efficiency was obvious. One always got a confession, eh, señor? Well, almost always. Some of the *ratas* died, and once in a while a *cerdo* escaped into madness and actually laughed while you were smashing out his front teeth.

At least, MacInnes decided, he was on the side of the angels. The occasional Hawthorne type assignment didn't count as good or evil. It was merely financial gamesmanship. He had saved innocent people from going to prison—in three cases, from life sentences. He had helped send some *to* prison. They belonged there, until some better way of protecting society could be found.

He had helped others in strange ways, such as the king who needed to find out whether his brother was plotting to kill him; such as the rich and highly successful doctor who wanted to know which of his patients was writing anonymous letters to the American Medical Association. The range of PSE was seemingly unlimited. It could help stop a war or start one. It helped countless psychiatrists in restoring patients to emotional health. The good, he reasoned, far outweighed the bad.

He poured himself another small drink. Take it

easy. There was a long night of drinking ahead.

He smiled. The PSE might, in time, reduce people to putting their lies only in writing, thus bringing about a rebirth of literacy. He chuckled, picturing Hawthorne and Edmunds bargaining, passing a pad back and forth, each scribbling his elaborate proposals on paper designed to self-destruct in exactly two hundred and forty seconds.

The phone rang. He got up to answer it, expecting to hear Vanessa's voice. The voice was raspy and male. It belonged to Craig Weymouth, an old friend and an assistant district attorney.

"Kevin!" he said, "What luck, catching you up here. I called your office, and they . . ."

"Yeah. Hi. How are you, Craig?" It sounded like work, and MacInnes had had enough work for one day.

"Okay, I guess." There was a short pause. "Fact is, old buddy, I'm sitting on the horns of a dilemma."

"Yeah." Assistant DAs were always perched on horns of dilemmas.

"This is really big. I need your help."

MacInnes fished out a cigarette, holding the phone with his shoulder. "What's the situation?"

Weymouth said, "Well you see, I've got this guy. He's an informer but not really an informer. I mean, he's not a pro, you understand, but he wants money. Now, he's got a fantastic story." He cleared his throat. "Assassination. A very big hit is being planned. Someone very big, probably of national importance."

MacInnes expelled smoke into the mouthpiece.

Some of it ricocheted back into his eyes. "So pay him and get the information." He blinked, turning his head.

"He may be conning me. It's not so much losing the money. If his story is true, I want to know how much of it is true and how much is embroidery. You know how it is. When these guys start laying it on they tend to build it. If it's true, this is too important to screw around with."

MacInnes glanced at his watch. Three-thirty. "Can you get him out here in a half hour?" If Vanessa got back, she could hole up in the bedroom for a while. It shouldn't take more than an hour.

Weymouth's voice was quietly relieved. "You're damned right I can. I'll bring him myself, sirens screaming, if necessary."

CHAPTER THREE

CRAIG WEYMOUTH WAS tall, about five years younger than Kevin. He had curly black hair, a thin, beaked nose, and a big mouth with a lot of white but irregular teeth. He shook hands with MacInnes, at the same time ushering in the heavyset man who accompanied him. "Kevin, this is Mr. Kaiser. Richard Kaiser."

Kaiser extended a flabby hand. MacInnes shook it, looking Kaiser over carefully. Kaiser was a three-hundred-pound man in his early sixties, with a big, fleshy face, thick-lensed glasses, and a rosebud mouth.

The two men moved into the room, Kaiser glancing around curiously. "You FBI or something?" he asked MacInnes.

MacInnes smiled. "Have a seat and make yourself comfortable, Mr. Kaiser."

Kaiser sat down in the chair MacInnes had just vacated, eyeing the bottle on the coffee table.

"Either of you care for a drink?" asked MacInnes.

"I'll pass for the moment," said Weymouth.

Kaiser said, "I wouldn't say no to a rye and ginger."

"Afraid I only have Scotch. We could send down to the bar. . . ."

Kaiser gestured, waving the offer away. "Naw, skip it. It ain't important. That goddamned Scotch tastes like medicine to me."

Weymouth eased himself onto the sofa, putting his feet up. "Mr. Kaiser, as I explained to you on the way out, Mr. MacInnes handles special assignments for us. I want you to tell him your story. He will make a tape recording of it and evaluate it for me."

Kaiser asked, "Does that mean I get my money or don't get my money?"

"Mr. MacInnes is going to help me decide that."

Kaiser shook his head. "I ain't giving you all the details until we make a deal."

Weymouth said, "Just tell Mr. MacInnes what you have already told me."

Kaiser shrugged. He glanced at MacInnes, who was fitting a fresh tape into the Uher. He turned on the machine, then sat down facing Kaiser.

"All right, Mr. Kaiser, suppose you tell me in your own words what this is all about."

Kaiser puffed out his cheeks thoughtfully. "Well, like I told Mr. Weymouth here, I'm a respectable citizen. I own my own cab. Like, there's about three hundred of us; we all own our own cabs." He crossed one fat leg over the other. "We got an association. As a group, we got a fleet of three hundred cabs, and that ain't so bad, brother. I'm on the *board of directors*." He paused to let the importance of his position to sink in. "We cooperate with the cops all the time. We see any crimes being committed, we get right on the old microphone. There's many a perpetrator been caught with our help."

MacInnes nodded. "Right."

"The way this thing happened, I'm waitin' for my old lady, havin' a couple of beers in Suggies Bar. She's at the parish hall down the block playin' bingo. Never liked bingo. Can't stand all them dames shriekin'. So I'm havin' a beer to pass the time. I can't leave the old lady go home alone with all this muggin' around. So I gotta wait for her."

He searched in the pocket of his skintight pants and found a crumpled package of cigarettes. "They got a new bartender there last night. One of them goddamned 'Ricans who can't hardly speak English. I'm so disgusted, havin' nobody to converse with, I takes my beer to one of the back booths, preferrin' my own company to this jerky 'Rican kid who can't speak no good English annaway."

He pulled out a bent cigarette and lit it. "I'm in the last booth on the left side. Right near the hall to the gents' and the telephone. I'm sort of slumped

47

down, half-asleep like. Drivin' a cab sort of takes it out of you when you get to be my age. Annaway, I'm slumped there, facing the back of the room, when these two guys come in and take the next booth towards the front. They think the dump is empty, which it is except for me and this dumb 'Rican bartender.''

"They start talking in low voices, but I could hear every word, and I'm telling you it scared the shit out of me." He dragged nervously on his bent cigarette. "They was talking about a big hit. A three-hundred-grand hit. I listen to them, trying to shrink under the table. I mean, they see me, I'm done. For that kinda dough, it's cheaper to knock me off than make new plans."

MacInnes smiled, picturing the three-hundred-pound cabbie trying to shrink under the table.

"It ain't no laughing matter, mister," said Kaiser. "Them guys was cold-blooded killers. I mean, there was ice freezin' all over the place. If one of them goes to the can, or the phone, I'm done. Even if they happen to look around when they're leavin', I'm done."

MacInnes said, "I wasn't laughing at you. I was smiling at your joke."

"What joke?"

"About it being cheaper for them to knock you off than change their plans."

Kaiser gave some serious thought to his new role as a stand-up comedian and decided to accept it. He grinned. "Yeah, but I wasn't jokin', buster."

MacInnes nodded, reaching for his own cigarettes.

"Well, I'm sittin' there shakin' like Jell-O, when I see my chance. Another guy comes in. He's about as fat as I am, and he heads right for the can. I say to myself, when this joker comes out, the second he passes my booth I'm going to slide out and duck behind the partition. They got one of the partitions that screens the hall to the can."

He crushed out his cigarette, tapping and scraping it all around the ashtray. "Well, that's exactly what I do. As soon as this guy passes, he gives me a couple of seconds of cover, and I dodge behind the partition. Then I go out the other side to the aisle where they got booths on one side and the bar on the other. I walk to the front of the bar, like I come from the john, and order myself another beer from the dumb 'Rican."

MacInnes shook his head. "Too bad you didn't get a look at them."

Kaiser held up his hand. "*Wait* a minute. After I have this beer I begin to get my courage back. I figure they don't know I been listenin', so I'll go back and take a look. I walk down the aisle slow like. They're talking, but shut up like clams as I go by. I go to the phone and call the parish hall to see whether the bingo is over, which I know it ain't. It's an open phone, and they can hear me. Then I hang up and walk past them again for another fast look."

Kaiser leaned back, sighing. "As much as I hate the taste of this stuff, I gotta have a drink." He poured a healthy slug of Scotch into one of the clean glasses on the tray. He held it up. "Well, gentlemen, that's the end of the free show. If you want to see Mademoiselle La Zonga take off her pants, you got to step into the tent and cross my palm with gelt.'' He tossed the Scotch down, grimacing.

MacInnes forced a laugh. That's what he got for giving Kaiser the idea he could roll them in the aisles. He hoped Kaiser had more to show than Mademoiselle La Zonga, whose pantless state would reveal nothing unusual in these uninhibited times.

He said, ''Mr. Kaiser, this instrument is a modern electronic device that measures psychological stress. I want to ask you a few simple questions and see what the machine says about you. I won't ask you for any details you haven't already given me.'' He paused. ''Okay?''

Kaiser looked puzzled but said, ''Okay. Fire away when you see the whites of my eyes.'' He rolled his eyeballs skyward.

MacInnes, who had been scribbling a few questions, looked up. Encourage this guy much more and he'd give up cab driving. He smiled. ''Okay, here we go. What's your name?''

''Richard Arnold Kaiser.''

''What's your favorite color?''

''Green.''

''Mr. Kaiser, did you ever steal anything from anyone?''

Kaiser reared back indignantly. ''Uh, what the hell. No.''

''Mr. Kaiser, you're a reputable citizen, a member of the board of directors of your association. You and your colleagues help the police. Why do you think you should be paid for helping law-enforcement officers prevent a major crime?''

Kaiser thought for a moment. ''I explained this to Mr. Weymouth. It's like, well, here I am, sixty-two years old. I been workin' my ass off for forty-five years, and I got nothing. Social security, shit! What will it buy you? A living? Like hell. I get too old and sick to drive my hack any more, what are me and my old lady going to do? It don't even hardly pay the rent.''

He tugged at his collar, which was too tight, even unbuttoned, with the frayed red tie pulled down slightly. ''It's like, well, there ought to be a big reward for something like this. But if it turns out there is, you can be damned sure Arnie Kaiser ain't going to see any of it.''

MacInnes nodded sympathetically. ''When you overheard these two men, what were they planning?''

''I told you, a big hit. A three-hundred-grand hit.''

''Can you describe them?''

''Yes.''

''Can you describe them *well?*''

Kaiser thought for a few seconds. ''Pretty well.''

MacInnes held up his hand. ''Okay.'' He re-wound the tape to the beginning of the short test and then played it through the PSE at reduced speed, watching the pen mark the roll of narrow chart paper. There was good stress for anger as Kaiser explained why he wanted money for the information. Deception stress on the answer to

"Did you ever steal anything from anyone?" Hardly a person alive hasn't stolen something, even if it goes all the way back to when he or she tried to snitch a dime from Mom's purse and got whacked. The remainder of MacInnes's questions brought no evidence of stress.

Weymouth had been watching MacInnes closely. MacInnes smiled, making a circle with his thumb and forefinger. Kaiser had been telling the truth about the incident.

Weymouth turned to Kaiser. "All right, Mr. Kaiser, we'll pay you the amount agreed upon. And if there is any reward, which at the moment is a pretty nebulous proposition, you have my word that your contribution will be fully documented for whoever is offering the reward."

Kaiser, who was following this statement with rapt attention, said, "Okay."

MacInnes started up the tape recorder again. "All right, let's get the details. What did they say to each other?"

Kaiser drummed the coffee table with his plump fingers. "Well, lemme see. This one guy, he's an Englishman. Real posh. Talks just like a college professor. The guy sittin' with his back to me, he has a Southern accent. Heavy. Mouth full of mush.

"They chitchat first about what they're gonna drink. The professor orders a double Chivas. Mushmouth asks for a bottle of Bud." Kaiser started to pick his nose but thought better of it and hastily withdrew his finger. "Then after the 'Rican brings the drinks and leaves, the professor says,

'This is a tough one, but you're going to like it. It's big, very big. Your budget could go as high as two, three hundred gees.'

"Mushmouth sort of whistles. He says, 'Who you want me to waste, Bonny Prince Charles?'

"The professor laughs. He says, 'I want you to find me a crazy with a gun. Pay out whatever is necessary to build him up and aim him in the right direction. Whatever is left is yours.'

"Mushmouth asks, 'What you mean, crazy?'

"The professor says, 'I mean a fanatic. I don't care where you get him or what he's fanatic about. Symbionese Liberation Army, or the Friends of Sirhan Sirhan Society, what the hell. Just find me a real nut who's sane enough to be out of the loony bin and reliable enough to do the job. The money's big. You can find a good one.'"

Kaiser paused, thinking hard. "You got to realize I can't remember the exact words. I'm sort of telling you this in my own way, with as much of the words as I can remember. Now this Mushmouth says something like, '*Huh-uh*. You want to set up somebody, it ain't gonna be me. First thing the crazy does is finger me. First thing you do is see I ain't gonna be able to be fingered.'

"The professor says, 'Don't be an ass. With this kind of lolly to play with, you can put a couple of layers between you and the crazy. The chap who knows you, well, you know what to do with him.'

"Mushmouth don't say nothin' for a while; then he says, 'Yeah, I reckon it could go that way. The question is, who's gonna do the real hit? I mean, you ain't depending on this crazy?'

53

"The professor says, "No. Maybe it'll be you. We'll worry about that later. The important thing is to find the *right* crazy. Aim him and be damned sure he shoots.""

Kaiser pulled out another of his crumpled cigarettes and lit it. "Then about this time I seen my chance and got my ass out of the booth."

Weymouth, who had been filling a chewed-up-looking black briar, lit it, sending up thick white clouds. He looked at MacInnes. "Political, obviously."

MacInnes nodded. "You had the booth dusted, of course."

Weymouth said, "Of course. We went in at four this morning—with a little cooperation from the security outfit that services the building. Don't think we got anything much, but they're still checking out what they did pick up."

MacInnes turned back to Kaiser. "Well, let's get those descriptions."

The Southerner, it developed, was redheaded, hair long but not quite shoulder length. Might have been a wig, but Kaiser thought not because the guy had freckles. His right eyelid had a noticeable droop. About thirty-five, medium height, a guess, but he didn't sit terribly tall. Slender. Short, turned-up nose. Eyes wide set, didn't notice color. Wearing a brown leather jacket and blue turtleneck sweater.

The professor had been wearing a blue pinstripe suit. Expensive. Light blue shirt and dark red tie. Tan, in his forties, light-colored hair modishly long. Bushy eyebrows. Thin nose. Didn't get as close a look at him as he did of Mushmouth.

During his army years, MacInnes had made a study of regional accents. He tried out all the Southern variations he could successfully mimic. Kaiser found this confusing and had a difficult time concentrating. It definitely wasn't Virginia. It might be South Carolina or Alabama; he wasn't really sure. In a way, they all sounded sort of alike to him.

With only a cursory knowledge of English accents, he tried out Eton Oxford, middle-class educated, Cockney-educated, and Australian. Yorkshire and other regional accents were beyond him. Here again Kaiser was confused, and agonized over his choice. He finally decided it might have been Australian or middle-class educated.

MacInnes stood up. "Well, Craig, I think that's about all I can do for you. I'll run the entire tape through the Dektor PSE, and if anything comes out funny, I'll get in touch."

Kaiser had been so obviously sincere in his attempts to repeat the conversation and to describe the two men accurately, that MacInnes doubted the existence of any padding. So, apparently, did Weymouth, who also stood up.

"Okay, Kevin. I want to get our identikit artists to work with Mr. Kaiser as fast as possible, so I think we'll take off."

At the door, Kaiser, still puzzled over MacInnes's role and status, held out his pudgy hand and said, "Who are you, anyway?"

MacInnes shrugged. "I'm Kevin MacInnes." He shook hands and eased the door shut as soon as

Weymouth got into the hall.

There was a fast rapping. Weymouth had forgotten something.

"How charitable are you feeling today?" he asked when MacInnes opened the door.

Thinking of the five hundred thousand, MacInnes said, "Pretty charitable."

Weymouth said, "One of my friends has a tough case. Name's Joel Friedland. He's the court-appointed attorney for this woman who has been indicted for murder one. The case is driving him up the wall. He doesn't know how to plead her." Weymouth sucked on his briar. "Long as you're up here, could you come in and see her tomorrow morning?"

He'd have to go into the city to collect his certified check anyway. "Sure, why not?"

Weymouth slapped his arm. "Great. I'll have Joel give you a call."

CHAPTER FOUR

WHEN VANESSA RETURNED, she was in one of her rare bleak moods. She strode in, dumped a couple of small packages on the sofa, and said, "Well, are we staying or going?"

"Staying." He was running the Kaiser tape through the PSE at reduced speed, watching the pen move up and down on the chart.

She went into the bedroom and slammed the door.

He lit a cigarette and continued to watch the chart until the tape played out. No embellishments to the story as far as he could see, and no need to call Weymouth. It was some story. Everybody would be getting into the act. The FBI, the CIA (after all, one of the plotters was an Englishman, wasn't he?), and God knew who else. Maybe even the president himself.

The pattern was clear enough. Oswald, Sirhan Sirhan, James Earl Ray, and the nut who shot Wallace, what was his name? The fanatics aiming at and shooting at President Ford.

Find me a crazy and aim him in the right direction. But first build layers and layers between the man or men who paid for the assassination and the crazy who pulled the trigger.

He copied Kaiser's tape on the Sony, then bundled the Uher tape and the charts into a large envelope for hand delivery to Weymouth.

Now this was a case worthy of MacInnes's talents. He mulled over ways to stay within the orbit of the investigation. This party would be by invitation only, and he'd simply have to promote some invitations. No harm too in checking some things on his own.

The Southerner with the droopy right eyelid, for instance. MacInnes had good contacts in the police departments of many of the larger cities. He could check Atlanta, New Orleans, Birmingham, Montgomery, Raleigh, and others. With thousands of redheads, the chances were slim, but this one just might be known.

He went into the bedroom. Vanessa had pulled a chair up to the floor-to-ceiling windows and was sitting, smoking and staring out at the soot-gray dusk settling over the vast airport.

"What's the matter?"

"Nothing."

"I thought we might go to Lutèce for dinner and

then maybe a show later."

She remained silent.

"Would you like that?"

She shrugged.

"Well, hell, if you don't want to, say so."

"I don't want to."

He lit a cigarette. There wasn't a woman in the whole world who wasn't difficult at times for no apparent reason, he told himself. Probably something to do with their second-class-citizen syndrome. What was Freud's despairing cry in his old age? "Woman, what in God's name do you want?"

"Well, what *do* you want to do?"

No answer.

He went back to the living room and poured himself a large drink. Why did these things always happen after a man had had a nerveracking, exhausting day and was ready to relax and have a good time? Remind himself to ask Weymouth for a Xerox of the identikit drawings tomorrow when he delivered the tape. Back to Vanessa. What was bothering her?

He returned to the bedroom, carrying his drink.

"Why are you giving me the old frigid shoulder? What have I done?"

She turned to face him. "I don't know. Sometimes I just wonder why we bother."

"Why we bother?"

"Why we bother to stay together."

He lit a cigarette, juggling his drink to reach for his lighter. "I thought we bothered to stay together because we enjoyed staying together."

"I wonder."

"Why?"

"I'm nothing to you but a high-class whore. Instead of twenty, you hand me a thousand and send me packing." She jerked the chair around to face him. "You don't like my friends. You never discuss your work with me. All we do together is eat, drink, and screw."

MacInnes mentally mopped his brow. "When my father felt affluent, he used to give my mother extra money and tell her to buy herself something nice. I'm sorry if you felt the money meant anything more than that."

It was true that the Tonys and Cecis bored him, but not all the jet-set types were boring. Many were interesting people: producers, actors, writers, musicians—people who did things. But even they were a bit hard to take. Egomaniacs all, with only one desire—to talk about themselves and what they were accomplishing. MacInnes was at a definite disadvantage. Like a doctor in charge of a VD clinic, he couldn't talk about his work.

"As far as your friends go, some I like and some I find boring. You undoubtedly find some of my friends boring too."

"Friends!" She glared at him. "Do you *have* any friends? I've never met anyone but clients and professional associates."

He bit his lower lip. Did he *really* have any friends? There were people he thought of as close friends, but they were so scattered over the world that he rarely saw them.

"Well, maybe I'm friendless," he said. He put his cigarette in the ashtray. "Maybe I'm just a peculiar type who doesn't deserve a woman as lovely and beautiful as you are." Some of his mother's blarney coming to his rescue.

She turned her head. "Oh, hell—"

"As far as my work goes, well, some of it I could discuss with you, if I thought it wouldn't bore you. Other things are highly confidential, and it wouldn't be sensible or honorable to discuss them, even if you were my . . . mother." He had started to say "wife" and switched just in time. "The kind of thing I work with isn't cocktail-party chitchat. It could be disastrous to my career."

She turned back to stare at him. "In other words, I'm so dumb and disloyal that I can't be trusted to keep my mouth shut?"

Why did women twist things around and put the worst possible interpretation on them? He pulled a chair over close to her and sat down, reaching for her hand. She reluctantly let him hold it.

"Look, dearest, this is the first time you've even indicated you were interested. I don't distrust you, and I certainly know you're not dumb. In fact, I'm damned sure you have a very high IQ."

He had employees staffing MacInnes Security, Inc., who were actually no brighter and probably no less a risk than Vanessa when it came to inadvertent spilling of confidential information. Probably his attitude had stemmed from his tendency to strictly separate work from play.

"Some of the situations I'm involved in are dangerous. And for you to have the information could put you in danger. I wouldn't want that."

She tugged her hand away. "Oh, hell!"

He certainly would never involve her in something like the Kaiser affair. Somewhere, some very powerful people were anteing up a hell of a lot of money to eliminate someone damned important. If he ever penetrated the layers leading upward from the Englishman . . .

"You're too precious to me to take that risk," he said.

"I feel sort of sick," she said.

The sudden shift startled him. Sick? Sick from the idea of his work?

"My stomach is flipping around." She jumped up and ran to the bathroom. He followed and stood outside the door, listening to her regurgitating agonizingly and noisily.

"Can I hold your head?"

"No!" came through the door, followed by a loud gasp. "Go away. I'm a mess. I don't want you to see me."

He went back to the living room. Too much rich food and wine. And probably several martinis before lunch.

He poured himself another stiff Scotch. It was going to be a lousy night. Maybe Vanessa was getting bored with him. Maybe she was ready to move on.

Draining the glass, he looked at his watch. Almost seven. He was hungry. He had been unconsciously anticipating that exceptional meal at Lutèce. Well, he had to eat somewhere. There were at least three, probably four, restaurants in the hotel.

He went back to the bedroom. Vanessa was now

in bed, propped up with several pillows, looking pale.

"Whoop it all up?"

She smiled weakly. "Hope so."

"Feeling better?"

"Some."

He put his hand on her forehead. Cool. "Think you'll be okay while I go downstairs and have some dinner?"

"Of course." She closed her eyes.

Downstairs he chose the restaurant specializing in steaks. It was called the Full of Bull or some such name, hard to read in phony Old English lettering.

He ordered a large porterhouse, French fries, and salad with Roquefort dressing, and a bottle of good Burgundy. The waitress, who had a frightened look on her face, asked, "Well, medium, or rare?" She might have been asking, "You're not going to kill me, are you?"

"Medium rare."

She scurried away. He wondered why he looked frightening. Had that last drink changed him into a Mr. Hyde? He felt one cheek tentatively, wondering whether it would feel cracked, and lumpy. Nope, smooth as ever. Had he been scowling threateningly?

When she returned with the wine, he decided that she just naturally looked frightened. Her mouth hung open, and her eyebrows were arched in a peculiar way. Or did she see something really rotten in his soul?

He ate the steak, bemused, and drank the whole fifth of wine, his spirits rising with the descending level of the bottle.

Finishing, he signed the check and added a larger-than-necessary gratuity for the frightened waitress. He strolled out into the chilly spring evening, overstuffed and in need of some air. He walked for more than a mile around the vast parking lot.

When he got back to the suite he found Vanessa reading *Vogue* and looking healthier.

"Feeling better?"

"Much."

He sat on the edge of the bed. "Still feeling sort of blah about me?"

She put the magazine down and stared at him soberly. "I don't want to be just a sex object."

"Look, honey, being a sex object in itself isn't bad. Most men would love to be sex objects. Sex is one of the most powerful motivating forces men and women have. What I think you mean is that you don't want to be sexually exploited."

She shifted impatiently, pulling the covers higher.

"If a woman has to go to bed with a man she doesn't really enjoy going to bed with, because she's a woman and in a weak position, that's exploitation."

He paused for a few seconds. "But I don't know how it can apply to you. A woman as beautiful as you are can certainly pick and choose. The fact that you are my mistress, in effect, and that I support you and give you money, is in this case sort of irrelevant, wouldn't you say? Unless you're the world's greatest actress, I would say you enjoy our lovemaking.''

"I do."

"Then what is it?"

She pushed her hair back. "You're cold. Oh, I don't mean in bed. I mean as a human being. You're a cold person. Sometimes I'm a little afraid of you.''

She had unwittingly touched a raw spot deep inside him. Sometimes he felt he was abnormally unemotional. Cold. Controlled, rather, he preferred to think. Yet at times, within, he was as sentimental as an Irishman getting drunk at his daughter's wedding. But sentimentality didn't mean you had any really deep feelings. Maybe he was just a shallow clod. Only that morning he had been thinking that eventually their relationship would undoubtedly end and that he would pass her on to some handsome and very rich fellow or she would, on her own, find someone else and leave him. Now the idea of losing her distressed him deeply, and his eyes burned and were slightly blurred. He turned his face away.

Sensing his despair, she clutched him. "Now I've hurt you!''

He sank down with her, surreptitiously burying his face in the pillow to dry his wet eyes. He hadn't cried since he was six years old, and he was damned if he was going to take it up again now.

It turned out to be a very good night after all.

Later they sat smoking and having a nightcap, and he told her about Hawthorne. She thought it was very funny, and she was astounded at the size of the fee. He could see that she was eyeing him with more respect. Not because of the money—she knew he was rich—but because of his skill in earning it. Maybe sharing some of his problems with her would give their relationship more depth.

He drifted off to sleep wondering about the woman charged with murder whom he had to test tomorrow.

CHAPTER FIVE

"YOU SEE," SAID Joel Friedland, "she stabbed him in the back. I want to plead self-defense; she swears it was an accident." Friedland had wavy black hair and a face so youthful that he might have still been in law school. "This is one of those cases of assault and abuse over a long period."

MacInnes, who was having a cup of coffee with Friedland in a restaurant near the jail, said, "She definitely should have stabbed him in the front."

"Yeah."

"How does she make it an accident?"

Friedland sipped the hot coffee cautiously. "Claims he stumbled and fell, and in doing so, caused her to trip and fall on top of him. Holding the knife, of course."

MacInnes shook his head. "Could have happened, I suppose."

Friedland said, "From the path of the wound, the medical examiner thinks the victim was standing upright when stabbed. However, he won't testify unequivocally to this. He admits it's just barely possible that the thrust entered when the victim was in a prone position."

MacInnes stifled a yawn. Making up with Vanessa could be strenuous. He was feeling definitely anemic, and she, bless her, would sleep until noon or later.

"The husband has a long history of abuse. There are at least eight neighbors willing to testify that he beat her up frequently. He'd been hauled into court a couple of times, once for beating one of the kids so badly he had to be hospitalized. A drunken sadist."

MacInnes nodded. "So what's the problem? I mean, why do you need me? Why won't an ordinary polygraph operator do?"

Friedland lit a cigarette. "One, she won't plead self-defense. Two, she won't take a polygraph test. Now you know what a backlog of cases we have here in New York. If she'd plead self-defense, the DA would recommend clemency. But she won't."

"Hmmm."

"So we've come up with a deal. You test her. If she's telling the truth about its being an accident, he'll recommend that the charges be dismissed. He's just going to waste a lot of the taxpayers' money trying to convict her anyway."

"I see."

MacInnes hated prisons for all the usual reasons, but he particularly resented them when he had to conduct PSE testing under the conditions they imposed. Prisons were not only uncomfortable, but they made him uneasy, and he worked better relaxed.

They were shown into one of the rooms used for legal conferences. It contained nothing but a table and four folding chairs. The chairs showed two layers of paint, both badly chipped. The table tilted slightly, one short leg reinforced insufficiently at the bottom with a folded cardboard that had contained a McDonald's Big Mac. The room stank of harsh disinfectant, smoke, and old sweat.

The woman was brought in by a plump, red-faced matron whose round chin sprouted a few black hairs. The prisoner was a woman about thirty, one of the world's losers if MacInnes had ever seen one. Dull brown hair, coarse strands of which strayed onto her pimply cheeks, bad teeth in a mouth turned permanently down, a bumpy nose, and expressionless brown eyes staring at him without interest or hope. Surprisingly, she had a good figure, evident even under the loose prison dress.

The matron seated her charge and then took up a post outside the door, in a position to watch the prisoner through the glass window.

Friedland said, "Mrs. Weedall, this is Mr. MacInnes. I've brought him here to try to help you. He's going to ask you some questions and will tape-record your answers. If he thinks you're innocent, his opinion will go a long way with the district attorney."

She looked at MacInnes, her dull eyes coming to

life with suspicion. "I ain't taking no polygraph test."

MacInnes said, "Mrs. Weedall, do you know what a polygraph test is?"

She stared at him blankly. "They hook up a lot of wires to you, like an electric chair."

MacInnes smiled. "Well, they do hook up a lot of things to you, but they're not all wires. They put an accordion tube around your chest to measure your breathing. They put a cuff on your arm to measure your blood pressure, just as the doctor does. They attach wires to your hands to measure the electrical resistance of your skin—"

She shook her head. "Well, like I said, they hook you up to a lot of things."

He took out a package of cigarettes and offered it to her. She took one eagerly.

"Mrs. Weedall, we aren't going to hook you up to anything." He held his lighter under her cigarette. "I'm just going to turn on my tape recorder and ask you some questions. You can answer them if you want to. If you don't want to, you don't have to. Okay?"

She thought about it, sucking on the cigarette, then said, "Okay."

MacInnes switched on the Uher. "Tell me how you happened to get in this terrible situation. I hear you and your husband fought a lot?"

Smoke curled from her nostrils. "He fought. I just tried to keep myself and my kids from getting kilt."

"Why did he attack you?"

"Drink."

MacInnes moved some dust around on the table with his thumb. "Why do you suppose he drank so much?"

She shrugged. "Who knows? But it was drink that done it. It was drink that made him mean as catshit."

He took one of the cigarettes from the package he had left on the table. "When people drink more than they should, there's usually something bugging them. You know what I mean? Fear, frustration, insecurity?"

This was beyond Mrs. Weedall. "I ain't no head doctor, mister."

He smiled. She was right. There were too damned many amateur psychiatrists messing up the world as it was.

"What did he blame you for, when he got mean?"

She looked down. "Different things. The kids bugged him a lot. He didn't want *no more* kids."

Friedland scraped back his chair and stood up. "Well, I think I'll leave you two to talk. Mrs. Weedall, as your attorney I advise you to answer Mr. MacInnes's questions. He's on our side, and you can trust him."

She shifted her glance to Friedland and nodded dumbly.

With a wave of his hand to MacInnes, Friedland tapped on the glass and had the matron unlock the door.

When the door clicked shut again MacInnes asked, "How many children do you have?"

"Three."

MacInnes said, "It's usually the wife who doesn't want any more kids. She has to do most of the work taking care of them."

She had been staring at the door. She turned slowly back to MacInnes. "You can say that again, mister. Three's plenty. Specially when you ain't rich. Not that Elwood wasn't always a good provider. Even with his drinking, he always worked steady and made good money."

MacInnes glanced at the ceiling, seeking inspiration. His mind was still a trifle fuzzy from lack of sleep. "So at least you don't fight about not having more children. Neither of you wanted any more children."

She compressed her lips briefly. "He didn't want no more kids, but he wanted plenty of sex."

He glanced at her with more interest. "Are you Catholic?"

"No."

"Then it shouldn't have been a problem. I mean, you have nothing against contraception?"

She shook her head. "I have one of them diaphragm things."

"So what's the problem?"

She hesitated, opened her mouth to speak, then shut it.

"You found sexual relations with him offensive?"

Her face flushed. "Mister, he got his kicks out of hurting me. If I told you the things he done to me . . ."

MacInnes held up his hand. "I understand." Ordinarily he considered himself unshockable, but there was something about this poor, hopeless woman that embarrassed him.

"He never enjoyed it unless he hurt me."

MacInnes finally lit the cigarette he had taken.

"Down at the clinic they told me he was a, a sadis, or something like that."

"Sadist?"

"Yeah."

MacInnes asked, "Why didn't you leave him?"

She shrugged. "Who's going to take care of my kids? He says I leave him he's going to take off for Australia or someplace, and I ain't going to *ever* get one cent from him for support."

She chewed on her lower lip. "And he woulda done it, mister. He was stubborn."

All MacInnes could say was, "I see." After a pause he said, "I'm curious to know why you won't plead self-defense."

She stared at him for a long time without speaking. "I wouldn't have my kids have that shame on their heads."

"Shame?"

"Knowing their mother killed their father. Even in a fight. Now, like, it was accidental, that could happen to anybody."

MacInnes thought about it for a moment, then came to a decision. "Mrs. Weedall, I believe you when you say you killed your husband accidentally. For the record I'm going to have to ask you some questions about it. Just relax and don't worry about them. Okay?"

She nodded.

"What's your name?"

73

"Erma Weedall."

"Did you ever steal anything from anybody, ever?"

She bit her lip. "No."

"Did you accidentally fall on your husband with the knife? Is that the way he got killed?"

"Yes."

"Do you like to go to the movies?"

"Yes."

"Did the knife go into your husband's back when he was standing up?"

"No."

"Did you deliberately thrust the knife into him?"

"No."

He played the short test through the Dektor at reduced speed. As he had feared, there was heavy stress on every question involving her husband's death. She had simply reached the end of the road and let him have it.

He smiled. "You're doing fine, Mrs. Weedall. Just calm down and don't be excited when I ask you these questions."

He knew that if he asked her the same questions four or five times, there would be less and less stress. She was puzzled as he continued to go through the routine, but she cooperated, sensing somehow that he was trying to help her.

Before the last test he tore a sheet of paper into four pieces and printed a word large on each segment.

The question, "Did you deliberately thrust the knife into him," was still producing some noticeable stress. Just before asking it this time he held up one of the squares of paper.

He said, "Read this word, please."

"Blue."

He held up another.

"Green."

He flashed the third square.

"Red."

As he showed her the fourth square, he stood up suddenly.

"Yellow."

He sat down.

"Did you deliberately thrust the knife into him?"

"No."

He ran the test through the Dektor. As he had anticipated, she showed more stress on the word "Yellow" than she did on "Did you thrust the knife." It was a delicate instrument indeed. The surprise of his standing up suddenly had given him the stress he needed.

He tore up the old charts, marking up the last one for Joel Friedland to discuss with the district attorney. Obviously the woman was innocent—as far as the chart was concerned.

He gathered up his equipment. "I think you'll find that you'll be out of here and back to your children soon," he said, tapping on the glass for the matron.

On his way to meet Hawthorne MacInnes felt vaguely nauseated. It was the first time he had ever faked a test, and doubts began to nibble his conscience. Now he was trying to play god with the damned machine. What right had he to become Mrs. Weedall's judge and jury? Suppose, having got away with it once, she killed someone else? No—the poor, hopeless creature would struggle on, on welfare, trying to raise her kids. She'd find another man, and maybe he'd be more kind. At least the chances were good that he wouldn't be a drunk who got his kicks sadistically.

Hawthorne greeted him in an office half the size of a basketball court. Thickly carpeted in a muted red-and-gold weave, large sofas and deep lounge chairs forming a conversation area at one end, with a huge free-form desk at the other—it looked more like the lobby of a small, exclusive hotel than an office.

As MacInnes had anticipated, Hawthorne had begun to see the light. He was effusively friendly during the exchange of checks.

MacInnes placed the certified check carefully in his billfold, which had certainly never contained a half million dollars before, and stood up.

Hawthorne said quickly, "Before you leave, I have another situation brewing that might just possibly—"

MacInnes glanced at his watch. "I have a plane to Tehran to catch. You remember, I mentioned the Shah?" He shook his head and sighed wearily. "My schedule is so full for the next month or so, I just don't know how I'm going to handle it."

Hawthorne's mouth drooped. "I could make it well worth your while to fit me in."

MacInnes snapped his fingers suddenly. "I've

just thought of a man who can help you." He was not acting. The right name had suddenly occurred to him. Wilbur Trott, a backwoods Alabama deputy sheriff so slow-witted that the Dektor people had been very reluctant to sell him a PSE, though Wilbur had, with much coaching, managed to pass the course. Wilbur was so dense that he would even have difficulty developing questions about hunting and fishing, which he knew. When it came to high financial wheeling and dealing, Wilbur would be like a ten-year-old trying to cope with Einsteinian physics.

"His name's Wilbur Trott. Southern boy, sounds sort of slow, but he's actually sharp as hell." MacInnes rubbed his chin, trying to repress a smile. "I'll have him get in touch with you."

He left, chuckling all the way to the elevator.

He then delivered the Weedall tape chart to Joel Friedland, and again felt a gnawing deep inside when Friedland raised his eyebrows at the results.

"I swear to God, I never would have believed it," said Friedland. "But it sure solves my problem."

MacInnes said, "You can't fool the old PSE, son, not when it's operated by an expert. Frankly, I wouldn't have believed it either, but well, there it is."

Friedland eyed him curiously, shaking his head.

MacInnes wondered if he suspected.

"Would you mind going over this with the DA? You can probably explain it better than I can."

MacInnes shrugged. "Not at all. But it's really quite clear. You can see that she stressed stronger on an irrelevant word such as *yellow* than she did on the key question.''

MacInnes's feeling of guilt continued through the meeting he and Friedland had with the assistant district attorney handling Mrs. Weedall's case, even though this harassed young man, only too happy to have the matter settled, accepted the chart with MacInnes's explanation eagerly.

Craig Weymouth's office was his next stop. MacInnes gave him the Kaiser tape and charts. After they chatted about inconsequentials for a few minutes, MacInnes asked whether he could have photostats of the identikit drawings of the assassination plotters.

Weymouth puffed his pipe for a moment and then asked, ''Why?''

MacInnes smiled. ''Who knows, I might run into one of them.''

Weymouth shook his head. ''The thing was taken out of my hands. Like five minutes after I gave the big boss the whole story.'' He emitted some more white clouds. ''However . . .'' He opened a desk drawer and took out a stack of photostats. He selected one of each man and handed it to MacInnes. ''If you ever tell anyone where you got these, I'll personally find you and cut you loose from your manhood.''

MacInnes would have phrased it differently. He smiled and tucked the drawings into his leather case. ''Thanks. If I develop anything, you'll be the first to hear about it.''

In the cab back to Kennedy, MacInnes studied the drawings carefully. It was such a nebulous thing. Where in the hell did you start?

CHAPTER SIX

IT WAS DARK, and he couldn't see the man clearly. The man's face was in deep shadow, and MacInnes was conscious only of an elongated egg-white forehead. "She was conning you, Mac. A dirtier, lousier bitch never lived. How come you never asked for *my* side of the story? What am I—some rotten vegetable you throw in the garbage can and put the lid on quick? You can't put the lid on me. She lied, she lied, she lied, she lied. . . ."

The voice tapered off, growing fainter, and the room brightened. MacInnes was in a narrow kitchen facing Erma Weedall. Her unkempt brown hair hung over one eye; the other was fixed on him, shiny with the glaze of madness. In one hand she held a big serrated knife, the blade triangular, tapering to a sharp point. She advanced slowly. He backed away until he was pinned to the wall. She raised the knife high and lunged. He tried to lift his arms, but they were strangely paralyzed.

"No!" The word was forced from his throat in a husky croak.

Vanessa shook him. "Kevin! Kevin! Wake up."

He sat up and turned on the bedside lamp, his forehead damp with perspiration.

Vanessa stared at him, the sudden light making her squint. "Bad dream?"

"Ummm."

She stroked his cheek. "Poor baby." She smiled. "The bogeyman almost got you, and 'Nessa saved your life."

"Bogeywoman," he muttered.

He got out of bed, slipped on his robe, and went to the living room, lighting a cigarette on the way.

How, he wondered, could he have been so stupid? In a spur-of-the-moment decision he had compromised everything he stood for. His integrity, his career, his whole life. And it hadn't even been necessary. Friedman would have got her off with nothing worse than probation, probably. An idiot act of chivalry. An idiot act because you don't play judge and jury with only one side of the story. In fact, you don't play judge and jury, period.

He poured himself a stiff Scotch and added a little water. After taking a small sip he set up his equipment and brought out the tape of his entire conversation with Erma Weedall. He started it through the PSE at reduced speed and sat watching the pen move up and down, marking its way across the narrow chart.

No deception stress showed as she talked about her husband's violence, his drinking, and his sexual abuse. She was telling the truth too when she talked of the shame that would fall on the heads of her children. This knowledge relieved him and nibbled away a portion of his guilt, but the core remained solidly lodged in his chest cavity, a sticky, heavy foreign object that he was afraid would always be there.

Vanessa came out to him, stifling a yawn. She bent over and put her arm around his shoulders. "It was really a bad one, wasn't it, darling?"

He smiled sheepishly.

"Was it—was it Vietnam?"

He shook his head, reaching for the glass of Scotch. He took a quick gulp.

"Nightmares don't mean anything," she said. "I have some dillies when I eat too much lobster."

He finished off the Scotch. "Yeah. Usually they don't. This one concerned a very recent experience. What happened was probably more traumatic than I realized."

She eased herself onto his lap. "Do you want to talk about it?"

He shook his head but then decided that he did want to talk about it.

He told her the story, editing it. If he admitted that he had deliberately faked the test she could ruin him. And who could tell, someday she might feel like ruining him. Women, he had found, could be the most vindictive of the species. His altered version was that the PSE results had been inconclusive, but he had stretched a point to give his opinion that Mrs. Weedall was innocent. No one could fault him for an erroneous opinion.

She cupped his cheeks with her hands and stared, her big brown eyes wide. "And you're upset because you *helped* this poor woman?"

He blinked. "Well, of course I wanted to help her. But I . . . well, I compromised my integrity in doing so."

"I don't understand." She removed her hands. "What else could you *possibly* do?"

MacInnes said, "*You* don't understand. I have a strong conviction that this woman is guilty." He shifted his legs slightly to move Vanessa comfortably closer. "I think what got to me was her statement about the shame her children would have to live with. It was so simple and naïve, and yet so heartbreakingly true. Nobody thinks about the children in these cases."

She tucked her face down into the crook of his neck. "I still don't see why you're upset. Even if she *meant* to kill him, the pig certainly deserved it."

"Nessa, it's not my right to sit in judgment."

She turned her face up and kissed him, silencing any further discussion. He wanted to continue explaining how a man had to live with his conscience, the importance of his integrity, but her tongue had slipped between his lips, sending small shock waves through him as it touched his. He eased to his feet, picked her up, and carried her back to the bed.

CHAPTER SEVEN

MACINNES LOWERED HIS newspaper as the big jet roared down the runway. Despite the millions of miles he had flown, he still found himself giving most of his attention to the aircraft during the seconds when it lifted off the ground and headed upward at a sharp angle. It was not fear; merely a feeling of alertness. His unconscious may have been pointing out that if anything drastic was in the cards, this could be the most likely moment for it.

He glanced past Vanessa and could see that they were now well above the clouds. His eyes shifted back to the newspaper.

"Damn," he muttered. He was staring at an item headed "Noted Financier a Suicide."

Vanessa, who had been looking out the window, turned to him.

"William L. Edmunds, multimillionaire real estate and auto sales magnate, was found dead early this morning in his luxurious Manhattan penthouse. According to the police, death was probably caused by an overdose of barbiturates, and a letter, the contents of which were not released, indicated clearly that Mr. Edmunds had taken his own life," MacInnes read.

"Rumors of the shaky financial structure of the Edmunds empire have been circulating in Wall Street. These, however, were largely discounted. Though the police would not confirm financial problems as the reason for Mr. Edmunds's suicide, a well-informed source has told this newspaper the contents of the letter indicated great and desperate pressures in this area. . . ."

"What's the matter?" asked Vanessa.

MacInnes folded the paper and let it drop to the carpeted floor. "Fellow I was talking to the other day committed suicide." He started to add, "I engineered his death with my little black box," then told himself to cut out the melodrama.

Would the four million dollars have put Edmunds over the hump? Why did men become so obsessed with money and power? Why should he feel guilty because the greedy son of a bitch couldn't face life without the clout of his big money? Of course, he would not have participated in Hawthorne's bargaining had he known, but then you probably participate unwittingly in all kinds of tragic situations.

Still, his stomach felt queasy.

"Was he a friend?" asked Vanessa.

"No."

She stared at him. "You seem so upset."

He smiled. "I'm not. Just sort of shocked."

She studied his face for a few seconds and then said, "I can see you'd rather not talk about it."

If he kept confessing his sins and his doubts to Vanessa, she would soon decide he needed a priest more than a mistress or, more likely, that he was a weakling who had to be mothered.

"You remember the Hawthorne deal?"

Vanessa nodded. "It wasn't that funny old man, I hope?"

"No, it was Edmunds, the man at the other end of the telephone. The one I put down."

"Oh." She found his hand and squeezed it. "I can see why you would feel badly."

He said, "Not really. I see myself as an innocent bystander. The subway motorman after someone has jumped right in front of his train."

She shuddered at the brutal image.

The *No Smoking* sign went off, and a flight attendant with his cart of bottles paused in the aisle beside them.

"Nothing for me," said Vanessa.

"I'll have a double Grant's on the rocks," said MacInnes.

The thin, cool night air of Mexico City was somehow exhilarating, and they walked briskly to the baggage-collection area and customs. A handsome young Mexican with a hairline moustache stepped up to them.

"Señor MacInnes?"

"Yes?" MacInnes spoke fluent Spanish but used it only when absolutely necessary. A form of one-upmanship.

"I am Feyas, Bernardo Feyas, the, how you say, assistant to Señor Arrosamena. He begs a thousand pardons that he is not able to meet you personally, but he has been delay."

"Señor Juan Hernández Arrosamena y Bela," said MacInnes, smiling.

"Ah, *si*. But we are not so formal these days," said Feyas. He bowed his head slightly. "Now if you will be so kind to permit, I will speed you through customs and escort you to your hotel." He was eyeing Vanessa eagerly.

"My secretary, Miss Peckham," said MacInnes.

He bowed deeper. "I am honored, Señorita Peckham." He turned back to MacInnes. "I have the special permission for your equipment."

They were hustled through customs and whisked away from the airport in a shiny, immaculate but ancient Packard limousine.

But for the employees in *serapes, sombreros,* and peasant skirts, the luxurious hotel could have been any Hilton the world over. The three-room suite was red plush and heavy-oak Spanish but comfortably spacious, with a private balcony. Señor Arrosamena had delicately booked the extra bedroom for MacInnes's secretary.

"I suppose Señor Arrosamena will be available tomorrow?" asked MacInnes.

"Ah, señor, I am sorry to say, no. The next day, or possible the next. He will fly with you personally to Guadalajara. Tomorrow I shall take you sightseeing and shopping.''

MacInnes nodded impatiently. ''Señor Feyas, Miss Peckham and I have explored your lovely city more than once, and my time—well, I'm not sure I can remain here indefinitely.''

''I'll be delighted to go shopping,'' said Vanessa.

Feyas turned to her gratefully. ''Ah, *si*. There is much of beauty to see. Our silver . . .''

MacInnes stared at him, unsmiling. You had to expect this sort of thing south of the border, but it still irritated. Fortunately, his schedule was relatively flexible at the moment. There were two projects waiting, but they could be postponed. A couple of days relaxing in Mexico City would be pleasant.

''Well, I suppose you must take Miss Peckham shopping. I may just loaf by the swimming pool and enjoy a bottle or two of your fine beer.''

Feyas was delighted. He bade them a hasty good night and hurried away before the forbidding American could change his mind.

· Later Vanessa came into the living room and said, ''Stop brooding and come to bed.''

''When I finish this drink.''

She came over and tousled his hair, her fingers cool on his forehead. ''You are like a big boy. You think you have done something bad and must punish yourself.''

''Don't be ridiculous.''

She gave his head a playful slap. ''You are the most transparent man I have ever known. Sometimes you are so transparent that I can see only your soul in there, gleaming like a hard diamond.''

Transparent, was he? Among his poker playing friends he was known as the great stoneface. Maybe he was just transparent to women. As for his soul . . .

She kissed him. ''Promise to wake me?''

He promised and watched her stroll languorously back to the bedroom. It was touching the way she seemed to think sex could solve all the big boy's problems. True, it certainly took his mind off them. But like a good belt of Scotch, the relief it brought was only temporary.

He could still hear Edmunds's tomcat wail of anguish and the clatter of the phone as it fell to his desk. Had that been the moment of truth—the instant Edmunds knew that he was through and that only the grave lay ahead?

But why should Vanessa think he felt guilty? He felt no guilt whatsoever. He merely tended to dramatize these things in his imagination. You can't take part in a man's death without reconstructing, analyzing, understanding your role. Death is not some trivial thing to be brushed away like a mosquito. Edmunds had been an old man. Probably he was simply tired, fed up, unwilling to cope with this new disaster, to exert the energy a fight for survival would require.

He drained his drink, crushed out his cigarette, and went to wake up Vanessa.

CHAPTER EIGHT

KEVIN LOUNGED BY the hotel's large pool, comfortable in a canvas chair, a glass of beer on the small table beside him. He idly surveyed the swimmers and sunbathers. They were mostly Americans and Europeans. Aside from some of the attractive girls, who might be hotel employees off-duty, the few Mexicans there would be rich, because the hotel was unconscionably expensive. Like the French, the Mexican girls were hipless and, though bikini clad, were poor competition for the thin-waisted, swelling-hipped Americans.

The thought of the expense of this hotel, and the life-style he was becoming accustomed to, led him to recount his blessings. During the last three years he had moved from the comparably modest income of an army colonel to the affluence of one who could drive a nineteen-thousand-dollar Mercedes, with a Mark IV Continental as a second car, who could roam the coast and inland waterways in his forty-foot cabin cruiser, and who owned a three-hundred-thousand-dollar ocean-front mansion with private beach and dock.

Yet for some reason, these luxuries were not as satisfying as he had expected them to be. After the novelty wore off, they were merely status symbols, producing friendliness or respect from strangers who would not ordinarily bother to be friendly or impressed. And who in hell needed this? Some inner scold, left in his core by his childhood conditioning, kept telling him that the only thing that counted was what a man *achieved,* what kind of human being a man made of himself, not the quantity or quality of material things he accumulated. What kind of a man was he? And what had he achieved? He smiled at the naïveté of his answer. *I am a protector of the innocent, a stalker of the guilty.*

"Colonel MacInnes!"

He looked up. A wiry little man dressed in powder-blue slacks and a yellow safari jacket, his dark-brown monkey face creased by a cynical smile, stood before him. The man's hair had turned white since MacInnes had last seen him.

"Señor Hergueta." MacInnes shoved the other chair out with his foot. "Sit down." MacInnes did not rise or offer his hand.

Hergueta slid into the chair and moved it closer. "So we meet again, my friend."

MacInnes smiled. Friend he wasn't. Carlos Hergueta, Colombian national, was a smuggler, thief, international blackmailer, narcotics dealer, informer. It was amazing that Hergueta had lived so long. He would sell you anything not screwed to the floor, including information. Hergueta ranged the world like an overactive, irritable chimpanzee, buying, selling, stealing. On a number of occasions MacInnes had bought information from him, and usually it had been reliable.

"What brings you to Mexico, Colonel?"

MacInnes said, "No longer, Colonel. I've retired."

"Ah!" Hergueta lifted his eyebrows in friendly disbelief. "So now you sit in the sun, an old man, content with your memories."

MacInnes signaled a waiter hovering nearby. "I work, but not for the United States government." The waiter sauntered up. "What will you have, señor?"

"*Gracias*. A tequila on ice will do."

On ice? Hergueta was the one who was getting old. Generally they belted it down straight, sometimes with a bite into a salted lime quarter.

The two men stared at each other silently. All previous meetings had been devoted strictly to business, with no attempt at amenities. Small talk would be difficult, as far as MacInnes was concerned.

"You enjoy your stay in Mexico?" asked Hergueta.

MacInnes said, "So far." It suddenly occurred to him that he might, even as a civilian, be able to make use of Hergueta. It was a thousand-to-one longshot, but what the hell, he had nothing to lose but a little time.

The waiter arrived with Hergueta's drink. MacInnes signed the check and, after the waiter left, said, "Carlos, there is a possibility that we might be able to do some business."

Hergueta raised his drink in a silent salute. "Ah?"

"When you finish your drink, we'll go to my suite. I have something I want to show you."

Hergueta pursed his thick lips. "Better to talk outside, Colonel."

MacInnes smiled. Being outside wasn't the protection it had once been. Electronic surveillance wasn't limited to bugging rooms. The table could be bugged. For that matter, a long-range sound pickup could be beamed right on them. But Hergueta was right. A stroll in the open would be safer.

"We will go to my rooms. You will look at what I wish to show you. Then we will return and stroll the grounds for our talk," said MacInnes.

Hergueta tossed his drink down, the ice clinking, and stood up. "You do not talk to me at all in the room, Colonel. That is understood?"

"Right," said MacInnes. He lowered his voice. "What I want you to look at is an identikit drawing. A police artist's drawing of a man described by a witness. You understand?"

"*Si.*"

In the suite MacInnes quickly extracted the photostat of the drawing of the Englishman from his locked attaché case. He handed it to Hergueta. The Englishman might well be known in the underworld of one of the dozens of big cities frequented by Hergueta. London, Melbourne, Rome, Tokyo, New York?

Hergueta studied the drawing carefully, then handed it back to MacInnes.

They left the suite silently and made their way outside.

Strolling toward the tennis courts, MacInnes said, "He is English or an Australian. I am interested in his name and whereabouts." He stopped, so that he could look squarely at Hergueta.

Hergueta said, "I do not know this man, Colonel." His eyes flicked nervously away from MacInnes's stare.

MacInnes said, "I could make it well worth your while to get me information on this man." He searched his mind for an amount large enough to impress Hergueta but not foolishly large. "I would say I would pay a thousand dollars for some hard information about this man."

Hergueta turned away. "I will see what I can do. I am doubt that I can help you."

"One thousand dollars if you can."

"*Sí.*" Hergueta hesitated, then said, "I must leave you, Colonel. Thank you for the refreshment."

MacInnes watched Hergueta walk briskly toward the hotel parking lot. He felt a surge of excitement. He didn't need a PSE to know that Hergueta had been lying when he said he didn't know the Englishman. Had he been frightened, or was the delay merely to demonstrate that he was truly earning his thousand dollars? If Hergueta was frightened, the Englishman might be a shark in the scummy waters of international crime. Interpol probably already had a make on him. MacInnes decided he'd probably hear no more from Hergueta.

CHAPTER NINE

IT WAS LATE in the afternoon when Vanessa and Feyas returned, both laden with packages. They deposited various boxes and bags on one of the giant sofas, and Vanessa said, "We had lunch in a really great Italian restaurant. You'll have to take me there again while we're here."

MacInnes, who had been pacing restlessly, said, "I didn't expect you'd be gone the whole day."

Vanessa began tearing open one of the packages. "Darling, we didn't leave until almost noon."

Feyas, MacInnes thought, looked definitely shifty eyed.

"Before we came back, we had a drink in a little *cantina*. It was full of real moustachioed brigands," said Vaness. *"Mucho machismo."*

MacInnes lit a cigarette. "I'm not sure that was very wise. Some Mexicans don't take kindly to us *gringos*." He had almost been killed getting out of a "little *cantina*" not many years back.

Vanessa looked at Feyas, smiling. "Oh, Bernardo would have taken care of them."

Feyas was glancing at the ceiling, as though it might be the only safe place to look. Finally he lowered his eyes and said, "The place was not too bad, señor, though I would not have chosen it to entertain the señorita. It was she who insist."

Feyas left quickly, murmuring something about calling tomorrow to see if he could be of further service while they waited to hear from Señor Arrosamena.

Vanessa said, "I can't believe it, but I think you are jealous."

MacInnes forced a grin. "And why shouldn't I be? You go off with a handsome young Mexican and stay away almost six hours."

She stopped unwrapping the package and stared thoughtfully at MacInnes. "He bought me all these things. With his own money. He insisted."

MacInnes stifled rising irritation. "Why did you let him?"

"He's in love with me."

"Oh."

"He probably spent two months' salary on these things."

MacInnes shrugged. "These Latins come on pretty strong. And Arrosamena is rich. Maybe he told him to spend freely entertaining us. You know, an expense-account thing.''

Vanessa frowned. "You don't think he's in love with me?''

MacInnes said, "No. That I wouldn't doubt. That's why I'm jealous.''

She pushed the package away. "It was his own money. I'm sure of it. It hurt, but he wanted to do it. He wanted to buy me everything I admired.''

MacInnes felt a tightening in his throat. "Are you attracted to him?''

"Of course. He's absolutely charming.''

MacInnes crushed out his cigarette, trying to maintain his forced smile. "Ready to trade in the old model?''

She stared at him for a moment, wide-eyed, not understanding. "You?''

He nodded.

She hurried over and hugged him. "Darling, I don't love him. I merely agreed that he was attractive.''

"Do you love me?''

She looked up at him. "I thought we had an agreement about love. I quote, 'We'll take life as it comes, day by day, and we won't worry about love. Who can define it, anyway?'''

"I remember. But you haven't answered my question.''

She pushed away a bit. "I can't. I've been living up to our agreement. I haven't thought carefully about it.''

"Think.''

She returned to the sofa and stared at the package. "You must pay him back discreetly, without hurting his feelings. I think he spent something over three hundred dollars."

MacInnes nodded. "Doesn't he understand our relationship? He's surely not so unsophisticated?"

"Oh, he understands."

And perhaps, MacInnes thought, she has no trouble making a choice because he would not be able to support her in the manner she was pleased to have become accustomed to.

"I'll take care of it," he said.

She stood looking at him, sensing the coolness and hurt beneath the casual tone he attempted. She came back to him.

"Kevin, I don't think you'll ever be able to really love any woman. What happened?"

He shrugged.

"How long were you married?"

"Six years."

"With no children?"

He shook his head. "That was by choice."

"You didn't want children?"

He reached for his cigarettes. "I was in the army, away a great deal. Wouldn't have been a proper father, all that sort of thing." He moved to the coffee table to pour himself a Scotch, asking her with a gesture whether she wanted one. She shook her head. "Lately I've been regretting it. The only real continuity we have is through our children. Unless, of course . . ."

"Unless you write a great book, or paint a great picture, or create a great invention?"

He smiled. "We all want some little morsel of immortality, I guess."

Vanessa said, "Male ego. I don't believe women think much about it."

He sipped his drink silently. Lately he had been having crazy thoughts about settling down and marrying again. Children. A real family. It wasn't too late, but soon it would be. Vanessa, of course, was not the answer. The difference in their ages. She might easily get bored and walk out on him. On the other hand, fifteen years wasn't an impossible gap. And she was the only woman he had known to whom he sometimes felt he wouldn't *mind* being married.

He leaned back in his chair and closed his eyes. "Why don't you relax a bit then we'll have a drink or two and we'll go to Fouquet's for dinner. Pretend we're in Paris." Suddenly Mexico City had lost its charm for MacInnes.

Later when he went to bed to wake up Vanessa, he trailed a wire with a tiny microphone into the dark bedroom and fastened it to the headboard. He almost always had to wake Vanessa, and she demanded it, because she was one of those who fall asleep seconds after head touches pillow.

After they made love and he lay with her in his arms, her soft breasts pressed against his chest, he asked, "Nessa, do you love me?"

"No."

"Are you sure?"

"Yes."

"What are your feelings for me?"

She was silent for a while. "I'm very attached to you. What would the word be, *fond*? I enjoy living with you. You're a good lover." She arched her back to press her belly tightly against him. "I like your making love to me."

"And that's all?"

He could feel her light breath warm on his neck. "I suppose so."

He kissed her. "Nessa, have you ever done anything you're terribly ashamed of?"

There was an almost inaudible gasp. "Yes."

"What?"

"I won't tell you."

"And you're sure you don't love me?"

She stroked his cheek. "Yes." There was a pause. Then she said, "And neither do you love me."

He pressed her more firmly, his hand wandering down her back. "I'm not so sure about that." He was becoming aroused and had no desire for further talk.

A half hour later, when Vanessa slept soundly again, he got up and carried the microphone and trailing wire back to the living room.

The sounds of lovemaking came softly from the tape recorder. He erased them as unwanted and voyeuristic invasions of their privacy. It was the dialogue, not Vanessa's faint gasps and moans, that he wanted for the PSE.

"Nessa, do you love me?"

"No."

He fed the slowed-down tape through the PSE, watching the chart with an intensity no professional case had ever provoked. On the word *no* the pen strokes closed in, blocking the area almost solid with stress.

A small surge of joy crept cautiously through him, doubting whether it was in the right house. What he saw was plainly deception stress. She was lying when she said she did not love him. Or maybe there was some malfunctioning of the equipment?

He studied the rest of the conversation as the chart moved slowly beneath the pen. There was normal stress on the "yes" to "Have you ever done anything you're terribly ashamed of?" Lesser deception stress showed on the answer to "Are you sure you don't love me?" and there was no stress on "And neither do you love me."

Again there was heavy deception stress on her answer, "I suppose so," to his question "And that's all?" following her summation of his attractions.

If he was to believe the Dektor PSE, she did truly love him. Or at least, at that particular moment, she believed she loved him.

He sat for a long time bemused, then finally returned to bed, where sleep came eventually.

Bright Mexican sun flooded the bedroom, waking MacInnes slowly, his blurry vision settling on a ceramic Aztec calendar hanging on the opposite wall. The design gradually became three dimensional and he was fully awake, his first thoughts of Vanessa. Her long golden hair was divided, part under the sheet and part outside, faintly perfumed and glossy clean. Which might, he thought sleepily, be the answer to the question whether the old man slept with his beard under the covers or outside. He gazed at her with deepening affection, happy in the knowledge that he was loved, even though the message had arrived through devious electronic trickery.

He slipped quietly from the bed without waking her and went to the living room to telephone for breakfast. Papaya, bacon, eggs, toast, and coffee for himself. Papaya and black coffee for Vanessa, should she happen to wake, which was doubtful. Hanging up, he hurried to the bathroom for a quick shower and shave.

Was he placing too much reliance on the PSE? he wondered, drying himself. Irony. If he couldn't trust his own interpretation of a PSE chart, what could he trust? He dressed quickly in fresh slacks and sport shirt. He was bending to wipe the dust from his loafers, when he heard the waiter rapping. He threw the soft paper provided for shoe polishing in the wastebasket and hurried to the living room to open the door.

"Buenos días, señor," said the waiter, rolling his cart into the room. "You would like breakfast on the terrace, no? Still cool. Sun not so hot yet."

"Fine," said MacInnes, buttoning his shirt.

The waiter pushed the cart across the large living room to the French doors. He opened them wide and started wheeling the cart through. He stopped suddenly, becoming as immobile as a mannequin. After a few seconds of paralysis he muttered, *"Madre de Dios,"* and backed into the living room, crossing himself.

MacInnes hurried to the terrace doors. He shoved the cart aside and stepped out into the sun. Hanging from the balcony above, a figure swayed slightly in the gentle breeze.

Carlos Hergueta, his tongue protruding from his

brown monkey face, dangled before MacInnes, his high-heeled ankle boots hardly a foot from the terrace flagstones.

The waiter, dry washing his hands, stood in the doorway bug eyed.

"A knife. Get a knife quickly," said MacInnes. "He may still be alive." He grasped Hergueta's wrist, feeling for a pulse. No pulse.

The waiter was still frozen. "Get a knife. We must cut him down!" MacInnes said, this time shouting. The rope was secured somewhere on the balcony above. Cutting him down would probably be quicker than trying to get up there.

Fumbling nervously the waiter brought a large pocket knife from his jacket and handed it to MacInnes, his hand trembling. MacInnes climbed to the wide concrete balcony rail and began sawing away at the rope.

"Call your manager. Doctor, police, ambulance. Be quick!" he yelled to the waiter.

The knife had been recently honed, and it cut through the strands faster than MacInnes had expected. Hergueta slumped to the flagstones. MacInnes jumped down and went to work, trying artificial respiration and heart massage. The protruding tongue made mouth-to-mouth resuscitation impossible, for which MacInnes was vaguely thankful. He knew all these acts were futile, but they had to be done. Hergueta was as dead as he would ever be. He could have been hanging there for hours.

Hergueta had gone seeking information once too often.

The manager, a young Mexican-American, to

judge by his California-accented English, was glossy haired and sleekly dressed. Accompanied by the portly hotel doctor, brown with a big moustache, they hurried to the balcony.

As the doctor knelt to apply his stethoscope, MacInnes explained the measures he had already taken. The doctor nodded gravely, then spent a minute listening intently. He shrugged and got to his feet, folding the stethoscope and cramming it partially into his jacket pocket.

They returned to the living room, which was now filling up with police officers, three in uniform and one in an ordinary dark suit.

Vanessa chose that moment to come out of the bedroom looking bewildered as well as seductively naked under her thin negligee. Conversation stopped as the seven Mexicans stared at her with apologetic and courteous admiration.

"What's going on?" she asked.

MacInnes put his arm around her. "Nessa, why don't you go back to the bedroom? There's been a nasty accident on the terrace." He tried to guide her gently in the right direction. "There's a dead man out there. Get dressed and we'll have the manager move us to another suite."

She pulled away and crossed to the terrace doors. She glanced outside briefly, then returned, looking pale. She went back to the bedroom and closed the door.

The official in the business suit was tall and thin. He was obviously in charge. He had the inevitable moustache and a mildly pock-marked face. Approaching MacInnes, he held out his hand. "Capitan Corando García,'' he said.

"Colonel Kevin MacInnes, U.S. Army retired,'' said MacInnes, shaking hands. Titles sometimes smoothed the way in Latin America.

"Ah.'' García scrutinized him carefully. "You know this man, perhaps? This man who has hanged himself on your balcony?''

MacInnes decided that it might be politic to switch to Spanish. He could see being delayed considerably in Mexico City while the wheels of investigation ground with exceeding slowness.

"Yes,'' he said, speaking rapidly. "I knew this man as Carlos Hergueta. I am sure you know him too. When I was on active duty, I had occasion to deal with him. Yesterday he approached me with an offer to sell certain information. I explained that I was no longer a buyer of information. However, the situation concerned a large shipment of heroin being readied to cross our border, and so I told him I would pay him one thousand dollars for the details.'' MacInnes smiled. "I was sure my government would reimburse me.''

García had been studying MacInnes's face, impressed with his fluency, yet maintaining a policeman's skepticism.

"And these details, señor, did you receive them?''

"No. We were to meet late this afternoon.''

García stared at him, still skeptical. The American would prefer to let the shipment get across the border, then make the arrest. In any event the plans would now be changed. *"Sí,"* he said. "Well, the *gusano* is no loss to us.''

He turned to the uniformed policemen and began giving them orders. MacInnes singled out the manager and asked that they be moved to another suite.

"I have no other so large, señor," said the manager. "I can move you to one with one bedroom only."

"That will do."

"I must get permission from *el capitán*. Nothing can be touched in a place where *un homicidio* is happen."

He moved away to speak to García. MacInnes could see García nodding, then García turned and came back to him.

"I have given permission for the hotel to move you and your lady and your personal effects to another suite. I must ask, however, that you remain available for further interrogation."

"Good. I'll be available."

"Why are you in Mexico, Colonel MacInnes?"

MacInnes rubbed his cheek thoughtfully. Arrosamena would not appreciate being involved in the situation. On the other hand, since he would be dealing with the police in Guadalajara, there was little point in trying to conceal it.

At that instant, Bernardo Feyas arrived, eyebrows raised at the number of men milling around in the living room and on the terrace. He hurried up to MacInnes.

While García stood listening, MacInnes explained the situation to Feyas.

Feyas shook his head, making small sounds of commiseration and irritation. "Señorita Peckham, how shocking for her. Is she all right?"

"I have asked the manager to move us to another suite immediately."

Feyas turned to García and introduced himself. "Señor MacInnes is a guest of Señor Arrosamena of Guadalajara."

García looked thoughtful. Arrosamena was a powerful man, considerably out of García's orbit. When Arrosamena spoke to the police, he would speak to *el comandante*. He turned and called to the manager, who was chatting with one of the uniformed policemen. "Señor, I have asked you to move the colonel and his lady to another suite. Please do so *at once*."

The manager nodded and hurried away.

MacInnes excused himself and went to the bedroom.

Vanessa was sitting by the windows, dressed in jeans and a loose shirt. Her bags were all packed. He could see that she was still a bit stunned.

"They'll be getting us moved shortly," he said.

She nodded.

"I could use some coffee." He thought about the untouched breakfasts on the cart. "Why don't we go down for some breakfast? I'm sure you could stand some coffee."

She stood up without answering and followed him out of the room. He told García where they were going, and she gave Feyas, who was busy telephoning Arrosamena, a faint smile as they left the suite.

In the restaurant she asked, "The man who was killed, did he have something to do with your work?"

He attacked his bacon and eggs while she sipped her black coffee. He was wondering what to do about Vanessa. Finding Hergueta on his balcony meant only one thing. War had been declared. Perhaps only a drastic warning? They surely would have no idea *why* he was looking for the Englishman. Would Vanessa be safer with him or in Palm Beach or with some friend in some undisclosed city? Away from him she might be kidnapped and used as a hostage.

"Yes," he said. "Do you have some friend in some out-of-the-way place like, say, Topeka, Kansas, that you could go to and stay with?"

She stared at him, smiling. "No."

He sipped his coffee. "I can't decide whether it will be less dangerous for you to stay with me or go back to Palm Beach."

"I think I'll stay with you."

MacInnes shook his head. "The man who was killed was working for me."

"I'm not afraid."

He'd have to pass the information along via the local CIA people. He might get some help in deciding what to do about Vanessa.

"Kevin, are you a spy?" she asked.

He smiled at her quaint way of expressing it. "No, I'm nothing more than I've told you. I'm the Lie King."

He saw skepticism in her face.

"Remember I told you some of the things I'm involved in could be dangerous. There's been nothing this sticky so far, though—at least, not since I left the army."

"You wouldn't tell me if you were a foreign agent, would you?"

He shrugged.

"You wouldn't work for any government other than ours, would you?"

He held up his right hand. "No, so help me God." He thought for a few seconds. "You mean in the sense of being an agent and working secretly against the interests of the United States? I might openly assist a foreign government or foreign national with a problem involving my specialty. The way General Motors might sell them Chevrolets."

They finished the meal in silence.

On the way through the lobby he stopped at the desk to find out whether they had been moved to another suite.

The clerk said, "Oh, Señor MacInnes, there is a message for you." He handed MacInnes a small envelope with "Col. MacInnes" scribbled on it in a hasty scrawl.

MacInnes ripped it open. Inside there was a single thin sheet, with a short paragraph in Spanish. He read, "The man you are seeking was born in 1925 in Liverpool. Name, Colin Head. Other names used: Lawrence Hawley, Calvin Harp. He is a mad dog. You would be wise to forget your desire to locate him. Send $1,000 to Account No. 2635H, Bank Heinrich Brum, Geneve."

He jammed the note into his jacket pocket quickly. It was the first free information he had ever received from an informant.

The clerk told him the maids were still cleaning the new suite, and it would be ready shortly.

MacInnes turned to Vanessa. "Let's take a little stroll in the sun." He planned to head directly for the American embassy, only a short walk away. Vanessa would be safe there while he tried to decide their next move.

CHAPTER TEN

THE AMERICAN EMBASSY in Mexico City is the second largest American embassy in the entire world, and probably the busiest. Since he had decided to tell his story only once, and to the right person, MacInnes had resigned himself to wasting considerable time being shunted from one lower-level staff member to another. Then he remembered that an old friend, Billy Tucker, was at the moment stationed there as a military attaché.

Colonel Tucker sent word out that he would be delighted to see his old friend if MacInnes would be kind enough to wait for ten or fifteen minutes, since Tucker was in a meeting.

The saying is that being a bird colonel is as far as you can go in the army without two special qualifications. The first is to be a member of the "club"—a West Pointer—and the second, to have some political clout. Tucker had the first but was evidently lacking in the second. Some ten years older than MacInnes, he had been a bird colonel for a long time.

Tucker's hair was already white, and it looked very white topping his florid complexion. He was delighted to see MacInnes and even more delighted to meet Vanessa. They spent the customary five minutes reminiscing. Then MacInnes said, "Billy, I've got something too hot to mess around with. I think I'd better tell it to your chief spook. It's definitely NKO."

"What's 'NKO'?" asked Vanessa.

Both men smiled. MacInnes said, "It means the information is strictly limited to those who *need to know only*." He turned back to Tucker. "Is there somewhere Vanessa can have a cup of coffee and wait for me?"

Tucker smoothed his white locks carefully. "Indeed there is, and I hope she'll let me have the pleasure of providing it." He picked up his phone and dialed.

MacInnes had on occasion worked with the CIA when an army case with international complications overlapped with them. These were largely unhappy associations. In general he had found the CIA people arrogant, superior, and secretive to the point of endangering not only the success of the operation, but also the safety of army personnel involved.

Adverse publicity may have brought about a

new policy. They seemed to be trying to change their image. Jack Mulcahy was a big man with a big warm grin, and MacInnes trusted him instinctively, at the same time warning himself to watch out for a con job. With tousled blond hair, blue eyes, and a fleshy Irish face, Mulcahy could have made a great priest. He filled a large Scandinavian pipe with a bowl that looked like an inverted volcano, packing it with very black tobacco, lit it, and leaned back to give MacInnes's story close attention.

MacInnes began with the cabdriver and described the whole situation in detail, leaving out only the fact that Weymouth had given him photostats of the identikit drawings. He had merely described the Englishmen to Hergueta.

When he finished, Mulcahy grinned. "Sort of sticking your nose into it, weren't you, bubba?"

MacInnes shrugged. "Hergueta being an international bastard, I thought he might know another international bastard. I had no idea the son of a bitch was local."

"And you were willing to invest a thousand of your own hard-earned cash?"

MacInnes said, "I can afford it," thinking of the half million he had hard earned in New York. He pulled out the note Hergueta had left and handed it to Mulcahy. "I imagine there's one hell of a tangle of law-enforcement agencies working on this, but since I am now on foreign soil, I think you're probably the right man to pass this on to."

Mulcahy took it. "You're absolutely right, bubba." He read it quickly. "I've heard about you. The Lie King himself, eh?"

He puffed on his pipe for a moment. "All over the world we're looking for that effing Englishman, and *you* have to find him here." He shook his head sadly.

"Tough," said MacInnes.

Mulcahy pointed the stem of his pipe at MacInnes threateningly. "You know what it means? It means that I've not only got to find the son of a bitch, I've got to keep him under close surveillance the entire time he's in Mexico."

MacInnes said, "I'm surprised Interpol didn't have anything on him."

Mulcahy shook his head. "Nary a word. Maybe this cabdriver's description wasn't so hot."

"It was hot enough for Hergueta."

"Unless he was killed for some other reason."

MacInnes smiled. "On my balcony?"

Mulcahy tamped his pipe down and relit it. "So what are you doing in Mexico, besides sticking your nose into our garbage?"

MacInnes described his business with Arrosamena. "As for sticking my nose into your problem—"

Mulcahy held up his hand. "I know. Billy's told me all about your background. I can trust you with my ass, and all that shit. We're brothers under the skin, and I must commend you, bubba, for being most helpful. At least we know the name the son of a bitch was born with. And if he is now known as Harp, it's a goddamned insult to my favorite beer."

MacInnes laughed but sobered quickly. He told

Mulcahy his problem with Vanessa. Should he ship her home, send her into hiding, or keep her with him?

Mulcahy thought about it. "Keep her with you. As far as we know the Englishman doesn't know *why* you want to find him. If you panic, he's liable to think it's more important trouble than he thought. He may abort his whole part of the job. Then we're in great shape. We know an assassination is being planned, and we haven't even a clue as to where to start looking."

MacInnes shifted uncomfortably. "To kill Hergueta, he must have figured it was pretty big trouble. I don't want to take any chances with Vanessa's safety."

Mulcahy said, "How could he connect you, man? He's a psycho, showing off to the gang. See, this is what happens to informers, even if what they tell isn't very important."

Could be, MacInnes thought. How could the Englishman possibly tie him in with the situation? On the other hand, Mulcahy obviously wanted to make patsies of them both. He wasn't going to look for the Englishman. He was going to let the Englishman look for MacInnes and Vanessa. Still, what was the alternative? Give up the job for Arrosamena and hotfoot it back to the States? They could find him there just as easily as in Mexico.

"I don't care for the idea of being bait in your rat trap."

Mulcahy waved his pipe gently, a tired Toscanini. "You, bubba, are going to be more than bait. He's a psycho, so of course, he's going to come looking for you. He's got to find out why you're looking for him. But you got nothing to worry about. The marines gonna be hiding in the bushes, protecting your every move.''

"Ha."

"What do you mean, ha?"

"The bastard comes around and kills both of us, and you're going to keep right on keeping him under surveillance. You rush in and put him out of the game and you're right back where you mentioned—up that famous creek without a clue."

Mulcahy stuck his pipe in his mouth and puffed, trying to look insulted. "Bubba, you think I would do that to a fellow-American?"

"Yes."

Mulcahy shook his head. "Look at it this way. If he wanted to kill you, he could have done so last night, right after swinging Hergueta from the yard-arm."

MacInnes said, "He wants information first, then kill. It might have caused too much noise trying to get information there at the hotel."

Mulcahy puffed thoughtfully for a while. "Look, bubba, you're not thinking this thing through. You're a trained agent, and we need your help, and goddammit, you're going to give it to us!"

"I—"

"Now, you look here, bubba! I do not see you as expendable. I see here an opportunity for you to help us get the kind of information we need. You will be given a goddamned fine cover story, a story that can lead to further association with our boy.''

"Such as?"

Mulcahy grinned. ''I haven't figured that one out.'' He thought for a few seconds. ''Try this one on for size. Your teenage daughter is in a Mexican jail having her life ruined by a ten-year narcotics rap. You are pulling powerful strings trying to get her out. If these fail, you want to hire a group of hard types to spring her by force. You know, storm the jail with submachine guns and a waiting helicopter. The kind of thing they pulled getting that guy out a few years ago. . . .''

MacInnes smiled, nodding, admiring Mulcahy's quick improvisation. Since the thought of having to deal with the Englishman had first hit him, MacInnes had been searching his mind for a credible cover story and had been stumped. How do you convince a shrewd and hardened criminal that a man who has devoted most of his adult life to law enforcement is after him to do business, not cause trouble? What better situation could bring a man of rigid rectitude to crime quicker than the agony of his nineteen-year-old daughter doomed to ten years in a *Mexican* prison? His work had taken him into a few Mexican prisons. Attica would be a country club in comparison.

''We'll make up an identity for one of our agents and actually slap her in the can. We've got some twenty-year-olds, you know. Sometimes our freaks down here get involved in the drug traffic, and we have to keep an eye on them.''

Mulcahy knocked some of the ashes from his pipe and tamped down the remaining tobacco.

"You'll go to the jail and visit her. She'll throw her arms around you and scream and sob and beg. If he has any contacts inside the jail, he'll believe you're legitimate."

MacInnes said, "Let's think about who told me to look for the Englishman to handle this job."

Mulcahy yanked open a drawer and extracted a memorandum. "No problem. Last night a dealer named, let me see"—he scanned the sheet—"named Ubaldo Galindo was killed in a shoot-out with the Mexican police. A contact in the States sent you to him. Ubaldo told you the Englishman was the only man for the job. The one man with enough *machismo* to pull it off."

MacInnes said, "That could be a bit shaky. If Ubaldo and Mr. X happen to be close, why would I have to go to Hergueta?"

"Ubaldo was going to get in touch with you but didn't. You got impatient."

There was one question MacInnes couldn't ask. Before he died, Hergueta had undoubtedly told everything he knew about the incident. Why would MacInnes be carrying an identikit drawing of Mr. X? He'd have to figure out the answer to that one on his own. He realized suddenly that he was sitting with every muscle tense. He relaxed them, one by one.

"Vanessa will have to be kept completely out of it. Otherwise, it's no deal."

Seeing Mulcahy's frown, MacInnes hurriedly said, "It would be a perfectly natural thing for me to do. Finding a hanged man on your balcony is a hell of a shock for a woman. I'd want to get her away while I straightened things out."

Mulcahy shrugged. "Okay. If you insist. I suppose it won't make too much difference. We'll pack her off to my sister in Acapulco. She'll be perfectly safe there."

"What about Arrosamena? He's liable to want me to go to Guadalajara any minute."

"Guadalajara." Mulcahy scratched his chin. "I think that's probably even better. Comisario Torrejón is a good man. Very cooperative. Less complications." He stood up, stretching. "We'll put your daughter in jail over there."

MacInnes found his way to the nearest men's room. Locking himself in one of the booths, he took the identikit drawings from his jacket pocket and systematically tore each photostat into tiny bits and flushed them down. Burning them would be safer, but the smell, in that particular men's room, might cause someone to push the panic button, precipitating a sort of wild in-house investigation.

Vanessa took some convincing. She was no fragile flower and preferred to take her chances with MacInnes. They talked her down. Mulcahy pointed out that she was untrained, that the situation demanded an experienced agent, that her presence, instead of helping, might endanger MacInnes.

An hour later a strange Mexican girl came up to MacInnes and threw her arms around him. Startled, he stared at Vanessa's dusky face, her long black hair, her bright yellow dress, intriguingly snug and short.

He held her tightly for a moment, feeling intensely possessive. This woman belonged to him.

She loved him. The PSE said so. A mawkish wave of sentimentality made him wonder if he would ever see her again. He cursed the impulse that had made him show the drawing to Hergueta. He had been in graver danger many times, but necessary danger. Part of the job. This he had invited. *Estúpido. Muy estúpido!*

She left the building with two of the embassy secretaries. Three Mexican girls on the way to lunch and shopping.

MacInnes had lunch with his daughter. She looked all of seventeen. Worn jeans, a thin T-shirt that outlined her braless nipples, no makeup, and long blonde hair that could have used both a shampoo and a great deal of brushing. Though not beautiful, her scrubbed face had an appealing freshness and a look of clear-eyed no-nonsense.

They shared a plate of sandwiches in Mulcahy's office. She was Deborah MacInnes, according to her new passport, nineteen years old, height, 5 feet 9 inches; hair, blonde; eyes, blue-gray; birthplace, New York, U.S.A.

MacInnes handed the passport back. "I don't envy you your assignment," he said.

She smiled. "I've had worse. A few days of getting rid the head lice and crab lice, and a month or so of diarrhea medicine, and I'll be okay." She flipped the passport thoughtfully. "I'd rather have my assignment than yours."

MacInnes nodded, his mouth full of ham-and-cheese sandwich.

Back at the hotel, MacInnes surveyed the new suite sadly. Without Vanessa it was empty, boring, stupefying. He fingered the .38 holstered under his loose-fitting sport shirt; the cigarette case that actually had cigarettes in it but, more important had a tiny camera so skillfully concealed that no one but an expert would find it; the felt-tipped pen that would fire a micro-dum-dum bullet a quarter of an inch thick and an inch and a quarter long, guaranteed to be fatal in vital areas when fired from up to ten feet away. It also functioned beautifully as a pen. There was a small wallet that contained a micro-tape recorder, flat enough to be disguised as five plastic credit cards, stuck together, unfortunately; and a scalpel-sharp knife taped to his right calf. The most exotic piece of equipment was his key chain attached to a souvenir square of Connemara marble containing deadly gas, a squirt of which would kill at a distance of up to two feet.

"What if he coughs or sneezes just as I squirt?" MacInnes had asked.

"See that he doesn't," Mulcahy had answered.

Mulcahy had fitted him out as a walking arsenal of death—his own death. If Mr. X or his crew caught up with him, and that was the whole point of the operation, they would undoubtedly frisk him.

Mulcahy had agreed that MacInnes could use his own judgment on how much of the equipment he could jettison, with the exception of the Connemara marble, which was top secret. He urged him fervently to at least keep the camera. A picture of Mr. X would be worth ten thousand words.

Feyas had called three times. While MacInnes was shuffling the message blanks, there was a polite rapping on the door.

He walked over and opened it cautiously. Feyas was in the hall.

"They tell me you are back, señor. I take the liberty of coming directly up, because Señor Arrosamena is now ready to return to Guadalajara, and I am concern about you and the señorita."

"Come in," said MacInnes, opening the door wide.

Feyas entered, looking around eagerly for Vanessa.

"Señorita Peckham will not be accompanying us," said MacInnes. "The shock of this terrible murder has depressed her and she has returned to the United States."

Feyas's mouth drooped.

"She may rejoin me in a few days. Would you be so kind as to see that her luggage is stored in some safe place?"

Feyas perked up. "Certainly, señor. It is my pleasure."

MacInnes closed the door. "Please have a seat."

Feyas sat down, back straight, occupying hardly six inches of the front of the cushioned chair. "Señor Arrosamena has asked can you be ready to leave for the airport at 4:00 P.M.?"

MacInnes glanced at his watch. "Easily."

Feyas started to rise.

MacInnes gestured. "Stay a minute. I'd like to have a chat with you. About Señorita Peckham."

Feyas sank back, his expression faintly apprehensive. Then his jaw became firmer. "I suppose I must confess to you, señor, that I am very, how do you say, very enamored of the lady."

"I know."

Feyas said, "I would consider it a very great favor if the señor would not mention this to Señor Arrosamena. He will be very angry with me."

MacInnes smiled. "Depend on it, I won't."

"Grácias."

"Señor Feyas, will you do *me* a very great favor?"

Surprised, Feyas said, "Certainly, señor, you have only to ask."

MacInnes searched for the right words. "You see, I feel very possessive about señorita Peckham. Of course, she is free to choose her own man. But while she is with me, I would consider it a great favor if you would allow me to reimburse you for the beautiful gifts you purchased."

Feyas thought about it, his mouth slightly open. "I can understand your feelings, señor. Yes, of course you may do so."

"Thank you." MacInnes quickly signed traveler's checks totaling three hundred and fifty dollars and handed them to Feyas.

Without looking at the amounts, Feyas stuffed the checks into his jacket pocket. "I will accept these on the basis of what you say, señor." He smiled sadly. "But I have the feeling you are trying to be kind."

"Not at all."

They shook hands, and Feyas left.

CHAPTER ELEVEN

ARROSAMENA WAS RICHER than MacInnes had thought. His private Gulfstream jet not only had a pilot, co-pilot, and steward, but also a luxurious lounge, sleeping quarters, and a sumptuously stocked galley.

Arrosamena did not look rich. About forty-five, with gray, closely cropped, curly hair, a brown face, and high Indian-inherited cheekbones, he could have been selling tortillas in the *zócalo*.

The plane had reached cruising altitude and the steward was busy serving—Scotch on the rocks for MacInnes, coffee for Arrosamena, and a Coca-Cola for Feyas.

Arrosamena studied MacInnes, his lively black eyes searching MacInnes's expressionless

Anglo-Saxon face. "Bernardo has told me of your unpleasantness, this international *bandido* who has been killed on your balcony. Please accept my sympathy."

"*Grácias,*" said MacInnes, sipping his Scotch. They were speaking Spanish. Arrosamena's English was barely understandable.

"I think, Colonel, that you are still working for your government. My friend *El Comandante* tells me this thief was known to you as an informer."

MacInnes nodded. "*Sí.*"

"I hope this problem will not interfere with the task I have hired you to do?"

MacInnes put his glass down. "I don't think it will, Señor Arrosamena. I hope not."

Arrosamena wanted MacInnes to prove that Arrosamena's son, Juanito, was dead. Even more urgently, he wanted MacInnes to prove to *la mamá* that Juanito was dead. A peculiar assignment for the Lie King.

Six months ago, Juanito, age nine, had disappeared. Strong evidence indicated that he had been kidnapped. Eduardo Torres y López, twenty-eight, black-sheep son of another rich and powerful family, had, it was suspected, taken the boy away in his car, molested him, and then killed him. Torres had a mistress, and there was no evidence indicating deviate tendencies, the police could think of no other explanation for the boy's disappearance and, they were certain, murder.

The police had a strong circumstantial case but no body.

Señora Arrosamena, alternating between hope

and despair, was on the verge of a breakdown.

After a month or so, Arrosamena had accepted the obvious. A nine-year-old, well dressed and obviously of the elite, does not disappear without a trace from a party at his grandmother's home in early evening. Juanito was obedient and well mannered. He did not wander. Had the exception occurred, and had Juanito wandered off, he was quite capable of telling his name, address, and position in society. He would have been returned to his parents forthwith. Even if he had wandered into the hands of criminals, unlikely in the rich, quiet neighborhood of *la abuela,* at least some money demand for his return would have been received.

Señora Arrosamena could not accept the obvious. Her other children, three older daughters and a son younger than Juanito, were neglected, even ignored, while *la mamá* grieved and tortured herself waiting for and seeking information about Juanito. There were servants, but teenaged daughters have problems they need to discuss with *la mamá,* especially in Mexico, where the new ways and the old ways are churning in chaotic flux.

"It is my fault that you have been involved in this nasty affair," said Arrosamena. "I had business in Mexico"—no Mexican calls it Mexico City—"and it coincided with your arrival. It was my intention to fly you to Guadalajara immediately, providing an opportunity to discuss the problem enroute. My delay has involved you in serious trouble, I'm afraid."

Latin courtesy, MacInnes thought, and little did

Arrosamena know what truth he spoke. Had MacInnes gone directly to Guadalajara, he would not have met Hergueta, and life would have remained much simpler.

MacInnes shrugged. "These things happen. Do not concern yourself, señor."

Arrosamena sipped his coffee. "Do you think you can help me, Colonel?"

MacInnes said, "I hope so, señor. I can't really tell until I have examined Torres. From what you have told me in our telephone conversations, I suspect he may be psychotic. Psychotics are uncertain. If their condition causes them to *believe* they are telling the truth, no instrument will indicate deception."

Arrosamena shook his head. "He is not so insane that he does not know that he killed my son and hid the poor child's body." His coffee cup clattered against the saucer as he set it down, his hand trembling. "Find out where he has hidden the child. I care not whether he confesses. It is *la madre's* mind we must save."

Arrosamena seemed unaware of the naïveté of his request. Revealing the location of the body would convict Torres more quickly than a confession. He could always claim that a confession had been forced by torture.

"I have read about you in the famous magazine of your country, *Newsweek*. You can get the truth from this unspeakable *pedazo de excremento*."

MacInnes nodded. Sometimes he regretted his reputation as a miracle worker. "I'll do my best, señor."

Arrosamena brought out a thick folder and handed it to MacInnes. "All the facts are here. I suggest you will wish to review them. There are many details, of course, which were too lengthy to include in our telephone conversations."

"*Grácias,*" said MacInnes.

Arrosamena turned to Feyas and in low tones began to give him instructions relating to Arrosamena's regular business activities, shuffling papers dealing with mining, oil, hemp, and other commodities.

MacInnes opened the folder. It was filled with newspaper clippings, affidavits from witnesses, police reports, and a lengthy statement by Torres. He began to read and make notes. The relevant facts sifted from the mass of documents were simple enough.

Fact one: Torres had been at the large party celebrating Grandmother's seventieth birthday. He was a friend of one of her many grandchildren. He had been seen leaving the party with Juanito. He maintained that Juanito had only accompanied him to his car.

Two: Torres had exhibited special fondness for Juanito, and on at least two earlier occasions he had taken Juanito for a brief ride in his blue Mustang.

Three: Two witnesses in the neighborhood had observed a boy of Juanito's approximate age and a young man of Torres's approximate age drive by in a blue American car with a shape similar to that of a Mustang. Neither could provide a more definite identification of occupants or car.

Four: Juanito was missed about 9:00 P.M. when his parents, sisters, and brother had assembled to leave *la abuela's*. El Comandante himself had directed the search. A hundred men had combed the area for a radius of several miles, investigating all empty houses, barns, wells, ravines, bushes, streams, and other areas where a small boy might conceivably come to harm. The search had lasted three days and had produced nothing.

Five: Torres claimed he had spent the entire night with his mistress, a surly woman ten years older than he. They had been drinking heavily, particularly Luisa, and her testimony about the time of Torres's arrival was confused.

Six: Torres's car had been examined. The police report noted that it had been extremely dusty, the tires mud caked. In the trunk, police found still-damp scuba-diving equipment, some of it also muddy. They had taken the scuba equipment but had not dusted the car for fingerprints or made any laboratory examination of the interior. They had noted, however, the presence of the international peace symbol finger-drawn in the dust of one fender. One of Juanito's childish proccupations in the days preceding the party had been drawing this symbol everywhere.

Seven: Torres had been arrested. The following day he had been released on the strength of his mistress's alibi. Two days later he had been rearrested on the basis of additional evidence. During his two days of freedom, Torres had washed and polished the car, scrubbing it in every nook and cranny both inside and out. The police, however, still had the muddy scuba equipment.

Eight: Mud on the scuba equipment had been identified as coming from a large lake of volcanic origin some ten miles from Guadalajara. The lake had been dragged, as far as practicable, without success. Certain areas were too deep for the dragging equipment. During the intervening six months, no body had surfaced.

Nine: Torres had been in prison for six months. He steadily maintained his innocence. A polygraph test had been given with his permission. The results had been inconclusive.

MacInnes finished his notes, closed the folder, and silently signaled the steward for another Scotch. It was going to be a tough one. Knowing Mexican prisons, MacInnes suspected that Torres had taken quite a beating during his six months of imprisonment. Yet he had not confessed.

The Scotch arrived. MacInnes lit a cigarette gratefully. He had managed to cut down to a half pack a day, and each one allowed came after long periods of self-denial. He really should concentrate on Torres, he thought, but his mind kept wandering to Mr. X. He decided to lock part of his arsenel in his attaché case, keeping on his person the felt-tip pen-pistol, the cigarette case-camera, the knife, and the deadly square of marble.

CHAPTER TWELVE

AT THE AIRPORT, Arrosamena was whisked off to some important meeting in one limousine while another stood by to take MacInnes and Feyas to MacInnes's hotel.

Feyas sat, ill at ease, feeling like a competitor for Vanessa's affections. MacInnes had decided Feyas wasn't much competition. Though not ill at ease, he was in no mood for conversation. He preferred to ride in silence, staring out the window.

Guadalajara was new to him. He had been in many parts of Mexico but somehow had never touched down in this, the country's second-largest city. Guadalajara, like so many Latin American cities, was a combination of the old, the modern, the seedy, and the typical Spanish. He could be in certain sections of Bogota, Madrid, Balboa, or New York. The smells might be somewhat different. Here it was burlap and dust, straw and pepper, auto exhaust and animal.

Many of the cars they passed were strange, as if some queer cosmic mutations had occurred in Detroit and the offending products had been secreted from the United States to avoid public alarm. Ford had been particularly affected: There were Galaxies with opera windows and Continental Mark IV trunk lids, and puzzling combinations of Maverick, Pinto, and Comet. MacInnes couldn't decide whether unbalanced parts inventories had victimized Guadalajarans or provided them a certain unique charm in transport.

Feyas had MacInnes quickly ensconced in a luxury suite at the Guadalajara Hilton. Torres's family, Feyas explained, insisted that Torres's lawyer be present during the interview. This might take a day or so, because *el abogado,* Señor Ortiz, was a busy man. In the meantime, MacInnes would meet with Comisario Torrejón and some of the lesser police officials involved in the case. A meeting with the comisario was scheduled for eleven the following morning.

Feyas offered dinner with almost visible reluctance, and MacInnes declined with thanks. He had a lonely dinner at the hotel, then returned to his suite to read a paperback, wondering whether X's curiosity would bring a visit this early. He had begun to think of the man as "Harp." Harps were for angels. The book began to bore him, and he decided Harp was not going to appear. He could go for a walk, inviting an approach under easier conditions for Harp. He decided against it. That situation might be more difficult to control.

He dug out the Torres folder, which Arrosamena had insisted he keep, and reread the prison psychiatrist's report. Skimming the lengthy document, skating rapidly over the flowery and honorific phrases, he studied the conclusions. ". . . *con evidente inmadurez emocional . . . personalidad antisocial . . . condiciones de inputabilidad . . . consideramos un sujeto peligroso. . . .*"

Emotional immaturity, antisocial personality, impotent, and considered dangerous. Certainly the ingredients for a kidnap murder involving sexual assault.

The irony of the psychiatrist's report struck him. Here was modern science at work—very inexact science, it was true, but still science. Under the same prison roof, the secret police had undoubtedly been practicing their medieval science on the defendant. He could well be missing a few fingernails. And further irony, when Torres came up to trial in the liberal Mexican courts, exhibiting his scars of torture, he would be released, guilty or not.

Kevin poured himself a large Scotch, checked the double locking of corridor doors, finished off his nightcap with a rationed cigarette, and went to bed. The suite had no balcony.

The hall of justice, an annex to the federal building, was reasonably impressive as government buildings go. In front was a large fountain surrounding a statue of a great eagle, its claw grasping a writhing serpent. In the fountain were figures of mermaids. One of the mermaids had acquired a polka-dot brassiere. Two uniformed policemen were having an arm-waving argument over who would wade out into the fountain to remove the offending article. MacInnes smiled. From the passion exhibited, he was certain the argument would continue for some time, probably until a superior officer came along with an executive decision. A small wave of nostalgia hit him. Idiots were alike the world over. The full-breasted sphinx in front of the army intelligence center headquarters building had frequently been similarly adorned.

After a brief wait in the reception area, MacInnes was escorted to Comisario Torrejón's large, well-furnished office. The Comisario was a man in his middle forties, five feet, eight inches tall, with dark black hair, oily brown skin, and metal-rimmed glasses. MacInnes noticed a portrait on one wall of the Mexican hero Benito Juárez, and the similarity between Torrejón and Juárez was remarkable.

Torrejón came around his desk, his hand extended. "Señor MacInnes, *bienvenido a México!* I have heard much about you from Señor Arrosamena, and I have been looking forward to meeting you."

"*Grácias.* I am honored to meet you, Comisario."

"I have also heard from your friend Mulcahy," said Torrejón, with a sly smile. "This morning we have incarcerated your poor 'daughter.' "

MacInnes nodded. "Silly child. I must do everything in my power to bring about her release. She must return to her home and be rehabilitated."

Torrejón chuckled, then became serious. He pointed his finger at MacInnes. "I have warned Mulcahy, and I shall warn you. There is to be no shooting, no violence, no bribing of guards. That is understood?" He stalked to his desk and sat down. "Should you violate my trust, you will both be persona non grata in Mexico."

MacInnes said quickly, "Understood, Comisario. I'm sure the young lady can be released on a legal technicality."

After offering MacInnes the box and receiving a polite refusal, Torrejón selected a small black cigar and lit it. "You will wish to see her, of course. Possibly late this afternoon?"

MacInnes smiled. "Fine." It wasn't really fine. He hated visiting Mexican prisons. He threw away the clothes he had been wearing after each visit. He had been saving some old slacks and a shirt he didn't like for the day he would need to spend interviewing and testing Torres. He had nothing put aside for "daughter." Regardless of his personal wealth, his Scots heritage made it very difficult for him to throw away expensive clothes. Dry clean and fumigate? Uncertain in Mexico. He would have to buy some cheap clothes in a local store.

Torrejón shuffled some papers on his desk. "Now, this matter of Torres. The man is most certainly guilty. However, as you know, we have no *corpus delicti*. Our evidence is circumstantial, and without a confession, he will undoubtedly get off." He puffed thoughtfully on his black cigar. "We are hoping this miracle of electronics you operate will succeed where we have failed."

MacInnes reached for his cigarettes. He had not had one since breakfast. "It may, or it may not, Comisario. But this I will say—it is far more efficient than torture."

Torrejón grimaced. "The old ways die hard."

MacInnes lit his cigarette. "Aside from moral repugnance, I can't understand the logic of it. After one or two belts with a rubber hose, many men will confess to anything."

Torrejón smiled wryly. "I'm afraid that's your logic, Colonel. One solves crimes so easily with a rubber hose." He stared at the end of his little cigar, uncomfortable. "As you know, we are trying to wipe out these barbaric practices. The city is filled with criminals who walk about free to rob and murder again because the courts have no confidence in confessions."

MacInnes brought out the Torres folder and spent the next ten minutes verifying a few points that had seemed ambiguous in the police reports.

"I suppose, Comisario, that there is no possibility that Torres took the boy swimming and that the boy drowned accidentally and that he used the scuba equipment to try to find him and bring him up?"

Torrejón hunched his shoulders. "Why? We are not so medieval we imprison a man for an accident, for bad judgment."

"Possibly fear of the Arrosamena family?"

Torrejón shook his head. "When you talk to this Torres you will understand. He is an arrogant young decadent with no moral values whatsoever. He cares nothing for family, his own or the Arrosamenas. He fears nothing."

MacInnes nodded, standing up. "Well, Comisario, I've taken enough of your time, and I appreciate your help." They shook hands again. As MacInnes turned to leave, he said, "Incidentally, Comisario, it would be helpful to our plans if my meeting with my "daughter" could be witnessed by as many of the prison staff as practical."

Torrejón looked puzzled.

"The more people who know about it, the safer I will be," said MacInnes.

Torrejón smiled. "Ah, *si.* Even one or two prisoners might accidentally observe this meeting, eh?"

Outside, a sargento had settled the matter; he stood bristling near the fountain, where one of the policemen, barefoot, with his trousers rolled up to the knees, was wading out to remove the mermaid's brassiere.

MacInnes took a cab to the Plaza del Sol, where he located a clothing store and bought two pairs of cheap rayon trousers and two equally inexpensive shirts. He then returned to the Hilton and had a larger lunch than he cared to eat. There was nothing to do until late afternoon but wait—wait for a visit from Harp or his representative, wait for an appointment for his interview with Torres.

He tried to take a nap, wishing he had Vanessa's ability to curl up and push a button, turning on instant sleep anywhere at almost any time.

He was drowsy but only half-asleep when the phone rang. He picked it up.

"Señor MacInnes, here we have a man by name of Felix Díaz who wishes to see you. Will you receive him?"

MacInnes said, "I do not know him. What is his business with me?"

There was a pause while the clerk inquired. "He is wish to speak to you with regard to the Torres case."

"Is he alone?"

"*Si*"

"All right, have him come up."

MacInnes was rarely anything but neutral in the early stages of a first meeting. Felix Díaz brought an immediate reaction of hostility. He was a typical Latin gangster, with hard face, hard eyes, an oily smile that was more of a sneer.

He sauntered in and sat down.

"What is it you wish to see me about?" asked MacInnes, still standing.

Díaz, who was lighting a cigarette, gave him a bored glance. "Señor, please sit down. I wish to discuss with you the case of poor Eduardo Torres."

MacInnes said, "What is your interest in the case?"

Díaz snapped his lighter shut with a loud click. "You may say that I am a friend of Eduardo Torres. Eduardo has many friends. They have asked me to come here to, how you say, represent them."

"I see." MacInnes sat down.

"Are you aware, señor, how much this poor boy has suffered, being in the hands of the secret police for six long months?"

MacInnes stared at him. There was no answer to that one.

"In a month or so, Eduardo will come to trial. He is as innocent as a *niño pequeño*. He will be freed. Now, the Arrosamena family has brought you here to provide further harassment. I say to you, go home, señor. Eduardo has suffered enough."

MacInnes lit one of his own cigarettes. "I am not here to harass Torres. I'm here to interview him and give my opinion of his innocence or guilt. If my interview indicates to me that he is innocent, I will report exactly that to the police. If such testimony is allowable under Mexican law, I will even testify on his behalf in court."

"You are being paid by Arrosamena."

Irritated, MacInnes spoke more sharply. "I am being paid to do exactly what I have described. My integrity is not for sale."

Díaz's oily smile broadened in disbelief. "No doubt, señor. However, I think you will be healthier if you go home."

"What the hell do you mean by that?"

Díaz held up his hand. "Señor, I am not a violent man. Unfortunately, some of Eduardo's friends are men of violence. They strike first, then think later. Already there is talk of killing you."

MacInnes took a light drag from his cigarette. "I see."

"I have convinced them it is only honorable to warn you."

MacInnes stood up. "All right. Now you have warned me. Our business is finished."

Díaz stood up. "I hope you will heed that warning, señor."

MacInnes moved closer to Díaz. He outweighed the skinny little pimp by at least fifty pounds. "Get out, or you will find that I *am* a man of violence."

Díaz walked to the door, trying not to hurry. Safely in the hall he turned and said, "I feel great sorrow for you, señor. You are young to die. I hope you have made your peace with Dios."

MacInnes slammed the door and walked away, muttering. It was too much. An international killer was stalking him, perhaps, and now he had a bunch of Mexican hoods on his tail.

He telephoned Comisario Torrejón and reported the incident. There was a long silence while Torrejón searched his memory.

Finally he said, "I do not know this man Díaz. Describe him in more detail, if possible."

"Very thin, about five feet eight, flashy dresser, small mouth, ears that protrude more than normal, small scar under his left eye, knife wound I would guess—"

"Ah! Alfredo Flores. A *malo ejecutante,* that one. Hmmm." There was a pause, and Kevin could hear Torrejón muttering. "I would advise extreme caution in any dealings with him, señor."

MacInnes said, "I do not plan to have any dealings with him."

Torrejón chuckled. "What I mean is, be exceedingly careful, señor. Have eyes in the back of your head."

"Yeah."

"More poisonous than a rattlesnake, Alfredo."

"Great."

"We shall keep an eye on him, señor. But you, too, must exercise great care. Be ever alert."

MacInnes thanked him and hung up. He wandered around the room, then poured himself a generous Scotch. Alfredo Flores was now providing a worrisome complication. If any of Alfredo's hoods jumped him, he would have to try some killing and maiming of his own. On the other hand, if they belonged to Harp, the scenario would be to let them take him to their leader. How in the hell would he know which was which? He could be killed while he was trying to decide. He decided to return the .38 to his personal arsenal.

He showered, put on the cheap rayon trousers and the too-tight-across-the-chest shirt, and headed for the *cárcel de mujeres,* keeping a wary eye on anyone who approached within two yards of him as he waited for a taxi.

At the prison, instead of being shown to a small conference room, he was asked to wait in the large reception area. Guards, matrons, and clerks moved about, paying little attention to him. A prisoner mopping the floor nudged his shoes. He moved his feet out of the way.

"Deborah MacInnes" came out in the custody of a shriveled little Indian woman, so old she could hardly totter, one eyed, without even a patch to cover her gaping, dried-out socket. Deborah jerked free from the ancient claw that held one arm and ran to MacInnes, throwing herself at him, sobbing.

He hugged her, smoothing her hair and comforting her. Only one day and God, how she stank! Decayed fish and sweat and excrement in rank and nauseating combination assaulted his nostrils, and there were real tears wetting his neck. He could already feel her bugs crawling through the hairs on his chest.

"Daddy, Daddy, you've got to get me out of this horrible place! I can't stand it!" Her shrieks were becoming hysterical. "The food—I'm dying of dysentery!" She beat his chest with her fists. "Get me out, do you hear! I'm covered with lice, and big roaches crawl over my face at night!"

He patted her. "Yes, dear, I know, I know. I'm doing everything I can."

"There are rats! Rats run over you! They bite people and kill them!"

"Now, now, try to calm down," he stammered. What a superb actress the girl was. Tears were streaming from her eyes, and she seemed genuinely hysterical.

The bystanders were now watching them— some sad, shaking their heads sympathetically, others smiling at the hysterical *gringa*.

He grasped her firmly by the shoulders and shook her gently. "Now calm down. I'm going to get you out of this stinking hole if I have to tear it down, stone by stone! Do you hear me? *Quiet!*"

Her shrieks subsided, but she was still emitting dry, racking sobs.

Of the two, she was certainly the better actor. He was having difficulty refraining from scratching his chest.

He spent another five minutes pretending to comfort her, promising to get her out quickly, then watched the ancient crone lead her away. He found what he hoped was the head matron and surreptitiously slipped her twenty dollars, whispering in Spanish, "My daughter, Señorita MacInnes. Please help her. Let her have a bath and a clean place to sleep and some food she can eat without becoming sick. She is not used to prison food."

The fat-faced woman quickly stuffed the bill somewhere under her voluminous skirt. "*Sí,* we take good care of her, señor. Believe me, she will get the best."

As he left the prison, itching all over, it suddenly occurred to him that maybe Deborah MacInnes wasn't the world's greatest actress at that. After a day in *la cárcel de mujeres,* she would only have to do what came naturally.

He felt a surge of pity for the poor immature American youngsters who got caught up in these situations. It looked like big money and little risk; then they found themselves facing ten years in a Mexican prison—or a Turkish or Greek prison.

Kevin was awakened by a steady tapping of metal against wood, as though the visitor might be knocking with the broad end of a key. He threw on his bathrobe and staggered to the corridor door, still half-asleep. He switched on the overhead lights.

"Who's there?"

"Calvin Harp."

MacInnes was fully awake in an instant. "I don't think I know you. And it's 3:00 A.M."

"I'm the man you asked Carlos Hergueta to find."

"Just a minute." MacInnes hurried to the bedroom and picked up the .38 he had left on the night table. He walked back and, holding the revolver about level with his belt, opened the door an inch. "Are you alone?"

"I'm alone."

MacInnes opened the door wide enough to see that there was only one man in the corridor and that the man's hands were both visibly empty. Backing away, the revolver still pointed at Harp's middle, he said, "Come in."

Harp stepped inside the room. He was slender, and slightly taller than MacInnes. "Put that thing away, mate. You're not going to shoot me now, are you?" He nudged the door shut with his heel.

MacInnes relaxed but did not lower the revolver. He stood staring at Harp for a few seconds. Dressed in an expensive tropical suit of navy blue, Harp had thick, tawny hair, the color of a lion's coat—assuming the lion shampooed frequently. It was cut mod long, with the "dry look," but every strand was in place. His eyes were the light arctic blue of a husky's, with the same overhanging shaggy brow and a slight oriental cast. If Hergueta's information was correct, Harp would be about fifty. He looked much younger. His skin was tight over prominent cheekbones, and there was no sagging around his underjaw or neck. He did not much resemble the Identikit drawing.

MacInnes motioned with the revolver. "Sit down."

Harp strolled to one of the lounge chairs and folded his lanky frame into it. "Put that thing away, mate. You're destroying the ambiance."

MacInnes said, "When someone has a man hanged on my balcony, he can expect me to be a bit nervous."

Harp grinned. He had an appealing smile, flashing teeth so perfect they were probably all capped. "I didn't kill Hergueta. He was long overdue, but I couldn't have cared less whether the sod lived or died. He had his uses."

MacInnes nodded. "Very strange that they chose my balcony."

Harp continued to smile. "That I must take credit for. I said to the lads, as long as you're determined to terminate the twit, string him up on the Yank's veranda. Bit of a giggle, eh?"

He crossed one long leg over the other. "I can see you're skeptical. Now let me explain something to you. There were a thousand logical reasons for eliminating Hergueta, but this being Mexico, you can be certain it would never be logic at work." He took a package of Gauloises from his jacket pocket and lit one. "Hergueta was seeing a *brujo* over in Tlaquepaque. The lads decided he was having the evil eye put on them. Armando's right leg has been knee-kicking every time he sits down, and he trips over things frequently. Pablo is certain the *brujo* is causing his already small penis to disappear into his groin. Every night he ties it tightly with a strong cord fastened to his wrist.

He's afraid to go to sleep. It may not be there when he wakes in the morning.'' Harp shrugged, smiling broadly. ''Candido keeps dreaming of a nun who is offering him a spoon and a plate with dog excrement on it. Others have similar complaints.''

MacInnes smiled, staring at Harp, mesmerized. Tlaquepaque, a suburb of Guadalajara, was a center of witchcraft. It teemed with good witches, *curanderas,* who could cure anything, and *brujos,* who could take good care of your enemies for you. Harp might even be telling the truth.

''I didn't find Hergueta's corpse a giggle,'' he said.

Harp nodded. ''Bad taste, I'll give you that. Especially in the presence of your beautiful companion.'' He offered the package of Gauloises to MacInnes. ''Sorry, I've been rude. Will you have one?''

MacInnes said, ''No, thanks. I'll get one of my filter tips.'' He stuck the revolver in the pocket of his robe, then reached for the cigarette case in his jacket, which he had flung over a chair. He opened the case, carefully aiming the tiny aperture at Harp's face, took a cigarette, and snapped it shut. As he put the cigarette in his mouth he saw that Harp now had a wickedly efficient-looking Colt automatic aimed at a spot right between MacInnes's eyes.

He lit the cigarette, forcing a smile. ''I thought we weren't going to play shoot-'em-up.'' He blew smoke toward Harp. ''Put it away. This is no goddamned cops-and-robbers deal.''

The pistol remained steady. ''I'm not a man to

be trifled with, Colonel. Why are you looking for me?"

MacInnes said, "I thought I had a job that might be of interest to you."

Harp's lips curled. "What possible job could you have that would interest me?"

MacInnes puffed his cigarette, wishing Harp would lower the pistol. He might well be a madman, the kind who gets his kicks killing. "I spoke to Ubaldo Galindo. He told me you were the only man he knew with *machismo* enough to pull it off." He flicked ashes into the tray. "He was going to tell me how to contact you, but he never got back to me."

"What brought you to Galindo?"

"A contact in the States."

"Who?"

"Tony Fiorenza." Fiorenza had been found in a Brooklyn swamp with the back of his head blown off only a week ago.

"Galindo is dead. Somehow I doubt that he would recommend me."

MacInnes shrugged. "He did. There could be big money in it." He dragged hard on the cigarette. "I offered him a percentage if he got me the right man. Someone smart enough to organize it successfully." Apparently Harp hadn't heard about Fiorenza, at least.

"You are lying to me, Colonel." The small black hole was still staring at MacInnes. "Hergueta said you had a drawing of me. A police artist's drawing."

CHAPTER THIRTEEN

MacInnes stared at Harp wide-eyed, puzzled. "Drawing?" he idly rubbed the burning tip from the end of his cigarette and tossed the butt in the ashtray.

"That's what I said."

"Why would I have a drawing?"

"That's what we're here to find out, Colonel."

MacInnes shook his head. "I had no drawing. Hergueta must have been trying to buy some time."

Harp crushed out his cigarette with his left hand. His right continued to hold the Colt rigidly. His eyes never left MacInnes. "I told you I had nothing to do with the decision to terminate Hergueta. He was currying favor with me, telling me about the Yank colonel asking questions. He had no idea the chaps were planning some black magic of their own.''

MacInnes turned his palms up. ''I don't understand it. Maybe he was trying to make his story more important.''

Harp sat and stared at him silently. At this angle his blue eyes were so pale that they were almost white.

MacInnes said, ''When you hear about the job I had in mind, you'll understand that I would not have been carrying a drawing of you. I've never heard of you. I was looking for a man with balls enough, and brilliance enough, to carry out a very difficult assignment. Galindo told me you were the only one he knew crazy enough to attempt it.''

Harp grinned, but it was an unfriendly baring of teeth. ''All right, let's hear the fancy tale you have concocted.''

MacInnes sighed wearily. ''I wish to hell it *was* concocted.'' He took the case he had left on the coffee table and opened it to lift out a cigarette, snapping another picture of Harp—he hoped. Without using a viewfinder, he might end up with some fine photos of the Countess Mara tie Harp was wearing. ''My nineteen-year-old daughter was caught with three kilos of cocaine hidden in her luggage. She has been sentenced to ten years. Ten years in *la cárcel de mujeres,* and she'll be completely deranged. She's an unstable child to begin with.''

He lit the cigarette. ''I've been spreading money around, pulling strings. I hope to get her out *le-*

gally. If that fails, I plan to take her out by force."
He pointed his cigarette at Harp. "Understand? I
can't leave my daughter in that place to die, mentally if not physically. I may be in the market for an
army, a helicopter, an aircraft to get her out of the
country—and a man to organize and lead the local
talent."

He could see that Harp was becoming interested.

"Armies are very expensive. How does a mere
colonel finance this elaborate scheme?"

MacInnes smiled. "I'm a rich man, Harp.
Haven't you heard of the Lie King? What would
the operation cost?"

"Lie King?"

MacInnes described his work briefly, and his
reputation, and mentioned the job he was there to
handle for Arrosamena. "Big people all over the
world pay thousands of dollars for my services. I
am no longer a mere colonel. I retired three years
ago. What would it cost?"

Harp finally lowered the pistol, carelessly shov-
ing it into the holster under his loose jacket. "Expensive, my friend. Very expensive."

He could see Harp doing some hard calculating.
How much would the traffic bear?

"*La cárcel de mujeres* would be easier than
some prisons I can think of. But nevertheless,
expensive. Might even run three, four hundred
thousand to mount an operation like this." He
glanced at MacInnes quickly.

MacInnes winced. He said, "I can handle it. If
necessary. Arrosamena's lawyers may be able to

swing it without the fireworks." He shrugged.
"I'd prefer it that way, of course."

Harp nodded. "Naturally. She might be hurt,
even killed in that kind of breakout." He stared at
MacInnes, still not entirely convinced, MacInnes
thought, but at least the pistol was no longer in
sight. "Your daughter's name is?"

"Deborah. Deborah MacInnes." MacInnes
tried an eager look. "If you have any contacts with
influence at the prison, I'd pay well to see that
she's made more comfortable. Decent food, clean
place to sleep and bathe, cigarettes, books."

Harp reached for his Gauloises and lit another.
"It's possible." He shrugged. "This PSE thing.
Does it really work? I'm intrigued."

MacInnes said, "Certainly it works. Want a demonstration?" Anything to keep the contact alive
short of shooting up *la cárcel de mujeres*.

Harp said, "Why not?"

MacInnes connected up the Uher and the PSE,
and when he was satisfied that everything was
functioning properly, he turned to Harp. "Now
I'm going to ask you five inconsequential questions. Tell the truth on four of them and lie to me on
one."

Harp smiled skeptically. "And you'll be able to
spot the lie? And these are to be innocuous questions?"

MacInnes nodded.

"I'll believe this when I see it."

MacInnes smiled. He switched on the tape recorder. "Ready?"

"Quite ready."

"Do you like French wines?"

"Yes."

"What's your favorite automobile?"

"Mercedes."

"In females, do you prefer blondes or brunettes?"

"I have no strong preference. Qualities other than hair color would influence my selection."

"Do you like Mexican food?"

"Yes."

"Which do you prefer, Scotch or bourbon?"

"Scotch."

MacInnes held up his hand. "Okay. Let's see where you lied." He rewound the tape, then started it through the PSE at reduced speed, watching the pen move up and down on the chart. In this type of parlor game, deception was difficult to spot. The lie would cause virtually no emotional stress. However, even in a game, it requires a little more mental effort to lie than to tell the truth. If your eyes were sharp enough you could spot the very faint and very subtle differences in the markings.

This was a tough one. No stress anywhere. Then he found it. Hardly noticeable, but it was there.

"You lied about Mercedes being your favorite automobile."

Harp was startled. He reached for the chart. "Let me see the bloody thing." He studied the long strip like a puzzled stock broker wondering what the hell was happening to the market. "They all look about the same to me."

MacInnes pointed to the deception-indicating

markings, using the end of his ballpoint pen. "That's where you said 'Mercedes.' The differences are very subtle. It takes quite a bit of training to read them."

Even if the photos were bad, MacInnes now had a tape for a voice print. He picked up the cigarette case and tried for another snapshot, then lit the cigarette hastily.

"So Mercedes isn't your favorite?"

Harp shrugged. "Hell no. Nothing the Krauts build is my favorite. I'm a good hater. Been at it since World War II."

He turned away abruptly. "I'll see what I can do about your daughter's comfort. It may cost you a thousand. I don't want anything out of it."

MacInnes nodded. "No, I can see that kind of money wouldn't be of much interest to you."

Harp turned back to him. "Why wouldn't it?"

MacInnes closed the PSE case. "Obviously you're a man of considerable intelligence." Better lay it on thick. "Well educated, powerful. You wouldn't operate outside the law for peanuts."

Harp smiled, neither pleased nor annoyed. "How soon will you know whether Arrosamena's lawyers can help you?"

MacInnes said, "In Mexico that could be three days or three years. I'm hoping I'll have some idea before I finish the job for Arrosamena." He thought for a moment. "In any event, I'm not letting Debbie stay there very long. She was hysterical when I saw her this afternoon."

Harp strolled towards the door. "Well, mate, if you want a shoot-up, it'll take a week or two to arrange. I'll be in touch with you about the *cohecho* for your daughter's comfort.'' He opened the door.

MacInnes said, ''The Torres family sent a punk around to threaten me. Said they were going to kill me if I stayed to *harass* young Torres. His name is Alfredo Flores. He wouldn't be one of yours would he?''

Harp turned back, the door open. ''Flores? No, he's not one of my chaps. But he's no punk. He's one nasty lad. I'd keep that firearm you carry handy.''

MacInnes said, ''Thanks.'' Great. Apparently he had underestimated Alfredo Flores.

''I can't help you there, Colonel. I don't mind a limited war against *la cárcel de mujeres,* but I'm not about to begin a wheel-spinning feud with Alfredo's people. No profit in it for either of us.'' He slipped out the door and closed it quietly.

MacInnes turned away, relieved and exultant. The contact with Harp had worked out better than he had hoped. The drawing was still a problem. His puzzled disclaimer had been the only way out he could think of, and Harp was acute enough not to buy that completely. It would stay in the back of his mind, nagging. It was lucky he couldn't run a PSE test on MacInnes. It was also lucky that some gut intuition had stopped MacInnes from showing Hergueta the drawing of the Southerner. Harp would certainly have made the connection.

The PSE was the real bait. Harp would be back to find out more about it. The PSE could be useful to a shark outside the law—even more useful than to an aquarium shark like Hawthorne.

Kevin double locked the door and went back to bed, where he found sleep impossible. He got up, poured himself a large Scotch, and sat drinking it and smoking, his half-pack-a-day rationing shot to hell. He must get back on it tomorrow. He missed Vanessa. When the Torres interview was finished they could be together. Harp was under control for the time being, and Flores would not be a problem. He got out the tape of their lovemaking and ran Vanessa's beautiful lie again, enchanted with the chart markings. The chart was more precious than ten thousand declarations of love.

At seven he called the Guadalajara number Mulcahy had given him. To his surprise, Mulcahy was there. They exchanged a few cryptic remarks, and Mulcahy decided he would be right over.

MacInnes ordered breakfast for two.

Mulcahy arrived, hardly recognizable in a mod-long chestnut wig, artificial tan, off-white safari jacket, and green slacks. He looked like a typical tourist. How these guys laid it on.

Mulcahy was aware of MacInnes's amused smile. "Don't laugh, bubba. If they are keeping an eye on you, the mere fact of my walking through the lobby could stir up a connection, even though I made certain no one saw me enter this particular suite."

MacInnes said, "I'm not laughing. I was just thinking the transformation is an improvement."

Mulcahy grinned. "This is the real me. Dashing, debonair."

The waiter knocked, and Mulcahy hurried into the bedroom and closed the door.

After the waiter left, Mulcahy returned and they settled down to eat. "Hergueta's information was a big help," said Mulcahy, buttering some toast. "Interpol was able to give us a good dossier on Harp."

In between bites of ham and eggs and toast, MacInnes gave Mulcahy a full report of the session with Harp, omitting any reference to the problem of the drawing. "I may have some photos for you. But it's pretty damned difficult to know whether you're aiming that cigarette case properly."

"No problem," said Mulcahy. "He'll be visiting you again, and from your description, he'll be pretty easy to spot. We can get some good shots of him."

Over coffee, Mulcahy gave MacInnes a summary of the Interpol report. Colin Head had been born in Liverpool. He had emigrated to the United States with his parents at age ten. He became an American citizen, joined the army, a volunteer, in World War II, airborne infantry. He rose from private to major and served with distinction— bronze stars, oakleaf cluster, purple heart, medal of honor. His postwar service was not so distinguished. He was allowed to resign following a brawl with another officer that had resulted in the other officer's death. He pleaded self-defense in the court-martial and was acquited, with off-the-record agreement that he would resign.

He attended college on the G.I. bill, completing a four-year course in three years. B.A., Columbia University, 1950. IQ, 163, genius level. He spent some time in Australia, then became a mercenary, leading revolutionary troops or training government troops in various African countries and banana republics. He had engaged in illegal arms traffic, terrorist activities for a fee, piracy, and other unsavory crimes. He usually affected an English accent but occasionally employed the south-New Jersey American he grew up with. He spoke fluent Spanish, Somali, and French. He was presently known as Calvin Harp.

"Quite a boy, Calvin," said MacInnes.

Mulcahy poured himself another cup of coffee. "Yeah. Whoever hired him, or had him hired, picked a damned effective operator to pull off an assassination. Your fat cabdriver was the luckiest break of the century."

"Any make on the Southerner?"

"Don't know. Domestic."

MacInnes said, "This Alfredo Flores can screw up the works. Harp doesn't want any war with the Flores crowd. You'd better give me plenty of protection until this damned Torres interview is out of the way. Harp probably won't come around if there's a chance of a brush with Flores."

Mulcahy sipped his coffee. "Oh, well, he'll come around after you've finished with Torres."

"Not if I'm dead."

"Yeah. That's a thought, bubba." He stood up. "I thought Comisario Torrejón was going to take care of that. I'll see what I can do."

"You're sure Vanessa's okay?"

Mulcahy slapped him on the back. "Never better. Did I tell you, we're engaged to be married?"

"Yeah," said MacInnes, smiling. "Keep your paws off of her or the company will be missing one fouled-up Irishman."

Mulcahy left, shaking his head.

MacInnes called Feyas and told him about Alfredo Flores, pointing out that the sooner the interview could be arranged, the better.

Feyas said, "I am shocked that the Torres family would engage in such dishonorable activities. I shall tell Señor Arrosamena immediately. Steps will be taken, Señor MacInnes."

He now had the Guadalajara police, the CIA, and Señor Arrosamena protecting him, and he was still reluctant to leave the hotel. When someone is out to kill you, the whole damned U.S. Army can't protect you. Ordinarily, with nothing to do but wait, he would have spent some time exploring Guadalajara on foot. He settled for sitting by the pool and drinking beer, taking an occasional swim. And even that nearly proved fatal.

He had dived from the high board, hit the water cleanly, and was arcing out near the bottom for his ascent to the surface, when he felt both ankles being clutched by powerful hands. He was dragged quickly toward the shallow end, water rushing up his nostrils. He struggled, twisting his body upward, conscious that at least two men were holding him under. One was riding his shoulders and the other holding his ankles. They quickly worked him up to a level shallow enough for their own heads to be out of the water and continued to hold him under.

He struggled wildly, his lungs bursting. There was a sudden flurry of activity, and he was wrenched loose. He surfaced, regurgitating water and gasping. A burley Mexican helped him to the edge of the pool, where he clutched the rail, still gasping. His attackers stood in the shoulder-high water eyeing him malevolently.

His rescuer said, "What are you trying to do to this man?"

One of his attackers said, "This *gringo loco* has been playing games, pulling people under. We decided to teach him a lesson."

The conversation was in Spanish, and MacInnes maintained a blank look but stared hard at the faces of his attackers. He'd have no trouble identifying them in a lineup.

"Such lessons can send you to prison," said his rescuer. "The *gringo* was not bothering anyone. I have been watching him. Now get out of this pool and leave the premises."

"Who are you to tell us to leave the premises?"

"I am an employee of the hotel. Shall I call the police and have you removed?"

The two men came slowly to the edge of the pool where MacInnes clung to the rail. They climbed out, nudging him roughly. One said in a low voice, "Go home, *gringo*. The next time you will not be so lucky."

MacInnes thanked the hefty Mexican, who was probably one of the hotel's security guards, and made his way slowly back to his suite. He telephoned Torrejón's office. Torrejón was out, and MacInnes reported the incident to the comisario's assistant. Then he called Feyas and repeated his report.

"If Señor Arrosamena does not arrange this interview soon, I will not be alive to conduct it."

Feyas stammered, "We are exerting every pressure, señor."

Kevin hoped he didn't sound hysterical to Feyas. His irritation had reached a peak. He wanted to concentrate on Harp and on ways to maintain contact with Harp, and Alfredo's hoods were keeping him virtually a prisoner in the hotel, injecting a stupid problem into a situation where there should be no problem. Late in the afternoon he would have to maintain the fiction of Deborah MacInnes with another visit to the prison. If Arrosamena was so damned powerful, why couldn't he hire some strong-arm buggers to keep Alfredo off his back?

This time the fat matron, beaming proudly, brought a sulky-looking Deborah out and led them back to a small chapel.

"Here, señor, you can talk with privacy to your disobedient daughter."

MacInnes had a difficult time holding back a grin. Deborah was sparkling clean, her hair tied back with a red ribbon. She was wearing what looked like the matron's original white confirmation dress. It was tied at the waist with a bright red sash.

Deborah dutifully threw herself in his arms.

Still beaming, the matron left them alone.

Deborah whispered, "What the hell are you doing to me? The fat *mamacita* threw me in a tub and practically scrubbed my skin off. She jerked me around like crazy and kept telling me what a bad girl I was to get in such trouble when I have such a distinguished *papá*."

"Sorry," MacInnes whispered. "I was just trying to make things easier for you. Things are better, aren't they?"

"I guess so. As soon as I grow another layer of skin."

She went into her act, clutching him frantically and screaming, "Daddy! Daddy! Get me out of this place!" Real tears were again flowing. The woman was incredible.

He comforted her, promising her again and again that he would get her out. Finally, deciding that she had created enough commotion for this visit, she became quiet.

"Can I bring you anything? Cigarettes, candy, magazines?" He had been so nervous about his role the day before that he hadn't thought of the obvious.

"I don't smoke," she said, her voice low. "And I don't want any candy. I'm so full of beans and tortillas that I poop all the time. And *mamacita* has supplied me with plenty of reading material, all religious."

"You *are* in bad shape."

"The thing to do is avoid the meat and rotten vegetables and fruits. As long as you can stick to beans and tortillas you're okay—if you don't mind put-putting like a motor cycle all night."

He bit his lip to keep from laughing.

"How long do you think it will be?" she whispered.

He shrugged. "We'll wrap it up as quickly as practical."

On his way out he slipped *mamacita* another twenty. *"Grácias, muchas grácias, senorita."* He smiled. "Please be gentle with my daughter; she is only a stupid child."

She ducked her head, smiling. *"Recibo con agrado.* I will take good care of that young lady. You will see that she is much improved in her morals."

He had asked the cab to wait. He walked to it slowly, glancing to the right and the left and turning for quick looks over his shoulder. He opened the door. When he saw the figure crouched in one corner he threw himself back. A pile driver hit him from behind, sending him plunging into the car, half on the floor and half on the seat. In a second the pile driver was on top of him, slamming the door. The cab roared off, the three men thrashing around in the small space like a wildcat and two dogs caught in the same garbage can.

MacInnes fought with every dirty trick he knew. He karate chopped, kneed in the groin, eye gouged, jammed elbows into hard bellies, writhed and kicked, and threw his body around like a maniac. There was such a tangle of arms and legs that MacInnes even grabbed his own foot at one point and stopped himself just in time before twisting it backward.

MacInnes was heavier than the two Mexicans, but they were both wiry and strong. One finally got MacInnes's left arm up behind him in a tight half nelson while MacInnes had one of them by the throat with his left hand, twisting the attacker's Adam's apple loose from its mooring. He hoped it was the bugger who was breaking his left arm. A sudden thud brought a flash of excruciating pain to his head and then blackness.

CHAPTER FOURTEEN

KEVIN REGAINED CONSCIOUSNESS painfully, his head reeling with knife thrusts that seemed to penatrate right to the center of his brain. He wondered fuzzily whether he had been blinded, it was so dark. He could smell earth and sun-baked clay. He seemed to be tied to a wooden chair, his arms strapped to its back, his ankles tied to the chair legs. He could move his feet slightly, enough to feel the texture of hard earth underfoot. Dim shapes of black and less black appeared gradually, and he decided he wasn't blind after all.

From the smell, and the hard earth, he suspected that he was in an adobe hut or house and that the night outside was moonless, with almost no light penetrating the room.

There was no one else in the room, he was certain, but outside, or in another room, were sounds indicating some activity. The thud and crunch of metal trying to cut into hard earth, the clink of an occasional rock being struck.

"*Caramba,* this earth is hard!" The voice was low and somewhat breathless. "How deep must we go in this *concreto*?"

Silence. Another voice, gasping, said, "A meter should be ample."

For Christ's sake, the bastards were digging his grave! He tugged frantically at the ropes binding his arms. No give. He rocked the chair back and forth, trying to loosen them, each movement sending flashes of pain through his head. Nothing seemed to loosen.

"That *maniaco* has wounded me grievously. I should be seeing *el médico,* not digging."

The other voice said, "I, too, am injured seriously. This is no task for a man who is ill, whose throat cannot swallow."

The sound of digging stopped. A match was struck, and in a few seconds the smell of strong Mexican tobacco drifted faintly into the room.

MacInnes considered the fact of his death. He had been in other situations involving the strong possibility of death, but these situations had always involved movement, action. There had been no time for philosophical considerations, no time to sit like a prisoner awaiting execution, wondering what the cessation of living meant.

If it was only oblivion, and he suspected it was, then Lucretius had a point. With oblivion there were no regrets. Those who consider death somehow feel they will be hovering around after death, regretting all the fine things they are missing—the sensual joys of the flesh and the intellectual joys of the mind, the love of family and friends, the eternal curiosity about what tomorrow will bring.

So he would not really be missing Vanessa long. Only a few minutes.

There was always hope. Why, for instance, hadn't they killed him immediately, then dug his grave? Was it only because when murder is done it is better to be able to hide the evidence fast?

One of the men groaned. "*Amigo,* we must return to work. Alfredo will have anger of gigantic size if our task is not completed when he arrives."

"*Si,*" the other said. He sighed deeply. "My throat pains me greatly."

The sounds of digging started, noisier than before, indicating a brisk pace that MacInnes found disheartening. So Alfredo was coming to supervise his execution. Or could there be a last-ditch deal? To show a man his grave and say, "Now will you cooperate?" could be powerfully persuasive. No, Alfredo would enjoy killing him more. Nor would he be able to trust MacInnes to keep any bargain offered.

There was just one faint possibility. His mind clung to it with the desperation of an alcoholic certain that there was another bottle hidden somewhere.

He heard the sound of a car approaching. The sound was faint, yet very clear. Though the distance seemed to be great, the almost absolute quiet of what was probably desert or farmland brought the gradually increasing rumble to him with ominous certainty. Alfredo was arriving.

It was only minutes, but it seemed an hour before the car finally pulled up and stopped with a small squeal of brakes.

After a few muttered words with the diggers, Alfredo entered the room carrying a lighted candle in a small saucer. He held it high for a few seconds surveying the room and MacInnes with sardonic amusement. Then he placed it on a crude wooden table near MacInnes and said, "So our arrogant *gringo* Colonel is no longer so arrogant."

Trying to look humble, MacInnes said, "No, you've convinced me. I'm ready to cooperate." He smiled. "The case certainly isn't worth my life, that's for sure."

Alfredo shook his head in mock sadness. "I'm afraid the time for cooperation is past."

"Why?"

Alfredo put his hands on his hips. "For two reasons, *gringo*. First, you have insulted me. No one has long to live who insults Alfredo Flores." He reached for his cigarettes, lit one, and tossed the burning match at MacInnes. It fell on his lap, but fortunately went out quickly and lay there on his trousers sending up wisps of smoke. "Second, even if I could forgive that, I would not be such a fool as to trust you to keep any agreement made here tonight."

MacInnes said, "Look at it this way, Señor Flores. I have told Comisario Torrejón of your threats, and I have told Señor Arrosamena of your threats. Now if I disappear, they're both going to make life very uncomfortable for you. You will be needlessly inconvenienced with many interrogations. And this whole thing can be settled quite simply.''

Alfredo puffed on his pungent cigarette. ''Neither Torrejón nor Arrosamena concern me in the slightest.''

MacInnes said, ''They should, Señor Flores. Comisario Torrejón has told me that if I am harmed, he will have you tracked down like a rat and killed. There won't even be any interrogations.''

Alfredo snorted. ''Torrejón! That pissant has no *macho* for starting a war with me. I will chase him right out of Guadalajara.''

MacInnes shifted uncomfortably, the ropes cutting his arms. ''Señor Flores, let me tell you in all sincerity that I am thoroughly fed up with this situation. Get me a piece of paper and I will write a letter to Señor Arrosamena. I will tell him I have become convinced of Torres's innocence, that I have strong moral objections to the torture he has been subjected to, and that I am resigning from the case and returning to the United States''

He paused for a few seconds, meeting Alfredo's stare with bland honesty. ''Furthermore, I am a rich man. I can pay heavy ransom for my life. You can more than double what you are receiving from the Torres family.''

Alfredo studied him contemptuously, but MacInnes could sense that the idea of the letter interested him. After all, the letter might be of some use. He could still dispose of MacInnes after it was written.

MacInnes said, "You could even keep me prisoner until more letters are written by me to Torrejón and Arrosamena and mailed to them from the United States. In the meantime, I will have one hundred thousand dollars transferred to your account in a Swiss bank."

He could see Alfredo wavering. Why not? He had a stacked deck. How could he possibly lose?

Alfredo tossed his cigarette on the floor and ground it out with his booted foot. "Very well— we shall see about this letter. You have stationery in your luggage?"

MacInnes nodded. "In the gray attaché case."

Alfredo went to the door and called, "Pepe, bring in the *gringo's* small gray case. It is somewhere in my car."

They had cleaned out his suite. He wondered how they had managed that.

After a moment, Alfredo stomped out to supervise the search. He returned shortly, followed by Pepe carrying the case, with the second grave digger bringing up the rear. The men were the same two who had tried to drown him in the hotel pool. He was glad to see that they looked as damaged as he felt. The one called Pepe had a black eye and a torn eyelid. His nose was puffy, and there was dried blood on his upper lip. Some front teeth seemed to be missing, but that may have been a prior condition.

The other one had lost part of his right ear.

MacInnes remembered then that he had done some biting, too. The man's face looked as though it had come in contact with an electric sander. The two were regarding him with venomous hostility, but their hostility was toned by alert caution.

The case was locked, and Alfredo seemed to regard this as something of a personal insult.

"The combination is seven right, three left, six right." said Macinnes.

Alfredo managed it on the second try and opened the case. It contained mostly correspondence relating to current assignments, but there was also a supply of printed letterheads and envelopes.

Alfredo turned to the men, who were standing near the door. "Manuel, untie the *gringo's* arms."

Alfredo laid out paper and envelopes on the table, then closed the case and threw it aside. Manuel, whose face looked like bloody pulp, came over and untied MacInnes's arms, first giving him a clout in the face with the heel of his open palm. The blow almost knocked MacInnes off the chair. Ears ringing, he flexed his arms and hands, trying to get rid of the thousands of needles of pain from impaired circulation.

Both Pepe and Manuel were wearing revolvers. With them in the room, he wouldn't have a chance.

"Señor Flores, I have heard an interesting thing about what one of your enemies has been doing." MacInnes took the felt-tipped pen from his shirt pocket and uncapped it. Now speaking English, MacInnes said, "He has visited a certain *brujo* in Tlaquepaque." MacInnes picked up a piece of his stationery and placed it on the table in front of him as though preparing to write. "Have you been feeling any pain in your lower abdomen and testicles?"

"Who is this enemy? What *brujo*?"

MacInnes put his finger to his lips and continuing to speak in English, said, "I can see that your men are superstitious peasants. Should we discuss this curse that has been placed upon you in their presence? It may frighten them, or they may repeat it, making you a figure of ridicule."

Alfredo's hard, oily face showed a mixture of rage, fear, and curiosity. He turned. "Pepe, Manuel, go to your car and wait for me there."

As they left, Alfredo reached for his own revolver and held it in his hand loosely. "If this is a trick, *gringo*, I will blow your stupid head off. Now who is this *brujo*, and what is this curse?"

"I am told the *brujo's* name is Entravino Tentera, and I have heard the curse, but I do not know the name of your enemy."

"Entravino Tentera." Alfredo moved closer. "He will place no more curses." He spat on the ground angrily. "What is this curse?"

Alfredo was now about five feet away. MacInnes pointed the pen at him tentatively, as though emphasizing a point, and said, "The curse was this: May everything that moves through your bowels be as though embedded with razor blades, causing excruciating pain. May the testicles of

Alfredo Flores wither away until they become no larger than a pimple in his crotch. . . ." MacInnes let his voice drop to an inaudible mumble. The goddamned gadget had better work, or MacInnes was going to be a dead Lie King.

Alfredo moved closer. "Speak louder. I did not hear the last—"

He was now only three feet away. MacInnes pressed the indented firing lever with his fingernail. Simultaneously with the slight jerk of MacInnes's hand and a sound softer than a baby's sneeze, Alfredo clutched his chest with a startled look on his face.

"Pepe!" he shrieked, and stumbled backward, collapsing on the earthen floor, his eyes already glassy. As he hit the ground, the revolver fell from his hand and skidded several feet away.

MacInnes, whose ankles were still tied to the chair legs, lurched to his feet and moved desperately toward the revolver, which had fallen about seven feet away. Hopping and dragging the chair from side to side, he moved slowly toward it. Movements too violent could trip him and send him sprawling helplessly.

But Pepe was already looming in the doorway, his revolver drawn, unsure what all the commotion was about. MacInnes dived for Alfredo's revolver, the chair banging him painfully in the spine as he fell. His hand scrabbling in the dirt frantically, he managed to get the revolver in his fist just as a bullet ripped through the back of the chair, showering splinters of wood on his neck. He rolled, took quick aim, and squeezed off two shots in rapid succession. One caught Pepe between the eyes, the second, right in the mouth. Pretty good shooting, considering the circumstances.

That left Manuel. If he could only get rid of the damned chair. . . .'' Pepe's body lay blocking the one door, and in the dim candlelight MacInnes could see no other opening, aside from a very small window. With pitch blackness outside, the light made him vulnerable. Dragging the chair on his back, he crawled to the table and grasped one leg, upending it. The saucer fell, sending the candle sputtering to the ground. He hastily moved closer and blew it out.

He was now in almost complete darkness, and the silence was total. He strained his ears listening for any movement, either in the room or outside. There wasn't even the sound of his own breathing.

Had Manuel taken off? It would be dangerous to assume that he had. Kevin wondered if he dared put the revolver down and try to untie himself.

He shoved the revolver into his belt and went to work on the knots binding his ankles, listening for the slightest sound and wishing he had the hearing of a blind man. As his pupils adjusted, the door and window now outlined themselves as dark gray.

The window became blacker. A voice whispered, ''Señor Alfredo, what has happened? Are you there, Señor Alfredo?''

Grasping the revolver, MacInnes whispered in Spanish, ''I am here, Manuel, wounded. Pepe is dead. The *gringo* is dead.'' He groaned faintly, then resumed in a whisper, ''You must get me to a hospital.''

"Si," whispered Manuel. "I must make a light."

"The candle is on the floor. Do not trip over poor Pepe when you come in. He is right in the doorway."

MacInnes could hear movement as Manuel came around the house to the doorway. He held the revolver trained on the gray rectangle. A blacker shape appeared. As Manuel struck a match, MacInnes was already firing. One in the belly, one in the left cheek, and one in the chest for good measure, all three shots squeezed off while the match was still burning in Manuel's hand.

The match fell to the floor with Manuel, and MacInnes was again in darkness. He lay there for a moment, listening. He was sure there were no more outside, but why take chances? He had literally snatched himself from the edge of the grave, and life was suddenly very precious. He again stuck Alfredo's revolver in his belt and began another bout with the knots, working by touch in the dark and keeping a wary eye on the gray rectangles of door and window.

The knots were very tight. He broke a fingernail on one and turned his thumbnail back painfully on another, but they gradually loosened and he was able to get first his right leg free, then his left.

He stood up on numb feet and moved cautiously to the door, Alfredo's revolver again drawn. The bodies of Pepe and Manuel were blocking the door so effectively that he had to step on Pepe's belly to get through.

There were a few stars, but most of the sky was

overcast, and there was no moon. He could make out the shapes of two cars, the cab and Alfredo's big white Mercedes. Now satisfied that he was completely alone, he approached the Mercedes and opened the door. The overhead light flicked on, revealing the luxurious interior of the Mercedes 450. Some of MacInnes's luggage was in the back; the rest was probably in the trunk. The keys were conveniently in the ignition.

He slid in and started the big engine and flicked on the headlights. The car was pointed toward his former death cell, and he got his first good look at it. As he had suspected, it was an abandoned adobe hut, grass thatched, in the middle of what was probably farmed-out or ranched-out dry earth.

He backed up slowly and maneuvered until the headlights found the rough dirt road. Perhaps he would come back tomorrow and look at his grave in daylight. He dismissed the notion as childish.

He was so angry that he made the sleepy night clerk get the manager out of bed.

"But señor, you telephoned that your luggage was to be picked up and taken to Casa Arrosamena!"

MacInnes yelled, "I did not telephone! And you do not give away a man's luggage on the strength of a goddamned telephone call."

Comparatively unruffled, the manager studied him curiously. "Señor, have you perhaps been in an automobile accident? You will let me call *el médico*?"

MacInnes was suddenly aware that he ached and hurt all over. His clothes were ripped, and his face probably looked as though it had been massaged with a cactus plant. His voice now quiet, he said, "No. I will go to my suite and bathe, and then I will decide whether I need to see a doctor."

Stripped for his shower, he studied his wounds in the bathroom's full-length mirror. He was indeed a mess, but mainly he was splotched with bruises and abrasions, with only a couple of gashes, which had stopped bleeding but might need stitches. The lump on his head was sizable, and he should probably be checked for concussion. Shrugging, he stepped into the shower and gritted his teeth as the warm water flowed like acid onto his abrasions. He dried himself gingerly, applied antiseptic to his wounds, took two aspirin, and fell into bed.

CHAPTER FIFTEEN

KEVIN WAS AWAKENED by the too-loud jangling of his bedside telephone. He picked it up, glancing at his watch: 11:00 A.M. At least he had had a few hours of rest.

Comisario Torrejón was in the lobby and desired to come up.

MacInnes slipped into his bathrobe and lit a cigarette, forgetting that his rationing plan called for none until after breakfast. Then he remembered, but since he felt like a basket case without much longer to live, he decided he would not worry about the rationing for the time being.

Torrejón entered the suite with a jaunty step. He was carrying MacInnes's gray attaché case. He handed it to MacInnes. "This, I believe, is your property, Colonel."

"Please sit down, Comisario," said MacInnes. "I'm surprised you found it so quickly."

Torrejón explained that the hijacked cabdriver, once he had regained consciousness, had reported the theft and had described the American he had driven to the prison. Luckily the report had come up to Torrejón, probably because an American was involved, and he had recognized the description. A widespread search had been organized. They had located the car early this morning, largely through the help of a *campesino* who lived a half mile away and had reported to the searchers that he had heard shots fired nearby during the night.

"And what do we find, Colonel? We find that Guadalajara's criminal element has been practically wiped out overnight."

MacInnes smiled. "It is not an experience I would wish to repeat. It wasn't easy."

Torrejón studied MacInnes's battered face. "I can see it was not. And I shall marvel to my dying day that you have been able single-handedly to wipe out these despicable scorpions. You had no help, Colonel?"

MacInnes shook his head.

Torrejón stared at him, his expression a mixture of wonder and faint skepticism. "I would appreciate your describing how this was done."

MacInnes told him, making one substitution. Mulcahy would not appreciate his talking about the pen. He told Torrejón that he had grabbed Alfredo's pistol and shot him with it.

Torrejón listened, his mouth slightly open. "You are one *hombre valeroso* Colonel." He stroked his chin thoughtfully. "We saw the grave they had dug for you. One meter deep, almost a meter wide, and two meters long."

"I heard them digging it."

Torrejón nodded in happy wonder. "You have removed a very painful thorn from my side, Colonel. I shall be eternally grateful." He stood up to leave. "We shall ask you for a deposition, but this can wait until your health has improved." He reached in his pocket and brought out MacInnes's felt-tip pen. "I believe this is also yours, Colonel."

MacInnes took it. "Yes, thank you."

Smiling, Torrejón said, "It is a most curious pen, Colonel."

MacInnes nodded. "Yes, and quite valuable. I'm glad you found it."

As Torrejón opened the door, MacInnes said, "The Mercedes belonging to Flores is in the hotel parking lot, I presume. I left the key with the manager."

"*Grácias,* we have it," said Torrejón, and left.

MacInnes took more aspirin, reflecting that he had not responded to Torrejón's praise very graciously, at least by standards of Latin courtesy. But then, Torrejón would probably excuse him on the grounds of *gringo* ignorance. The truth was, he was in no condition to be hospitable to anyone. He wondered if he had a cracked rib, since it still pained him to take a deep breath. Probably should have X rays. Check his skull too. Instead, he went back to bed and was asleep immediately.

In midafternoon a telephone call from Feyas woke him. The interview and testing of Eduardo

Torres had finally been arranged. For tomorrow. Great. Now that he was half-dead they were ready for him to go to work. He mumbled an acknowledgment of the appointment and went back to sleep.

By early evening he was again awake, and he now got up and crept around the suite, bones and muscles making each movement agonizing. But there was definite improvement. He was even hungry. He wondered if he could eat a steak. Tentatively opening and closing what felt like a cracked jaw, he decided he could not. Filet of sole or hamburger, probably.

He poured himself about three fingers of Scotch, added a little water, and downed it slowly, feeling the soothing anesthesia flowing into his bloodstream. A cigarette and a second drink gave him the numbed strength to dress.

He selected the darkest and least noisy of the hotel's three restaurants. From the appearance of his face, he might have just lost the world's heavyweight title, then gone directly from the ring to be shaved by an insane barber.

He ordered a double Scotch on the rocks, a thick seafood soup, a fish platter with French fries, a half-bottle of Chablis, apple pie, and coffee.

The waitress was staring at him curiously. "Señorita," he said in Spanish, "I have been in an accident, and I have not eaten since yesterday. I would appreciate it if you would hurry things along."

"Señor," she said, "I am so sorry that you have been injured. If you have not eaten since yesterday, is it wise to put into your stomach the strong Scotch? The wine, of course, will give you strength."

MacInnes said, "Please. I am accustomed to the strong Scotch, and I need it for strength."

She raised her eyebrows. "As you wish, señor."

The Scotch arrived, and he sipped it cautiously, lighting a cigarette. On a very empty stomach, and after two large drinks he had had upstairs, he might not be able to get himself up from the table. On the other hand, his many pains had miraculously disappeared. It would be good to maintain this happy state.

While he was meditating, almost oblivious of his surroundings, a figure slid into the booth and a large tanned hand was thrust across the table. "Colonel MacInnes, I believe."

He shook the hand. Calvin Harp had a painfully strong grip.

"Allow me to congratulate you. You look awful, mate, but I understand Alfredo Flores doesn't even look."

MacInnes said, "That's true. Will you have a drink?" News traveled fast in Guadalajara's iniquitous circles.

Harp said, "Thank you. I will indeed."

MacInnes signaled the waitress, and Harp soon also had a double Scotch in front of him.

He lifted it. "Cheers."

MacInnes raised his own glass and nodded.

After taking a drink, Harp said, "Why do you need me to lead your army, Colonel? A man who can put down Alfredo, Pepe, and Manuel in one evening . . .''

MacInnes toyed with his glass. "Some luck there. Anyway, I'm sure you'd be better at it than me."

Harp lit one of his Gauloises. "Of course, you don't know the local talent."

MacInnes said, "That would be one problem."

Harp sat studying him silently. He was obviously seeing a new MacInnes. "Tell me, mate, is it true that you really took on three of them? Alone?"

MacInnes sipped his drink, trying to make it last. With a half bottle of wine to go, he might be badly hung over tomorrow if he kept at the Scotch. "Yep. And it may be that you inadvertently saved my life."

"*I* saved your life?"

MacInnes described the ruse he had used to get Alfredo to send Pepe and Manuel out of the house. "If I hadn't had your story of Hergueta and his *brujo* fresh in my mind . . ." He took another drink. "What in holy hell could I have possibly told Alfredo to con him into having Pepe and Manuel leave?"

Harp grinned. "Glad to have been of service, mate. I must say it was an inspiration." He drained his glass and waved to the waitress to order another round.

She brought MacInnes's soup.

"I'll skip the drink," said MacInnes. "Will you join me in a meal?"

"No, thanks. I've had dinner." He lit another of

his French cigarettes. "I've been thinking about it, and I'm damned if *I* can think of any story that would have made Alfredo send them outside."

MacInnes buttered some bread. "Suppose I had cocked my head and pretended to hear noises outside?" He started in spooning up his soup. He was ravenous, having not eaten in more than thirty hours.

"No good. Even if he bit, which I doubt, he would have sent only one to investigate."

Harp played with his second drink thoughtfully, turning the glass around in his fingers but not drinking. "I think your daughter is doing about as well as you could hope, as far as prison life is concerned."

MacInnes raised his eyebrows but continued eating.

"It seems that one of the senior matrons has taken a fancy to you, and your daughter is under her wing. She has a clean, small room to herself and is leading the upright life of a convent novice."

MacInnes nodded, tearing off more bread. "I slipped the old girl a couple of twenties, but you never know whether that sort of thing is going to do any good."

Harp quit playing with his whiskey and took a drink. "Any word from Arrosamena's lawyers?"

MacInnes said, "They tell me the prospects are favorable. Whether that means anything, I wouldn't know."

Harp took another drink. "I'd like to engage your services for about ten minutes."

The waitress arrived with MacInnes's fish platter and the bottle of Chablis.

While she was clearing the soup plate away and setting up the main course, Harp lifted the bottle from the ice bucket and looked at the label. "They have a nice Pouilly Fuisse here. Try it the next time you want a white wine."

MacInnes picked up his fork and started eating. The huge platter contained shrimp, mussels, filets of fish, crawfish tails, and other pieces of seafood he could not identify. "I'll do that," he said. When the waitress finally had everything arranged to her satisfaction, she left. MacInnes said, "You mentioned something about engaging my services for ten minutes?"

Harp smiled. "One telephone call."

In between bites, MacInnes said, "Somebody telling you lies?"

"That's what I'd like to find out."

MacInnes poured a glass of wine, offering the bottle to Harp.

Harp shook his head. "Thanks, I'll stick to Scotch."

MacInnes salted the French fries. "My talents are at your disposal, providing you'll let me finish dinner. This is the first meal I've had since lunch yesterday."

Harp said, "No hurry. I'll be making this call at ten. And of course, I expect to pay."

MacInnes shook his head. "No charge. You've been kind enough to look into my daughter's situation. And if Arrosamena's lawyers get her out, you will have wasted a certain amount of time with me. Consider it *quid pro quo*."

Harp smiled. "If you insist." He finished his drink and stood up. "I'll see you in your suite later."

MacInnes stopped him. "Better come a half hour or an hour early if you want to make your call at ten. I need some time to work out a proper sequence of questions." He glanced at his watch. "Say nine-fifteen?"

Harp moved his chair to one side. "You're the expert. I'll be there." He turned and strode off swiftly.

MacInnes ordered cheddar with his apple pie and sipped strong black coffee as he ate. He felt like a well man. The curative powers of alcohol and a full stomach were amazing, even if only temporary.

Still feeling somewhat crippled, though in no real pain, he took a slow walk through the lobby and around the hotel grounds, then returned to his suite to set up his equipment. He attached the tape recorder to the telephone, tapped the line for his extension handset so that he could monitor Harp's conversation, and then checked the PSE.

Harp arrived promptly at nine-fifteen. He threw himself on one of the big sofas, put his feet up, and immediately got down to business. "The situation is this. I've had an excellent offer for a truckload of rather heavy equipment. No narcotics, in case you have some hangups because of your daughter's situation. The fact is, I have hangups in that direction myself." He flipped open his box of cigarettes. "My intuition tells me there's something phony about the deal. My intuition has not always

185

been right. It may be that nature dealt me less than the share of female hormones every man is alleged to have.''

MacInnes smiled, burping silently. He was splendidly satiated with food and drink.

''My problem is, there's one spot along the road we have to travel that is perfect for ambush. It's the only road into area we use for a landing strip.''

MacInnes stared at Harp trying to surpress a yawn. It was not that he was uninterested; fatigue was simply catching up with him again.

''Of course, we're always prepared for trouble, and give better than we receive. The point is, if it's a hijack, it's a no-win proposition for us. I have a truckload of equipment worth several hundred thousand, and he has no money. I may lose a couple of good men and at best get away with my cargo.'' He crushed out his cigarette and immediately lit another. ''Furthermore, if we leave a few bodies around, the police will put three and three together and we'll have to find a new airstrip.'' He paused. ''Am I elucidating the problem to your satisfaction?''

''Perfectly. You want to find out whether his intentions are honorable.''

''Exactly.''

''Do you have any evidence at all to back up your intuition?''

Harp thought for a few seconds. ''Not really. He's an Ecuadorian, and I've never done business with him before. Also, he agreed to my first price, which is about thirty percent high, for bargaining purposes. But some Latins are that way. Too proud or too obtuse to haggle.''

"Did he come to you through a reliable contact?''

Harp shook his head. "I approached him. Heard a rumor he was in the market for certain items.''

"What's the purpose of your telephone call? As far as the Ecuadorian is concerned?''

Harp thought for a few seconds. "Really only to set the exact time for delivery. Tentatively it's now between 0200 and 0400.''

"Hmmm." MacInnes felt his bruised cheek gingerly. "Ordinarily you'd simply say, 'We'll be there at 0320,' or something similar?''

"Right.''

"We need to prolong the conversation. I've got to see different levels of stress to give you an accurate answer.''

Harp got up and paced for a moment, hands thrust in his trouser pockets. "I suppose I could jolly him along a bit, expressing concern about his having the money there, that sort of thing.''

MacInnes said, "Okay. Let me see what I can do.''

While Harp continued to stroll up and down, MacInnes scribbled some questions on a yellow legal-size pad. He worked away for about ten minutes, cutting and rephrasing.

He handed the revised questions to Harp. "Can you get through all these without making him suspicious?''

Harp read the sheet carefully. He finally nodded. "I think these are all right. He may think I'm a bit peculiar, but not enough to queer the deal if he's on the level. If he's not . . .''

"If he's not, it doesn't matter."

"Right."

It was now ten minutes till ten. They sat waiting in silence, MacInnes heavy lidded and sleepy after his big meal. "If I seem to be unsociable, it's because I'm damned tired and sleepy. I had an exhausting evening yesterday.''

Harp said, "I can understand that, mate.''

"Help yourself to a drink if you want one.''

"Thanks. I'll take a raincheck.''

At ten o'clock Harp picked up the phone and gave the operator a number. MacInnes started the tape recorder and picked up his extension.

Speaking in Spanish, Harp said, "Señor Prima?''

"Yes?''

"You are well?''

"Very well, señor.''

"You have had a good dinner?''

There was a pause. "I have had a good dinner, but I do not understand your concern, señor.''

"I am concerned that you have been discreet. The road we travel is a lonely one. Have you considered this possibility? We both have much to lose.''

There was another pause. "Have no fears, señor. We have been most discreet.''

"The road is ideal for ambush.''

"Ambush?''

"*Si*. Are you prepared for this possibility?''

Señor Prima chuckled. "Do not worry, señor. My people are most discreet. There will be no ambush.''

Harp said, "I am also concerned about payment. It must be *in full,* as agreed."

"Certainly. You will be paid in full."

"You will have the total amount agreed upon?"

"Absolutely."

"Very well. We shall be there at 0310."

"0310 noted, señor."

There was a soft click, and the connection was broken.

Harp turned to MacInnes. "Well, Colonel, what's the verdict?"

MacInnes started the tape through the Dektor. "This will take a little time. It's not as simple as the little parlor game we played the other night."

As the chart flowed through the PSE, MacInnes wrote the dialogue underneath the pen markings. Harp again started pacing the large living room slowly, pausing on each turn to stare out the windows at the lighted swimming-pool area below.

Finally MacInnes finished the long strip. He ran it through his fingers, double checking. "Well, Señor Harp, the answer is abort. Your female hormones must be working okay." He lit a cigarette, trying to remember when he had started the pack. "Your intuition is correct."

Harp came over. "I'll be damned. Are you certain?"

MacInnes said, "Sure. Look, I'll show you." He pointed to the beginning of the strip. "See, here where you've asked, 'You are well?' there's no stress at all in his answer. When you ask, 'You have had a good dinner?' we see the beginning of some mild stress. He's nervous, wondering what kind of game you're playing. When you mention the lonely road, the possibility of ambush, his answers show even more stress. See the lines getting closer together and more even in height?"

Harp muttered, "The bloody thieving crook."

MacInnes said, "Wait a minute. Up to this point the stress could be caused by normal reactions. Fear, nervousness. Or it could be caused by his wondering if you were on to him. Now, when we get to the last important statement, 'There will be no ambush,' 'Certainly. You will be paid in full,' and 'Absolutely,' see what happens. Very heavy deception stress. Compare the heaviness of the blocking with the other stress." He looked at Harp. "See the difference?"

Harp said, "I do indeed." He hurried to the telephone and picking it up, asked the operator for a number. In a few seconds he said, "Theresa, plan B. And not a minute to lose," and then replaced the handset.

He turned back to MacInnes, lighting a cigarette. "You have done me a great service, mate, and I appreciate it. I would say you're one up on me."

MacInnes shrugged, smiling. "Glad I could help." He gathered up the long ribbon of chart strip. "If it's not violating security, what's plan B? I'm curious."

Harp said, "Plan B, we keep them under close surveillance until they give up and leave the staging area. We follow them until they are considerable distance from the airstrip. Then we have a meeting—a confrontation, you might say. If Señor Prima has the sum agreed upon, which I now doubt, we take them back to the airstrip and hold them there until the cargo can be brought up. Fair enough?''

MacInnes asked, ''And if they do not have the money?''

Harp shook his head. ''Then it's possible that Señor Prima will return to Ecuador in a box.'' He turned and headed for the door. ''I've got to hurry off, mate. Thanks again. I'll be in touch.''

After the door closed, MacInnes went to the bathroom and washed his hands. They were already clean. Was he getting a Lady Macbeth hangup? More blood on his hands. He shrugged. Better Señor Prima's blood than Harp's. With Harp dead, there would be little possibility of finding out whom he had been hired to assassinate.

He wearily dug out the Eduardo Torres folder and began to study it. After all his problems with Alfredo, it would be ironic if it developed that Eduardo was actually innocent.

CHAPTER SIXTEEN

SEÑOR FEYAS ARRIVED at ten-thirty, impeccably
dressed and visibly shocked at MacInnes's appearance. He held his hands out, palms up.
"Señor, I am devastated to see you injured. El
Comisario has informed us of the situation, and
Señor Arrosamena wishes me to extend his
greatest sympathy and to tell you of his indigna-
tion that this has happened to you. He is prepared
to pay a substantial bonus."

"Combat pay," said MacInnes, trying to smile.

"I do not understand."

"In our army, soldiers on combat duty are paid
extra."

"Ah, *si*."

MacInnes said, "Señor Feyas, I would like you
to do me a favor."

"Certainly."

"In this interview with Torres, I would like you to function as interpreter."

They walked down the corridor to the elevators. "But señor, your Spanish is perfect."

MacInnes said, "You are very kind. However, let us say that I might miss some subtle nuance. Actually it will be to our advantage if Torres does not know that I speak Spanish during the early stages of the interview."

They entered the elevator. "Ah, *sí,* I understand."

The prison was much larger, and much grimmer, than *la cárcel de mujeres*. Situated in the southern-most district of the city, it sat in the heart of a corregated metal *bárrio,* a slum of shacks of various sizes and shapes clustered around the walled compound like a thousand-acre junkyard. The frontal facade of the prison was vaguely similar to the Alamo. Atop the walls, a double apron of barbed wire added its spiky warning.

As the limousine approached the main entrance Arrosamena's driver had to slow to a low-gear walking pace as they worked their way through the crowds, mostly women and children, massed near the gates. It was almost time for visiting hours to begin. At the signal, Feyas explained, these visitors would press into the entrance, where they would be searched and admitted to the open courtyard beyond. The women carried baskets of food and other articles for husbands and boyfriends inside. Street vendors threaded noisily through the crowd selling food and drink, socks, soap, cigarettes, and other items to add to the baskets.

When Feyas and MacInnes left the car and moved toward the gate a cheer went up from the crowd.

"What was that all about?" MacInnes asked as they hurried into the building.

"They have been waiting for us, señor. The officials would admit no one until we entered. Now the people know that visitation can begin."

"They were waiting for *us*?"

"Sí, señor."

"Ridiculous."

"At the reception desk they were greeted silently, with knowing looks. Guards moved forward to relieve MacInnes of his two attaché cases.

They were quickly guided down the left corridor some fifty feet where they stopped in front of a door marked *Dispensario*. Waiting in the corridor was a tall, gray-haired man who was introduced to MacInnes as Coronel Arias, chief of the prison.

"I hope you will find our dispensary suitable for your purpose, Señor MacInnes. If there is anything you need, you have only to ask."

The double doors were swung open. After a glance inside, MacInnes stepped back, startled. The room was indescribably filthy. Strangely, there were no cobwebs, but the dust was a quarter of an inch thick, and the smell drifting into the corridor was nauseating. All prisons tended to be offensive in this respect, but this odor was completely intolerable. He had worked in prisons where the smell of sweat and urine was strong enough to make the eyes actually smart with irritation. In the United States, the pine oil, Lysol, and metallic odors were even unpleasant. In this old stone building the mustiness of a damp cave heightened the sweat-urine smell, but the odor emanating from the room was that of a colony of rat carcasses putrefying on a hot day.

One of the guards, who seemed immune to the odor, started into the room with the PSE cases. MacInnes caught his arm and said, "I shall need this room cleaned from top to bottom with plenty of hot water and detergent and considerable amounts of disinfectant." He turned to the warden. "*Coronel*, I cannot work under these conditions. While they are cleaning this room, I'd like to speak to your medical director."

The warden snapped his fingers at the guards. "*Acelerar!*" To MacInnes he said, "*Sí señor*. Would you please to wait in my office?" He gestured down the corridor, and MacInnes followed as he strode off. Feyas, who had been listening with his mouth slightly open, said he would go in search of Señor Ortiz, Torres's lawyer.

The warden's office had an ancient air conditioner clacking away, and the air was breathable, though the door to the hallway was warped and would not close tightly. Motioning for him to enter, the warden left.

One large window faced on the courtyard, and MacInnes stood there waiting, watching a scene more suggestive of some Hogarthian marketplace than a prison. Apparently the prisoners had to supply their own clothes; the only uniforms in sight were those worn by the guards. As MacInnes watched, he could see prisoners taking off their shirts to augment tablecloths and other materials in erecting privacy screens between trees and rocks and light poles. Beyond these skimpy coverings conjugal rites were being performed in the sort of semiprivacy that would have delighted a voyeur. MacInnes turned away. It was the only sensible thing he could think of about the Mexican prison system.

The office door scraped open, and the prison doctor entered and introduced himself. He was a chalky-faced young man with intensely black hair. As they shook hands MacInnes noticed that Dr. Garza was a big man whose white hospital coat would be just about the right fit for himself.

"You are enjoying your stay in Mexico, señor?" asked the doctor, glancing curiously at MacInnes's battered face.

"Not particularly," said MacInnes, "though on previous visits I have found your country delightful."

The doctor shook his head. "You have been injured in an accident? Many of our drivers are insane Indians."

"You might call it that. Doctor, may I ask where you received your medical training?"

Doctor Garza's very black eyebrows rose. "Please, señor, let us not waste time sparring around. I was trained in your country, and I interned at Bellevue. I know and smell filth just as you do. But this is my country, which doesn't make it better or worse, just different.''

MacInnes shrugged. "I'm just curious about your *dispensario*."

Garza's lower jaw protruded a bit in irritation. "That so-called *dispensario* has been closed except for solitary-confinement prisoners since I have been here. I use my office to examine and treat patients. The chief is playing games with you as he does with everyone.''

MacInnes smiled. ''As you said, doctor, it's your country. I'm not a crusader. I have a job to do. I'll do that job even if it means rolling over your chief. Then I'll leave the place just as I found it. In the meantime, I'd like to be friends, and I'd like to borrow the use of one of your lab coats.''

Garza grinned. ''*Muy bién, señor*. No offense intended.''

''And none taken, Doctor Garza.''

Garza left and returned quickly with a freshly laundered coat.

MacInnes thanked him and slipped on the sparkling white garment, thinking how futile the white jacket was in this dung heap—like wearing a tuxedo for a trip through the sewers.

Garza left, and MacInnes sat slumped in a chair, his back to the window, until one of the guards returned to tell him that the room had been cleaned—to his satisfaction, they hoped.

The room still stank, but it had been scrubbed down, and the smell of disinfectant overrode the stink.

Feyas returned, accompanied by a fat little man with a small moustache and a large smile. He shook hands with MacInnes. He said in English, "Señor Feyas tells me he is to act as interpreter. I must warn you I will have no American browbeating of my client."

He had to be kidding, MacInnes thought. "Señor Ortiz, all I plan to do is ask him some questions, which I will tape record."

Señor Ortiz's big smile remained fixed. "Very well. I must protect the rights of my client."

Eduardo Torres was brought in in hand and leg irons. They covered skin areas raised and callused and highlighted by pink new skin where open wounds had healed. One guard remained several paces behind Torres with an automatic rifle at the ready. The prisoner's eyes were blinking as if adjusting to the bright light of the room. His eyes were sharply blue and full of confidence. He had defeated these people at their own game for six long months. His narrow, aquiline nose and narrow lips gave him a delicate, effeminate look, a look marred by several ugly scars above the eyes. He stood erect but glanced nervously around, taking in the barred window and the holding cell in one corner.

MacInnes turned to Feyas and barked, "Tell these stupid guards to remove those irons and wait in the hall. Especially you," he yelled, pointing to the guard with the weapon, and motioning for Feyas to translate.

Taken aback, Feyas said, "Señor!"

"You heard me!"

Feyas turned to the guards and bellowed MacInnes's commands.

One guard shrugged, then produced the keys to the restraints and removed them roughly. Both guards then left the room, the second closing the door with a bang.

"Please sit down, Señor Torres," said MacInnes, motioning to a chair. "I am Kevin MacInnes, and I am here, as you have been told, to question you with regard to the disappearance of Juanito Arrosamena. This is Señor Feyas, my interpreter."

Torres remained standing. "I speak English. But if you are going to have an interpreter, I must insist upon having *my* interpreter."

Ortiz said, "I will be your interpreter, Eduardo, if such is necessary."

"Do you know exactly why I am here?" MacInnes asked Torres.

Torres sat down. "*Sí*, you are going to run a lie detector on me."

MacInnes said, "That is basically correct. But first I am going to tape record an interview with you."

Torres grimaced. "In that case, señor, I must insist upon having my own tape recorder to have *my* record of this interview." He spoke in Spanish. MacInnes looked blank and waited for Feyas to translate.

MacInnes then asked Ortiz, "Can you obtain a tape recorder for your client?"

Ortiz nodded wearily and left the room.

MacInnes reached for his cigarettes and offered them to Feyas and Torres. Feyas declined, but

Torres accepted eagerly. MacInnes lit Torres's cigarette, then lit his own.

In Spanish, Torres said, "*Grácias*. Señor, if you'll excuse my saying so, you look as though you yourself have been in the hands of the secret police."

MacInnes waited for Feyas to translate, then smiled. "I met up with an unfriendly friend of yours named Alfredo Flores."

Torres looked blank, then said in English, "I know no one by that name."

"Perhaps your father knows him."

"My father!" Torres made a faint regurgitating sound.

MacInnes asked, "You are not on good terms with your father?"

"My father is a stupid man. A typical bourgeois with no thoughts more deep than how much money he can cheat from his fellow bourgeois."

"And your mother, are you on good terms with her?"

Torres's nostrils wrinkled in contempt. "My mother is more intelligent than my father. She considers herself to be a modern, liberated woman. In short, she is a whore who does not ask for payment." The last comment was made in Spanish, and Feyas looked horrified. That a son would speak of his parents in this brutal manner was almost sacrilegious. He translated reluctantly.

When he finished, MacInnes nodded. He was beginning to understand Torres.

Señor Ortiz returned with a cassette recorder.

Breathing hard, he switched it on and showed it to Torres.

MacInnes said, "So now, Señor Torres, we both have tape recorders. I want you to know that I'm going to run a series of tests relating to your knowledge of the missing boy, Juanito." He paused to stare at Torres. "I have seen in your records that you studied psychology at the university. Have you had any experience with the polygraph before?"

"No. None."

"In that case, you should know that I will review completely each question I intend to ask you. This will be done before the actual examination. I will ask no question that has not been reviewed with you. Do you understand?"

"Si, señor."

MacInnes asked several irrelevant questions to establish the necessary emotional controls. Torres was relaxed and confident. He saw no threat at this point. He answered each question quickly and calmly, even the interspersed "hot" questions, such as, "Do you know who was responsible for the boy's disappearance?" and "Did you do away with Juanito?"

MacInnes paused to offer Torres another cigarette, which he accepted with a small gesture of relief. Lighting it for him, MacInnes asked, "Do you understand the questions, Señor Torres? Do you agree to answer them truthfully during the test?"

Exhaling smoke, Torres said, "Certainly. I am innocent."

"Fine. Now I'm going to ask you to read words from some cards I will show you. As I hold up each card I want you to read out loud in a clear voice what is written on the card." MacInnes brought a set of cards from one of his attaché cases. "Now, if you will, let us practice this test."

MacInnes slowly displayed the cards one by one, and Torres read aloud. "*Sangre. Contrabando. Verde. Equipo de bucear. Felicidad. Lodo. Cabello.*"

When he had read the last card Torres sat back and smiled broadly.

MacInnes frowned. They were no longer friends. "Señor Torres, I am going to ask you to excuse me while I study the answers you have given me and prepare for the examination." He turned to Feyas. "Señor Feyas, would you ask the guards to return and take Señor Torres to another room? Perhaps he would like to confer with his *abogado*?"

Abogado Ortiz glanced at his watch. "Señor, I am a busy man. Let us finish this examination."

MacInnes gave him an amused stare. "Señor Ortiz, I am sure the Torres family is paying you well for your representation. You will have to give me sufficient time to handle this in my own way." He smiled thinly. "Or perhaps you'd like me to continue alone?"

The guards entered sullenly, followed by Feyas, and one of them clamped Torres's leg and wrist cuffs into place. They marched him out, Ortiz following, grumbling and again consulting his watch.

Feyas asked, "Will you need me here, señor?"

Scratching his chest surreptiously, MacInnes said, "No, I'll need a half hour or so to study the charts. I have a feeling they're going to be difficult." He opened the PSE case and began to set it up. "As a matter of fact, when he returns I intend to conduct the rest of the examination in Spanish. So you won't be needed to interpret."

"I would like to observe the finish, if I may?"

"Fine," said MacInnes, his mind occupied with setting up the equipment. "Take a coffee break and come back in half an hour."

As Feyas left, MacInnes was already playing the tape through the PSE. He watched the pen with grim concentration. He was itching everywhere he had hair. Head, armpits, chest, groin, and even his back, where as far as he knew, he didn't have any hair. The place was infested with lice, and his skin was literally crawling. He gritted his teeth, trying to ignore it, trying to refrain from scratching. Give way and he'd be clawing himself all over like a madman. The Chinese had the death of a thousand cuts. He was being executed with the death of a thousand itches.

He rocked his shoulder blades roughly against the back of the chair, scraping them from side to side. It didn't help.

He lit a cigarette and forced his attention back to the charts. As he had suspected, Torres's tension level was extremely high, and this tended to mask his responses. The stress he showed varied little between the "hot" questions and the irrelevant questions, though two of the "hot" questions were sufficiently abnormal to make a case. The "No" in answer to "Do you know who was responsible for the boy's disappearance?" and the "No" to "Were you responsible?" were somewhat thicker and more blocked with stress than the control questions. The answer to "Did you do away with Juanito?" showed no more stress than many of the control questions.

Wriggling frantically, the itching in his crotch almost unbearable, he studied the responses to the words Torres had read from the cards. Here, at last, was something. He momentarily forgot the itching. Torres's reading of the words showed heavy stress on the key words, *sangre,* blood; *lodo,* mud; and *equipo de bucear,* diving equipment. The irrelevant words had almost no stress.

Of course, Torres had been interrogated on the mud on his diving equipment and knew they suspected him of taking the body out to the deepest section of the lake. This alone could cause heavy stress, but not the blocked deception stress on the chart. And the deception stress on *blood.* Why stress on blood? If there was blood in Juanito's death, only Torres knew. He could have been strangled or drowned or hit on the head, as far as the police were concerned.

Suddenly the whole situation became clear to MacInnes. He allowed himself the temporary relief of some frantic scratching, then opened the door to the hall and went in search of the guards.

He found Feyas in the reception area in a sober conversation with a shapely, almost beautiful woman in her forties. Her clothes indicated New

York or Paris shopping trips, and her black hair had been lovingly sculptured by an artist.

Somewhat embarrassed, Feyas said, "May I present Señor MacInnes. Señora Torres."

Señora Torres gave MacInnes a searching, bitter look, then turned her back on him.

MacInnes looked at Feyas. "I am ready to proceed with the examination, señor. Would you be kind enough to locate the prisoner and his attorney and ask them to return to the *dispensario*?"

"Certainly, señor," said Feyas, and hurried away.

MacInnes stared for a few seconds at Señora Torres's back, on the verge of saying something to express his sympathy. He genuinely pitied her. Then he remembered Alfredo Flores and decided his sympathy might be misplaced. Still, it was probable that she knew nothing of Alfredo. Father would handle that. Father probably had his mistress or mistresses. It was said that almost every successful Mexican had his "little *casa*," his home away from home. For this he was judged stupid only by his son. Mother, deciding that she was entitled also to have affairs, now had a son accused of murder, a son who labeled her a whore. A simple Freudian trauma, if you were a Freudian.

He turned and headed back to the lice-infested *dispensario*.

Feyas returned with Señor Ortiz, the guards, and Torres. One of the guards started to remove Torres's irons. MacInnes stopped him, bellowing in gutter Spanish that he was to leave the prisoner under restraint and get the hell out of the room.

Señor Ortiz's mouth dropped open. Torres looked stunned. The guard nodded, frightened, and hurried into the hall.

Torres's eyes moved to the charts laid out on the table, first confusion, then panic flitting across his face.

MacInnes turned to Ortiz. "*Señor abogado,* I don't know what your client has told you, but you should know that he has lied to me, and I now know he is most certainly involved in the disappearance of Juanito Arrosamena."

Ortiz squirmed uncomfortably.

Torres gestured wildly, his chains clanking. "What are those papers? What have you done? When am I to be tested?"

MacInnes said, "You have already been tested, Señor Torres. I decided to test you on a more accurate instrument than the polygraph."

Ortiz said, "I must protest this, this trickery."

MacInnes wheeled to face him. "Trickery indeed! Would you say it's trickery such as the pills you slipped Torres when you came in?"

Ortiz flushed, then clamped his mouth shut, his fat jowls quivering.

MacInnes turned back to Torres. "You lied to me when you said you knew nothing about the polygraph. You were exposed to it in school. In fact, you were the hit of your psychology class when you succeeded in defeating a demonstration test of the polygraph. Isn't that a fact?"

Torres was suddenly hit by the realization that MacInnes had been speaking Spanish the entire time. "You bastard, you speak perfect Spanish!"

MacInnes yelled, "What difference does that make? You've been speaking English most of the time. Have you exchanged any confidential information with your lawyer in Spanish?"

He lowered his voice. "I am not going to play games with you any more, Torres. No more of the soft games I have been playing, and certainly none of the hard games your countrymen have been playing." MacInnes stared at the scars on Torres's forehead.

Torres gestured again frantically, his chained right hand following his left in an upward arc. "Yes, Señor MacInnes, you see what these animals have done to me. But you can't see it all, because of my clothes. Do you know what it feels like to have wires wrapped around your testicles, and the switch turned on?" Tears began to roll down his cheeks. "Do you know what other unspeakable things these animals have done to me?"

MacInnes turned his face away. No wonder the Mexican courts set murderers and thieves free by the hundreds. These stupid idiots and their torture.

"Well, I didn't confess to them," Torres yelled, "and you are no different!"

MacInnes turned back to Torres. "Ah, but I am. You said it yourself. They are animals, *and* they were never sure of your guilt. I am sure, and you now know that I do know."

Torres rocked back in his chair. "How do you know? I was not attached to your machine, so you have nothing."

MacInnes said, "You were attached, señor, by

your voice. That's all the attachment that is needed. I am prepared to show you how it works so that even you can understand."

Torres's thin lips curled. "I shall wait to see this miracle of nonsense."

MacInnes said, "Good. Now I'm going to ask you a series of questions. I'll ask each question twice. The first time I ask the question I want you to tell me the absolute truth. The second time I ask the question, I want you to deliberately lie to me." He paused and lit a cigarette, this time neglecting to offer the package to Torres. "Do you understand? And Torres, just forget the autohypnosis bit and the tensing of your muscles to try to beat this test. It doesn't work on this instrument. As a matter of fact, if you want some more of those pills, let me give you some of mine. They are much stronger, but they won't help you either."

Shaken, Torres glared at his lawyer. "Why are you sitting there like a stupid clod, saying nothing? What are you good for, Señor Ortiz? I want my mother in here."

Ortiz opened his mouth, red-faced, then closed it with a snap, like a fat frog catching a fly.

MacInnes said to Ortiz, "By all means, bring Señora Torres in if she wishes to observe."

Ortiz got up and left hurriedly, glancing apprehensively at Torres. He returned with Señora Torres in less than two minutes. She strode into the room, her nose tilted high, her face grim with the concentrated anger of a flamenco dancer.

MacInnes pulled out one of the crude wooden chairs for her. "Please be seated, señora," he said. ''Your son does not believe that my electronic truth machine can tell whether he is lying or telling the truth.''

She stared at MacInnes as she sat down, then gave her son a quick glance. ''Nor do I, señor,'' she said.

MacInnes nodded. ''I am about to demonstrate it to your son. I'm glad you're here to witness this demonstration.'' He explained the simple procedure to her, then turned to Torres. ''Remember, first the truth, then a deliberate lie.''

Torres nodded.

''Is today Thursday?''

''*Sí.*''

''Is today Thursday?''

''No.''

''Are we in Mexico?''

''*Sí.*''

''Are we in Mexico?''

''No.''

''Did you take the boy Juanito?''

''Uh, no.''

''Did you take the boy Juanito?''

''Uh, yes.''

''Did you hide the body of Juanito?''

''No!''

''Did you hide the body of Juanito?''

''Uh, yes.''

''Is your mother in the room?''

''*Sí.*''

''Is your mother in the room?''

''No.''

MacInnes reached into his attaché case and

brought out some sample sheets illustrating chart markings characteristic of a truthful response and a deceptive response. He handed one to Torres, another to Señora Torres, and a third to Feyas. He ignored Ortiz, who had taken a seat in one corner, behind Torres. The situation was obviously beyond his capabilities, and he didn't want Torres to be reminded of it.

MacInnes said to Torres, "Now I want you to study these patterns, because when I run your answers through the psychological-stress evaluator, you'll be able to read your own lies from the charts."

Perspiration stood out on Torres's scarred forehead. His hands shook as he stared at the sample chart markings.

The chart strip moved slowly through the PSE, and MacInnes hastily printed the questions and answers under the chart markings as the slowed voice came over syllable by syllable. In a matter of minutes he had a reading of the five questions and the ten answers. Luck was with him—the markings followed the standard patterns so closely that even the uninitiated could compare them easily.

He shoved the tapes at Torres. "Now do you see what is on that chart when you said we were not in Mexico, that it was not Thursday, that your mother was not in the room? Do you see the markings for your answer that you did not take the boy Juanito? That you did not hide the body?"

Torres looked, then threw the charts on the

floor, tears again rolling down his cheeks.

MacInnes gathered them up and handed them to Señora Torres. "Señora, please compare these and tell me whether I have been unfair to your son."

He lit another cigarette. "Señor Torres, there's another mother grieving and on the verge of a breakdown because she cannot accept the fact of her son's death. You and I know that he is dead. *She* must know and accept it, or she will go out of her mind. Are you prepared to bring more tragedy to the Arrosamena family?"

Torres stared at him blankly.

Kevin turned to Señora Torres. "Señora, do you see the obvious truths of these charts?"

She shook her head but remained silent.

He looked back at Torres. "I'll tell you what your test has revealed to me, Torres. You were not alone in this situation. There were two or three of you. You had been drinking too much tequila. You decided to go for a swim. I think your original plan was to kidnap Juanito and obtain a big ransom."

MacInnes crushed out his cigarette. "Your stupid *papá* does not give you nearly enough money, does he? So in your drunken bravado you saw yourself tapping the Arrosamena millions. Then, when you got to the lake, and you all stripped for a swim, other things happened, didn't they?"

Señora Torres said quickly, "Do not answer, Eduardo!" She turned to MacInnes. "My son belongs in a hospital, not here. My son is sick, sick in the mind."

Torres flushed. "Sick in the mind, am I? You bitch in heat, you're the sick one! Do you think I have not known what you've been doing? Do you think I have not observed you, that I have not watched you through the window as you spread your legs for Pablo, the gardner, for Reinaldo, the chauffeur, for my father's *good* friend, Jaime? Shall I go on with the list, Señora Bitch?"

"Shut up!" screamed his mother. "You are insane!"

Torres banged clenched fists on his thighs, his chains rattling. "I hate you, you bitch!"

"Where did you hide Juanito?" asked MacInnes, his voice pitched deliberately low.

"Do not speak!" yelled Señora Torres.

Torres turned in his chair, his face twisted with loathing. "I'll speak if I wish to speak!"

MacInnes said, "Señora Torres, your son *did not* kill Juanito."

Torres's eyes widened and his jaw dropped. "*Brujo,*" he muttered.

"It was one of the others, wasn't it?"

"Sánchez."

"Why did Sánchez kill him?"

"He was only cutting him a little to make him scream. Juanito lunged, and the knife went too deep."

MacInnes said, "And they made you hide the the body. You were the expert diver."

Torres raised his hands to wipe his wet forehead. "Sánchez is a beast. He is a sadist. I did not want to hurt Juanito, only to play with him a little."

"Where is Juanito?" MacInnes kept his tone conversational.

"In the lake."

"Where in the lake?"

"There is an underwater cave about a hundred meters from the dam, near the east shore. I have explored it often."

MacInnes said, "That was a clever place to hide him."

Torres screamed, "I did not want to hide him! Sánchez will kill me for telling."

"There was another involved?" asked MacInnes.

"Breton."

"What did Breton do?"

"He fought with Sánchez. He did not like what Sánchez was doing to Juanito."

"And . . .?"

"Sánchez stabbed Breton too."

MacInnes shook his head. "And Breton, is he also in the cave?"

"Si!" screamed Torres, then collapsed, falling from his chair to the floor, sobbing and curling himself into a tight fetal position, his body shaking convulsively.

MacInnes stood up quickly. "Señor Feyas, would you please get Dr. Garza? Ask him to bring a sedative."

Señora Torres had moved hurriedly to Torres and was kneeling over him. "Oh my God, my God, my poor Eduardo," she sobbed, stroking his hair. "What has God done to us? What have we done to deserve this?"

Feyas hurried back, accompanied by Dr. Garza and the warden.

While Dr. Garza perpared a hypodermic, the

warden stood rubbing his hands together, smiling. "So the dog has finally confessed!"

MacInnes turned to him. "Warden, someday maybe they will wrap electric wire around *your* balls. I would love to be here to see it."

The warden's face turned cranberry red, the color even spreading to his scalp, where it gleamed through the sparse gray hair. He turned and strode away.

Feyas whispered to MacInnes. "Señor Arrosamena will be tremendously grateful, Señor MacInnes. Now perhaps the señora . . ."

MacInnes nodded absent-mindedly. Now that the job was done the itching had again become intolerable. "I hope Señora Arrosamena will soon be on the road to recovery," he said to Feyas. He turned to Dr. Garza, who had finished giving Torres an injection. "Dr. Garza, would you mind if I wait in your office? I'd like to borrow some isopropyl alcohol."

Garza bowed his head slightly, with a trace of a smile. "But of course, señor. You'll find it in the large cabinet next to the refrigerator."

In the doctor's office MacInnes quickly located the bottle of alcohol. He dropped his pants and doused his pubic hair thoroughly. He took off his shirt and sloshed alcohol on his chest and armpits. Then he bent over the wash basin and poured it on his hair, massaging his scalp vigorously.

The cabdriver sniffed the air, greatly puzzled. The *gringo* had obviously drunk enough to be staggering blindly; yet he was conducting himself in a remarkably sober manner. He shrugged. One

could never tell about the crazy *gringos*. He hoped
this one would not foul the passenger seat with
regurgitation or incontinence.

At the hotel, MacInnes showered, used delousing shampoo, and put on fresh clothes. Those he
had been wearing he wrapped in a newspaper.
Then he rang for the maid. He was explaining why
she should throw them in the incinerator, when
Mulcahy arrived, still in his safari jacket, wig, and
fake tan.

As the maid left with the package, still puzzled,
MacInnes said, "Thanks for the great protection
you gave me." His wounds were beginning to pain
him again.

"Don't mention it," said Mulcahy. "Of course,
I had to promise Torrejón five of those goddamned
pens, and you know they don't sell for peanuts,
bubba. Did you *have* to leave the damned thing
behind?"

CHAPTER SEVENTEEN

AFTER MACINNES TOLD Mulcahy what he could do with his pens, and with Torrejón, too, they settled down to an amicable drink. MacInnes described his meeting with Harp the evening before.

Mulcahy leaned his head back and grunted. "I'll be damned. That explains the four dead Ecuadorians."

"Four!"

"Yeah. They must have had their shoot-out on the old Borrico road. Since they were foreign nationals, Torrejón called to ask if I knew anything about them."

MacInnes poured himself another drink. "You know, I'm pretty damned sick of Mexico this trip. My nasty job for Arrosamena is finished, and I want to collect Vanessa and get the hell out." He added some water and sipped the Scotch. "I think I've got about as close to Harp as I can get. He may contact me in the States, and he may not. In my judgment, if I try to encourage this idea, he'll become suspicious. At least I've whetted his appetite for the PSE."

Mulcahy closed his eyes and thought about it for a moment. "I believe you're right. Incidentally, Vanessa is on her way. She'll probably be here around eight. I'm having her met at the airport."

MacInnes's aches and pains suddenly began to improve. It was a nice gesture on Mulcahy's part. Inside that cynical shell beat a heart at least the size of a walnut. Earlier, MacInnes would have estimated it as pea sized.

"I wanted her here when you collect your daughter from the pokey."

"Why?"

Mulcahy freshened his own drink. "Obviously Debbie will have to stay here with you. And I've got enough trouble without having you screwing around with one of my agents."

MacInnes said, "Oh for Christ's sake," and then laughed. On the other hand, it wasn't a bad idea. Vanessa wouldn't care for his sharing a suite alone with Debbie. Actually, she and Debbie were contemporaries.

"Why does Debbie have to stay here?"

Mulcahy gestured impatiently. "Because we've got to play this absolutely straight. You have an extra bedroom, right? She's your daughter. Where in hell else would she stay after you've rescued her? Furthermore, she's got to accompany you home to Palm Beach. Then after a day or so she can have a row with you and Vanessa, put on her jeans and backpack, and take off." He gulped some more of his drink. "This is very important to Washington. Now I've got to give up a good agent for months. Harp has a way of checking things out very carefully. It wouldn't be wise to have her seen around Guadalajara or Mexico city for a long time—say, six months."

MacInnes rubbed his chin thoughtfully. The two women were like creatures from different planets, and the thought of throwing them together was vaguely alarming. However, Mulcahy was probably right.

"When do I collect Debbie? Incidentally, is that her real first name?"

Mulcahy stared at him absent-mindedly. "Yes, her real name is Deborah. You pick her up tomorrow."

MacInnes smiled suddenly. There had been something phony about Mulcahy's concern over their sleeping arrangements. Female agents could take care of themselves when sex was involved, and they employed it or withheld it at their own discretion.

"Actually, her name is Deborah Mulcahy," said MacInnes.

Mulcahy grinned. "O'Reilly. She's my niece."

"You just couldn't stand the thought that she might go for me, right?"

"Oh shut up." He picked up his drink. "I don't know why I ever let her get into this rotten game."

Vanessa hugged him affectionately, but there

was something strange in her manner, some subtle restraint or fright, or perhaps she was just weary. She had looked at his face with dismay.

He held her at arm's length and stared at her. Her hair was still black, but she had cleaned away the fake tan. Though her hair had been dyed, it was probably now close to her natural color.

"I think I like you better as a brunette."

She thought about it for a few seconds. "Maybe I'll let it stay that way."

"Did you enjoy Acapulco?"

"No."

"Why not?"

She shrugged. "I was afraid you might be killed."

He couldn't think of an answer to that. "Care for a drink?"

"No, I had two on the plane."

"Dinner?"

"All right."

They went downstairs to the hotel's most lavish restaurant and ordered dinner, Vanessa silent and preoccupied.

He fiddled with his filet of sole *bonne femme*. His jaw was still too sore for anything that required vigorous chewing. "So how did you fill in the time?" he asked.

She looked up. She, too, had been toying with her food, not eating much. "Oh, Beth O'Reilly was very nice. In the mornings we went to the morning beach, and in the afternoons we went to the afternoon beach."

"How about Mr. O'Reilly? Was he nice?"

She sipped her wine. "Mr. O'Reilly was killed in

Vietnam. He was a career officer in the marines.''

"Oh.'' He went back to picking at his fish. He really didn't want to think about Vietnam. "The O'Reilly girl is posing as my daughter. She'll be staying with us for a few days."

"I know.''

"Does that bother you?''

"No. Why should it?''

"I don't know. You just seem sort of strange and preoccupied.''

She held her wine glass for him to fill. "Maybe I'm just a little depressed."

He filled the glass. "I'm sorry.''

She looked past him thoughtfully.

Kevin stepped out of the shower to find Vanessa at the wash basin brushing her teeth. She turned to look at him and gasped. His body was still a mass of bruises and abrasions, black, purple, and red.

"They did *that* to you, those men who kidnapped you?''

He toweled himself dry, gently. "You knew about it?''

She nodded.

"Mulcahy should have kept his big mouth shut.''

She rinsed her mouth, then replaced her toothbrush in the cabinet. "You killed all three of them?''

"Yes.''

"Was it necessary to kill *all three* of them?''

He slipped into his light cotton robe. "No I could have let one of them kill me." He pushed past her and stalked out of the bathroom. Did she think he was some kind of monster, that he had executed the three of them for beating him up?

He poured himself a drink. He could understand her shock. She had never played in such a rough league. First Hergueta being hanged on their balcony. That alone would be enough to send many women screaming home to Mother. Then to find that her lover was capable of gunning down three men, it was something she simply hadn't encountered in her little world of Tonys and Cecis. Killing Alfredo, Pepe, and Manuel had meant no more to him than stepping on three cockroaches—less, actually, because cockroaches were only offensive, not killers bent on exterminating Kevin MacInnes. True, Korea and Vietnam had blunted his sensitivity when it came to death. But any human had a right to kill in self-defense.

The silence in the suite began to envelope him like a plastic bag closing around his head, ready to cut off his oxygen. Had she gone to sleep? He certainly wouldn't wake her. He stood up, taking a deep breath, and went to the bedroom to see.

She was sitting on the edge of the bed, weeping silently. He went to her and sat by her, putting his arms around her shoulders.

"What is it, Nessa?" Tears baffled him, and he did not subscribe to the common belief that women cried for whimsical reasons. The women he had known did not. And he had never seen Vanessa cry.

She lowered her head. "I don't know. I feel so

rotten and useless and let down." Her voice was so faint that he had to strain to hear her. "I've been so worried about you. Then when I heard that you were safe and that you had killed those men, all of them, I felt . . . well, I don't know how to explain it."

He squeezed her shoulder. "You decided I was more cruel and ruthless than you thought, that you had to adjust to a different man than you thought you knew."

She raised her head, eyes still wet. "No, it's not that. You were fighting for your life. I understand that. When I saw what they did to you . . ."

He said, "But you have this picture of me carrying out a one-man massacre."

"No."

"Maybe if I tell you exactly what happened you'll understand there were no gratuitous killings."

She put her hand on his mouth. "No. You mustn't."

He pressed her hand close, kissing her palm.

"Kevin, what I mean is, you have too much of a puritan conscience to go around killing people."

He looked at her, trying not to smile. He had decided that he loved this woman, and he wondered whether his surreptitious PSE test had pushed him over the brink, giving him a sort of proof that she loved him? Well, why not? To love without being loved was futile. He couldn't imagine himself loving a woman he did not think loved him.

And if you loved a woman, you should try to be

honest with her. In which case should he tell her his Presbyterian conscience gave him not a single twinge about Alfredo, Pepe, and Manuel? The world was well rid of three murderous bastards, and although he had acted in self-defense, he was also actually happy with his role of exterminator. He decided it wasn't necessary to go into the matter.

He slipped her loose negligee down from her shoulders until it fell around her hips. He stared at her perfect breasts, then touched them gently as though they were fragile flowers, not to be bruised.

She looked down at them with the half-puzzled smile of the female who knows the power of her body to produce adoration but can't understand either the adoration or the sometimes indifference a half hour later. She pressed his hands tighter against her breasts, then wrapped her arms around his neck and sank back into the pillows, pulling him down with her.

They made love with slow and cautious restraint. His body was still encountering numerous sharp and unexpected pains, and all his muted groans were not produced by passion.

"Nessa, will you marry me?"

"No."

"Why not?"

"I just won't."

He pressed her tighter. "Is it the difference in our ages?"

"No. Of course not."

"What is it, then?" He released her and sat up,

staring at her in the soft light of the bedside lamp.

"I can't explain it."

"Are you married to someone hopelessly ill or stuck away in a mental hospital or something?"

"No. I was married once, but I'm divorced."

"Are you still in love with him, too?"

She sat up to face him. "Too?"

"I think you love me."

She smiled, then put her arms around his neck. "It's possible."

"Then why?"

"I'm afraid."

"Of what?"

She tucked her head down, resting her face against his shoulder. "I'm afraid it might turn into a disaster. Like my other marriage."

He stroked her hair. "Tell me about it."

"I can't. Won't."

He lifted her chin so that he could see her face.

She said, "Look, what difference does it make? Usually it's the woman who demands marriage and security. You have it all your way as it is now." She smiled, her lips trembling a little. "You're a rich man. What if we broke up? You'd have to pay alimony."

MacInnes said, "Aren't you glad I love you enough to want to take that risk?"

She studied him, her eyes wide with sadness and hurt. Her voice soft, she said, "I'm sorry. You'll just have to take me as I am, or . . . or else . . ."

He looked at her, cataloging her from toes to head as though she were the achievement of some great sculptor. Her toes were perfectly formed and wriggled a little when he touched them. His hand moved up to her beautifully rounded calves, her thighs, and paused to caress her soft black thatch, causing a tremor as his hand moved up her flat belly to the slight ridge of her ribcage, traveled over her soft breasts to her slender shoulders and neck, and plunged into the long black hair curtaining part of her cheek, to touch one perfect pink ear. Her lashes were long, and the wetness of her eyes made them shine.

He bent over to kiss her partly opened mouth, seeking the tip of her elegant little tongue. When it met his it was like touching a warm, damp peach, mildly charged to send electric ripples spreading down to his groin. He took her as she was.

Later she slept, as usual, and he prowled the living room. His chronic insomnia allowed him five or six hours' sleep at the most. Maybe it was all he needed.

He wondered what had been so horrible in her marriage. He sensed without knowing why, that she harbored some strong feeling of guilt there. He knew very little about her background. They had come together almost casually, and at the time neither of them, he was sure, had expected the relationship to last more than a few weeks. Her father, an American, had been an international businessman dealing in some commodity. He couldn't remember whether it was cotton or copper. His name had been Peckham, so she had not retained her married name.

She had grown up in Europe. A private school in Switzerland, a lycée in Paris. A year or so at the

Sorbonne. Her father had been killed in an accident on a German Autobahn, his Mercedes spinning out of control on a slippery winter night. Her mother had married again, and lived in Brazil. Rio.

And that was all he knew of the history of Vanessa Peckham. She spoke excellent French and German and, as might be expected, had a wide knowledge of, and interest in, French literature. What else went on behind that beautiful high forehead, he wasn't sure.

Up to now they had simply been strangers on a trip together, intimate refugees sharing their bodies and food and drink and sleep and showers and sheets and hotel rooms and aircraft seats, rain, wind, and sun, and conversation that seldom touched on anything really personal.

They were finishing a late breakfast, when Feyas telephoned from the lobby to say that Señor Arrosamena was with him and wished to see MacInnes.

Vanessa hurried to the bedroom to dress. MacInnes already had on slacks and a shirt.

Arrosamena may have thought he had accepted Juanito's death, but the fact of it was something else again. His face was drawn, and he looked ill. He offered his hand to MacInnes for a sad, limp shake, hardly more than a touch.

"The divers were out with the police at daybreak. They have found my poor Juanito and the other. There is no doubt of it now." He studied MacInnes's bruised face. "You have suffered much to help us, my friend, and I wanted to come here personally to thank you. You have my deepest appreciation.''

MacInnes stared at him soberly. ''I can understand how you must be feeling. I hope this knowledge will help Señora Arrosamena's recovery.''

''That is my earnest hope also, señor.''

''Will you have coffee, señor?'' MacInnes asked.

Arrosamena glanced at his watch. ''Unfortunately, I cannot stay. There are arrangements to be made. The funeral. It is very hard for my wife, and I must be with her.''

He stood up. ''I am lending you my *abogado* for the morning. He has the necessary legal papers from Comisario Torrejón for this, what do you call it? This *caper* your government is engaged in. He will go with you to obtain the release of your surrogate daughter.''

MacInnes said, ''That's kind of you, señor. When will I see your *abogado*?''

Arrosamena looked surprised. ''He is here. Señor Feyas.'' He glanced at Feyas.

MacInnes said, ''I didn't know Señor Feyas was a lawyer.''

Arrosamena walked to the door. ''Ah, yes. Feyas here is a man of many talents. Incidentally, he has your fee. You'll note that it is more than the agreed-upon sum, and this is not to be regarded as an error. You were asked to come here to examine a criminal, not fight a war.'' With another light clasp of MacInnes's hand, Arrosamena was gone.

Feyas, who had been silent throughout, said, ''It has been a terrible shock for Señor Arrosamena. There was little left of Juanito but bones. Fortunately the dentist had begun orthodontia, and the skull can be definitely identified." He reached in his briefcase and brought out an envelope. He handed it to MacInnes.

MacInnes opened the unsealed envelope and glanced at the single document. It was a bank draft for exactly three times the fee they had agreed upon. He whistled softly. "Señor Arrosamena is a generous man."

Feyas said, "*Si.* On the other hand, you could have lost your life. And no amount of money could compensate for that."

Vanessa emerged from the bedroom wearing jeans and a yellow pullover sweater.

Feyas blinked, then grinned. "The señorita has dyed her hair and is now even more beautiful than before."

While MacInnes watched with a twinge of unease, Vanessa went to Feyas and gave him a sisterly kiss on the cheek. "Bernardo, it's wonderful to see you again." She turned to MacInnes. "Kevin, we must take Bernardo to lunch at some really splendid place."

Feyas, whose face reflected pleasure and agony in split-second succession, said, "Alas, señorita, I'm afraid Señor Arrosamena has other plans for my day. Once our errand at the prison is done, I must hurry off."

"Prison?"

MacInnes said, "Señor Feyas and I are going together to collect 'daughter.' He has the necessary legal documents."

She pouted. "Then I suppose we'll have to take *daughter* to lunch."

The more MacInnes thought of it, the more he disliked the idea of having Debbie with them as his daughter. It would be a constant reminder of the difference in his and Vanessa's ages.

Feyas looked at his watch. "Señor, if it would be possible to leave now? Señor Arrosamena has much for me to do in making the sad arrangements."

MacInnes waited in the reception area while Feyas presented his documents to the duty officer of *la cárcel*. This formality was quickly over, and the fat matron appeared, leading a seemingly relieved and fearful Debbie. She was wearing her patched jeans and thin T-shirt and carrying her backpack by its straps.

She rushed to MacInnes and clung to him like a frightened child. "Daddy, they're going to let me go, aren't they? It's not some kind of trick? What happened to your face? Who hurt you?"

He patted her head. "No, it's all right, dear. You're leaving with me." He took her shoulders and held her a few inches away. "I sincerely hope this has been a lesson to you, Debbie," he said, his voice stern.

Feyas stood watching with an amused smile.

The matron said, "Señor, you must immediately buy her some clothes. She has nothing suitable for a young lady."

MacInnes had another crumpled twenty ready and slipped it into her hand. "Thank you again, señora, for taking such good care of her.''

The matron tucked her chin down, smiling. ''She will be a good girl now, señor, I am sure. But you must buy her clothes.'' She pointed to her own ample bosom and said, ''That undergarment she wears, it is scandalous.''

MacInnes said, ''How true. One can see everything, no?''

All the way to the cab Debbie clung to him so tightly that he almost had to carry her. Feyas opened the door for them, then shook hands with MacInnes and hurried away.

Debbie flung herself into a corner of the cab and said, ''God, am I glad to be out of that dump!''

MacInnes gave her a warning glance, indicating the cabdriver.

She returned his look resentfully, indicating that she knew the act must continue but had done nothing to compromise her role.

''I suppose you'll need a good delousing,'' he said.

She shook her head. ''I'm okay. *Mamacita* has had me in the nun's room. Very clean.''

''The nun's room?''

''They have a resident nun. She's away on a pilgrimage or something.''

''Oh.'' They rode in silence for a few minutes.

''Debbie, there's one thing I wanted to mention. The girl I'm, uh, living with . . .'' He paused, wondering just how to phrase it. ''Well, I'm, uh, very much in love with her, and I hope to marry her.''

''So?''

"She's only two or three years older than you are."

She grinned. "So what? You're young and healthy." Then she looked at his battle-scarred face. "Or are you?"

He smiled. "Oh, I'm healthy enough. Actually I'm only twelve years older than she is." Three years off made it sound so much better somehow. "The point I'm trying to make, we'll be sharing a suite, and tomorrow we'll be going on home together. Now I don't know what you kids call us plastic people currently. Is *square* still the word?"

"She's square?"

MacInnes said, "It's possible that you would so characterize her.

Debbie squeezed his arm affectionately. "If she makes you happy, Daddy, that's the important thing."

He was becoming irritated. "The thing I'm trying to say is that you two are poles apart in the life-styles you prefer. I hope you'll try not to get in each other's hair."

She threw herself back in her corner. "You're just afraid I'll make you look *old*. You don't *want* me at home." She began to weep. "Oh, Daddy, you don't *want* me any more!"

This damned kid could cry by just turning on a faucet somewhere. He slumped into his own corner. To hell with her act; he wasn't going to participate for the benefit of one crummy cabdriver. Let the cabdriver think he was the meanest papa in town.

Her sobs gradually quieted, and he looked over

in time to see her give him a big, wet wink.

They entered the suite to find Vanessa sprawled on one of the sofas, waiting for them. She stood up, and the two women made their lightning appraisals of each other.

"Vanessa, this is Debbie MacInnes O'Reilly. Debbie, this is Vanessa Peckham, my fiancée."

Vanessa gave him a quick glance that said they were by no means betrothed but she wouldn't argue the point.

"My God, you're *the* Vanessa Peckham!" Debbie held out her hand excitedly. Out of the corner of his eye MacInnes saw Vanessa shake her head barely perceptibly as she took Debbie's hand for a brief squeeze.

"What have I been harboring, a celebrity?" MacInnes asked.

Vanessa turned to Debbie quickly. "You must feel frazzled, just getting out of that horrible place. Would you like a bath and rest? Let me show you to your room." Before Debbie could answer, Vanessa took her arm and steered her to the second bedroom. The door closed with a loud click, leaving MacInnes alone.

He picked up his day-old *New York Times* and sat down to bring himself up-to-date on man the disaster maker. The same old problems that were never solved. Some of them would probably do as well left alone, like some untreatable disease that either got better or killed you. The Common Market, for instance. How many years had he been following the problems of the Common Market? Twenty? At least. In daily doses history moved with the speed of a crippled turtle, with occasional eruptions along the way to shake hell out of both you and the turtle.

He wondered what the hell they were doing at such length. Talking, of course. And why had Debbie said, "*the* Vanessa Peckham?"

He strolled over and rapped on the door.

Vanessa opened it a crack.

"How about lunch?"

Vanessa said, "It's only twelve-thirty."

He said, "Yes, but by the time you get yourselves together and we locate a good restaurant it will be one or one-thirty."

"We're talking." She closed the door.

In a moment she opened the door wide and they trooped out, glancing at him as though he was some sort of curious animal, and marched into the other bedroom, closing that door.

He decided that if they were not ready in ten minutes he would go to lunch alone. On the other hand, that would not only be pretty boring, but it would make him a boor in Vanessa's book. He poured himself a drink, resigned to waiting. He was eager to get out of Mexico. The session with Torres had shaken him more than the problems of Alfredo and Harp combined. The abject misery of the mother and her psychotic son, the barbarism of the police-state interrogations, the filth, the horror of the crime itself . . . In the future he would leave such cases to the psychiatrists, where they damned well belonged.

The women finally emerged, Debbie neatly dressed in slacks and sweater, undoubtedly Vanessa's; although she was obviously braless, at least her nipples did not show through. He personally enjoyed the sight of nicely shaped breasts but resented the display in public. He didn't like other men staring at his women. And temporarily, Debbie was one of his women, like it or not. He noted that Debbie's hair had been brushed vigorously and looked almost clean.

They cabbed to one of Guadalajara's better-known restaurants, a place named Tekare. It was in a penthouse, and both the food and the view were excellent—which was fortunate, because the conversation was not. It was spasmodic and awkward, confined largely to innocuous subjects such as the weather, travel arrangements, and sightseeing they might have attempted but would not have time for.

Without mentioning it, MacInnes decided he would have liked to visit Tlaquepaque. After all, the damned witches had saved his life. He again asked Debbie why she had referred to Vanessa as *the* Vanessa Peckham. Both women brushed him off by ignoring the question with a quick burst of unrelated conversation. He had a definite feeling that he was being left out, ganged up on, and in general treated as the unwanted third in the crowd. He concentrated on the view.

It was near midnight when he completed the statements he had promised Torrejón, one an affidavit concerning the Alfredo Flores incident, the second a report on his examination of Eduardo Torres, with charts and a copy of the tape to accompany it. After dinner at a rather dull nightclub, the women had yawned themselves to bed early.

Kevin was pouring himself a nightcap when he heard the familiar rapping of key against wood. As he had expected, it was Harp.

Harp sauntered in, dressed impeccably as usual, and threw himself on one of the sofas.

"Well, mate, I see you got your daughter out without any fireworks."

MacInnes held the bottle up questioningly. Harp said, "Yes, thanks."

"I believe you have better intelligence sources than the KGB," MacInnes said, pouring Harp a drink. "It only happened this morning."

Harp accepted the drink. "Well, mate, as old J. P. Morgan is reputed to have said, 'The secret of my success is the accuracy of my intelligence sources.'" He held his glass up. "Cheers."

MacInnes said, "I've been wondering how I could get in touch with you. We're leaving tomorrow."

This also was not news to Harp. "Your daughter is all right?" he asked.

Like any worried father, MacInnes hesitated. "She seems to be repentant. I just hope the hell she stays out of trouble. You never can tell with these kids today."

Harp crossed his long legs, displaying one beautifully polished ankle boot. "No, you can't, can you? There are times when I'm glad I have no children."

MacInnes sipped his drink. "You made out all right with the Ecuadorians?"

Harp gave him a quick look. "Oh yes. Bit of a dust-up but no hands lost, thanks to your electronic clairvoyance." He tossed off the rest of his drink and stood up. He strolled over to MacInnes and held out his hand. "Well, we probably won't be seeing each other again, mate. But it's been a pleasure knowing you."

MacInnes stood up and shook hands with Harp, smiling.

Harp said, "Even though I'm a thoroughly reprehensible fellow, I think you sort of like me, don't you?"

MacInnes gripped his hand warmly. "I do, Harp. You're a well-organized man." He was thinking with some surprise that he actually did like Harp. It had started, MacInnes decided, when the Alfredo Flores incident proved to Harp that MacInnes was as tough as he was. Harp's respect had been obvious since that evening. Remembering the Interpol report, MacInnes had found himself making excuses for Harp. A distinguished army career blown to hell by a covey of stuffed-shirt, desk-bound officers doing what seemed necessary for public relations. The fight probably hadn't even been Harp's fault. He was not the type to fight when there was no profit in it. So the stuffed shirts had turned a killer for the right into a killer for the wrong. And in today's world, the two professions were mixed up very easily.

Harp turned on his heel and left quickly with a brief smile and wave of his hand.

MacInnes was stretching, wondering if he could sleep, when Debbie's bedroom door opened and she came into the living room, rubbing her eyes. She was wearing what looked like an Indian blanket made into a poncho. It reached almost to mid-thigh, leaving a considerable area of long, bare legs.

"What the heck is that you're wearing?"

She yawned. "It's in lieu of a bathrobe, which I do not own. I sleep in my skin." She sat down in one of the lounge chairs, her poncho hiking very high. She tucked it between her legs. "I heard voices and thought it might be Uncle Jack."

He shook his head. "There was a fellow here on business, but it wasn't Mulcahy. I imagine he'll pop in tomorrow before we leave."

She yawned again. "You wouldn't have a joint tucked around somewhere, would you?" She glanced at his face and said, "No, I can see you wouldn't."

MacInnes said, "Would you like a drink?"

She said, "I suppose so. I can't get the taste of *la cárcel* out of my mouth. I think it made me more nervous than I thought. Particularly *mamacita*."

He poured her a drink. "Why *mamacita*?"

"She was on my back day and night, reforming me. Did you ever hear of pulverized kneecaps? That's what I've got. We did a terrific amount of praying." She took the drink he handed her and gulped it. "I've got a lot of hangups there anyway. I was a very good Catholic until I was about fifteen."

"I guess I shouldn't have tipped her. But it did get you a clean room."

"Yeah."

"Debbie, what the hell is this about Vanessa? I must be stupid, but what has she done to be well-known?"

Debbie twirled the ice cubes in her glass briefly. "I promised I wouldn't tell you."

MacInnes said, "You might as well. I'll find out one way or another, now that my curiosity has been aroused."

She gave him an amused smile. "Don't you read the *Times* Sunday Book Review section?"

He rubbed his forehead. "No. Not in a long time." During his early years in the army he had read a great deal, carrying on through interest stimulated in college. The army provided plenty of time for reading. There were periods of furious activity, then long periods of apathy when you tried to keep the troops busy with make-work projects and training. In recent years he had read only for entertainment, and lately he had been finding it increasingly difficult to find books that entertained him.

"Well, if you were up on things literary, you would know that Vanessa has written a couple of very successful novels. She has also translated several terrific modern French novels. For a while she was also very active in women's liberation." Debbie raised her arms and stretched, unconscious of the embarrassing exposure brought by the rising poncho. "Being beautiful, she has had a hell of a lot of valuable publicity."

MacInnes averted his eyes. There was something incestuous about being intrigued by his "daughter's" highly personal parts.

This new image of Vanessa disturbed him. He had accepted her as a delightful, bright, but lazy girl, a rich man's plaything, as Grandpop might have put it, a girl beautifully designed for lovemaking and the sympathetic, ego-bolstering companionship a man needed. A treasure of a woman but still a woman whose interests would be centered on her man. Instead, she had a career of her own. She really didn't need him.

"In addition," said Debbie, "she happens to be very rich. Haven't you heard of Barker-Peckham Copper?"

He stared at her, startled. "That family?"

"Yep." She stood up. "I'm going back to bed. Thanks for the drink. And don't tell her I snitched. You promised."

"I did not."

"You better did. Or I'll tell her you tried to ball me." She made her way back to the bedroom and closed the door.

He sat for a moment trying to adjust. Even his being rich meant nothing to her.

He went on to bed and woke up Vanessa.

"No," she whispered. "Daughter might hear us."

He gave her a sharp slap on the rear. In the struggle that followed, MacInnes won, but it was semi-rape.

CHAPTER EIGHTEEN

IT WAS THE third day it had rained. MacInnes sat in his study staring at the water streaking down the floor-to-ceiling windows and at the blurred ocean beyond, almost black under the high white breakers rolling toward the beach. He had just finished reading Vanessa's second novel, which had a white cover because he had reversed the dust jacket. After thinking it over, he had decided to play along with her game, whatever it was, and had given no indication that he knew any more than he had known before Debbie arrived. He had had difficulty in finding even one of her books. He visited all the bookstores in Palm Beach, West Palm Beach, and other nearby towns. Since the copyright date of the book he finally located was two years old, this was understandable. It had been written when she was twenty-two or twenty-three. Her first novel, according to the book jacket, had been published when she was twenty.

The novel was a sensitively written story of a young woman's unhappy love affair, her trip through drugland, and her eventual suicide.

He closed the book and locked it in the bottom drawer of his desk. He wondered how much of it was autobiographical. Told with such depth of understanding, large portions of it must have been experienced by Vanessa or some intimate friend. Or perhaps not. Maybe she had just researched her story skillfully.

His feelings about Vanessa had been changing. He no longer thought of marrying her. And he speculated endlessly on why she had refused to marry him. Perhaps, with his middle-class origins, he wasn't good enough for the social-registerite Peckhams? Lady Chatterley and the gamekeeper? On the other hand, considering her intelligence, he couldn't imagine Vanessa's being this sort of snob. Perhaps her explanation had been true—her other marriage had been so devastating that she couldn't face the risk again. But why conceal her identity? The very rich were terribly sensitive about people pursuing them for their money. Could the answer be as simple as that? Perhaps the man who provided her disaster had married her for her money?

Li Duc, a very compact, neat little oriental, came into his study. She was the female half of the Korean couple who took care of his house.

"You wish coffee, Colonel?" she asked.

He turned to her. "Thanks, Li, I would like a cup."

She glanced out the windows at the teeming rain. "Miss Vanessa will get very wet."

Vanessa had gone shopping. Spending more of *his* money. What a giggle, as Harp might have put it. "Well, it's warm. Won't hurt her."

Debbie and Vanessa had done nothing but shop since their arrival. Of course, it was understandable. Debbie had no wardrobe whatever. She had finally left early this morning, carrying nothing but her backpack. Most of her new clothing was going to Washington via parcel post. He was glad she was on her way. Instead of being at each other's throats, the two women had closed in and shut him out, which was probably preferable, but it had been lonely for MacInnes.

Li slipped out so quickly and silently that he didn't even notice that she had left. He had helped Li and her husband, Bill Duc, emigrate to the United States. The job the Ducs' sponsor had promised had lasted only a few months. Bill, who had insisted upon Americanizing his first name, had sought out "the Colonel." Though he had been a minor civil-service clerk, Bill Duc had been raised on a farm, and he was an expert gardener. Li was a good cook and a meticulous housekeeper.

They were happy, particularly since MacInnes did not mind that they had three children, ages six, eight, and nine. Their children would have a fine American education, because with all their living expenses paid the Ducs could save almost every dollar of the liberal salary MacInnes gave them.

The young Ducs would have university educations; become doctors, lawyers, architects. MacInnes hoped that prejudice would not discourage them. If they were good at their professions, they could move ahead in spite of it.

Li had just finished placing a tray with coffeepot, cup, saucer, sugar, and cream on his desk, when the phone rang.

MacInnes picked it up. "This is Balamur calling person to person for Mr. Kevin MacInnes," whined the operator.

"This is MacInnes. You mean Baltimore?" he asked.

"This is Balamur calling person to person—"

"Kevin MacInnes speaking!" he yelled.

She connected him, and another voice came through. "Hi, Mac. This is Ellery Kimbal."

"Ellery! How are you? It's great to hear from you!" Ellery Kimbal was a fairly high government official, and he had helped MacInnes many times in the early days of MacInnes's new career. Kevin owed Ellery Kimbal.

"Understand you've been in Mexico?"

MacInnes said, "Yeah, and I'm damned glad to be back. How's Edith?"

"Fine, Mac, fine. I've got a little problem, Mac. A young protegé of mine, named John Hall, has himself in a bind over in Stateline. I'd appreciate it if you could pop up there and give him a hand?"

"Sure. What's it all about?"

Kimbal's drawl came over slowly. "Well, I don't know quite what it's all about. None of the details, understand. It's one of those things. A twelve-year-old girl was raped and murdered. John is chief of detectives. He has himself a suspect, but he sort of feels it's not the right guy.''

MacInnes groaned. "God, Ellery, I just got off one of those child-molester cases, and I resolved I'd never take another one."

There was a long pause. "I know how you feel. But I'd appreciate it if you'd help me out on this, Mac."

He couldn't turn down Ellery Kimbal. MacInnes said quickly, "Okay, Ellery, I'll take it on. But you know, if this suspect is psychotic, I may not be able to help much."

"I understand. And I do appreciate it, Mac."

Kimbal gave MacInnes directions for getting to Stateline, in Maryland, right on the Pennsylvania border.

When Vanessa returned, she found MacInnes in a surly mood. She had been wearing a transparent plastic raincoat and was now holding it disgustedly. "My God, these things are hot! I should have taken an umbrella."

He stared at her glumly.

"What's the matter?" she asked.

"Oh, hell!" He stared out the window. "I've got to go up to a little jerkwater town in Maryland. Another one of those damned child-molester murders. I'd resolved not to take any more of them."

"So why did you take it?"

"The fellow who asked me, well, I owe him a lot. Couldn't refuse."

She left to hang the dripping coat in the bathroom, then returned.

"No point in your going," he told her. "Be boring for you, and I'll only be gone a couple of days."

She came over and bent to kiss him. "I don't mind going, if you want company."

"It's a wide place in the road. Nothing for you to do."

She left him and slumped in a chair, vaguely annoyed. "Whatever you wish."

"Too bad Debbie left. She would have been company for you while I'm away."

Vanessa smiled. "Debbie was interesting, but I'm glad she left, you old lecher."

"What do you mean, lecher?"

"She had a thing going for you."

"Come on!"

"No, really. She told me quite frankly that the only reason she didn't try was that I had her out-classed."

He shook his head, unbelieving. "Well, that's true enough. But I can't imagine . . ." Secretly he was amazed. He supposed it was typical of the no-holds-barred honesty the kids went in for. "I thought I played my role of father very well. There was certainly no thought in my mind . . ." He paused. "Actually, I thought of her in terms of, well, a daughter." Mulcahy had been more astute than MacInnes had thought. Women were a continuing mystery. Sneaky. He would have characterized Debbie's attitude toward him as amused, tolerant contempt.

Finally he said, "Probably she was just putting you on."

"*Oh* no."

"Well, I did nothing to encourage her."

"I'm not saying you did." Vanessa came over and sat in his lap. "She told you about me, didn't she?"

He was silent for a few seconds. "Yes, she did. And I don't understand why you chose to keep it a big secret."

"I didn't."

He looked at her.

"Really. I just egotistically assumed you knew about me. Then when I finally realized you didn't, I decided that maybe it was better that way."

"Why?"

She put her hand on his cheek. "Why? Because you're an ego-centered male chauvinist. And you'd probably be turned off if you knew that I was smarter and better educated than you are."

"And richer," he said.

"Not richer."

He wondered why she wasn't richer.

"My father left me a trust fund that gives me about twenty-five thousand a year. My mother has the rest. And we aren't even on speaking terms."

"Oh." He really didn't care whether she thought she was smarter and better educated. He had his own ideas about that. "Well, for your information, I do not agree that you're smarter and better educated. As for being a male chauvinist, that's completely wrong."

She wriggled into a more comfortable position. "That's what all you male chauvinists say."

"Look, I'm in complete agreement with all the sensible aims of women's lib. Equal rights, equality in pay and opportunity and all that. Where you lose me is in this unisex bit." The unisex idea irritated him beyond all logic. "I think the differences in the sexes, both physical and emotional, are one of the most wonderful and intriguing things about human existence. I can't understand this business of feminizing boys and masculinizing girls until they meet in some neuter land where they're almost alike."

She patted his cheek again. "Maybe they'd enjoy each other's company more if they had interests in common. Of course, the other kind of relationship is simply swell for the man. He hunches over the television set for hours watching football or drinks beer with his friends while the wife does all the work. It's strange that all the "feminine" things are boring hard work, like cooking, sewing, mopping the floors, vacuuming, washing dishes, being nursemaid to the children, and dozens of other tedious or back-breaking jobs."

He decided the argument was becoming banal. "The world is full of injustice. Consider the number of men who work hard to earn a living while their wives take it pretty easy on the housework bit. They spend most of the day kaffee-klatsching or watching game shows or soap operas on TV."

He pulled her around and kissed her. "How many floors have you scrubbed recently?"

She separated their lips enough to hiss, "I'm not married."

"I will admit you're superior in one way."

"What?"

"You're much more creatively talented. I read one of your books."

"Which one?"

"Dim Star."

"What did you thnk of it?"

He was silent for a while. "I thought it was sensitive and well written. Do you have a copy of your first one? I'd like to read it, too."

The idea seemed to depress her. "No. That is, not with me. There are probably some stored in the basement of my house." Her voice was unusually flat.

"You have a house"

"Yes."

"Where?"

"In New York. On Sutton Place. My father left me that, too." She sighed. "Though how he expected me to maintain it on twenty-five thousand a year I can't imagine."

"It's closed up?"

"No, I lease it."

Her head sank to his chest. She seemed weary and spent. Finally she said, "I don't think I'll write any more novels."

"Why not?"

"I don't know. It seems sort of futile."

He had been secretly proud of her accomplishments and found her attitude upsetting. "I think that would be terrible."

"Why?"

He stroked her gleaming black hair. "I'm not enough of a literary critic to know whether you're a major talent or a minor talent or what, but even if you only entertain a few hundred thousand or a few million people I would say that's a major contribution. You owe it to the world."

248

She looked up at him. "Why do I owe it?"

"Every human being owes the world his or her best. If you have been given a talent you owe it in return."

"Why?"

He kissed her. "So that you can be proud of being a human being."

"Pride!"

"Well, maybe that was the wrong word. So that you can feel it's worthwhile being a human being. So that life can have some meaning." He kissed her again. "Woman does not live by bread alone. Unless you're a male chauvinist."

She smiled, but it was a weary smile that discounted the naïveté of his Panglossian optimism. "A while back I decided I would live for today. To write a book you've got to care about tomorrow."

"And you don't?"

"Most of the time I think not."

Her attitude disturbed him. "Maybe you should come to Stateline, Maryland, with me."

She rested her head on his chest again. "I'd rather do that than stay here alone."

They remained silent for a long time, the rain slashing against the windows, the weight of her body, curled comfortably in his lap, pleasant and reassuring. He wondered idly whether the idea of her being more intelligent and better educated would really make any difference to his supposed colossal male ego. But was she, really? As he understood it, the Sorbonne was a collection of colleges similar to Oxford. As far as a classical French education was concerned, she was probably exceptionally well educated. But that was only a specialized segment of education.

During the years he had attended the University of California at Berkeley, it had ranked among the top five universities in the country. MacInnes felt that such rankings had very little bearing on the kind of person you were. He resented graduates of some schools who seemed to wear a cloak of superiority that, as far as MacInnes could see, had no justification. The stockbroker he dealt with, for instance, was charming, but beneath the charm MacInnes sensed that Hodkins felt himself immensely superior, socially. Why would a man whose attainments were on a par with those of a professional gambler and racetrack tout consider himself superior to MacInnes?

MacInnes and Vanessa arrived in Stateline shaken by the violent turbulence of the low-altitude feeder-line flight from Baltimore. The only time MacInnes became seriously concerned when flying was in heavy turbulence. He knew what wind shear could do to a plane in landing. Mopping his damp forehead, he guided Vanessa to the car-rental agency.

As in a thousand other small towns throughout America, Stateline's best hotels were motels several miles from the center of the city. This was good for the car-rental business.

A mile from the airport the car conked out.

Walking down the busy highway grumbling to himself, MacInnes finally found a filling station and called the car-rental agency. He hiked back, reflecting that he had disliked Maryland ever since his days at Fort Holabird, a thousand years ago. This was unfair, since he had seldom been outside the metropolitan Baltimore area. "Balamur," he muttered.

The car-rental service truck eventually arrived, and the crew cheerfully installed a new battery. Then he and Vanessa proceeded to the motel and checked in.

"You'd better drive me into town," MacInnes said to Vanessa, "or you may be stuck out here for the rest of the day. On the other hand, dammit, let them pick me up."

He telephoned John Hall and announced his arrival.

"Be right out," said Hall.

MacInnes went to the bathroom to wash. Hall was probably a bright young upward-mobile or he would never be a protegé of Ellery Kimbal. At least Kevin wouldn't be dealing with the usual smalltown slob who got his spot on the police force because his cousin was the mayor.

Vanessa decided she probably wouldn't need the car anyway. The motel had a swimming pool and a restaurant. "Maybe I'll start working on another book," she said.

The day suddenly became more bearable. "Great!" he said, kissing her. "That's really great!"

He took the Dektor cases to the lobby to wait for Hall, afraid that Hall might be another handsome young man like Feyas. It was a silly attitude, MacInnes decided, since you couldn't keep a showcase jewel like Vanessa hidden. She had had, and would continue to have, the opportunity to meet thousands of handsome young men.

Through the plate-glass window he could see a new Chevrolet wheeling up to the curb. A young man wearing a light blue checked sport coat and dark blue knit slacks got out. He had blond hair, mod styled and fluffed up to cover his ears except for the lobes. His face had a freshly scrubbed look. His stride, as he approached the lobby, was long and had an athletic bounce to it.

"Mr. MacInnes? I'm Detective John Hall."

They shook hands, smiling.

"It's a real pleasure meeting you," Hall said. "I've heard a lot about you, and I've been looking forward to working with you."

"Glad to meet *you*." MacInnes said, picking up the cases. Hall insisted on carrying them.

MacInnes said, "Ellery Kimbal is a good friend and thinks highly of you."

"The feeling is certainly mutual."

"Be careful with those cases. Delicate electronic equipment."

"Don't worry." Hall eased them into the back of the car with the delicacy of a lab technician handling a flask of nitroglycerine.

As they rolled onto the main highway, Hall said, "Mr. MacInnes—"

"Call me Mac."

"Okay, Mac, thanks. What I was going to say, this is one of those cases where you feel you can't leave any stone unturned. I arrested the suspect, but I have a gut intuition that I may have the wrong man." He took the center lane to pass a little old lady dawdling along at forty. "I'm fighting the whole department on this one."

"Why?"

Hall glanced at him quickly, then back at the road. "Well, there's plenty of circumstantial evidence pointing to him. Incidentally, his name is Carter Morton."

"You just don't believe he did it?"

"No, I don't. The man simply doesn't have the guts."

MacInnes said, "You're treading on dangerous ground with that statement. You realize that, don't you?"

Hall was looking in the rear-vision mirror. "Yeah, that's true. But after you've looked at the file and talked to Morton—" He broke off and muttered, "Damned stupid bastard."

MacInnes turned and glanced out the back. A teenager in a red Corvette was tailgating them, his hood about three feet from the Chevy's rear end.

"These damned tailgaters cause more pileups on this road. Excuse me a minute while I take care of this creep." Hall whipped into the slow lane, let the Corvette pass, then pulled behind him and turned on his siren. In a few seconds he had the Corvette off to the side of the road, and MacInnes watched, amused, while he gave the youngster an angry, arm-waving lecture.

Hall returned to the car quickly, his face flushed. "Sorry for the interruption, but these idiots really burn me. A few months ago a close friend of mine was killed in an accident caused by one of them."

MacInnes said, "Not at all. I enjoyed seeing you

give him hell. I can't stand them either."

Hall was well educated and had no trace of regional accent. He bore no resemblance to the smalltown southern cop MacInnes was accustomed to dealing with. MacInnes asked, "How long have you been in law enforcement, John?"

"About five years. This was my first job after college. I really didn't want to stay in a small town, but it's been a good job. And I've got a good boss. Director Bush is okay. So I stayed and pushed my plans off."

"Plans to do what?"

Hall waved to a passing state-police car. "Well, I really had planned to get an investigator's job in Washington. For a government agency or the Senate or something. I have the contacts, but I decided against it."

MacInnes glanced at Hall. It would be easy to picture him with the Bureau or the Secret Service. They couldn't possibly be paying him enough to stay in Stateline. "Are you married, John?" he asked.

"No."

"Don't you know the girls in Washington are a lot prettier than around here?"

Hall smiled, keeping his eyes on the road. "Okay supersleuth, you got me. My girlfriend not only lives here, she loves this town."

The public-safety building was a clean, modern brick structure in the center of the town. The center city itself was neater and more orderly in layout than generally found in the area. In the building's parking lot the police cars and other equipment were new and obviously well maintained. Hall pulled into a space marked CHIEF OF DETECTIVES. A fair title for an officer his age.

Director of Public Safety Bush was a genial grasshopper of a man, tall, slender, all arms and legs. He welcomed MacInnes warmly. MacInnes complimented him on the size and appearance of his operation. Smiling, Bush acknowledged that Stateline had a strong public-safety department. The town leaders had been farsighted. After chatting another minute or two, Bush suggested that Hall get the Carter Morton file together and then show MacInnes to the office he was to use.

After Hall left, Bush said, "I'm afraid your talents are going to be wasted here, Mr. MacInnes."

MacInnes said, "So far I'm a bit confused, I'll admit. On my way in I saw what appeared to be a very complete crime lab. You must have a polygraph section?"

"Yes, we do. One of the finest, we believe."

"What do they say about Morton?"

Bush shook his head. "Basically inconclusive, but pointing toward guilt. However, the evidence is so strong, we literally have an airtight case." He took a half-finished cigar from his ashtray and lit it. "As you well know, exceptionally nervous and high-strung people can play hell with a polygraph. It has been of little use to us in this case. But the other evidence is overwhelming."

He pushed his swivel chair back and stood up. "However, John Hall is a conscientious policeman, and he has a gut feeling that Morton is not guilty." He strolled to the windows and looked out, his hands on his hips, his pipe-stem arms and elbows forming tremendous triangles. "I believe in backing my men all the way. I must also consider the fact that if Morton is by some strange miracle innocent, we have a dangerous killer at large. We don't want to miss any bets in this situation."

Hall returned carrying a bulky manila folder. With a wave to Director Bush, MacInnes accompanied Hall down the corridor to a small office. About ten by ten feet, it contained a steel composition-top desk, steel bookcase, swivel chair, telephone, steel pedestal coat rack, desk lamp. A clean blotter was on the desk, a legal-sized lined pad in the center. Everything was new, but the office had apparently not been used, and everything was covered with dust.

"Damn," said Hall. "I told Timothy to clean this office this morning." He left the room and returned quickly with an older man in blue prison clothes. The prisoner carried a bucket of water in one hand and rags and furniture polish in the other. A mop was under his arm.

"I told you to do this early this morning, Timothy."

The old man fidgeted uneasily. "Yessir, Mr. John. I'll get it done right away."

Timothy shook so badly that the water in the pail had circular shock waves on top. MacInnes quickly moved out of the way.

Hall said, "Let's have a Coke and let Timothy mop up."

They walked down the corridor and into a

lounge and snack area, where MacInnes could look through large plate-glass windows into the communications center. As he watched the activity going on behind the glass, Hall handed him a chilled can.

"Timothy is our town drunk. He's doing another thirty days and is well into drying out again," said Hall.

MacInnes shook his head sadly, then asked, "How many cars do you have on the street, John?"

"Never less than thirty. Our jurisdiction covers nearly ninety square miles."

"That's a substantial area," said MacInnes.

"It keeps us plenty busy."

A tall young man came in the room. Hall introduced him to MacInnes as "Elmer Peters, our ax man."

Peters laughed, slightly embarrassed. "Lay off, will you!"

Peters was called to the phone and left quickly. Hall took MacInnes on a quick tour of the building, introducing him to various men enroute. They ended in the detective division, a large room on the second floor with Hall's office in one corner, a small room created by floor-to-ceiling glass panels.

"Why did you call Peters the ax man?" asked MacInnes.

Hall laughed. "Oh yes, I meant to tell you about that. Do you see those two corner windows over there?" He pointed to two large casement windows on either side of an outside corner of the building. "The telephone company had a main telephone cable running across this property before the building was built. They refused to move it. The damned silly thing dragged on in the courts so long that the city finally just built the building right over the cable. It came in that window and went out that one." He pointed out the path of the cable. "We moved into the new building, and the detective division was put in this room. The cable was not only an eyesore, but in spite of plastic wraps, it let in a lot of damned frosty air in winter." He laughed again. "About two months ago old Elmer just took a fire ax to it, and ten thousand telephone lines went dead. Ma Bell was furious, but somehow we got it all straightened out."

MacInnes chuckled. "Good for old Elmer."

Hall said, "Yeah, we had to protect old Elmer. Every damned one of us wished he had had the guts to do the same thing. This kind of bureaucratic nonsense can drive you out of your mind."

MacInnes wondered whether old Timothy had finished cleaning the office. He didn't care for the way the case was starting. He'd had to wait while they cleaned the *dispensario,* and this clean-up business, which he had never encountered before, loomed as some sort of evil omen.

"I expect old Timothy is finished by now, wouldn't you say?" he asked Hall.

Hall, who was glancing through a half dozen telephone messages, said, "Probably." He handed the Morton file to MacInnes. "Why don't you go ahead down and familiarize yourself with the file. I'll be down in about a half an hour and we can discuss it.''

The office had been cleaned thoroughly, but MacInnes found the strong odor of pine oil overpowering. He opened the single large window, slamming it high. A startled Timothy leaped from the bushes under the window. He had a brown paper bag in his hand, the neck of the bottle within plainly visible. MacInnes put his finger to his lips. Reassured, the old man crawled to another bush.

MacInnes sat down and opened the file. Photos of the deceased, a child named Sheere Lima. He shuddered and turned them facedown quickly. Her dress and underwear had been ripped off, leaving her thin, bruised body with only socks and sandals. She had been raped, beaten, and strangled.

MacInnes was a fast reader. He made his way through the stack of documents at a rapid pace, summarizing the relevant facts. Sheere Lima's body had been found in Harding Park, a large wooded area in the southeastern section of the city. The park was only three blocks from her home. She had been reported missing the evening before. An organized search party consisting of police and volunteers had located the body about 1:00 a.m. It was partially hidden in some undergrowth. Near the body they found her torn dress and her small white change purse. The purse contained a five-dollar bill and thirty-five cents in change. The five-dollar bill had apparently been given to her by her attacker, since her parents agreed that she had had only some change for ice cream.

All known sex offenders in the area had been questioned immediately. There were only five, and they all had unshakable alibis. It had taken the Stateline police and the computer two days to catch up with Carter Morton, because his record was in Pennsylvania. He had lived in Labelle, a city about fifty miles from Stateline. Morton, a bachelor, had been a schoolteacher there for thirty years. After he retired, he became involved in two incidents concerning children, both girls.

In the first case, charges had been dismissed at the request of the girl's parents. Morton had been a friend of the family. The child had not been harmed or even frightened. Morton had merely taken her to his apartment and given her a bath. He claimed that she had asked to take a bath, and the girl had substantiated this statement. He had bought her some toy boats to sail in the tub, and she was anxious to try them out. The parents felt the police should have a record of the incident, but they were not sure that Morton's actions had been any more than an old schoolteacher's eccentricity.

The second incident had been similar, but the girl had been a stranger, and the parents had pressed charges. Here again he had done nothing but take the child to his apartment and give her a bath. She had not been harmed or frightened, and she admitted that she had willingly agreed to take a bath so that she could play with her new boats. He had not touched either child. Brought to trial, Morton had received a suspended sentence tied to mandatory psychiatric treatment.

The evidence against Carter Morton was strong

indeed, as Director Bush had indicated. The girl's autopsy placed the time of death between six and eight the evening before. At five-thirty, Morton had been sitting on a bench in the park with Sheere Lima. Three witnesses had identified him in a lineup as the elderly man they had seen sitting with Sheere, helping her read a comic book. The witnesses were Harvey and Grace Nelson, a couple out for a predinner stroll, and Millicent Wagner, a librarian.

A search of Morton's apartment in Stateline had turned up Sheere Lima's underpants. There was no doubt of the identification, since Sheere's mother had sewn name tags in all her garments when the child had gone to camp that summer.

They also found a collection of photographs of naked children, mostly girls, some pornographically posed.

MacInnes shook his head. It certainly looked open and shut.

John Hall popped his head in the door. "How are you making out?"

MacInnes closed the file. "I'm wondering what you need me here for."

Hall came in and sat down. "I know it looks bad. I just have this goddamned feeling that the guy is a harmless voyeur. He never touched those other two kids."

MacInnes held up his hand. "But John, think of the million-to-one coincidence you'd have to have in a town this size to have *two* sexual deviates of this type in the same location at approximately the same time."

Hall said, "There have been bigger coincidences. For your information, Harding Park has a couple of nicknames, Screw Valley, and Grooving Grove. It's been a hangout for all kinds of sex for years—hetero, homo, deviates, and a number of drug-abuser types who go in for some really weird stuff." He rubbed his forehead wearily. "We try to keep an eye on it, but the damned place covers about five hundred acres, a good part of it heavily wooded."

MacInnes pushed the folder aside. "Well, John, we'll see what the old crystal ball says." He wanted to get the damned job over, get the hell out and back to Florida. "Why don't you have Morton brought in, and I'll get to work."

Hall gave him a two-fingered salute and said, "Right on, Colonel."

As he stood up, MacInnes said, "I meant to ask, do you have a photo of a girl in your files? She should be somewhere between nine and twelve years old."

"Probably. I'll check," said Hall, heading for the door.

MacInnes stopped him. "Wait a minute. I've just remembered, I've got one."

Hall said, "Fine. That'll save some time." He left, leaving the door open.

In cleaning out his billfold some weeks earlier, MacInnes had found a snapshot of his former wife when she was twelve. He had always been intrigued by it. There was something in the clear-eyed, wise, perky innocence of the child's face that he found endearing. If they had a daughter, she would be like that. He had thrown out all the other photos of Joanne. For some reason he had held on to this one. A sort of memento of what might have been. Or more likely, a *memento mori*. It had remained stuck in the back of his billfold, unnoticed, for years. He found it and placed it facedown on the desk.

Carter Morton, age fifty-eight, looked closer to sixty-eight. He was short and thin, gray haired, with bulging watery blue eyes large and myopic behind black-framed glasses. His tongue flicked nervously over thin lips as he sat down in the chair MacInnes indicated. He gripped the armrests tightly, as though afraid the chair might suddenly move and dislodge him.

It was hard to imagine this mild, inoffensive-looking little man as a brutal rape murderer. MacInnes reminded himself that it was not his job to judge, to have opinions. A man is innocent until proven guilty. It was up to the prosecution to prove that he was guilty. Yet with the evidence he had seen, the man was probably guilty, and try as hard as he could to be objective, the sight of Carter Morton disgusted him.

"Do you know why you are here, Mr. Morton?"

Morton said, "Apparently I'm to be given another lie-detector test." Although he was obviously nervous enough to fly out the window, his school teacher's voice came forth sounding firm and authoritative.

MacInnes switched on the tape recorder. "That is correct."

He leaned back in the swivel chair and said, "It

263

has been established that you were with Sheere Lima a short time before her death. You've admitted this, have you not?''

"Yes, but I didn't kill her. I left shortly after those people saw me. When I left, she was still sitting there, reading the comic book.''

"You left with her panties in your pocket.''

"I've explained that.''

"Explain it to me, Mr. Morton.''

Morton's lined face reddened. ''I bought them from her. I know it was wrong. I gave her five dollars for them.''

"You went off into the bushes with her while she took them off, right?''

"No! Absolutely not. She slipped them off right there. No one was around then. I didn't even look.''

MacInnes's lip curled. ''You didn't look?''

"No.'' He struggled to continue, his mouth working but no sound coming out. ''Well, maybe I saw a little out of the corner of my eye.'' MacInnes noticed that his knuckles were white, he was still gripping the armrests so hard. ''You don't understand. Three times a week I have to drive back to Labelle for psychiatric therapy. They show me pictures of naked girls and give me a nasty electric shock every damned time. Then they show me pictures of grown-up whores and I don't get a shock. This is supposed to make me prefer grown-up whores.''

MacInnes asked, ''What has this to do with your buying Sheere Lima's underpants?''

"I'm trying to explain. An alcoholic has got to

learn to be with people who are drinking and refuse to drink. The world is full of liquor and people who drink. To be cured, I've got to learn to be with young girls, talk to them, without giving way to any deviate impulses. So it was *all right* for me to be sitting on the park bench with Sheere Lima, talking to her. I helped her with words she didn't know in the comic book. The world is as full of young girls as it is of people who drink. I can't disappear into limbo where there are no young girls." Perspiration began to roll down his face. "It was *wrong* of me to offer her five dollars for her underpants. Obviously I am far from being cured. But I swear to you I didn't harm her."

MacInnes fingered the snapshot of Joanne. There were some people who reacted with strong guilt stress to the suggestion that they might have committed any crime, no matter how farfetched. He had to have this type of reading from Carter Morton.

He showed the picture of Joanne to Morton. "Do you know this girl?"

Morton studied the snapshot carefully. "No, to the best of my knowledge I have never seen her before."

"Four weeks ago she was brutally raped and murdered in much the same way Sheere Lima was killed. It happened in Baker, about seventy miles from here."

Morton said quickly, "I know nothing about it."

"Did you buy this girl's underpants and then do away with her?"

"No, absolutely not."

So much for the guilt-complex control question. MacInnes carefully fitted the snapshot of Joanne into its former place in his billfold.

"Now Mr. Morton, I'm going to ask you a series of questions about Sheere Lima. I want you to answer each question truthfully. Do you understand?"

"Of course."

MacInnes stared at Morton, his mind almost mechanically beginning to probe, trying to reach out to the man on the other side of the desk. In many instances a relay would seem to click and he would feel the subject's thoughts almost as an echo in his own mind. In this case, he could feel nothing.

"Is your name Carter Morton?"

"Yes."

"Regarding Sheere Lima and the girl in the picture I just showed you, will you answer every question truthfully?"

"Yes."

"Do you like the color blue?"

"Yes."

"Do you know who killed Sheere Lima?"

"No."

"Do you like the color black?"

"No."

"Did you kill Sheere Lima?"

"No."

"Do you like the color pink?"

"Yes."

"Did you attack the girl in the picture?"

"No."

"Does the number thirteen mean anything to you?"

"No, I'm not superstitious."

"Do you suspect someone of killing Sheere Lima?"

"No."

"Do you know for sure who killed Sheere Lima?"

"No."

"Did you kill Sheere Lima?"

"No sir!"

MacInnes said, "All right, Mr. Morton. That's the end of the test. I'm going to have an officer take you back to your cell. I may ask you to come back later after I've had a chance to go over your charts." MacInnes picked up his phone and dialed the duty sergeant on the intercom. He bent his head over the pad he had been scribbling on as they waited, glancing up only when the policeman came to lead Morton away. The officer was a hefty six feet two, and he might have been carrying a laundry sack through the door, a blue laundry sack with two limp legs attached to it.

MacInnes glanced at his watch. Six-thirty. He telephoned Vanessa and told her to go ahead and have dinner without waiting for him. Morton had been so nervous that Kevin was certain the charts were going to be sheer hell to interpret. Sheer hell. Sheere Lima. If he didn't finish the job tonight, they'd miss the flight to Baltimore in the morning.

"Do any writing?" he asked her.

"A little. Mostly I swam and read."

"What did you read?"

She sighed. "A novel by a male chauvinist pig."

"Oh. Did you write furious notes in the margins?"

"No!"

He laughed. "Okay, dearest, expect me when you see me."

She said softly, "Wake me up."

He crossed the square to a restaurant near the public-safety building. He had a quick double martini. He needed something more potent than Scotch. A large hot roast-beef sandwich with mashed potatoes took most of the buzz away, and a cup of black coffee obliterated it completely. He left to return wearily to work.

The building was almost empty and had been so for long hours now. MacInnes was standing by the window of the unlighted office he had been given to use. The lights of the parking area outside came through the window throwing MacInnes's shadow on the front wall of the small room. He had gone through two packs of cigarettes and was now working on a pack he had borrowed from one of the officers in communications. After a long minute he turned and walked back to the center of the room and stood looking at the charts he had taped to the wall at eye level. He couldn't see the details of the charts in the darkened room, but he stared at the wall anyway.

He had never struggled with such peculiarly

confused PSE charts before. He had considered every detail of the pen markings again and again, even resorting to a magnifying glass, something he rarely used. Morton had shown good stress on the revelant questions, but he had shown strong stress on the control questions also. For every answer MacInnes could dredge up, ten other solutions could be plausible. The thought of giving up and calling the examination inconclusive loomed. He rejected it. Dammit, he'd figure the damned thing out if he had to stay all night. He hadn't become the Lie King by walking away from problems and calling them inconclusive.

Should he consult with another examiner? Who? No one knew as much about the PSE as he did.

He had run the recording in every mode and speed, but he turned on the lights and began to run certain chart combinations again. He watched despairingly as they rolled out in the same configurations that had already baffled him.

His mouth was dry and pasty. He turned to the door in disgust and went down the corridor to the ready-room area to buy another cup of the foul black liquid from the coffee machine. At least it was wet.

Two detectives came in. One was Ax Man Elmer. The other, whom MacInnes had not met, said, "Dammit, Elmer, you really are a hardass. I told you not to bust that kid with the red bell bottoms."

Elmer waved his arm. "Goddammit, Pete, you told me not to bust him, but you didn't tell me he was the mayor's nephew.''

Pete yelled, ''I tried to tell you, dammit, but you had your big mouth going so fast I couldn't get a word in!''

The two men noticed MacInnes. Elmer turned to Pete and said, ''This is Mr. MacInnes. You were off-duty when he showed up. He's working on the Morton case.''

Pete offered his hand. ''Glad to meet you. I hope they finally got somebody in here who can nail that son of a bitch.''

MacInnes said, ''You think he should be nailed, huh?''

Pete stuck some coins in the coffee machine. ''Hell yes. If they'd put that creep away the first time they caught up with him, a little girl would be alive today. This psychology shit is for the birds. I've never seen it change one of those bastards yet.''

MacInnes took a swallow of the muddy, disgusting poison, shuddered, then poured the container down the drain. ''How do you guys stand this stuff?''

Elmer slapped his shoulder playfully. ''Guts of iron, man, guts of iron.''

MacInnes said, ''Well, I've got to go back to the glue factory. Take it easy.'' He turned and, with a brief wave, made his way back to the office.

He sat staring at the charts. He hadn't been kidding when he said glue factory. If any man had a mind full of glue, Carter Morton had more.

A half hour later he was still staring at the

charts, half-hypnotized by the strokes of the pen. Suddenly certain areas began to look different. By God there *was* deception stress! Excitedly he got up and began circling the chart areas with a red felt-tipped pen. There was an obvious pattern. Why hadn't he seen it before?

He was lighting another cigarette when John Hall looked in.

"Didn't expect to see you still here," he said. "They got me out of bed. Some stupid damned thing about the mayor's nephew."

MacInnes turned to face him. "I heard."

"How you making out?"

MacInnes said, "All done. Finally."

"And?"

MacInnes hesitated. He hated to put down a good man's hunch. "The guy's a bag of worms, John, but the signals indicate to me that he's your man."

Hall looked at the floor and was silent for a moment. "Well, I guess that's the way it is then." He turned. "Come on, I'll drive you back to your pad. It won't hurt the mayor's nephew to pee in his pants for another twenty minutes."

Back in the suite, MacInnes found he was too exhausted to sleep. It was the kind of exhaustion that leaves the nerves taut, the mind alert but scrambling aimlessly from worry to worry. He had no desire to wake Vanessa. If his cases started becoming as tough as this one, he couldn't keep it up. He'd be just another run-of-the-mill PSE examiner turning in "inconclusives" right and left. Maybe he was losing his skill. It had taken him so damned long to see the pattern of Carter Morton's guilt.

He poured himself a large Scotch, added some water, and sat there drinking it, finding some ease from the headache the hours of chain smoking had given him. After a second drink he relaxed enough to doze for a while, half-asleep but half-conscious of being in a chair and being slightly uncomfortable.

At 6:00 a.m. he was fully awake again. He found Vanessa's portable and typed up his report, then stuffed it in a large brown envelope with the charts and the Uher tape. He addressed the envelope to Director Bush and took it out to the sleepy night clerk. John Hall would have it picked up. He went back to the suite and took a shower and shaved. Case closed.

CHAPTER NINETEEN

KEVIN AND VANESSA were lazing away the morning under a beach umbrella, enjoying the warm, salty breeze and the muted rumble of the surf. MacInnes had taken a brisk swim and he was now propped on one elbow watching Vanessa, who was scribbling away in a fat loose-leaf notebook. She had been spending an unusual amount of time writing since the trip to Stateline, but she wouldn't let Kevin read anything she had written.

"If it's good enough to be published, then you can read it," she said.

He was curious. If she was writing about him, about their life together, what would show up in print? What would be her point of view? How much was she ready to expose? Not only was he curious, but he felt vulnerable as well.

Li Duc came plodding through the sand to them. "Man at house wish to see you. Won't tell name. Say it is about musical instrument."

Musical instrument. Harp? He got to his feet quickly and put on his terrycloth beach robe.

The man waiting for him was tall and well-built and had curly gray hair. His face was long and thin, elongated by a high forehead and receding hairline. His large gray-blue eyes appraised MacInnes carefully.

"Colonel MacInnes?"

"That's right." MacInnes half-turned away. "Probably you'd better come into my study."

The stranger followed him into his study and, after he closed the door, offered his hand.

"Jim O'Connor of the Bureau."

After a brief handshake, O'Connor produced his credentials.

MacInnes glanced at O'Connor's identification card, then went to his desk and pulled out a small notebook. "Washington or local?"

"Washington."

MacInnes found the number he wanted and dialed. "Who should I speak to there?"

"Ask for Herb Browning." O'Connor smiled. "It's a pleasure to deal with a careful man."

After a brief wait, Browning got on the line.

MacInnes introduced himself and said, "I have a man in my office who says he's James O'Connor of the Federal Bureau of Investigation."

Browning said, "Right. That's just where Jim O'Connor should be, in your office."

"Would you describe him, please?"

Browning described O'Connor, right down to the small mole on the right side of his chin.

"Okay. Thanks."

"A pleasure. Glad you're being thorough."

MacInnes turned back to O'Connor. "You're here about Harp, of course. And if he did decide to deal with me, which I doubt very seriously, this is just the type of cute trick he might try to test me. He's a very shrewd character. And FBI cards can be counterfeited easier than passports."

O'Connor dropped into a chair and stretched out his long legs. "Right. And we're hoping to hell he will get in touch with you." He sighed deeply. "Frankly, we've lost him."

"Where?"

"New York, of course. I'm sure you know the problems of surveillance in New York."

MacInnes smiled. "I know. You can have ten men on a guy and still lose him in Grand Central Station."

O'Connor scowled. "Macy's. It shouldn't have happened."

MacInnes said, "Can I offer you coffee or a drink?"

O'Connor thought about it, then shook his head. "No thanks. Too early in the day for a drink, and I've got coffee nerves already. I'm in charge of this buggering Harp project."

MacInnes rubbed his face. It was sticky with dried saltwater. "I wish I could help you," he said, "but I'm afraid it's very unlikely that Harp would trust dealing with me on anything this important."

O'Connor brought out his wallet and extracted a small card with a single telephone number on it. He handed it to MacInnes. "This number is manned twenty-four hours a day. It will be answered, 'Jeanine's Massage Spa.' Your code is, 'Is Nicolette available?' From there on, play it by ear. If you are calling from a safe number, leave it and I'll call you as quickly as they can reach me, probably within an hour. Otherwise, leave whatever information you can."

MacInnes riffled the pages of his notebook thoughtfully. "Sure. But as I said, I don't believe Harp will contact me. In Mexico it was different. Knowing my background, he could find it credible that I might break the law to get my daughter out of a Mexican prison and that I might help him with an illegal deal as a sort of consultation-fee payment." He glanced out his big glass wall overlooking the sea. Vanessa was under the umbrella, her ballpoint pen moving over the pages of her notebook. "But up here, I would probably revert to type. One hundred percent on the side of law enforcement."

O'Connor's long face became longer and more melancholy. "You're probably right." He reached into the leather envelope he had had tucked under one arm and extracted a manila file. "These are Mulcahy's reports. I'd appreciate it if you'd read them carefully and tell me whether there is anything you can add about this guy's personality or character that might help us."

MacInnes took the file and went back to his desk. There were excellent photos of Harp taken on the street. Two not-so-sharp shots had been produced by his cigarette-case camera. He read Mulcahy's reports carefully. Mulcahy had been very thorough. When MacInnes finished, he closed the folder and thought for a while.

"Mulcahy seems to have covered the ground. What could I add? Harp is a very vain guy and has a superb tailor somewhere. Since the tailor could be anywhere from London to Bombay, I'm afraid that isn't much help. However, you could nose around some of New York's choice establishments—you know, where you pay five hundred bucks for a suit? You might just luck out. At least you know he's in the city."

O'Connor took the folder and stuffed it back in his soft leather case. "Thanks. We're at the point where we'll try anything."

"Were you able to get a line on the Southerner?"

"Nope."

"That droopy eyelid should have been a help."

O'Connor stood up. "Well, it wasn't. At least, not so far."

MacInnes walked with him to the driveway and watched as he drove away in an old Chevrolet with KRAMER'S APPLIANCE REPAIR SERVICE printed on the door.

It was really getting too warm to eat breakfast on the patio, but when you were rich enough to have a patio overlooking the ocean, you felt impelled to use it instead of the comfortably air-conditioned dining room. Later in the summer common sense would drive them inside. Li Duc brought out the morning mail. She handed it to Vanessa, who had finished and was sipping coffee. Vanessa shuffled through the envelopes, putting MacInnes's mail in one pile and hers in another, including all letters addressed to "Mrs. Kevin MacInnes."

"Oh, here's one from your friend in Stateline, Maryland," she said, handing it to him.

MacInnes put down his cup and opened the letter.

"Dear Mr. MacInnes," John Hall had written, "I have some unpleasant news for you, but I feel that you are the sort of man who would wish to face up to it and make whatever reassessments are necessary. Maybe a good cop shouldn't rely on hunches, but it's probable that we also rely too much on lie detector tests. Yesterday Carter Morton killed himself. Somehow he conned old Timothy into giving him an empty wine bottle. He smashed it and cut his wrists. A Xerox of the note he left is enclosed. Incidentally, we caught the right guy. A drunken kid without any record at all."

On the left, under Hall's signature, was typed, "cc w/enclosures to President, International Society of Stress Analysts."

Unbelieving, MacInnes lifted the page and stared at the copy of Carter Morton's note. It was addressed "To Whom it Should Concern," and said, "This is a deathbed declaration of innocence. Apparently your electronic devices have found me guilty, and you're going to stop looking. The deck is stacked against me, and I do not have the strength to face your Kangaroo Court. So I go to face my maker with two curses in my heart, a curse for Him for giving me such a miserable, warped existence, and a curse for you for not being more discerning, for not searching harder for the real killer. Perhaps now you will *search*." He had signed, "Carter Morton," with a heavy flourish, and had added, "P.S. Do not blame poor old Timothy. He had no idea of the use I planned to make of his empty wine bottle."

MacInnes paled under his tan, and the coffee he had drunk rose slightly in his throat. He swallowed hard, a wave of dizziness sweeping over him.

Vanessa, who had glanced up, said, "Kevin, what's the matter? Are you ill?"

He handed her the letter and the note, then got up and walked down to the beach. John Hall was certainly bitter, sending a letter to the society. Was he out to ruin him? He supposed he deserved it.

In a couple of minutes Vanessa followed him. She put her arm around his waist. "I know it's horrible for you." She hugged him. "Everyone makes mistakes. You're entitled to a mistake."

"Not one that big," he muttered.

"Kevin!"

He squinted at the blue water. "Face it, I'm washed up. Through."

"Don't say that. It's not like you to . . . to give up."

He turned away. "Give up? Who could trust me?"

The rest of the day he sat in his study staring

into space, occasionally rising to pour himself another drink. He could eat neither lunch nor dinner. The Carter Morton report had been a wild-assed guess, wrong as hell. How many times had he conned himself into making a wild-assed guess—and lucked out? He'd never live this one down.

Vanessa came in from time to time to try to comfort him, but finding him completely unresponsive, she finally left him to brood alone.

By evening his spirits had risen a little. Very little. Hardly noticeable. "You know," he said to Vanessa, "I was injured down there in Mexico. That blow on the head. I may have a concussion. I should have it checked out."

She stared at him gravely, glad of any break in his depressed apathy. "That might well be it," she said.

Vanessa waited up for him, a measure of the seriousness of her concern. Ordinarily, it would be difficult for her to remain awake.

They went through their usual rituals, but he found that he could not perform. He had become some kind of sexless zombie.

The next day he entered the hospital. After four days and every possible test, he was pronounced as healthy as a thirty-year-old. No concussion to blame.

The doctor suggested he consult a psychiatrist about his impotence and the dizzy spells, and recommended a well-known therapist. It was depressing that he could not blame his failure on concussion, but he was glad to leave the hospital.

A woman down the corridor, obviously in excruciating pain, had screamed for many hours each day.

He made an appointment with Dr. Roman and had a consultation with him the following day.

When he returend to the house, Vanessa was waiting for him, hesitant to ask about the session but deeply concerned.

He smiled. "Oh, he said there's nothing much wrong with me that a good rest and some diversion won't cure. The impotence is purely psychological and obviously temporary. I've had a traumatic experience that has been more of a shock to me than it should have been." He glanced at her. She was smiling. "I'm going to lay off work for a couple of months. Swim, play tennis, read some good books."

Actually that wasn't at all what Dr. Roman had said. MacInnes wasn't sure of exactly what Dr. Roman had said, but he had the impression that Dr. Roman felt that if MacInnes came to him two or three times a week for the next ten years, they might get to the bottom of his problem. He had disliked Dr. Roman from the first moment of their meeting, and he had reasoned that if he did not like or trust Roman as a therapist, the association would be unsuccessful. The alternative seemed to be to go it alone or try to find another psychiatrist.

He wondered whether Vanessa believed him. If she knew anything about psychiatrists, she would know that you don't get off that easily. The human mind is infinitely complex, and apart from some harried doctor in a mental institution, no psychiatrist would be likely to dismiss a patient on the basis of one consultation.

"You didn't like him," said Vanessa.

He looked down. "No, I didn't like him. I decided I'd try to work out my own therapy."

Vanessa said, "It sounds sensible enough. Get your mind completely off professional problems for a month or so."

"It'll give me a fresh perspective."

Rather than freshened, Kevin's perspective became dimmer and more clouded. For the first time in his life, tennis bored him. He got no pleasure in it, and his game, once more than competent, became awkward, plagued by ludicrously poor timing. The good books he planned to read or reread either disturbed or bored him, and his shortened attention span left him floundering through the long descriptive passages of *Moby Dick* and other classics.

He carried on continuing arguments with himself over Carter Morton. Many good, dedicated doctors had buried more than one honest mistake without finding their lives ruptured. Carter Morton had probably only been the catalyst that unleashed some deeper emotional disturbance in Kevin. But what? Why was he becoming a zombie who could find no pleasure in anything? He had always enjoyed good food. Now he ate with no more interest than placating an empty stomach.

His relationship with Vanessa deteriorated subtly. After a few more unsuccessful tries at sex, he gave up. He found the situation too humiliating.

He felt like a eunuch. They reached an agreement, almost unspoken, that one day soon he would be over his problem, and they would wait it out. He told himself ironically that what he had was no worse than an aggravated case of gonorrhea, the gonorrhea being hardly worse than a bad cold, as they said in the army.

He called Josh Berger, the bright young manager of his West Palm Beach office, to find out how things were going. He hadn't spoken to Josh in three weeks, since he had first informed him of his prolonged vacation. Things were going surprisingly well. He had expected to lose some business, but Josh was holding his own, even bringing in new accounts. He had been thinking for some time that he should give Josh a piece of the action, even though he was only twenty-seven. A stock deal where he could pay off the cost of the shares through the profits they earned. He mentioned this.

Josh was both confused and grateful. After stammering slightly he said, "That's wonderful. I really appreciate it." There was a long pause, and he then said, "Mac, when are you coming back? You know, we're doing okay, but we haven't been getting any of the real *big* ones, the kind that depend on a big rep."

MacInnes wondered what kind of reputation he had left.

"Has anyone been really hot for me to handle something personally?" he asked.

Josh said, "Well, no, but when you're here these things just seem to percolate in."

So much for his reputation. Word did get around. There were comparatively few experts in his profession, and gossip traveled rapidly from coast to coast.

Only one thing seemed to ease the pain of his boredom—Scotch. It gave him no real pleasure. It relaxed and numbed and made the days pass. Normally he had been accustomed to having a couple of drinks before dinner and perhaps two more during the evening. Now he started at breakfast, with two ounces in his coffee. His intake was steady but well spaced, and he never became incapacitated or obnoxiously drunk; he was just moderately high all day and most of the night.

It worried Vanessa. "You're drinking too much and not eating enough, and it's going to ruin your health," was a frequent comment, expressed in different ways.

He smilingly and affectionately asked her not to nag.

The nights were long, and he started playing games with the PSE.

Question: "Kevin MacInnes, do you believe in God, I mean a God that has some interest in the actions of human beings?"

Answer: "No."

What did the chart say? Heavy deception stress. Childhood conditioning. Apparently he still believed in a personal God. That was interesting, but what did it signify? A rational versus emotional schism. What should he do, abandon his intellectual convictions and run back into the arms of Jesus? He doubted whether it would even be possible.

Question: "Are you a coward, Kevin MacInnes?"

Answer: "No."

Read the chart. Heavy deception stress. Now what the goddammed hell was he supposed to be afraid of? When had he ever flinched or turned away in line of duty?

Question: "Kevin MacInnes, are you an honest man?"

Answer: "Yes."

He watched the pen move up and down on the one syllable. "Yes." Heavy blocked deception stress. What the hell was wrong with the goddammed machine? He hastily tested it with control questions. Is today Thursday? Is your name Kevin MacInnes? Are you temporarily impotent? Do you like the color red? Did you ever steal anything? Are you sexually attracted to men?

The answers all came out right. He wasn't sexually attracted to men, he liked the red, and it was Thursday.

Of course, the answer was that *honest* was too broad. We are all dishonest at times, without even realizing it.

Question: "Why can't you accept the fact that you made a serious but honest mistake in testing Carter Morton, a mistake without malice in it, and go on from there?"

Answer: "I can, and I will."

Chart: heavy deception stress. In other words, he couldn't and wouldn't. Ridiculous. Was he supposed to let a crapped-up deviate ruin his life? Carter Morton's preoccupation with naked little girls had put him in the wrong place at the wrong time like an appointment in Samara. He was, MacInnes agreed, immediately responsible for Morton's suicide, but there were other factors, important ones.

Question: "Do you have a low opinion of yourself?"

Answer: "No."

Chart: Heavy deception stress. Okay, so he had a low opinion of himself.

Vanessa came out of the bedroom. She hadn't been falling asleep so easily since the arrival of the letter from Stateline. She looked at the equipment, suppressing a yawn. "Practicing?"

"You might call it that."

She sat down, staring at him curiously. "Maybe you should get back to work. Maybe it would restore your confidence. Maybe you should never have stopped."

"Maybe."

"I mean, like diving right away after you've taken an awful, painful bellyflop."

MacInnes thought about it. "I don't think I'm afraid of making mistakes. If I'm afraid, I'm probably afraid of finding out what it has done to my reputation."

Vanessa poured herself a Scotch and water, unusual for her at that time of night. He refreshed his own drink.

"Still, isn't it better that you faced it? If it's as bad as you think, you can still fight your way back. You don't lose a talent such as yours just like that, overnight."

MacInnes said, "Maybe you're right. I'll practice on you."

She half-rose. "Now wait a minute."

"Sit still. This won't hurt a bit."

She sank back.

"Is your name Vanessa Peckham?"

"Yes."

"Is today Thursday?"

"Yes."

"Are you happy here?"

"Not at the moment."

"Would you rather be with someone else?"

"No."

"Did you ever steal anything?"

"No." She held up her hand. "Let me change that to *yes*."

"Have you ever masturbated?"

She flushed, "What a silly question. Hasn't every normal person, at one time or another?"

MacInnes said, "Inhibitions die hard. It causes stress, whichever way you answer it. It's a control question."

She said, "Okay, the answer is yes."

"Did you love your father?"

"Yes."

"Do you love me?"

She gave him a long look. "Is that necessary, Kevin?"

"Do you love me?" he repeated.

"Yes, Kevin. I love you."

He lit a cigarette. "Okay, let's see what the chart says." He started the tape through the PSE and bent over watching the pen markings.

Minutes passed while the chart strip rolled relentlessly by and curled onto the floor. Normal,

normal, normal, no stress on the obvious truths, slight stress on the "steal" and "masturbate" questions. The answers to the last two questions scribbled their way to completion. His spirits took a deep dive. He looked at his cigarette, which had long since burned itself out in the ashtray. He lit another.

"It would seem that you didn't love your father and that you don't love me." There was heavy deception stress on both answers.

There was a lengthy silence. Vanessa finally said, "Apparently whatever I say, I'm going to be wrong. If I say you must be mistaken, I'll destroy your confidence. If I say you're right . . ."

He gathered up the chart strips. "Look, honey, you couldn't destroy my confidence on these. Some charts are very difficult to interpret. Others are as simple as ABC. A child could read these."

She glanced at them without interest. "I always thought I loved my father." She bit her thumb gently. "Of course, I hated him at times. Doesn't every child?" She looked at Kevin. "And I thought I loved you. Maybe I don't."

MacInnes said, "You did once. Now you don't. It's understandable. How can you love a eunuch?"

"Love should be more than sex. And why are you so sure I loved you once?"

MacInnes ground out his cigarette impatiently. "Because I tested you once when you didn't know it."

She lifted her glass and took several swallows. "What a disgusting thing to do."

"Why? I loved you, and I wanted to ask you to

marry me.'' He finished off his own drink. ''But I didn't think you loved me. I wouldn't want to marry anyone who didn't love me.''

Maybe the answer was more simple than he thought. Love was not a constant thing. You gained it or lost it day by day, week by week, month by month, year by year. So if it was such a chancy thing, why attach so much importance to it?

Vanessa poured herself another drink. ''You know,'' she said, ''when we started together we had only one emotional cripple to contend with. Me. Now we have two. Complicates things, doesn't it?''

MacInnes stared at her.

''You wondered why I wouldn't marry you.''

MacInnes reached for the bottle, then decided there was still enough in his glass. ''You said it had to do with your unhappy marriage.''

Vanessa said, ''Well, that was true. But it didn't mean much because I couldn't explain it to you.''

''No, it didn't,'' he said, his voice very low.

She took a sip of her drink. ''Well, you see, my problem is, I killed my baby.''

CHAPTER TWENTY

HIS MIND RACED frantically, unbelieving. She had had an abortion, that was it. Some women reacted that way, he supposed, especially with these religious groups calling it murder.

"An abortion isn't—"

"This was a whole, live baby, four months old. Her name was Wanda. She was named for Bob's mother. The name means wanderer." She began to cry silently, tears forming and creeping down her cheeks. "My little wanderer."

He hurried to fall beside her, taking her in his arms and cradling her head against his chest. He could feel the wetness of her face through his thin shirt. "What happened?" He hugged her tighter.

"Nothing. She just died. It was one of those

inexplicable crib deaths.'' Her voice broke. ''She didn't smother herself or anything. She just died.''

He kissed her forehead. ''Why do you blame yourself?''

''Because I didn't have time to love her. I . . .'' She began to sob and couldn't continue.

She cried for a while, then became calm enough to explain. Her first book had been a tremendous success. Wanda was born just about the time she was finishing her second book. She was excited and preoccupied with it. The nurse took care of Wanda. The nurse was a cold, efficient woman. In retrospect she knew later that Wanda had been fed, diapered, and bathed efficiently, but she had not been loved and cuddled. And without warmth and affection, some babies just die.

''Even little animals will die if you take them from the mother and they have nothing warm and loving to cling to,'' she said.

He didn't know what to say. He continued to pet her and stroke her hair. ''There was no malice in it. You didn't mean to hurt her.''

She sniffled. ''You didn't mean to make a mistake about Carter Morton.''

''Look, you were young and inexperienced. The situations are not comparable. I can understand your sorrow but not your feeling of guilt. There's no reason for you to feel guilty.''

''Reason!''

Of course, there'd be no logic in it.

''Someday you'll have more children and love them dearly. It will make up for Wanda.''

''Never!''

"Why do you say that?"

"I could never have another baby. That's why I couldn't marry you. I knew that's what you wanted."

She reached for the bottle and poured herself another drink. He had never seen Vanessa drink so much. Probably she wanted to get drunk. The ultimate loss of control, as far as she was concerned.

She asked him, "Don't you think one can feel guilty about being stupid and insensitive and negligent?"

"Maybe you should be seeing a good psychiatrist."

She took a big gulp of Scotch. "I have. Several. All they've helped me do is live with myself from day to day. I could no more have a baby than you could go out and handle a really big case." Her words were becoming a little slurred.

"I can handle a big case any time I want to."

"Then why don't you?"

"Because, love, you have to be asked to handle a big case."

He poured himself another. He was not spacing them very well tonight. But then, if she was going to be drunk, he might as well be drunk too. He was beginning to feel sorry for himself. His one thin hope had been that when he managed to pull himself together she would be there. Now it was apparent not only that she did not love him, but that she had her own wounds, a wound too grievous for his love to heal.

"Maybe the nurse cuddled the baby quite a bit

when you were not around. It's pretty hard not to cuddle a baby.'' He swirled his drink idly. ''Remember, you were preoccupied.''

She shook her head. ''I wish I could believe that. But I know it isn't true.''

''Why?''

''Because you sense these things. If I could just remember one instance of her showing Wanda any affection . . .''

She stared blankly for a while. ''I can't remember Bob and me doing anything except stand over the poor little thing and look at it adoringly. It was a living, breathing toy. A doll. I was much more interested in my book. I suppose I'd make a lousy mother anyway.''

He sipped his drink, unsure of the direction to take. ''Was there an autopsy?''

''Yes.''

''And they found absolutely nothing?''

''Nothing.''

''It was probably something medical science hasn't learned to detect. There are a lot of cases like that, you know. Adults, too. Cardiovascular arrest. No torn heart muscles or anything. It just decides to stop.''

She drank deeply, uninterested. ''I don't believe it was that.''

''Well . . .'' He was becoming so fuzzy minded that he couldn't think of anything.

She pulled away from him. ''I'll tell you what we'll do. We'll play that old game of yours. But this time, *I'll* ask the questions.''

He rubbed his chin. ''Well, I'm not so sure . . .''

"We'll play. What's a source for the gander must be a source for the goose."

He'd never seen Vanessa drunk before. "Do you always get witty when you're drunk?"

"No. That was a lousy pun."

"I thought it was pretty good."

Vanessa said, "You're probably drunk too. Come on, start the tape machine."

He reluctantly switched on the Uher.

"Is your name Kevin MacInnes?"

"Yes."

"Are we in Florida?"

"Yes."

"Do you still love your first wife?"

"No."

"Do you hate your first wife?"

"No."

"Have you ever had erotic fantasies about making love to a little girl?"

"Not since I was a little boy."

That one hurt. It reminded him of Carter Morton. It was not like her to stick the knife in and twist it. "I think that question was sort of rotten," he said.

"It was a control question."

"Oh, I see."

"Do you like swimming in the ocean?"

"Yes."

"Do you love me?"

He hesitated briefly. "Yes."

She waved her hand. "All right, that's enough. Run the charts."

Shaking his head wearily, he stopped the Uher,

rewound, and started it through the PSE at reduced speed.

As the chart strip moved slowly under the pen, he got up and started to leave the room. Let her interpret the damned charts. He lurched slightly, unsteady on his feet, which annoyed him, because he never allowed himself to get drunk enough to stagger.

"You stay here and read the charts to me," said Vanessa.

"No."

He glanced at her grim face and said, "All right. Will you kindly allow me to go to the bathroom?"

"Permission granted."

He went to the bathroom and stayed much longer than necessary, sitting on the toilet lid and smoking several cigarettes. He was afraid to read the charts. The situation was bad enough. They would probably make it worse.

When he returned, he found her trying to do her own chart reading.

She said, "It seems to me that you lied about not having fantasies about little girls. Look, it's a lot different than the other answers I know are true."

He glanced at the strip. "That's only mild, normal stress, probably caused by my being angry at you for being cruel enough to rub my nose in Carter Morton." He ran the strip through his fingers. "Now there's real deception stress. See the even, heavy blocking?"

She read the words she had scribbled under the pen markings. It was the "No" to "Do you hate your first wife?"

He rubbed his cheek. It felt numb, as though the dentist had given him Novocaine. "That's news to me. I wasn't conscious of it."

She gathered up the long strip, sliding it quickly along to the last "Yes." It was the same heavy, even blocking. Her face collapsed into an expression of utter hurt and defeat. She sank back and buried her face in her hands.

He suddenly understood that she, too, had been depending upon him, on his love, to pull her life together. What irony. Two broken reeds leaning on each other.

He put his arms around her. "Dearest." He shook her gently. "Dearest, the machine is not infallible. It probably isn't even working properly. Look, I *do* love you. I believe it with all my heart." He hugged her. She was weeping again, trying to stifle small sobs that welled up. "Look, I don't even mind that it said you don't love me. I know you did once, and I believe you will again when I'm . . ." He hesitated. "When I'm a whole man once more." Whole man. God, how corny could you be? Were they playing some soap opera? But sex was important, and his impotence, combined with his brooding apathy, could be enough to cool any woman's love.

In the morning, Vanessa decided that they should separate for a while. Alone, perhaps they could figure out things better. He tried to persuade her to change her mind, but she remained stubbornly determined to leave. They argued all morning until his pride finally made him give up.

At the airport she said, "I would suggest you see

another psychiatrist, except that I have no confidence in them any more. They haven't helped me much." She cupped his face in her hands. "And Kevin, maybe some other girl would solve your problem. Some girl who doesn't know about your failure with Carter Morton."

MacInnes said, "You want to get rid of me permanently, is that it?"

"That's not what I meant *at all*. I hope it wouldn't be permanent. I meant casual sex with someone else, even a prostitute, just to get you functioning again."

She was certainly a strange woman. "You wouldn't mind that?"

"Of course not. Whatever happens with us, I don't want you to be impotent. Maybe you should see Masters and Johnson."

MacInnes said, "Only if you go with me."

He kissed her and held her tightly; then she pulled away and walked through the boarding gate alone.

The big house was unbearably silent without Vanessa, which was peculiar, because Vanessa was anything but noisy. The Ducs, Bill and Li, always moved around so quietly that one hardly knew they were there. The house was as quiet as a little lake he had visited in Ireland where it was said that no birds ever sing. What was it called? Glendaloch?

He turned on the stereo and began selecting albums and tapes. Starting with Beethoven's Ninth, Toscanini, he turned the volume high enough to send rumbling vibrations clear out to the ships at sea. The Seventh would be next. Then *Don Giovanni,* some Haydn, Bach, Brahms, and Bruckner. Shubert's "Trout" and Beethoven's Archduke Trio.

The Ducs came and stood in the doorway of his study, inscrutably curious and concerned.

In a brief silence while he turned over the records, MacInnes asked if they would join him in a drink. They both accepted a small glass of Scotch but refused to sit down. The effect was of drinking a toast, and he felt he should stand up and join them.

"Mrs. Wirroby say can you turn volume down prease?" said Bill Duc.

Mrs. Willoughby, his septuagenarian neighbor, was an old grouch. "Tell her to sit back and enjoy the greatest music in the world."

"She say she like Rawrence Welk. You want to play loud, play Rawrence Welk."

"Lawrence Welk," said Li, who did better with her l's.

MacInnes poured himself another drink. "Oh, Christ." He turned the volume down. With the volume high, he could think of nothing but the music. With it lowered, his mind kept wandering into channels he wanted to avoid. He thought vaguely of taking his boat out and drowning himself.

Vanessa needed him. Why had she left? She needed him more than he needed her. It was in her face when she saw the chart that said he didn't love her. Goddammed lousy screwed-up PSE.

His impotence, he decided, had put the biggest

strain on their relationship. His depression would probably lift one of these days, but the other was a disaster. Maybe he had been made impotent permanently. He would kill himself.

She might be right about solving it with some other woman. She had been intimately linked to the events of the past month, a period of critical self-examination and failure. The suicide of Hawthorne's friend, what was his name? Mrs. Weedall, Eduardo Torres, Carter Morton.

Another woman would be a problem. Even in these permissive times, they required some pursuit, some effort. In addition, the embarrassment of possible failure made him uneasy. It would have to be a prostitute.

He had had only one experience with a prostitute. At age sixteen, early in the Eisenhower administration. The pill had not been invented, and few high school girls carried diaphragms. Although many females were available for almost anything short of actual intercourse, obtaining the ultimate was not as easy as the studs around the high school bragged. At least, not with the girls MacInnes knew. One evening he went with a group to a house in San Francisco. It was a pleasant, if brief experience. It remained in his memory in vivid detail, like a very short, full-color porno film.

The girl first collected his ten dollars briskly. She was a pretty brunette in her early twenties, and she quickly unzipped her dress and wriggled out of it. She was wearing nothing underneath. It was the first time he had been that close to a naked woman. She smiled, told him to undress, then went efficiently about the business of squatting over a basin and douching herself with some blue liquid. She patted herself dry with a towel, then bounced onto the bed, ready. He was still awkwardly taking off his clothes.

She glanced at his equipment and said, ''Wow!'' which he was even then sophisticated enough to guess she probably said to all her customers. Wetting her fingers with saliva, she annointed the end of his penis and then guided it home. With a few churning bounces of her buttocks, it was all over. He dressed and left, pleased that he had at last achieved the total experience, though disappointed that it hadn't lasted longer. Ten dollars was not small change to a junior in high school in 1953.

He decided that this type of prostitute would never cure his impotence.

He thought of Vernon Brown. Vernon ran a restaurant and cabaret in the back country some distance from town. He also engaged in some high-class pimping. MacInnes Security had once solved a worrisome problem for Vernon, who was very grateful. He had a fine chef, and it was sometimes worth driving the fifteen miles to enjoy one of Frioli's specialties, though MacInnes usually had to fight Vernon to pay the check. MacInnes wanted no freeloading on Vernon Brown. Vernon's operations were such that MacInnes Security might have to refuse certain assignments.

MacInnes dialed his number.

''Hi, Mac,'' said Vernon. ''I know, a table for two at eight, right?''

MacInnes said, ''Well, no, not exactly. I've got

sort of a problem. My girl left me.''

"That beautiful blonde chick left you? Man, that's bad. Real bad.''

"Yeah.'' She had been a brunette when she left him.

"So you want a table for one?''

MacInnes said, "No, I had a replacement in mind.''

It took a few seconds for MacInnes's delicate way of putting it to penetrate. "Oh, *yeah,* I gottcha. You want a girl.''

MacInnes said, "Yeah. You got anyone reasonably young and intelligent?'' No matter how beautiful, one of Vernon's gum-popping crackers would turn him off even in good health.

"You mean, educated like?''

"Hmmm.''

Vernon thought for a minute. "Hey, I got just the chick for you. You want a college grajuwait? I got a college grajuwait for you.''

"Is she attractive?''

"Oh hell, man, sure. You know I don't have no dogs around. She don't come cheap, either. Three bills for the evening.''

MacInnes, who was not familiar with going rates, said, "Okay, send her over.'' He was suddenly depressed. It probably wouldn't work.

Heather McCloud had the fair complexion of a real blonde, and she reminded MacInnes a bit of Debbie, Mulcahy's niece, except that "daughter'' always looked a trifle seedy, whereas Heather might have just stepped out of a shampoo commercial. Her long, straw-colored hair actually gleamed. Also unlike Debbie, she wore a discreet amount of makeup. She did not have Vanessa's beauty, but she was slender, with a good figure, and her face was pretty in an appealing way, with a freshness he would not have expected in a professional. Probably she hadn't been in the business very long.

She was shown into the study by Li, who carried her small overnight bag. She shook hands with MacInnes coolly. Except for her clothes, she might have been the visiting nurse on her rounds. She was wearing white stretch pants like a second skin and a white halter that set off her breasts, her tanned and nicely molded shoulders, and her equally trim and bare midriff.

"Li, would you please put Miss McCloud's bag in one of the guest rooms?" he said.

Li left quickly, bobbing her head.

"Well, Heather, it's nice to meet you."

"Thank you. Should we get the sordid commercial part out of the way?"

For a moment the word *sordid* confused him, and he thought she was suggesting that they go right to bed. Then he realized it was money. They always collected in advance. Which made sense, he supposed.

"Oh, sure." He removed a picture from the wall and unlocked his small safe. He never carried much cash with him, but he kept a couple of thousand in the safe for emergencies. He found six fifty-dollar bills and handed them to her.

"If we accomplish what I hope to accomplish,

there'll be another hundred in it for you,'' he said.

She gave him an anxious look. "I'm into almost everything but S and M," she said, tucking the bills into her purse. "I don't go for S and M."

"Oh hell, nothing like that. I'm not a sadist—or a masochist!"

She seemed relieved. "What shall I call you?"

"Mac will be fine."

She sat down, crossing her long, shapely legs elegantly. "Well, Mac, what's the program?"

MacInnes said, "I thought we might have a drink, dinner, get to know each other, and then take it from there."

She reached in her purse for a cigarette. "Fine. I'll have a Cinzano and soda."

Keeping her wits about her, this girl. He lit her cigarette, then went to the small bar to make her drink.

"Vernon says you're known as the Lie King, and you're a brilliant man."

He laughed. "To Vernon, anybody who can read the *New York Times* is brilliant." He handed her the drink. It had all the intoxicating power of a glass of iced tea.

She said, "Thanks. Well, let me keep my image with the brilliant Lie King. I'm interested in your work because I'm going to be in a related field."

"Oh?"

"I'm beginning my first year of law school in the fall. I'm going to specialize in criminal law."

"Law school!"

She grinned. "Yes, and let me cover the banalities before you're tempted to ask. Why is a nice, well-educated girl from a good family like me in this business? Answer: I do it because it's an easy way to make a lot of money, and I prefer it to slinging hash. What I make in the summer gives me enough to live comfortably through the whole year at school. Furthermore, I absolutely cringe inside when men call me Portia.''

"I won't," he said, pouring himself a drink.

"Second question. Am I not afraid that this kind of work will spoil me for marriage, that I won't dare tell my husband-to-be, and I'll live in constant fear of being recognized by one of my former customers? Answer: I do not plan to marry.''

He lifted his drink. "Suppose you fall in love?''

She wrinkled her nose. "Love is an illusion that quickly fades.''

"I think you just don't like men.''

She blinked her long lashes at him. "I *love* men. It's just that the career I've planned is more important to me.''

He'd read somewhere that many prostitutes were frigid. He wondered if this was her problem.

Li came in to announce dinner. Both Li and Bill had sensed for some time that MacInnes was in trouble, and they had doubled their efforts to please him. Tonight Li had outdone herself in culinary inspiration. They started with smoked salmon and capers, moved to vichyssoise, then to pompano en papillote steaming in sliced-open parchment bags, with a chilled bottle of Pouilly Fuisse to revitalize the taste buds as they ate it. Cheese, fruit, and perfectly brewed freshly ground coffee followed. It was the first meal MacInnes had enjoyed in weeks.

Heather, who had attacked each course with obvious enthusiasm, said, "You really have one hell of a cook out there in the kitchen."

MacInnes said, "Yes, that's Li. She's the cook. I sent her to one of those Cordon Bleu cooking schools. She's great with oriental cooking too, of course."

"She could open a restaurant."

"Shssh!" said MacInnes.

Over coffee they discussed philosophy, which had been Heather's major. Herbert Marcuse was one of her idols, and she almost made a communist of MacInnes, who sweated to defend the American democratic system with its checks and balances, regardless of its venality and inefficiency.

They finally got around to discussing MacInnes's problem.

"My God, that *is* serious," said Heather. "I should have majored in psychology." She thought about it, smoking and sipping her black coffee. "Can you think of any kind of exotic eroticism that might be particularly exciting to you?"

He thought about it. "No." Normal sex had always been exciting enough.

"Would you like to pretend to rape me? I'll fight back if you promise not to hurt me."

He said, "That sounds like S and M to me."

"Not if you don't hurt me. I don't mind a wrestling match." She giggled. "I had plenty of those before I . . ." She paused. "Before I decided to change my approach to the problem."

He put his coffee cup down. "Suppose we take a shakedown walk along the beach first?" He wanted to postpone the encounter.

They took their shoes off and walked for about an hour on the hard-packed wet sand, letting the breakers roll over their feet.

Back in the house, Heather said, "You must understand that I've never had this problem before, and I'm going to have to improvise."

She suggested that they first take a shower together, get all lathered up and slippery with soap, and see if that inspired him. They stripped and got into the shower together and began getting lathered. The water had to be reduced to a trickle because it kept washing the soap away. It was an unusual sensation, clutching her slippery body while she churned and wriggled against him, but it did not achieve the desired result. He turned the water on full, and they washed the soap away.

Toweled dry, they stood looking at each other, she biting her lip and staring at his limp member with grim determination. They went to the bedroom and lay down while she tried oral stimulation. It gave him a tingling, pleasant sensation but brought no tumescence.

"Come on, you, stand up or I'll bite you off," she threatened.

She tried giving him a mineral-oil massage. This, too, was pleasant but unsuccessful. He washed away the oil in another shower.

She stalked into his study and searched through his albums until she found a record from Casablanca. "I'm going to dance for you," she said, slipping the record from its dust jacket. "I worked my way through my junior year as a professional belly dancer." She put the record on the turntable.

"Belly dancing is the oldest known dance form. Women used it in the earliest fertility rites to symbolize the act of love and the agony of childbirth and"—she grinned—"to attract a mate." She lowered the stylus, and the wail of Middle Eastern music began.

He sat down, the leather sofa cool against his bare skin. She began to dance, slowly at first, her hips swaying gently, her pelvis undulating in lazy thrusts. As the music increased in tempo her churning became wilder and more abandoned. She moved close to him, and the graceful belly dancing became the furious bump and grind of burlesque, her legs spread, her pelvic thrusts bringing her vulva within inches of his face. It was exciting, and he loved it—but nothing happened.

She finally gave up, exhausted and covered with perspiration. She seemed ready to cry.

"You were really terrific," he said. "Honestly, it was tremendously exciting. It should have brought a dead man to life."

Dead man.

She left him, to take a shower. She returned, still toweling herself, with new resolution. "Why don't we just lie down together and try ordinary foreplay? Maybe we're making this more complicated than it really is."

He had decided by now that nothing but time or a psychiatrist was going to help him, but as long as she was willing to continue he was agreeable. There was a certain amount of pleasure and excitement in looking at her and in touching her naked body. They lay down and went through the ritual of kissing, licking, and fondling.

After a while she sat up and said, "I'm beat. I can't think of anything else except to try the rape bit. They say every man has an atavistic urge to take a woman by force."

He smiled. Remembering his awkwardness in the role of father with Debbie, he said, "I'm afraid I'm not a very good actor, but we can try."

She jumped up and ran to a corner of the room and crouched, cowering, both hands covering her pudenda. "Please don't touch me!" she whimpered. "Please, please."

He picked her up and carried her to the bed and dropped her on it. She grabbed a pillow, clutched it to her body, and flipped over onto her belly. He turned her over with a struggle, but while he was trying to pull the pillow away she twisted back onto her belly. He tried again, this time exerting more force, and succeeded in holding her down on her back and extracting the pillow. He fell on her, clamping her tightly to him as she continued to struggle, her legs locked together. He finally managed to get his hand between them as she tossed and bucked and emitted small cries of terror. He thrust his knee brutally between her legs and managed to open them further.

"Ouch!"

"Now I've hurt you."

"That's okay," she gasped. "Go ahead." She kept writhing and twisting.

He relaxed. It was no use. For a couple of minutes he had become totally immersed in the role of rapist and would have carried it through had he been capable.

They went back to the study and had a nightcap. This time she accepted a very large Scotch. He was a weirdo but a safe weirdo. "I've never felt so completely frustrated," she said.

"It's not your fault," he said. "You've certainly worked very hard for your fee."

She looked at him over the rim of her glass. "That's because I like you. If I hadn't, I would have gone through the motions very quickly and left."

MacInnes said, "I appreciate it."

"You really must see a good psychiatrist. It's such a waste for a man like you to be impotent."

He lit a cigarette. "Suppose I'll have to."

"Would you like me to stay and try first thing in the morning? Some men wake up with an erection."

He shook his head. "Early morning is a blah time for me, even when I'm in good shape."

He got out another two hundred dollars and gave it to her. "For combat action beyond the call of duty," he said.

She tucked the bills away, pleased. She kissed his cheek. "Call me when you're better. It'll be on the house."

He thanked her. If he was better, he wouldn't need her, but it would be ungracious to mention that.

He retrieved her overnight case, saw her out to her Volkswagen, and watched her drive away.

The next morning MacInnes fainted.

Luckily the living room carpet was thick and softly cushioned with sponge-rubber underpadding. Bill Duc brought him around with a cold washcloth and drove him to Dr. Himmelstein's office.

Himmelstein, a bronzed little man with gray hair, was known to be one of the best general practitioners in this very affluent area. He peered at MacInnes over his half-moon glasses.

"What is this? A month ago I give you every test known to medical science, and now you're fainting. Did you see Dr. Roman?"

MacInnes said that he had but that he had decided not to continue with Dr. Roman.

Dr. Himmelstein grunted and began his examination. Later his general questions led to the subject of MacInnes's drinking. He made MacInnes track down and itemize his daily drinking habits. MacInnes was shocked when he confronted himself with the facts. He was nipping away an ounce to two ounces every hour, almost a quart of Scotch a day, and he generally drank a bottle of wine with dinner, usually eating very little.

"You'll kill yourself with this kind of drinking," said Dr. Himmelstein.

He wanted MacInnes to enter one of the local sanitariums that specialized in alcoholism.

Dr. Himmelstein was right, of course—he'd have to cut down on his drinking. But he had the willpower to do it himself. He didn't need any damned hospital.

"I'll cut it out on my own. I don't need any hospital," he said.

Himmelstein shook his head doubtfully. "It's not easy, especially when you're using it as a crutch for a very serious emotional problem. If you didn't like Dr. Roman, we'll find somebody else.''

MacInnes stood up. "Give me a week or two to see if I can't lick it on my own. I have some business in New York. When I get back, if I'm not better, I'll call you."

He had decided suddenly that he wanted to go to New York and talk to Vanessa. What it would solve, he did not know; he just felt that he had to see her.

New York was in the midst of one of its sultry, airless heat waves—the kind of weather in which suicides and murders jump from two or three a day to fifteen or sixteen, keeping the medical examiner's office frantically busy.

MacInnes had not had an alcoholic drink since speaking to Dr. Himmelstein. His only prop had been three 5-milligram Valium tablets a day, one in the morning, another in midafternoon, and the third at bedtime. These kept him so drowsy that he slept a good part of both the day and the night. Thus, he was only vaguely depressed to find that Vanessa had checked out of the Lombardy, where she had told him she would be, and had left no forwarding address. He would find her, as soon as he could get himself awake.

He telephoned the New York office of Barker-Peckham Copper. After being shunted from one employee to another he finaly reached an executive high enough to tell him that Miss Peckham had no active interest in the company and that though she sometimes appeared at annual meetings, they had no idea where she was. He suggested that MacInnes contact Miss Peckham's attorney, Bill Jordan, of Jordan, Sands, and Freehold.

MacInnes telephoned Jordan and explained his problem.

Jordan was noncommittal. "I really haven't heard from Vanessa in months. I wouldn't know where you could reach her."

Jordan would, of course, first want to find out whether Vanessa wanted to see MacInnes. "If you hear from her, would you please tell her that I want to see her, urgently? And that I'm staying at the Lombardy?"

Jordan promised that he would.

MacInnes stayed on Valium for two more days waiting for Vanessa to call. He was sure that Jordan would telephone her and that she would then get in touch with him.

The phone never rang, and there was never a message waiting. He called home daily, hoping she had written or telephoned.

He called her publishers. It was not their policy to give out addresses of their authors. They would forward mail, but they couldn't in this case because they had no current address and hadn't heard from Vanessa in more than two years. They gave him the name of her agent. The agent hadn't heard from her in more than two years either.

He began making the rounds of the restaurants she and her friends frequented, having a drink or two in each place, the Valium regime abandoned. La Côte Basque, Lutèce, La Grenouille, Elaine's,

Nick's. No one had seen Vanessa in some time. He returned to the Lombardy drunk and panicky. He sent out for a bottle of Scotch and sipped himself into a stupor.

During the week that followed, he prowled Manhattan's upper East Side, reasoning somewhat fuzzily that if she had left the Lombardy she would be somewhere around Sutton Place and refusing to consider the idea that she could just as easily be in Rome or Paris.

Working uptown from 50th Street, he criss-crossed the area from the East River to Fifth Avenue, working north as far as 86th Street. He stared at thousands of female faces and visited hundreds of bars, pausing in his search every half hour or so to perch on a stool with a drink and a cigarette.

In the back of his mind he knew that it was insane, that he should be in a hospital, not carrying on this futile search. But like an obsessed roulette player he kept playing the game, walking miles each day and drinking more than he had been drinking in Florida.

In one moment of panic, he thought he was developing delirium tremens. He had seen Vanessa three times, and when he had caught up with her, he had faced a startled stranger. Then he followed a man who looked like Calvin Harp but gave up when the apparition seemed to float down a subway entrance.

He telephoned Dr. Himmelstein and got the name of a hospital not far from Sutton Place.

The Herman Martingale Memorial hospital was

a cube of shiny white brick nine stories high, and from the number of chauffeured limousines waiting and parked nearby, it catered to those who could well afford a drinking problem. MacInnes stood staring at the spotless glass entrance doors and wondered whether old Herman had been a drunk. Deciding to give the matter careful consideration before going in, he wandered around the corner to a place with apple-green doors labeled PETE'S BAR.

It was cool and dark in Pete's, so dark that MacInnes could see little but the lighted clock advertising beer at the far end of the room. It was the cave he needed to crawl into while he wrestled with the problem of Herman Martingale and his memorial hospital.

As his eyes adjusted to the gloom he found a stool, hiked himself up, and rested his tired elbows on the bar. The stool was big, old-fashioned, and comfortably padded. The bartender greeted him with the faraway smile of a brother tippler well on his way to nirvana. He served MacInnes a Scotch on the rocks with a liberal but unsteady hand, filling the glass to the brim. MacInnes felt at home in Pete's. Other bars had made him feel somewhat less than welcome, particularly in the late afternoon and evening, when he was becoming glassy-eyed and too deliberate in his movements. He knew in his heart that he would never be unwelcome in Pete's.

MacInnes sipped his drink thoughtfully. At least when he decided to turn himself in to Herman Martingale he would be conveniently close.

In a pinch they could even carry him there. In the meantime, he found the atmosphere and the companionship ideal for philosophical contemplation.

Most of the other customers, he soon discovered, were either dropouts or sneakouts from Herman Martingale. The sneakouts kept a wary eye on the doors, remaining anonymous but occasionally responding with good-natured obscenity to the remarks of one of the dropouts, whose comments varied around the subject of their being bad kids who would not get any pudding for lunch if they were caught.

A white-haired old man sitting next to MacInnes, who was immaculately dressed and might have been a retired banker, asked, "Are you a refugee from Herman Martingale?"

MacInnes turned to him. "No, I'm trying to decide whether to enter."

The old man said, "Give it a try. They succeed with a number of their patients."

MacInnes had sized him up as one of the dropouts. "But not with you, apparently."

"Well—" The old man smiled at him. "That's a long and boring story." He held out his hand. "I'm Howard Krampell. I'm a retired professor of mathematics."

MacInnes shook hands. "Kevin MacInnes."

"And?"

MacInnes asked, "And what?"

"You didn't say what you do, or did. That's the most interesting thing you like to find out about a stranger."

"I'm a retired seeker of the truth."

"You're joking."

MacInnes grabbed his drink, gripping it hard. "No, I'm serious."

"You're too general. We're all seekers of the truth in our own little areas. Philosopher, writer, historian, mathematician."

MacInnes took a long swallow. "I seek the truths lurking in the minds of men who refuse to divulge it."

"A psychiatrist."

MacInnes muttered, "Christ." He was misleading his new friend, but he was reluctant to talk about his work. "I'm known as the 'Lie King'," he said.

Krampell shifted his eyes to look beyond MacInnes, losing interest. The new man might even be too far gone for Herman Martingale.

MacInnes decided he'd better explain his work. He gave Krampell a brief résumé.

Krampell's attention returned. "That's most interesting," he said. "And being chairman of the lie detectors, or whatever, so to speak, has driven you to drink. Why?"

MacInnes said, "I don't know. The truth is a rock. Turn it over and there are too many maggots squirming around in the sun."

Krampell reached for his drink. "There's poetry in that statement, my boy. Sheer poetry."

MacInnes didn't agree, but the point wasn't worth arguing. He lit a cigarette. "One thing I can't quite understand is why I sometimes feel ashamed of doing with electronic equipment what the psychiatrist does with words, with therapy."

Krampell drained his shot glass, then rapped sharply on the counter with it. "The psychiatrist invades the patient's mind to try to help him. You invade it to try to trap him and send him to prison."

MacInnes said loudly, "No! More often to keep him out of prison when he's innocent."

Krampell watched the bartender refill his glass with colorless liquid. Vodka was the big seller in Pete's Bar. "There's that side of it too, of course."

MacInnes asked, "Isn't it healthier for everyone concerned for the truth to come out? Guilty men need to be restrained. Society needs to be protected."

Krampell said, "You mentioned the maggots under the rock."

"Remember," said MacInnes, "I don't put them there. I uncover them. They're the same maggots the psychiatrist must find."

Krampell sipped his vodka, following it with a gulp of beer from a glass in front of him. "Perhaps you should be more philosophical. There must be many who are from time to time made sick by what they find—garbage collectors, surgeons, undertakers. Now you see, that's where I've had it over you. In the realm of pure mathematics the mind works freely, joyously, in celestial spheres quite removed from human ugliness."

MacInnes fiddled with his drink. "So why do you have a problem with alcohol?"

Krampell waved one heavily veined hand gently. "I'm an old man very near the end of the road. My mind is no longer keen enough to wallow in those celestial spheres." He turned to MacInnes, smiling. "What else is there to do? Once a man is old and is no longer making any contribution, no one is very interested in him any more."

Krampell paid his bill and tottered out before MacInnes, brooding over it, could suggest that there were probably other ways he could contribute.

As the day passed other men joined MacInnes and told him their life stories—dull, repetitious tales punctuated by long silences while the speaker struggled with a lapse of memory. A sort of euphoria settled over MacInnes. He had no desire to go anywhere. He would sit in Pete's for the rest of his life, his mission to lend a sympathetic ear to these desperately lonely people.

He left his stool once to call the Lombardy and Bill Duc in Florida. No messages, no letters.

He returned to the bar and again wrapped himself in his cloak of euphoria.

The bartender touched his arm gently. "We're closing up, sport." It was a different bartender, but this one, too, seemed glassy eyed. MacInnes glanced at the lighted clock, which he could still read, though the numbers were fuzzy.

"You close at three in the afternoon?"

"It's three in the morning, sport."

Unbelievable. MacInnes scooped up his change from the wet bar, got up, and walked stiff-legged out to the street, which was dark and deserted. He wondered which direction would be most likely to produce a cruising cab. Unable to decide, he turned left and began walking, his gait reasonably steady. The summer night had turned cool. He decided he would walk to the hotel.

As he passed the dark, cavernous opening of an old apartment building he was conscious of some quick foot-scraping movements in the shadows. He veered quickly to the curb as two figures rushed him. The first man hit him, tackling MacInnes chest-high and bringing him down to one knee. The danger, combined with the impact, was almost as good as a quart of black coffee. In falling, MacInnes managed to shift the weight of the first attacker enough to keep from being knocked flat. His senses amazingly alert, he grabbed the foot of the second man, who was trying to kick him in the head. He twisted it hard, sending this one lunging into the gutter.

The first man now had MacInnes's neck in the crook of his arm and was squeezing with maniacal pressure. The second man had scrambled to his feet, and MacInnes saw the glint of a knife blade. With a mighty effort that strained every muscle, he pried and jerked the strangling elbow loose and twisted the first man's body between himself and the descending knife. The knife wielder stopped his thrust just in time. He aimed a kick at MacInnes's head, the toe of his heavy work shoe connecting with MacInnes's temple. The shock of the blow temporarily blinded him.

Stunned, but not completely out, MacInnes karate chopped at his first opponent's neck, missing and hitting the man's shoulder. His attacker gave a heave that knocked MacInnes backward to bounce his head against the pavement. Another foot slammed into his chest.

The last thing he remembered was the gleam of the knife again descending, and the screeching of brakes and the flashing lights of a police car.

CHAPTER TWENTY-ONE

THE VISITOR HAD shoulder-length black hair and a trimmed beard that framed his face in a style reminiscent of Lincoln, but the effect was spoiled by the addition of a black moustache that made his face altogether too hairy. When he removed his wraparound sun glasses, MacInnes recognized him instantly. The glacial blue eyes with their special tilt could belong to no one but Calvin Harp.

"You don't look too bad for a man at death's door," said Harp. He sauntered over and collapsed into the room's single comfortable chair.

MacInnes said, "I was at death's door a month ago. I've been backing away hastily ever since."

MacInnes had spent his first three days in intensive care. He had a concussion, two broken ribs, and a fractured ankle, and the knife had nicked his lower intestine. Very lucky, said the doctors, that it had not hit his liver or spleen too. The intestine had been repaired neatly, and no infection had developed.

There had been a few visitors. A small item had appeared in the *News* headed, " 'Lie King' Mugged, in Critical Condition." When he was well enough to be visited, his old friend Craig Weymouth, the assistant district attorney, had dropped in for an embarrassed few minutes. Apparently Kevin's downhill tumble was widely known. A Presbyterian minister had called, because the hospital had marked him P for Protestant. Bill Duc had flown up at his own expense. The police, of course, had been there. The Pink Lady volunteers kept him supplied with books and magazines. Vanessa had not appeared. He was sure she could not be aware of his condition.

He was happy to see Calvin Harp. It had been a lonely month.

"I've been hearing some sad things about you, my friend," said Harp.

"What sort of things?"

Harp stroked what MacInnes was certain was a phony beard. Harp was too vain to dye his hair or beard. "I heard you've become a rummy—that you flopped on an important case and you've been headed for Skid Row ever since." He held up his hand. "Not that I believe it."

MacInnes said, "Why not? It's more or less true."

Harp grinned. "Look, mate, we've got to get

you straightened out. I had you pegged for one tough *hombre,* not the kind of man who could be thrown by reverses.''

MacInnes reached for his package of cigarettes. In his limbo-like zombie's existence in the hospital, he found it easy enough to ration them and seldom smoked more than six to ten a day. "I suspect toughness has very little to do with it,'' he said.

"Why do you say that?''

"Depression can settle on anyone, strong or weak.''

Harp produced his inevitable Gauloises. "I can't see a man as controlled as you are taking to drink, however.''

MacInnes lit the cigarette he had been holding. "I think that's probably no longer a problem.'' For a month he had been too sick to drink, and he had no desire to start again. Yesterday the doctor had told him he could order some wine with his dinner. He hadn't bothered. He was ashamed of the drinking. It had almost cost him his life. The depression he couldn't do much about, but he was determined he would never again give way to such a stupid escape. If it was suicide he was after, he would do it neatly.

Harp said, "If I'm being too personal, stop me. But I suppose your girlfriend's leaving you wasn't easy to take either.''

MacInnes turned his mouth down slightly but said nothing. He did not wish to involve Vanessa in any way with Calvin Harp.

"I *am* being too personal.''

MacInnes said, "Your intelligence sources are phenomenal, as I have said before. Why are you so interested in my personal life?"

Harp smiled, his even, white teeth as sparkling as ever. "You did me a good turn in Mexico, mate. I've been fascinated by the possibilities of that black box of yours ever since."

MacInnes said, "It's good to know someone is still interested in it."

Harp said, "I can't believe *one* mistake has finished your career."

"It caused a man to take his own life."

Harp grimaced. "Do you think you've lost your skill?"

MacInnes dragged on his cigarette. "No. Of course not. The results of that test were obviously inconclusive. But for some reason I was determined to give them a firm answer, and I managed to hallucinate myself into finding one. I wouldn't do it again. I'd simply call the test inconclusive."

"Learned your lesson, eh?"

"Yes, indeed, the hard way." He crushed out the cigarette. "If you're going to make a wild-assed guess, label it that and let the client act at his own risk. My problem is that most of my wild-assed guesses have been right. But ninety percent of the time I never even need to guess; the charts are clear enough."

Harp tossed a package he had been holding onto the bed. "Little something to help you pass the time. Give you some giggles."

MacInnes tore off the wrappings. The last giggle Harp had given him was a hanged man on his balcony. The gift was a book by Woody Allen, whose humor MacInnes particularly liked.

"This is very kind of you. Thanks," he said, smiling.

"How much longer are you going to be an invalid?"

MacInnes riffled the pages of the book. "I'll have to stay here another week or two. Then I'll be hobbling around with a cane for a month or so." He put the book down. "I think I'll enjoy this. Thanks again."

"My pleasure."

"I'll probably stay in New York for a couple of months," said MacInnes. His leg pained him, and he shifted his position. "The ankle was a pretty bad break. I want the same doctor to follow through with it. I'd hate to end up with a permanent limp, and he's supposed to be one of the best in the field."

Harp nodded. "Best not take any chances." He stood up. "Well, just thought I'd drop by and say hello. Glad you're making a good recovery."

MacInnes said, "Thanks for coming."

At the door Harp paused. "Daughter okay?"

"I hope so. The only time I hear from her is when she needs money."

Harp smiled, making a circle with his thumb and forefinger. "That's the way of the world, mate. I'll drop by again if I have a chance."

"Good. Be glad to see you."

After Harp left, MacInnes lay still for a long time, thinking. Theoretically he should call the number Jim O'Connor had given him. He had memorized it and then torn the card up. Ordinarily when he memorized anything he never forgot it, but apparently the concussion had knocked this particular number right out of his mind. He could call the Washington office of the FBI. However, if Harp had any contacts on the hospital staff, an open call such as that might be a giveaway. Besides, the bastards had written him off. Everyone had written him off. Who could trust a rummy? Craig Weymouth hadn't even mentioned the case when he had visited MacInnes.

To hell with them. Let them fight their own war. All he could tell them was Harp's current disguise, which could change in fifteen minutes. He drifted off to sleep.

Two evenings later Harp dropped in again. He was carrying a copy of *Playboy*. He tossed it on the bed. "Here you are, mate, feast your eyes on these lovelies. If they don't raise your depression, maybe they'll raise something else."

MacInnes laughed.

"Remember, mate, as long as there are chicks like that in the world, a man has every reason to live."

The television news was on, and they both looked at the screen briefly. Senator Herbert Crispin was smilingly disposing of an interviewer's somewhat hostile questions. Then the scene shifted to a fire in the Bronx.

"I can't stand that son of a bitch," said Harp, referring to Crispin.

MacInnes said, "If he's elected, I'm emigrating to Australia."

The polls were showing that for the first time in history a third-party candidate stood an excellent chance of becoming president of the United States. Herbert Crispin was that candidate.

"I'll tell you, mate, this man is a Hitler in creep's clothing," said Harp.

MacInnes smiled. As a man of the people, Crispin wore clothes straight from the cheapest discount stores. And even though badly fitted, on him they looked good, because he was youthful, in his late thirties, and remarkably handsome. His voice was sheer music, making the most banal statements sound profound. A virtuoso can look good even in rags.

"I must admit, he's got me worried," said MacInnes. The polls showed thirty-five percent of the country undecided. The remainder was almost evenly divided among the Republicans, the Democrats, and Free America, Crispin's party. "But when you get right down to it, I have confidence in the good common sense of the American people. Let's hope it prevails."

"I wish I could share your optimism, mate," said Harp.

They chatted about politics. MacInnes was not surprised to find that Harp shared most of his own liberal views. A thorough individualist, Harp was still antiestablishment enough to be for the underdog.

MacInnes had finished college in the bland fifties, without strong political convictions. He had gone immediately into the army to get his required service out of the way. Because of his aptitude for languages and his exceptionally high IQ, he had been pushed right into army intelligence. He had stayed on—whether through a romantic desire for adventure or because he was exceptionally good at his job, he was not sure. To some men nothing is more satisfying than excelling. Probably both had something to do with it.

As MacInnes saw more of the world—Europe, South Korea, Vietnam, and several small countries in Latin America—and perfected himself in languages, he began to evolve a political point of view, somewhat left of center.

In Latin America he had watched the CIA set up one repressive regime after another in countries so poor that ninety percent of the population lived on the borderline of starvation. Ruled by medieval-minded landowners who regarded peasants as not quite as valuable as animals, these countries were usually ripe for revolution. It had been MacInnes's job to train intelligence units of the armies that kept the ninety percent from eating the rich for breakfast. He had resented it. Democracy had no hope in these countries. There was no strong middle class to implement it and preserve it. Communism, MacInnes had decided, was probably inevitable. The larger countries, such as Mexico, were different, of course, and he felt democracy had a chance of working in them.

Harp stood up and stretched. "Well, time to pack it in."

MacInnes stifled a yawn. "Been good to have some company."

Harp lit one of his Gauloises. He stood, apparently trying to decide whether to say something further. "Right now I am working on one of the biggest projects of my life. Its success depends upon infinite attention to detail and absolute certainty that the people I'm working with are straight and are doing exactly what I tell them to do."

MacInnes was no longer sleepy. He reached for one of his own cigarettes.

"I wonder, would you consider putting that black box to work for me?"

MacInnes lit his cigarette slowly, deliberately remaining impassive to hide the excitement and tension churning inside.

Harp took it for hesitation. "It wouldn't be you and me teaming up against the law, mate. It would be you and me teaming up to keep my associates straight." He eyed MacInnes sharply. "As it was in Mexico."

MacInnes flipped ashes from his cigarette, though there were not yet any to flip. "Why not?" he said.

Harp smiled. "Naturally, there will be a big fee in it."

"I would expect that."

"I'll want your services exclusively for a period of two months. How does a thousand dollars a day strike you?"

MacInnes shifted his injured foot. "Sounds fair enough."

"You will have to be virtually incommunicado during the time you're working for me, however."

MacInnes crushed out his cigarette. "Just how incommunicado?"

Harp said, "You'll have a comfortable suite in a

house I have rented for the project. From time to time you'll monitor and analyze telephone calls for me. The rest of the time you'll have to occupy yourself reading and watching television."

MacInnes shook his head. "In other words, I'll be a prisoner." He reached for another cigarette. "I'm going stir crazy in this hospital as it is. I can't wait to get out. Besides, I'll probably have to see the doctor about once a week. My ankle is worth more to me than sixty thousand dollars any day."

Harp sat down, chewing thoughtfully on his lower lip.

"Look," said MacInnes, "I can understand your not wanting to trust anyone any farther than you have to, and I don't resent your not trusting me. I'd like to help you just to get my hand back in, to prove something to myself. And ordinarily I could probably stand being cooped up for a couple of months for that kind of money. But it just doesn't seem practical at this time. I'm trying to fight off depression. I want to go to some good Broadway shows, concerts, eat meals in good restaurants, try to work up some interest in life once more."

Being a prisoner in Harp's house was too much. It could be a sentence of death for MacInnes.

Harp said, "Let me think about it. Maybe we can work out some kind of compromise. Obviously it's important for you to see the doctor as often as he thinks necessary."

MacInnes said, "The other things are important too."

Harp stood up. "All right, let me think about it,

mate." He walked to the door. "Relax," he said, and with a wave of his hand, he left.

MacInnes sat propped in his uncomfortable hospital bed, his mind in a turmoil. He hoped he hadn't queered the deal. But he had to have some flexibility, some room to maneuver. If he was a prisoner, closely guarded, Harp might easily succeed in his mission. Either way, MacInnes stood to lose. He would know too much and be an ideal candidate for elimination.

He pushed the button that turned on the television set. Senator Herbert Crispin appeared again. He was being interviewed on a talk show. MacInnes watched and listened, grinding his teeth. How could people be so goddammed stupid? The man was such an obvious fanatic, probably even psychotic.

Those who remembered John F. Kennedy—and MacInnes remembered him well—generally agreed that Herbert Crispin was even more charismatic. But here the similarity ended. Crispin had appeared suddenly out of obscurity to attract millions of disgruntled, militant citizens to his Free America party. He had become a religion. He had a cure for the yoyo bouncing of inflation-recession, unemployment, crime in the streets, income-tax inequities, inefficiency in government, graft, and the bureaucratic fat cats feeding at the public trough.

A complete demagogue, he had a promise for every powerful interest group. His cure was to free America from foreign influences, to return to the old American ideals of integrity, honor, honesty, forthrightness, cleanliness, Godliness, and no crime. To return to the conditions prevailing in the good old days of Vanderbilt, Jay Gould, Boss Tweed, John D. Rockefeller, and all those other sterling citizens who had not been influenced by foreign guile, dishonesty as a way of life, and low moral standards. Crispin had obviously never read Lincoln Steffens.

Though Crispin's political beliefs were to the right of Genghis Kahn, he had the support of the most powerful labor unions, many of the multinational corporations, big oil, and big blue collar. If you were of Italian, Irish, Polish, German, or Scandinavian descent, he led you to believe that the foreign influences so destructive were Jewish, black, and Hispanic. If you were black, it was the Jews and Hispanics. If you were Jewish, you were generally skeptical, though one rabbi had jumped on the Crispin bandwagon and raised a million dollars for him.

Even Tommy Fragment, the famous evangelist, was in the Crispin camp. As a result, Jimmy the Greek was offering odds of 5 to 3 on Crispin. Jimmy had confidence in Fragment's judgment. Fragment prided himself on being a confidant of all presidents and always supported a winner, though on occasion he had to do some fast footwork in his final endorsement.

MacInnes punched the television button with a disgusted thrust, blotting out Herbert Crispin. He picked up the issue of *Playboy* Harp had given him and began to leaf through it, scanning some of the articles and pausing to study some of the more seductive nudes. One photo caught his eye. There was little similarity in appearance, but something in the abandoned posture of the model reminded him of Vanessa. She had long auburn hair and was sprawled naked on a pebble-textured beige bedspread, her eyes almost closed, her lips slightly open, the tips of two upper teeth showing. Her full breasts were flattened somewhat by the position, but her nipples stood up in firm little points. Her legs were raised, bent at the knees. The left leg formed a triangle, with her foot resting on the spread. Her right leg was raised higher, so that her heel rested on her left knee. The position left her pudenda exposed, but it had been skillfully re-touched to show only a trace of her labia majora.

As he stared at the pink crease he felt a definite stirring in his midsection, a stirring that quickly became a startling rigidity. He couldn't believe it. By God, he was cured! One lousy picture had done what all the efforts of Heather McCloud had failed to do! Good old Harp, the wonderful son of a bitch!

CHAPTER TWENTY-TWO

IF HE COULD only remember the number O'Connor had given him, everything would be so much simpler. Jeanine's Massage Spa. Ask for Nicolette. Number? Figures floated hazily in his mind. The Washington area code, then . . . six three four? No, six eight four. Then nine five four eight? That was it! He scribbled it down quickly, to be safe.

Should he use the phone in his room, which went through the hospital switchboard, or hobble on his crutches to the pay phone in the corridor? If Harp was having him watched, using the pay phone would look suspicious. It was a big hospital and unlikely that the switchboard operator would have time to listen in or that she could be in Harp's employ. Still, there would be a record of a Washington call. Phone records were not top secret. It would be easy for some other employee to look at them. The pay phone was better, as long as no one saw him, and there'd be no record. He found a dime in the change in the drawer of his night table.

He put on his bathrobe, reached for his crutches, and hopped-swung his way out into the corridor. It was long past visiting hours, and the hall was deserted. He got himself into the booth awkwardly, deposited the dime, and dialed. When the operator asked for more money he told her to reverse the charges.

He heard a female voice answer, "Jeanine's Massage Spa."

"Will you accept charges for a call from New York from Mac?" asked the operator.

"Yes."

"Go ahead, New York."

"Let me speak to Nicolette," said MacInnes.

"This is Nicolette."

"Nicolette, I'm in room 603 of the East Medical Center Hospital, and I'd like to see you as soon as possible."

"Yes."

"I would advise being *very* inconspicuous."

"Of course. Thank you."

The connection was broken. Balancing on one foot, MacInnes pushed the folding doors open and maneuvered his crutches into position. He had just hopped out, when an orderly came sauntering into view, carrying a mop and bucket.

MacInnes pretended to be leaning against the booth to rest. As the man approached, he said, "It's hard to get used to these damned crutches."

The man smiled sympathetically. "Need any help?"

"No, thanks. I'll manage."

The man went on past, and MacInnes hopped his way back to his room. Had the orderly seen him leave the booth? He thought not.

Within an hour a white-coated young intern came into the room. Holding a chart board, his stethoscope dangling from one jacket pocket, he approached the bed. "So how are we tonight?"

MacInnes put down his book. "Okay."

The doctor attached the stethoscope and bending close, holding the end against MacInnes's chest, said, "Nicolette sent me."

In a voice so low it was almost a whisper, MacInnes gave him a rapid summary of the situation. He ended by saying, "I have no idea where Harp's house is, and it's going to be very difficult if not impossible for me to communicate with you once I'm locked into this thing. Everything will hinge upon your being able to follow me to it, pinpoint the location, put a tap on the phones."

The doctor nodded, folding up his stethoscope. "You're doing fine, fella. We'll have you out of here before you know it." He stuffed the stethoscope in his pocket, walked to the door, said, "Sleep well," and was gone.

The following evening Harp returned, accompanied by a younger man. They entered, the young man stepping aside deferentially to let Harp go ahead of him.

"Colonel MacInnes, this is my young friend Morris."

MacInnes shook hands with Morris. Morris was a husky six-footer, clean cut, with neatly trimmed black hair parted on one side. He might have been an FBI man fresh from Fordham Law School.

Harp said, "Morris is my right-hand man. I hope you're going to be seeing a lot of him."

MacInnes smiled. He couldn't imagine why he would wish to see a lot of Morris.

Harp sat down in the comfortable chair. Morris took the straight-backed wooden one.

Harp said, "I've given a lot of thought to our problem, and I think I have a compromise that may satisfy us both. You'll be able to leave to visit the doctor and to make a reasonable number of trips to theaters and restaurants." He extracted one of his Gauloises and lit it, eyeing MacInnes over the flame from his lighter. "With only one condition. Morris here will be your bodyguard. He will accompany you everywhere. You'll have no communication with anyone except in his presence."

MacInnes grinned. It was a better deal than he had expected. "All right, Harp," he said, "though I don't know why you don't trust me. I played straight with you in Mexico, didn't I?"

Harp held up his hand, smiling. "I'd trust you with my life, Mac, and did. It's just that the pressures are very great on this deal, and I'm a very cautious man. Which is one of the reasons I've been able to live as long as I have."

MacInnes said, "Okay, Harp. If I can get out once in a while, I certainly don't mind having Morris for company." Even with a bum ankle, he could take Morris if he had to. Morris might be younger and stronger, but MacInnes had fifteen years of experience on him.

They came for MacInnes on Saturday. His luggage, including the PSE equipment and other bags stored at the Lombardy, had been picked up earlier by Morris, so MacInnes was encumbered by nothing but his two aluminum canes and the clothes he was wearing. He had had one hell of a job getting his trouser leg over the light cast on his left ankle.

On this trip Morris was accompanied by a small, knotty-faced, taciturn man name Hank, who rarely spoke in more than a grunt.

The nurse wheeled MacInnes down to the cashier's office, where he wrote out a check for the remainder of his enormous bill. The hospital had billed him weekly until they found out his net worth, then had eased up.

He had been practicing with the canes, and he made it out to the cab without difficulty. He had noticed that Hank was carrying a lightweight fold-up wheelchair. He'd said, "I don't think we'll need that." Hank had merely shrugged.

Morris gave the driver an address in the east eighties. They helped MacInnes into the roomy Checker. MacInnes stifled a few qualms as they wheeled away from the safety of the hospital. When you're dead, you're dead. When you're ahead, you're ahead. Stay ahead. The silly rhyme popped into his head and wouldn't leave.

Even with heavy traffic they reached the address in about seven minutes. It was a high-rise apartment, red brick and older than its neighboring boxes. Morris paid the driver and led the way to the elevator bank. They rode to the second floor, walked down a long corridor, opened a fire door, and descended to the first floor. To speed their passage, Morris and Hank virtually carried MacInnes down the steps. They exited into an open passageway that led to the back of an apartment building facing on the next street. Descending a few steps to the basement entrance, they went in. Morris gave a quick code rap on the door of the back basement apartment. It was opened by a woman wearing a white uniform. She was middle-aged and smiling.

Before MacInnes was quite aware of what was going on she had persuaded him to remove his jacket and shirt. She shaved his face, then applied foundation cream, powder, lipstick, eye shadow, and false eyelashes. After pulling a loose-fitting yellow dress over his head, she completed his tranformation with a woman's wig, long, black, and lustrous. He stared in the morror. He made a handsome woman, he thought. She then had him sit in the wheelchair, and she spread a lightweight lap robe over him, covering his trousers and feet. She asked him to tuck his obviously masculine hands under the robe.

His disguise complete, she wheeled him out of the apartment to the elevator, rode up to the first floor, and wheeled him through the lobby to the building's entrance, one street away from the building they had entered. A black, chauffeur-driven limousine was waiting for the lady and her nurse. The nurse helped the lady into the back seat, keeping the robe tucked carefully around her legs and feet the entire time. She folded the wheelchair, put it in the back, closed the door, and joined the chauffeur in the front seat. The limousine eased away from the curb.

Harp was indeed a careful man. If the FBI located his house this trip, it would be a miracle.

The limousine had opera windows, and they were so smoky-dark that MacInnes could see nothing but blurred images outside. The glass between the back seat and the chauffeur's compartment was also smoked. He couldn't even see the Cadillac's hood, only the fuzzy outlines of the two heads in the front seat. In short, he wasn't going to have the faintest clue where they were going.

They drove for about a half an hour, making so many random turns that MacInnes gave up on the mental map he had been trying to construct. There were several long stretches, with gradual curves, but they were obviously seeking to confuse him. The driver could have simply been going up and down the East River Drive.

Finally they turned sharply and entered a garage. A door descended quickly behind them, and a bright overhead light popped on. At least it was a townhouse, one with its own ground-level garage. The distance from street to garage had been too short for any other type of house.

They entered the house from the garage, and Morris helped MacInnes up the stairs to his suite on the third floor. It consisted of a modest living room, a bedroom separated from the living room by an archway with folding doors, and a bathroom. The living room and bedroom had obviously been one large room. The furniture was simple, boxy and comfortable, the upholstered chairs and sofa covered in light-colored fabrics. The floor was thickly carpeted in a maroon and black weave.

On the table in the living room Harp had placed a stack of books, current bestsellers, bottles of Grant's eight-year-old Scotch and Jack Daniels, three cartons of cigarettes, and a bowl of fruit. There were a color television set and a small wood-paneled refrigerator.

He was going to be living underwater. All the windows were of green glass and sealed for air-conditioning. Whatever was outside would remain a mystery.

He eyed the bottles of whiskey and decided against a drink. He was sure he could now drink moderately if he chose to, but he decided not to risk it until this complex job was finished. Turning away, he caught a glimpse of himself in a mirror hanging over the sofa and whirled to see the strange woman who had invaded his room so quietly. Chuckling at his absent-mindedness, he removed the wig and went to the bathroom to wash away his makeup.

He heard the clicking thump of a lock being turned, and the hall door opened. He really was a prisoner.

Harp came in, smiling. "Everything comfy, mate? Like your quarters?"

MacInnes said, "I don't care much for being locked in. When I said I was going to be a prisoner, I didn't expect it to be literally true."

Harp slumped into a chair. "For your own protection, mate. The fewer people who see you, the less you're involved, right? The less you know, the safer you'll be."

"What if the goddamned place catches fire?"

Harp laughed. Pointing, he said, "Right outside that window you'll find a fire escape. All you'd have to do is smash the glass out and trot down the steps."

MacInnes looked at the window, wondering if there really was a fire escape there. Not that he was really worried about fire. He was just feeling testy about being locked in. He said, "This job is beginning to worry me. What are we going to do, rip off Fort Knox?"

Harp lit one of his Gauloises. "Getting cold feet? It's not to late to call if off."

MacInnes stared at him. "No, I'll stick it out." He picked up an apple from the bowl of fruit and bit into it. His mouth still tasted of lipstick, even though he had scrubbed it with soap. "That was certainly an elaborate procedure, getting me here. Did you think some one might tail *me*?"

Harp emitted a cloud of blue-gray smoke. "Don't know why they should. However, they just might be watching Morris. As we say in Old Blighty, he is known to the police."

"Oh."

"Morris can shake any tail, but with a gimpy leg slowing him down . . ."

"I understand."

Harp flashed his white, even teeth. "Okay, so we're all set." He stood up. "After your long confinement, I know you're anxious to see some bright lights. I've arranged for Morris to take you to dinner and the theater tonight." He crushed out his Gauloise impatiently. "Isabel will be up about five to fit you out with a disguise."

"Not as a woman, I hope."

Harp laughed. "No." He went to the door. "Though I must say you were some tasty dish, mate. I saw you when you came in." He went out, and MacInnes heard the bolt clicking into place.

Morris took him to dinner at Giambelli's and then to a Broadway musical comedy. This time they were both fitted out with wigs and moustaches. MacInnes had curly brown hair, not quite an Afro, with a brown, bushy moustache that matched perfectly and tinted glasses that gave the world an unreal look. Morris became a shoulder-length blond, with a Vandyke beard to match. Security measures were not elaborate. The limousine dropped them off on a deserted street in the Bronx. They walked a block to the Grand Concourse and hailed a cab.

MacInnes enjoyed the evening. After almost six weeks of hospital, he would have enjoyed dinner at Chock Full O'Nuts. He limited himself to one bottle of beer with the dinner and tried to chat with Morris. Morris was not a brilliant conversationalist, but he was interested in MacInnes's specialty, primarily from the criminal's point of view. He was eager to know how to beat the polygraph and the PSE. MacInnes assured him it couldn't be done, with a good examiner in charge. MacInnes knew of methods the KGB had devised for its operatives, methods that sometimes defeated both instruments, but he certainly was not going to share them with the underworld.

Morris was annoyingly alert, and he stuck to MacInnes like a third withered arm, useless and embarrassing. Every word MacInnes spoke to anyone, even his orders to the waiter, was monitored with suspicious attention to every inflection. If Morris maintained this type of vigilance, MacInnes's only hope would be his visits to the doctor. Unless he underestimated the FBI, the "intern" would be present at these examinations. Unfortunately, so would Morris.

For three days MacInnes lived the life of a hermit. He read and watched television. He paced the length of the two rooms back and forth incessantly, both as an outlet for nervous energy and to become accustomed to walking again. His ankle was much improved and did not pain him as much as formerly when he put his weight on it. Hank brought him his meals, which were generally excellent. Both Morris and Harp dropped in each day for a brief visit, probably to keep him from feeling completely isolated. He had been promised another evening in town soon.

He was finishing his dinner and his one bottle of Heineken's, when Harp unlocked the door and came in. He was carrying a telephone handset with a plug-in jack cord.

"Time to put the old black box to work," said Harp.

MacInnes swallowed the last of his beer and lit a cigarette. "Thank God. Anything to break the monotony."

MacInnes had decided he would play any PSE work straight. Harp was shrewd enough to read the simpler charts. MacInnes could probably confuse the issue and discredit Harp's associates, but that would just prolong the situation pointlessly. Harp would either line up a new crew or become suspicious and terminate MacInnes with extreme prejudice. Better let them organize the thing and then nip it in the bud. The nipping depressed him. Before it was done, probably either he or Harp would be dead.

Harp said, "I plan to make three telephone calls. One at eight o'clock, the second at eight-thirty, and the last at nine. The men receiving them will be in telephone booths in different cities." He lit one of his cigarettes. "I don't know how we're going to structure these conversations, because I don't know what's going to be said. I'm concerned mainly with two issues. One, the amount of money to be paid, and second, the reliability of the people involved. Are they telling the truth about their willingness to do the job? And more difficult, are they capable of doing it?"

MacInnes said, "Hmmm."

"Can we do it?"

"I don't think you'll be able to measure capability. You can find out whether the guy *believes* he can do the job.''

Harp said, ''I'll settle for that.''

MacInnes said, ''Keep in mind that we've got to have some comparative readings. You'll have to ask at least three types of questions. Give me two or three innocuous questions that are certain to bring truthful answers. Then one or two designed to fluster the subject. Make him angry, afraid, or embarrassed. We need to get a picture of his normal stress pattern. Then when you get to the truth-or-lie questions, make him repeat the answer. For instance, if he says, 'X wants ten thousand,' you ask, 'How much did you say X wants?' Or you may even just elicit a 'yes' from him by saying, 'did you say X wants *ten thousand*?' ''

Harp said, ''I think I have the picture.''

''Isolate the statement you want to test. If he sandwiches a lie in with a long, completely true statement, it may be difficult to detect.''

MacInnes began taking the phone apart to attach the tape recorder and his extension handset.

Harp said, ''I understand. Hey, why are you attaching another phone?''

''I have to monitor the call.''

''Why? You'll have it on tape.''

''I've got to adjust the volume so that we'll have a tape that will give us a good chart. The guy may be speaking an inch from the mouthpiece, two inches, three inches, four. He may even vary it by leaning closer at certain times.''

For some reason, this seemed to annoy Harp.

"Are you sure it's necessary?"

"Of course. What difference does it make? As you say, it's got to be on tape. I've got to hear it, if that's what's worrying you. How could I analyze the charts otherwise?"

Harp began to pace the room. "I'm a little touchy tonight. You're right, of course."

MacInnes decided that what really annoyed Harp was discovering that MacInnes had an extension phone tucked away in his gear and could, theoretically, have been listening to Harp's telephone calls. Theoretically. MacInnes had considered the idea and abandoned it. Having no plug to fit the wall jack, he would have had to remove the wall plate and splice into the wires behind it. It couldn't be disconnected quickly. In fact, even a plug would be risky. Listening to a conversation he might miss the sound of the lock clicking. And even if he heard the lock, could he unplug and hide the phone in the second it took to open the door?

Harp glanced at his watch. "Well, we're ready for number one. Are you switched on?"

MacInnes said, "Yep," simultaneously turning on the Uher.

Harp dialed. MacInnes had once been able to read the numbers by the length of the whir of the dial, but he was out of practice, and none registered as he listened.

A voice said, "Hello."

"Yes. Red?"

"Yes."

"What time is it?"

"Thirty five seconds after eight o'clock."

Harp asked, "This is Thursday, isn't it?"

"Yes."

"What have you to report?"

"My intermediary thinks he may have found the right man. Black boy. SLA." The voice was slow and Southern. Probably the man that Kaiser, the cabdriver, had seen with Harp.

"What does he want?"

"Fifty for himself, seventy-five for the black. The black has a terminal illness. He insists this is the minimum. Wants it for his family."

Harp asked, "Was that fifty for the intermediary and seventy-five for the black?"

"That's right."

"Are you sure you know what you're doing? Do you have confidence in this man?"

Some resentment surfaced. "Why not? He's a good man. He's handled some very big projects."

"What took you so long, for Christ's sake? Have you been screwing off with some chick instead of getting your tail moving to organize this thing?" asked Harp.

The other voice was now muted and angry. "What the hell! You know these things take time. What did you expect me to do, put an ad in the goddamned newspaper?"

"Okay, okay, calm down," said Harp. "I was out of line. I shouldn't have needled you that way. Keep up the good work."

"Okay."

"Stand by for another call at nine-thirty at the other number."

"Okay."

Harp replaced the handset. He turned to MacInnes. "All right, wizard, let's roll the charts."

MacInnes started the tape through the PSE. He scribbled the words under the chart markings as paper inched by. Nothing difficult about this one. Red was a good boy.

As the last answer moved by, MacInnes said, "You've no problem with this man. He's as clean as a sunny day in April."

Harp smiled. "Nice you didn't say 'hound's tooth.' Most of them look rather slimy to me." He lit a cigarette, glancing at his watch. "I rather expected Red would be. We've had dealings in the past."

The intermediary's name was Chuck and he had a Midwestern accent. He checked out as truthful all the way, but he expressed some reservations about his choice. "Red told me you wanted a nut case. I got one. He's a fanatic, but he knows what he's doing, you understand? We might be safer with a pro. You understand?"

"When I talk to him, we'll decide that," said Harp.

Harp dialed the third number.

"Harvey?"

"Yeah man, that's me."

"You've been talking to Chuck?"

"Yeah man, Chuck and me, we got a deal."

Harp asked, "You think you can handle it? I'm wondering if you've got the guts. A lot of blacks turn chicken when they get in a corner."

There was a sharp intake of breath. "Looka heah, you white racist son of a bitch, you lucky you talking to me on the phone. You tell me that to my face, I kick the shit out of you."

Harp said, "Okay, take it easy. I just wanted to find out if you really cared about blacks. You see, I'm black myself."

"You black?"

"Yeah."

"Son of a bitch!" The voice was pleased.

"Chuck says you want seventy-five."

"Yeah man, but you understand, it ain't for me. I only got about six months, man. Sickle-cell anemia. Hell, if it wasn't for that, I'd wipe old Sentuh Rice-crispies for you free. I mean it! I got to protect my family."

"Careful!" Harp's voice was sharp.

"I mean it, man, I hate that mother so much I'd do it free. I'm telling you—"

Harp cut in, "All right. Chuck will be in touch with you." He hung up quickly.

Harp turned to face MacInnes, and they stared at each other. It was worse than ripping off Fort Knox. The target was Senator Crispin. What a world-wide stinkeroo that would make! There would be an investigation bigger than Watergate. The American people were sick of political assassination, and they were not likely to believe any damned committee that tried to lay it in the lap of one crackpot. This time the press wouldn't stand still for it. Since John F. Kennedy, a whole new breed of investigative reporters had risen to scourge the evil and the corrupt.

MacInnes took a deep breath. "So you're going to knock off Crispin."

Harp continued to stare at him, without answering.

MacInnes said, "Well, he'll be no great loss to the country." If he didn't appear totally committed, he probably would never get out of the house again until the job was done.

Harp relaxed. "Right you are, mate. Think of how many millions of lives would have been saved if some dedicated Germans had managed to get Hitler."

MacInnes nodded slowly. It was the old argument, means and ends.

"You seem a little white around the gills, mate. Developing qualms?"

MacInnes smiled. "Whoever knocks off Crispin will be doing the country a big service. If I have any qualms, they're strictly concerned with getting caught." He lit a cigarette, snapping his lighter shut vehemently. "Christ, this will bring the biggest investigative crackdown in history."

Harp said, "I wanted to keep you out of that part of it. That stupid black . . ."

"I'm in it up to here," said MacInnes, holding his hand level with his throat. "And in it I stay. I'll consider the risk a contribution to America's future."

Harp slapped MacInnes's shoulder gratefully. "Good man. As you say, the investigation will turn the country upside-down. That's why every detail has to be planned perfectly. The trail has got to stop right at the black. And we'll see that it does."

"The intermediary's got to go," said MacInnes.

Harp thumped his fist against his open palm thoughtfully. "Yes, of course. Possibly even Red, too. I hate to do it, but this is too big to take any chances. Chuck may have told someone about Red."

MacInnes asked, "Any chance that Red might have stashed an envelope away somewhere as protection?"

Harp grinned. "I rather think not. Red is one of the smartest operators I know, but he's almost totally illiterate. He can barely write his own name."

MacInnes looked skeptical. "In these times? I find that hard to believe."

Harp said, "It's true. Red grew up on a poverty-stricken little farm in the wilds of Louisiana. What schooling he was forced to take just didn't take. I suspect there weren't many truant officers roaming the bayous in those days."

Harp thought of everything. He even picked an illiterate associate who couldn't hide a written document for protection. Of course, he could leave a tape, but that would be a rather elaborate ploy for someone like Red.

Harp said, "Well, let's get that player piano to work on the black. See what kind of tune he's given us."

MacInnes ran the charts on the black. Harp paced the floor, chain smoking.

Harvey was a bad boy. He lied about practically everything. Sickle-cell anemia, how much he hated Crispin, how he would do the job free, how he wanted to protect his family.

"Well now I'm really earning my keep," said MacInnes. He showed Harp the charts. "This baby has lied about everything significant." MacInnes traced the solid blocking with the blunt end of his ballpoint pen. "He isn't terminal, he doesn't hate Crispin, he wouldn't do the job free, and he isn't planning to give the money to his family. Maybe he just plans to grab it and skedaddle to Uganda."

Harp studied the chart markings. "I had a feeling he was a phony. But as I've mentioned before, my intuition is not always right."

"It's working okay tonight."

Harp was bemused. "Yeah. Well, this calls for some fast footwork." He unplugged the telephone, wrapping the wire around it. "I'll have to take the other extension too, Mac."

MacInnes disconnected the other extension and handed it to him, looking grim. "You'd better let me remove the induction coil from your phone. We'll need it the next time we want to tape."

Harp handed him the phone. "It isn't that I don't trust you, Mac. I simply work on the sound intelligence principle that nobody should know any more than he absolutely has to know to perform his function well." Harp walked over to the Uher. "Incidentally, let's clean this tape." He rewound, then set the machine on Record and waited until it erased the few minutes of telephoning. It was fine with MacInnes. He had picked up all three conversations on the little Sony, which was lying unnoticed under the chart spillovers.

After Harp left, MacInnes sat smoking and brooding. The world *might* have been saved the holocaust of World War II if someone had assassinated Hitler. With hindsight, having read about Buchenwald and Auschwitz, he would have joined the assassination team with enthusiasm. On the other hand, some other Nazi leader might have stepped in and carried on. The German people, at least the unthinking masses, were ripe and eager for what Hitler offered. Still, moderates might have prevailed.

With Crispin out of the way, a big threat to America's free institutions would be removed. It was a tempting thought. In some cases, maybe the end did justify the means? Was it always true that "the end is the means," as some philosopher had written? Terrorist means did not always produce a government that had to be maintained by repression. The Republic of Ireland had been born with the aid of terrorism, and today it was as much of a democracy as you would find in the Western world. The birth of Israel had had its share, and no repressive dictatorship had developed.

He shut off this line of thinking abruptly. He had a debt to help preserve America's freedoms as they were, and they included Herbert Crispin's right to run for office. Watergate had proved that America was healthy enough to handle Crispin, even if he was elected, which MacInnes doubted.

He found some flimsy second sheets in the attaché case containing his stationery and other records. He cut one sheet into strips an inch and a quarter wide. Taking a pad to give him a writing surface, and a ballpoint pen with a fine tip, he went into the bathroom. There was a lock on the bathroom door. Seated on the toilet lid, he filled two of the strips with microscopic writing on both sides, providing all the information he had. At least they would know that the target was Senator Crispin. They would know that he was in a townhouse with a ground-floor garage. There were not many of those, he hoped. They would know the disguises already used and the method of evading surveillance when MacInnes left the hospital. He asked them to provide him with a weapon, a .45 or a .38, on his next visit to the doctor.

His hand cramped, he finally finished. Taking a bent-open paper clip, he painstakingly removed the tobacco, bit by bit, from one of his cigarettes, being careful not to tear the paper wrapping. He wasted three cigarettes in the process but finally managed to empty one with the paper intact. He then rolled up the strips tightly and slid them into the wrapper, pushing them with his pen until they were flush against the filter. He moistened the tobacco slightly and filled the remaining inch of the tube, packing it down delicately so that it would have an even, solid look at the open end. He flushed the surplus tobacco down the toilet. His last step was to mark the outside of the filter with a tiny ink dot.

MacInnes entered the examining room with Morris attached like a Siamese twin. Morris was wearing his blond wig and Vandyke.

The "intern" said, "Sorry, only patients in the

examining room." He turned to MacInnes, "How're you doing, Colonel?"

MacInnes said, "Pretty well, I think. This is my bodyguard, Mr. Brown. I keep him with me at all times."

The intern grinned. "I'm not going to kill you. I'm only going to take the cast off so Dr. Bunner can look at your goddamned ankle." He turned to Morris. "Okay, but just make yourself inconspicuous, will you? It's going to be a little crowded in here when Dr. Bunner comes in."

MacInnes sat on the examining table. He pulled out his cigarettes and stuck one in his mouth. He held the package out to the intern and said, "Still bumming, Doc, or have you finally managed to give them up?"

The intern took the cigarette and stuck it in his mouth. "Still bumming, dammit."

MacInnes said to Morris, "The doctor is trying to give them up. He smokes only when he can bum one."

Morris, who had moved to a corner of the small room, smiled.

MacInnes swung his feet up on the table. He lit his cigarette, then held the lighter out to the intern, who was starting to take the cast off. The intern shook his head. He removed the cigarette from his mouth and stuck it in his jacket pocket. "Dr. Bunner would chew my ass out from here to Times Square and back if he caught me smoking while working on a patient. I'll save it for my next cup of coffee."

Dr. Bunner came in and examined MacInnes.

Morris watched, fascinated, but his eyes were fastened on the ankle. The intern had managed to get himself partially between MacInnes's right side and Morris. MacInnes felt a very slight tug on his jacket.

Dr. Bunner decided the ankle wasn't doing as well as it should be. His back to Morris, he winked at MacInnes when he said this. MacInnes had better come back next week, and in the meanwhile, maybe he'd take it a little easier on the walking.

In the corridor MacInnes saw a ravishing brunette hurrying toward him. It was Vanessa!

She threw herself into his arms. "Kevin! Where in hell have you been? What's happened to you?"

He took her shoulders and held her away from him, lovingly. "Where in hell have *you* been? I looked for you for days."

Vanessa lowered her eyes. "I know. I talked to Bill Duc. He told me about how you'd been mugged and been in the hospital over a month. I rushed to the hospital, and they told me you had gone, and they didn't have any address for you other than the hotel."

MacInnes said, "Then you were smart enough to talk to Dr. Bunner, and he told you I was coming for an examination?"

Morris stood there glowering. This was not good. Harp wasn't going to like it.

MacInnes said, "You didn't answer my question. Where have *you* been?"

"I've been up at Martha's Vineyard writing the novel you told me to write."

He pulled her tightly to him. "Nessa," he said in almost a whisper, "I'm cured. And the depression is about gone too. Also, I'm not drinking."

She looked up at him. "Was it . . ." She took a small breath. "Was it another woman?"

He laughed. "No. A magazine. I was looking through a copy of *Playboy*."

She smiled, vaguely astonished.

Morris was making impatient sounds, clearing his throat.

MacInnes said to Vanessa, "This is Max Brown, my bodyguard. Max, this is my fiancée, Miss Vanessa Peckham.

Morris nodded stiffly. Vanessa just looked puzzled.

MacInnes said, "Nessa, I'm on a very important case. It requires my presence twenty-four hours a day. It may be a month or six weeks before we can get together."

Her face fell. None of his cases had ever separated them before. "But Kevin . . ."

He turned her face up to look at him. "Trust me. You know I love you dearly."

She stared at him, still puzzled.

"Are you at the Lombardy?"

"Yes."

"Maybe my client will let me off one night to take you to dinner. Did you finish the book?"

"Of course not. A book takes months to write."

"Then the best thing would be for you to go back to the Vineyard and do some more writing." He shook her affectionately. "And for God's sake give me your address there."

She gave him her address, but her voice was flat. He wondered if she thought he was giving her a fast shuffle. He wrote the address carefully in his little book.

He gave her another hug, and kissed her. "I'll be counting the days, darling," he said.

"Okay," she said, but there was definite hurt in her voice.

Morris hurried him to Grand Central Station. They took a train to Stamford, Connecticut. At Cos Cob, Morris glanced out the window and saw that conditions were right. He hurried MacInnes off the train. Two other men suddenly decided that Cos Cob was just the place they had planned to get off. There was only one cab, and Morris commandeered it quickly, waiting while MacInnes limped his way there. The two agents looked wildly around for transport. The place was empty as only a very smalltown commuter station can be in midafternoon. As they drove away, one of the agents was telephoning, the other still glancing around hopefully.

The cab took them to White Plains, where they waited for the limousine on a deserted side street.

Back at the house, MacInnes locked himself in the bathroom to see what gifts the intern had dropped in his jacket pockets. A microtransmitter sending out a constant signal. No good. Its range was about two miles. White Plains was at least ten, probably more, from Cos Cob. And the cab would certainly have been more than two miles from the station by the time they turned up even a local squad car. The cabdriver had taken off like a jet when he found they wanted to go all the way to White Plains.

In his other pocket he found a beautiful little set of pick-lock tools and a Mulcahy special, the soft-tipped pen with the lethal bite.

Where in hell could he hide the transmitter? Harp might have some kind of electronic sweeping device that would pick up the signal. And if the FBI hadn't zeroed in on it by now, it was unlikely that they ever would. Using the pick-lock tools he managed to take it apart and disconnect the power cell. He left the bathroom and threw the pieces in the small PSE spare parts kit.

The pen reminded him of his deadly key chain, with its square of Connemara marble, the only weapon left from his graveside confrontation with Alfredo Flores. He had been somewhat apprehensive about carrying it around. Suppose the gas were accidentally discharged or leaked into his pocket and wafted its way up to his nostrils? He dug around in his suitcase and found it, then transferred his keys from his regular ring. He was going to need all the protection he could get.

With the pick-lock tools he could get out of the room—and into any other room. He could also get killed doing it.

He sat down in the living room and eyed the unopened bottles of Scotch and bourbon longingly. A little nerve medicine would be most welcome. Perish the thought, lest you too perish, he told himself. Give thought to the task at hand and forget the booze. Objectives, one, two, three. One, target. Solved. Two, plan of action. Unsolved. But Harp, being the meticulous planner he was, would eventually have it all on paper, minute by minute, second by second. Objective number two, get a look at Harp's plan. Too early. Objective number three. The buck must not stop at Harp. The money behind the killing, and the man or men who dished it out. Who was he, or they? Who in hell would want Crispin killed? Liberals, yes. But liberals were notoriously reluctant to assassinate. Also, if more than one of them was involved the story would already have been leaked to the *New York Times*.

Communists? The native brand was not nearly rich enough to buy Harp. And if it was a Marxist terrorist group such as the SLA, they wouldn't buy Harp; they'd feel quite capable of doing the job themselves. The Soviet Union or a third-world power? What possible motive? The more confusion in the United States the better, as far as they were concerned. And Crispin's election would indeed bring confusion and chaos. Talk about polarization. The United States would be polarized as it had never been before. The Vietnam war would be a Little League game in comparison.

Vanessa. How he missed her. She was the good news and the bad news. She hadn't abandoned him. Good. Would she understand and wait? Yes. She'd figure it out. Bad? Knowing that she hadn't abandoned him made the risk he was taking so much harder.

He heard the lock thump, and Harp came in.

"Morris tells me your beautiful friend was at the hospital." Harp was annoyed.

MacInnes looked up. "Lucky, wasn't it?"

"Why lucky?"

"Now she won't have the police looking for me. If she thought I had just disappeared, she might decide I was in trouble. After all, I was kidnapped and almost killed in Mexico, and she knew about it."

"I see."

"I should have called Bill Duc, my houseman, and told him I was going away for a month or two to convalesce. I'd better do that. I wouldn't want the police feeling there was anything mysterious about my whereabouts during this period."

"I see." Harp looked as though he had found a fly baked into his muffin. "What I don't see is why you were tailed. Morris was well disguised."

MacInnes said, "I was wondering about that myself."

Harp stared at him, his light blue eyes locked on MacInnes's. "Some explanation must have occurred to you?"

"Sure. Obviously they're keeping an eye on me. When a man becomes a drunk, a man who has been sixteen years in army intelligence, many of them in the top echelons, they are no doubt concerned about who he might take up with and what he might tell them. I might be ideal pickings for the KGB, right?" He glanced at the unopened bottles. "After all, they have no way of knowing I've reformed, do they?"

Harp relaxed. It was a good answer. "I put the liquor there to test you, of course."

"It's no problem, believe me."

"Morris said you mentioned another meeting with your friend. Dinner?"

MacInnes said, "That was a stupid impulse. I don't want her involved with me in any way until this thing is over."

Harp went back to the door. "You're right, of course. I'll get a telephone so you can call your houseman."

When he returned, MacInnes called Bill Duc and told him he was driving to California for a long vacation and would be out of touch for a month or so. Yes, he was feeling fine. And no, there was no need for him to bring either car up; MacInnes was renting one.

Harp had been eyeing the unopened bottle of Scotch. He said, "I think you're wise to stay off this stuff." He picked up the bottle, opened it, and poured himself a drink. "I feel in the mood to have a drink with you. Will you have a beer while I soothe my ruffled feelings with some Highland dew?"

MacInnes said, "Sure. Why not?" He plucked a bottle of Heinekens from the small refrigerator and opened it.

Harp lifted his drink. "Well, here's confusion to our enemies."

"Skoal," said MacInnes, tasting his beer. "May your life be interesting," he said to himself. It was a fairly mild curse, but then, he was feeling benign. If Harp was planning to eliminate Red, MacInnes was probably on his list too. He'd have to see that it didn't happen before the showdown showed him up. It would happen soon after Harp made the last

PSE call he needed to make. How in hell would he know when *that* call was made? Probably he would want to keep checking on Red and the others right up to the event, at least to the day before the event.

MacInnes said, "I'm really befuddled in speculating about the people behind this." He held up his hand. "Oh I know you're not going to tell me. I'm just curious about *your* vulnerability. It surely must have occurred to you that they may have plans for you?"

Harp laughed. "The fool thinks I don't know who he is. That's my protection. The whole deal was arranged by telephone, through intermediaries."

"But you know."

"Damned right I know, mate. I have good intelligence sources in Mexico."

MacInnes shook his head wonderingly. "Other than some deranged liberal, I can't imagine who in hell would want to knock off Crispin. It wouldn't be a liberal. Assassination isn't their bag."

Harp tossed down his Scotch and poured himself another. "Mate, your eyes would bug right out of your head if I told you the name of the man behind this. You would be absolutely astounded."

MacInnes toyed with his beer glass, still three-quarters full. "Whoever he is, he has plenty of money. Your services don't come cheap."

Harp smiled. "My fee is one million dollars."

MacInnes whistled softly.

"I estimate that half of it will be clear profit."

MacInnes looked impressed. He was. "Since

he's so rich, hasn't it occurred to you that he, too, may have excellent intelligence sources? That he may know you know?"

Harp rubbed his chin. "I doubt it."

"Still, it might be wise to have some protection stashed away somewhere."

"Such as?"

MacInnes thought for a few seconds. "Say a tape of his voice showing incriminating knowledge of the situation. A voice print could identify him as thoroughly as fingerprints." He drank some more of his beer. "Have you talked to the top man?"

Harp said, "Yes indeed. He wanted to speak to *me*." He chuckled. "Maybe he had a PSE on the wire testing me."

MacInnes filled his half-empty glass. "Maybe you should test him on the subject."

"What subject?"

"Whether he knows that you know who he is."

Harp considered the suggestion, pouring himself another drink. "Could it be done without compromising my situation?"

"I think so. But aside from what he knows, suppose he simply decides to play it absolutely safe. Dead, you can never lead investigators to anyone connected with him."

Harp locked his fingers behind his head and leaned back. "How would you test him?"

MacInnes stared at him thoughtfully. "Perhaps you could make it in the form of a complaint. Say, 'Now you know who I am, but I don't know who you are, right?' Then when he answers that, go on to complain about being at a disadvantage in the

deal. Demand some kind of extra security."
MacInnes reached for his cigarettes, then put them
away without lighting one. "I assume you only got
part of the money. When do you get the rest? After
the job is done?"

"Before."

"What assurance has he that you'll perform?"

Harp smiled. "My reputation. I've never yet
failed to keep my part of a bargain."

MacInnes rubbed his forehead wearily. "If investigators, both law enforcement and press, decide it's a conspiracy, what's to stop him from
throwing you to the wolves?"

"What would that solve? I'm a mercenary. Just
another step toward Mr. X."

MacInnes interrupted him. "Not if you left a
suicide note with a plausible reason. Let's say
you're a Marxist terrorist, an SLA member."

"Mate, it won't wash. I've always been on the
side that could buy me."

"So the SLA bought you."

Harp just shook his head, smiling.

MacInnes knew the argument was weak. He
needed a tape of Mr. X's voice. It might be the only
slender thread leading to him. Thread? Not even
that. A fragile strand of spiderweb. Mr. X
wouldn't be a public figure whose voice was well-
known, or he wouldn't have spoken to Harp.

But with his voice on tape, investigators could
painstakingly compare with a thousand, even several thousand other voices. How many politically
minded multimillionaires were there?

Harp said, "You know, you're as cautious as I

am." He poured himself another drink. "I wish I could trust you completely. You'd make a fine devil's advocate. I'd profit by discussing all the details with you."

"I've always been curious about why you don't."

Harp held up two fingers. "A couple of reasons. First, your background. You might get an attack of conscience and revert to type."

MacInnes laughed, genuinely amused.

"What's funny?"

"The idea that a man engaged for sixteen years in international intelligence operations would have a conscience. I don't know where you'd find a more cynical, cold-blooded bunch of bastards anywhere."

Harp stared at him, some of his assurance shaken. "That may be. Nevertheless, you strike me personally as a right-minded chap with a conscience. Faulty intuition, perhaps, but that's how I feel." He made a steeple with his long, bony fingers. "Strangely enough, that's one of the things I like about you. I would be sadly disillusioned to find you cynical and cold-blooded."

MacInnes wondered whether he should be touched by this endorsement. "What's your second reason?"

"The picture you showed Hergueta. Whatever his faults, Hergueta was not a man to embroider information."

MacInnes's mouth turned down. "That damned picture. If you remember, you were pointing a .45 at my head at the time. To explain it would have been too involved and confusing, and you might not have believed it. Actually, it was a simple mistake on Hergueta's part. Did he tell you the picture *looked* like you?''

"No, he said it was a very poor resemblance."

"Well, there's your answer. The picture I showed him was not of you. While I was in the army I occasionally bought information from Hergueta. When he approached me at the hotel, I suggested that we might do business. I had a drawing in my suite that I wanted to show him. It was an Identikit drawing of a fellow who called himself Robinson Finch. This man embezzled about three hundred thousand dollars from a client of mine. It was thought that he might be hiding out in Mexico. Since I had to be in Mexico anyway, the client asked me to look into the possibility."

MacInnes paused, out of breath. He took a few swallows of beer. "Now, Hergueta said he would go to my suite and look, but not a word must be spoken in the room. He was afraid it might be bugged. So I showed him the picture and we went back outside. He said, 'I do not know this man, señor.' We walked on a bit and it occurred to me only incidentally that he might know how to reach you. Remember, I was expecting to hear from Ubaldo Galindo. When I described you, and that was merely as 'the Englishman,' I thought I made it clear that this was a second situation. Apparently, Hergueta was confused and connected them as one."

MacInnes lit a cigarette and stared belligerently at Harp. "Now goddammit, I did not wish to go into this involved explanation. I chose to simply deny the whole thing. My client's problem was none of your business. I try to give my clients the same confidentiality a lawyer gives his clients."

Harp chuckled. "I wish you had. It's been gnawing at me like a crossword puzzle with only one word missing." He sipped his drink. "What did Hergueta say about 'the Englishman'?"

"He said, 'I do not know this man, señor, but I will inquire around.' "

Harp leaned back and stretched. "You know, all this chitchat has led me to one conclusion. I've been making this thing too damned complicated." He reached for his French cigarettes. He was now smoking the filter-tip version, MacInnes noticed. "Your original suggestion is the simplest. There's no reason in the world why the old bastard shouldn't be told that I know and that I have hedged my bets. If he puts out a contract on me he's dead."

He lit the cigarette and sat staring at MacInnes, grinning. "In fact, there's no reason you shouldn't know. I don't owe the old son of a bitch anything. If he had trusted me, it would be different."

MacInnes literally held his breath. Finally he released it gently and said, "Naturally I'm very curious."

"Would you believe Chad Worrowby?"

MacInnes laughed. "You're kidding." Chad Worrowby was a billionaire Oklahoma oil man, notorious in his support of the far right. He had invested millions in Crispin's political career.

"I'm not joking, mate."

369

MacInnes asked, "Why kill him? He could just cut off his money. Are you serious?"

"Absolutely."

"I don't understand it."

Harp puffed on his cigarette. "Mate, Crispin has all the money the law will allow him to spend, and it's still pouring in."

"But why is Worrowby turning on him?"

"Because he has created a Frankenstein's monster. Crispin is a nut. Crispin has a bunch of wild-assed young economists working on his progam behind the scenes. One of the first things he plans to do is declare a national energy emergency. He's going to nationalize energy, from top to bottom, even if he has to send Congress home and go to the people for backing. He'll get mass support for it too. Everyone feels he is being gouged by the oil, natural-gas, and utility companies. Crispin's theme will be that since the oil companies claim they can't produce enough, and find new fields, without charging the same blackmail the Arabs are charging, then the government will step in and do it for them. Nobody believes their self-serving surveys of the amount of oil and natural gas they have left in the ground anyway. And nobody believes the utilities have to double their light and heat bills. They've never been controlled with the consumer in mind. All these government agencies are loaded with industry-oriented people—in fact, many former executives of the companies they're supposed to regulate."

"Son of a bitch," said MacInnes in wonder. "It sounds like a good idea."

Harp laughed. "You see, even you are impressed. Think of the millions who have to drive to work, who have to sweat blood to pay heat and light bills that are two, three, and four times what they used to be."

Harp poured himself another drink. "Well, let's get the old bastard on tape." He stood up. "I suppose you need your other phone too?"

"Yep," said MacInnes.

Harp left to get MacInnes's extension handset. MacInnes had counted five drinks of at least an ounce and a half each. Harp had a good capacity. He wasn't showing it in any way, other than perhaps his unbending to tell MacInnes about Worrowby.

When he returned, MacInnes set up the Uher and attached the other phone.

Harp dialed a ten-digit number. The phone was answered by a man with a thin, reedy voice.

Harp said, "Tell *numero uno* that it is urgent that I speak to him immediately. I'll be waiting for his call." He broke the connection while the other voice was protesting that it might not be possible.

They sat waiting. Harp said, "You have no idea of the appeal of this man Crispin. Being rich, you wouldn't understand how the quality of life has deteriorated for the lower-middle and middle-middle classes. A man comes home from a hard day's work to eat ground round that turns out to be half gristle, a steak tough as a buckskin glove, a turkey breast so hard it bends the carving knife. He yells at his wife, and his wife cries. His heat bill that used to be seventy dollars a month is now two hundred and seventy. He can't get new windshield wipers on his car without paying out fifty dollars. His savings are dwindling because his income can't cover his outgo."

MacInnes smiled. "I thought you were richer than I am."

Harp said, "That may be, mate. I keep in touch with some of my men. They aren't so rich."

"Your men?"

Harp looked away. "I, too, was an officer in the army once. But that's a story I don't care to go into."

The telephone rang. MacInnes flipped on the Uher.

"Is this Mr. Smith?" asked Harp.

"Yes."

"Mr. Smith, first let me tell you this line has been electronically swept. There is no possibility of a bug, so we can talk freely."

"About what?"

"I want you to understand that I do not appreciate your keeping me at a disadvantage. You know who I am, but I don't know who you are, right?"

"That's right. But you're being magnificently paid, in *advance*. What business is it of yours who I am?"

"I've made it my business to find out, Mr. Worrowby."

The western drawl became sharper. "My name is not Worrowby."

Harp said, "Oh but it is. I've identified you conclusively. I have also identified two of your associates, Earl Montgomery and Victor Watson."

"What the hell is this all about, anyway? Blackmail?"

"Not at all. The project of taking care of Senator Rice Crispies will go through as planned. I just want you to know that I do not trust you. I have compiled sufficient evidence to indict you and your associates should anything happen to me. Is that clear? Should I meet with an accident, say, the FBI will within hours receive tapes and other documents."

There was the sound of heavy breathing at the other end. "So that's what's bothering you. You damn fool, I'm tempted to abort the whole project."

Harp said, "That's your privilege. However, you'll deliver the final payment, regardless."

"Listen, you could be killed by the police in carrying out the project."

Harp whistled softly. "Let's hope not. However, my friend is not unreasonable. He'll take into consideration the circumstances surrounding my demise."

The voice at the other end became harsher. "All right. You have nothing to fear from me. Just don't telephone me again, understand?" There was a click, and Worrowby had hung up.

Harp poured himself another drink. "Let's run that tape. I'm curious about whether this was necessary."

MacInnes ran the tape through the PSE. Worrowby showed plenty of stress on almost everything, but his statement "That's right, but you're being magnificently paid," showed a different kind of stress. The two words "That's right" were heavily blocked with deception stress.

MacInnes showed it to Harp. "You see, I was right. He did know that you knew who he was."

Harp stood up. "Mate, you've done it again." He collected the phones and the Uher tape with Worrowby's voice on it, and left.

During the three weeks that followed MacInnes monitored and tested a number of calls. Chuck had found a real SLA black who tested out one hundred percent honest. There were calls concerning a panel truck and two cars. There were several conversations with Red. From these MacInnes gathered that the event was to take place in or near Madison Square Garden. Whether before, after, or during Crispin's speech, he was not able to determine.

He had three visits to the hospital. After each, Morris demonstrated his amazing versatility in evading surveillance. One involved waiting three hours in a deserted subbasement of the Waldorf, then emerging as dark brown Hispanics in soiled white coats, ostensibly bus boys.

One of Morris's ploys evidently failed, however, because among the things the intern kept dropping in his jacket pockets was a note that read, "You are in a house at 675 East 81st Street, Manhattan. Need help, break window and blow whistle." The whistle was the type only dogs can hear. They even had dogs working on it, for Christ's sake. He was also supplied with a small Beretta automatic, a poison capsule, another key chain complete with marble square, and another soft-tip pen. In the small room Dr. Bunner and the intern were able to block Morris's view easily, and MacInnes decided it was no longer necessary to dig tobacco out of Vantage cigarettes. He put the latest information on the same tightly rolled strips of paper but simply slipped them to the intern during the examination.

He wondered what they expected him to do with the poison capsule.

The day Kevin had been dreading finally arrived. He would have to get out of the room and look for Harp's plan. How many people were in the damned house anyway? The chauffeur, a short, beefy redhead; Isabel, the matronly makeup artist who probably subbed as housekeeper; and of course, Harp, Morris, and Hank. Who else might he stumble upon in the dark? Did Harp have any pressure-type burglar alarms under the carpets? How about other electronic protection devices?

He waited until 3:30 A.M. If they were not all asleep by this time, they never would be.

The lock was easy enough. They had simply reversed an ordinary double-locking Sager, leaving the latch on the outside and the key entrance plate on the inside. He had it open in about three minutes. He slipped the Beretta and the whistle into his jacket pocket, put both pens in his shirt pocket, and carried his small, pen-sized flashlight. A small notebook and a regular ballpoint completed his equipment.

The corridor was narrow and thickly carpeted.

Besides his own, there were two other doors. He went to each door and listened. No snoring or heavy breathing. Still, these old houses were solidly built. One wouldn't necessarily hear soft snoring, or perhaps even loud snoring.

He crept slowly down to the second floor, using his light only when necessary. There were five doors on the second floor; one, probably a bathroom, was slightly ajar.

He stood there for a moment in the dark, listening and thinking. Why was he taking this risk? He could simply go outside and blow the whistle. They had as much evidence against Worrowby as they'd probably ever get right in the house, they could take Harp and his whole crew. They'd lose Red, Chuck, and the black, but these men were small fry. Still, all the loose ends should be tied up. If he copped out now, they wouldn't say much, but the word would go around that he had lost his nerve. A matter of pride? How proud the dead man doth look! What a pile of horseshit, pride. Yet he knew he would continue right to the goddamned end, driven by motives so stupid they were incomprehensible to him. How could a man with his high IQ be so feeble-minded?

The slightly opened door was a bathroom. He listened at the other four doors. No sounds. Should he assume they were all bedrooms? There were five of Harp's staff in residence that he knew of, and six rooms other than his own on the two floors. Harp would probably have a suite. Perhaps two of the second-floor rooms were his. Or there might be another member of the crew.

He moved carefully down the steps to the first floor. Front door, hall. On one side of the hall, small living room and small dining room, connected by an archway. Kitchen probably back of the dining room. On the other side, two closed doors. One of them was probably Harp's study, and this room might well be rigged with an alarm system. The second door, away from the front, would be most likely. It had a lock on it, and the other did not. He knelt and examined the carpet carefully. It looked all right—not that the damned thing would show. He played the light around the edges of the door, then sighed with relief as he saw it. A small keyhole set directly below the lock. A key-type alarm switch. A minute with one of his pick-lock tools shut off the alarm. He went to work of the regular lock. It was a Medeco, and damned difficult. It took him about ten minutes. He glanced at his wristwatch. 3:45 A.M.

Harp's study was large and comfortably furnished. About fifteen feet by twenty-five, it extended to the back of the house and included a small private bathroom. Bookshelves covered two walls. The other two, on the side and at the rear of the house had heavily draped windows.

One end of the room contained a large desk and upholstered swivel chair; the other, near the door, had a long, wide sofa, an equally long marble coffee table, and three lounge chairs.

MacInnes closed and locked the door carefully. The dark red drapes were thick and opaque. He decided it would be safe to turn on the desk lamp.

The desk was beautifully polished mahogany,

about six feet long, with three drawers on each side and a center drawer above the knee space. On top was nothing but a spotless desk blotter, a large ashtray, a clock under glass that had four brass balls slowly turning, and a lined legal-size pad with nothing written on it.

Each drawer had its individual lock, and they were tough little bastards, he could see. Not so tough to open, but tough to open gently, without leaving any scratch marks or indications of forcing.

All seven drawers were locked. Eeenie, meenie, mynee, mo. If he opened all seven he'd be there for what was left of the night. Which drawer would Harp lock his plans in? He stared at them, wishing ESP would give him a lead. No flash of revelation. He always locked his own more important papers in the bottom drawer for some reason. Say, the left-hand bottom drawer.

He dropped to his knees and, sweating, fiddled with the delicate lock, trying to move the bolt without forcing it and, possibly, jamming it in the open position. It was years since he had completed his course in Breaking and Entering, recently renamed Defense against Sealed Premises. He was rusty.

There were a couple of small keys on his ring, and he decided to try then. Miraculously, one of them flipped the bolt.

Another lock clicked.

The door opened slowly as MacInnes stared, his throat suddenly full of cement.

Knotty faced little Hank stepped in, a very new

and shiny blue steel .45 in his hand.

"You lousy son of a bitch," he said between clenched teeth. "I told Harp he was a fugging idiot for trusting you."

He swaggered over to the desk. "Get up. I'd blow your crapped-up brains out, but I know Harp ain't gonna want his carpet dirtied up."

MacInnes stood up, holding the keys. "Just a minute, farthead—you see these keys? Harp gave them to me. He wants me to go over the god-damned plan."

Taking a deep breath, MacInnes thrust the keys in Hank's face and dug his fingernail into the indented border to release the mechanism.

A soft swoosh sent a small white cloud of droplets into Hank's face. He smiled, as though his girlfriend had playfully squirted him with Arpege. Then he gasped, half-turned, his knees buckling, and collapsed. He made hardly a sound hitting the soft, thickly padded carpet.

Still holding his breath, MacInnes rushed from the room and down the hall to the front door. Fumbling with the two double-locking latches, he finally got it opened and stumbled outside to take a deep breath of New York's corrosive smog.

Coughing softly, not from the gas but from the smog, he stood on the sidewalk assessing his situation. He had really blown it this time. Might as well walk away and leave the rest to the FBI.

On the other hand, had he? There had been very little noise. He took a deep breath and, holding it, went swiftly back to the study. Grasping Hank by the feet, he managed to drag him into the hall, lungs bursting with the effort. He rushed to the front door, which he had left open, and took another minute of deep breathing. Then he went back to Hank, picked him up, and carried him out to the pavement.

He blew his soundless whistle. There was a faint bark not too far away, and in seconds two men appeared out of the dark from somewhere.

In a whisper MacInnes said, "Get rid of this bastard; he was about to blow my cover."

In the deep shadow, MacInnes recognized his friend the intern and smiled. "Don't try mouth-to-mouth resuscitation, Doc," he whispered. "He's had a dose of gas."

The intern asked softly, "Are you okay?"

"So far." With a small wave, MacInnes went back to the house, pausing at the front door to take another deep breath. He hurried into the study, pulled back the drapes, and opened two large casement windows. Leaning out, he breathed some more smog. He could feel a strong draft from the East River rushing in from the opened front door.

He shut off the desk lamp and went back to the front door. Hank's body was gone, and the neighborhood was as still as a crematorium at dawn.

And dawn wasn't far away. He glanced at his watch, barely able to see the hands in the dim light from the street lamp about sixty feet down the block. 4:10 A.M.

Estimating that he had given the room long enough to ventilate, he closed the door and went back to the study. He switched on the desk lamp, locked the hall door, and sat down in Harp's swivel chair. He placed the Beretta on the desk. This time anyone who came through the door would be shot first and questioned later.

The plans were not in the bottom drawer. Only a stack of ledgers. Fortunately the small key opened all the drawers. He found the plans in the middle drawer on the right.

As he had guessed, Harp had documented the operation with military precision. He went through the sheaf of papers, scribbling in his notebook frantically, filling page after page with notes and small, rough drawings of Harp's diagrams and charts.

At 5:15 light was filtering in through the drapes, which he had not completely closed. He gathered up his notes, put the plans back in exactly the same order, locked all the drawers, then glanced carefully around. Everything in order. Close the windows and pull the drapes.

On the way to the windows his foot struck Hank's automatic, which had been lying unnoticed on the carpet. He was slipping. He picked it up with his handkerchief and carried it to the bookshelves. Kneeling before a floor-level shelf, he pulled out two thick and dusty volumes of Gibbon's *Decline and Fall of the Roman Empire* and shoved the pistol to the back of the shelf. He replaced the books and stood up. Harp was not likely to be browsing through the *Decline and Fall* during the next few days. He then quickly shut the windows and closed the drapes.

He locked the door, turned on the burglar

alarm, and crept back upstairs to his suite, where he undressed quickly and fell into bed, first making certain that the Beretta and his notes were snugly hidden under his pillow.

His nerves were too taut to allow sleep. He lay there exhausted, half-dozing, his senses as alert as those of a wounded animal waiting for an attack.

Isabel brought up his breakfast at eight o'clock. Harp came in almost on her heels.

"Has Hank been up here?" he asked MacInnes.

Grumpily MacInnes said, "No," and leaned to pour himself a cup of coffee.

"I wonder where in hell he's gone."

MacInnes stared at him blankly, bad temperedly, as though saying, "How in hell would I know, locked in this damned suite?"

Harp glanced quickly into the bathroom, then opened the doors of both closets, giving MacInnes an apologetic look. Then he left, muttering to himself.

Alone, MacInnes found himself eating his bacon and eggs ravenously. It had been a hard night. After he had cleaned up all the toast and rolls he poured himself more coffee, lit a cigarette, and picked up the copy of the *New York Times* Isabel had left with his tray.

A front-page item caught his eye, causing him to spill coffee from the cup on its way to his lips. Crispin was speaking at Madison Square Garden *tomorrow night!* A week and a half before the date he had estimated. He had a few seconds of panic. He'd have to get the plans to his friends late tonight. Then a surge of wild elation ran through him. The goddamned job was almost over.

Panic returned. Today, tonight, sometime before tomorrow, he would be scheduled for termination. A terminal termination. He finished the coffee, his hand shaking slightly. He lit another cigarette.

Break the window and blow the whistle!

Calm down, you chickenshit bastard, he told himself. He swallowed two 5-milligram Valium tablets and sat waiting for them to take hold. Euphoria gradually crept over him. Slipping the automatic and his notes into the pockets of his robe, he locked himself in the bathroom to shower and shave.

He dressed slowly, slacks, open-neck shirt, jacket, loafers, accompanied by a careful distribution of weaponry. Transferring his keys to the chain holding the unused marble square, he dropped it in his left jacket pocket and tucked the spent number in one of his suitcases. Automatic in right jacket pocket. The two deadly pens he clipped into his shirt pocket. Notes in inside jacket pocket. Whistle, cigarettes, handkerchief, billfold, and his small container of Valium tablets went into his trouser pockets.

He turned on the "Today Show" and sat seeing and hearing nothing. Isabel brought him lunch, but fifteen minutes later he couldn't have told you what he had eaten.

He was desperately drowsy but didn't dare

sleep. Sleep would leave him vulnerable to a quick injection or a crack on the skull with a blunt instrument. Later, at night, into the limousine he would go, off to the river in a pair of concrete overshoes. Harp would send Morris to dispatch him. Perhaps Morris and the chauffeur. Not good. Two's company and three's a crowd.

He occupied his mind memorizing Harp's plans. Spend your last hours on earth doing something constructive.

Late in the afternoon Harp came up to see him, alone. He was looking worried but did not mention Hank's disappearance.

Sinking into a chair near MacInnes, he said, "Well, mate, as you have undoubtedly read in the newspaper, our job is just about finished. And I know you'll be delighted to know that *your* job is completed."

MacInnes forced a smile.

"So it's back to the beauteous Vanessa and a resumption of your carefree life. I hope this job has helped lift your depression."

MacInnes said, "Oh it *has*." If he lived to enjoy it.

"Good." Harp reached in his pocket and brought out a thickly filled envelope. "Our agreement was for sixty days, and while we're eleven days short of that, I am of course paying you in full." He handed the envelope to MacInnes. "You'll find 60 one-thousand-dollar bills. Count them, please."

MacInnes attempted to look grateful. He glanced into the envelope, took out the stack of notes, and riffled them briefly. "No need to count. I know you wouldn't cheat me." He replaced the money and stuck the envelope into his inside jacket pocket.

Harp chuckled. "Your trust is touching. But I really wish you would count them."

MacInnes shook his head, smiling.

Harp said, "We're evacuating these premises early in the morning. I've arranged for you to leave tonight."

MacInnes said to himself, *I was afraid of that.*

"I have reserved a suite for you at the Rye Town Hilton, which is some thirty miles from New York. Morris will drive you out there tonight. I suggest you stay out of Manhattan until the clamor dies down. Why don't you join your friend in Martha's Vineyard? You can rent a car up at the Hilton and drive on to Massachusetts."

MacInnes said, "That's a great idea." Harp sounded so sincere that Kevin almost believed him. However, they wouldn't let him go until the job was completed if Harp was on the level. He hoped Morris wouldn't bring company.

Harp stood up and held out his hand. "It's been a pleasure working with you. I hope our paths cross again someday."

MacInnes shook hands, smiling.

"Can you have your gear all packed by nine o'clock?"

"Sure."

Harp left with a small wave of his hand.

MacInnes, who had stood up to shake hands, sat down with an idiotic smile on his face. The irony of his position struck him. He had been feeling vaguely guilty about his two-faced role, his betrayal of Harp. In books agents somehow never had to smile, agree, play a despicable part, never had to be the false friend who slipped a knife into you while you slept. In books the agent rushes about gathering information tight-lipped and heroic. The enemy literally thrusts information upon him while he remains sturdily uncommitted.

The agent in books never kills first, with a lethal pen or squirt of poison gas. He waits until the enemy has half-killed *him*. Then, with both arms yanked loose from their sockets by torture, the agent kicks the enemy to death.

He chuckled, with a touch of hysteria in it, because he had difficulty stopping. Harp was sending him off to be executed, and MacInnes had been feeling uncomfortable about betraying Harp. Childhood conditioning dies hard, if at all.

If he lived, he would donate Harp's sixty thousand to a fund for indigent families of agents who were too clean and forthright to shoot first. But since they existed only in books, he supposed he would have to find some other worthy charity. Admittedly, he was too much of a Boy Scout himself to keep the money.

Morris loaded MacInnes's equipment and luggage into the trunk of a big old Chrysler Imperial. Harp probably didn't want to get the limousine all bloody. At least the car had clear glass windows.

With an ice cube in his chest, MacInnes saw that they were going to have company. The redhaired chauffeur was at the wheel.

"We might as well all get up front. Plenty of room," said Morris, offering MacInnes the center seat.

MacInnes opened the right rear door. "I'll sit back here. I like to stretch out." He climbed in and wedged himself in the right-hand corner.

Morris said, "In that case, I'll join you." He opened the left side and slid in, keeping his distance from MacInnes.

MacInnes slipped his right hand into his jacket pocket, curling his fingers around the butt of the automatic. With his thumb he flicked the safety off. Then he adjusted his jacket so that the pistol was pointing directly at Morris. They might kill him, but he was sure of one thing—Morris Noname was going with him.

The garage door opened, and they were on their way.

"I hear the Rye Town Hilton is a pretty nice place," said MacInnes.

"Yeah," said Morris.

What do you converse with your executioner about? The weather, the Mets? Chimpanzees who learn to speak sign language? Visitors from outer space? He had had a number of evenings out on the town with Morris and had found conversation with him almost impossible. In fact, the evenings became so boring that MacInnes preferred to stay in and read. Even the gourmet meals were not worth it, particularly when his companion demanded a bottle of ketchup and sloshed it on everything. MacInnes had a mental image of an enraged chef out in the kitchen spitting in their soup.

They drove along in silence. Up the East River Drive, across the Triborough Bridge, and on to the turnpike to Westchester.

At Rye, where they should have turned off for the Hilton, the chauffeur switched to the Cross Westchester parkway headed for the Tappan Zee Bridge, which spanned the Hudson River. A very high dive, if that's what they had in mind. Impractical. Fairly heavy traffic on the Tappan Zee.

MacInnes started to call to their attention that they were now speeding away from the Rye Hilton, then thought better of it. He'd make the first move when the time came, but he wasn't sure this was the right moment.

The chauffeur took the turnoff for Brewster. Lonely country up there. Roads that wound around for miles with nothing in sight.

MacInnes decided he preferred more heavily populated areas.

"Morris," he said, pointing his jacket pocket at Morris's chest, "I have a very lethal automatic in my pocket aimed right at your chest. Tell that monkey to turn off and head back to the Rye Hilton before I give you a heart unplant."

Morris giggled, reaching for his holster. He said to the chauffeur, "He thinks he can con me with the old rigid-digit-in-the-pocket trick."

"Last warning, Morris," said MacInnes. He squeezed off two quick shots, blowing hell out of his jacket pocket. Morris's .45 tumbled to the floor. Morris belched blood copiously down his chest as he fell back into his corner.

The chauffeur glanced back, then hastily turned to the front. He was traveling about eighty.

MacInnes picked up Morris's pistol and stuck it in his belt. Then he untangled the Beretta from his tattered pocket and stuck the barrel against the chauffeur's neck. "Slow down and turn off, dammit. We're going back to Rye."

The chauffeur pressed harder on the gas. The speedometer rolled up to ninety. He said, "Shoot me, man, and we're both dead."

"Slow up, you crazy bastard!"

The speedometer moved to ninety-five.

"What's the matter with you?" yelled MacInnes.

"Throw both pistols up here, man, or I'll kill us both."

The speedometer climbed to one hundred.

The damned Chrysler would probably do a hundred and twenty. There were curves on the Brewster parkway that wouldn't even take ninety.

"You'll get it you son of a bitch!" yelled MacInnes. "A thousand pounds of engine right in your face!"

"Shit on you!"

"Back seat walks away!" yelled MacInnes, "You hear me, *back seat walks away*! He wished he could believe it. He tried to lean past the driver and turn off the ignition. The driver moved his thick body to block MacInnes.

"Throw both pistols up here!" he yelled.

The speedometer rose to a hundred and five.

The bastard was insane or bluffing with a manic game of chicken typical of one of Harp's combat infantrymen. Rage built up in MacInnes. The son of a bitch wasn't going to bluff him. He slashed wildly at the driver's fat neck with the barrel of his automatic, the sight gouging out a thick ridge of blood. "Slow down or I'm going to blow your goddamned head off!"

The speedometer held steady on a hundred and five.

MacInnes bent over the back of the front seat and shot the driver in the right kneecap. He wouldn't be pressing that frigging gas pedal down very long now!

The chauffeur ripped out a shriek of pain. Holding the steering wheel with his left hand, he reached for his own pistol with his right. MacInnes slammed the butt of his automatic down on the hand before it reached the holster.

The sharp thunder clap of an exploding tire sounded, and the two-and-a-half-ton car started to career wildly. The driver struggled to hold the wheel with his left hand. The Chrysler veered crazily from side to side, then headed straight for a concrete abutment. MacInnes dived for the floor.

Ripping metal screeched as the side of the car scraped and bounced, then headed straight into a solid wall. The crash rang out with the sound of a hundred garbage cans being struck by a diesel locomotive.

The reverberations died down, and there was silence. Then the Chrysler's horn, shorted by the impact, started up a shockingly loud moan, like a dying man at the mike of a rock amplifier.

MacInnes lay in the back, literally covered with blood.

A car pulled up, brakes squealing. In a moment, men began to pry at the crumpled metal.

"Christ what a mess," said a voice.

"Looks like MacInnes has had it," said another.

"I'm okay," said MacInnes.

The blood covering him was Morris's blood. Fate had tossed Morris in front of him like a pillow, and Morris had been cut in half. The driver, who had the engine in his lap, was an unrecognizable mass of bloody pulp.

They extracted MacInnes. He stood up. He walked up and down the grass verge. He was whole and unhurt. "Back seat walks away!" he yelled, and began to laugh hysterically.

The intern put his hand on MacInnes's shoulder. "Take it easy, man, you're fine."

MacInnes turned, recognizing him. "Doc, what the hell is your name? I want to shake your hand." He held out his bloody hand. He was drunk with the knowledge of being alive.

"Ron Cohen," said the agent, clasping MacInnes's hand, blood and all.

The other agent, a tall Irishman with curly black hair, said, "I've got to stop that horn. It's driving me up the wall."

The state police sirened up, one squad car following another.

Ron Cohen and the other agent, Tom Bascomb, had a short conference with the occupants of the two squad cars, producing identification. MacInnes stood by smoking, still giddy with half-hysterical euphoria.

They opened the Chrysler's almost undamaged

trunk compartment and transferred MacInnes's luggage to Ron Cohen's Buick. In forty-five minutes he was back in a suite at the Lombardy.

MacInnes stood under a hot shower and scrubbed Morris's blood away.

He put on fresh clothes and went out to the living room. A bottle of Scotch had appeared. The two agents had drinks in front of them and were studying MacInnes's notes.

Cohen looked up. "We thought you could use a drink."

"That was good thinking." MacInnes poured himself a healthy two fingers.

Cohen said, "We're trying to decide whether to take Harp tonight or wait and see whether he tries to go through with it." He lifted his glass. "In any event, Jim O'Connor agrees that we should reassure him. He may take off in a panic when Morris doesn't return."

MacInnes sat down. He was mentally weary and physically exhausted. He couldn't imagine how they would reassure Harp.

Cohen picked up the telephone and gave the operator a number. When it answered he said, "This is Sergeant Sullivan of the Westchester County Police. Are you Mr. Harp?"

There was a silence while Harp spoke.

"Your name is Timothy Nolan? Do you have anyone named Harp living there? You see, we've had a very bad vehicular crash on Route 684. All three occupants of the car are dead, but one of them we've identified as Morris Brown said 'Harp' and gave this phone number before he died."

There was another pause while Cohen listened. "Do you have any acquaintances named Morris Brown, Fred Reagan, or Kevin MacInnes?"

Cohen waited, then said, "I see. Thank you. Sorry to have disturbed you."

Cohen replaced the phone, smiling. "Never heard of any of you. We must have one of the digits in the phone number wrong."

MacInnes said, "I don't think he'll abort. He's got a million bucks tied up in this thing, and if he's confident that I'm dead . . ." He paused. "Incidentally, I assume there really is a Sergeant Sullivan who knows that I'm supposed to be dead? Harp will check."

"There is, and he does," said Cohen.

Cohen had a long telephone conversation with Jim O'Connor. It was decided to keep the house staked out and opt for rounding up the whole crew tomorrow evening. MacInnes would accompany them. If Harp was disguised, MacInnes would stand a better chance than anyone else of recognizing him.

MacInnes took two Valium tablets and went to bed.

CHAPTER TWENTY-THREE

MADISON SQUARE GARDEN was born almost a hundred years ago on the site of an abandoned railway station at Madison Square. Eventually it moved and became a shabby, vast arena at 50th Street and Eighth Avenue, where for many decades it offered major sports events, housed political conventions, and thrilled millions of New York children with the annual visit of the Ringling Brothers circus. Now it's back at a railway station—on top of one, in fact. In spite of the efforts, or lack of efforts, of the Landmarks Preservation Commission, the developers demolished Pennsylvania Station and perched a gigantic complex of tall glass box skyscrapers and the new Madison Square Garden right over the tracks, driving railway travelers completely underground.

From the street level this new round Garden looks like a macro version of an avant-garde church or synagogue. From the air it becomes a phallic symbol, attached as it is to a tall, slender glass skyscraper.

Placed in the heart of a seedy, declining neighborhood, these glittering buildings stand out like a bejeweled film star at a Salvation Army Thanksgiving Day dinner.

The site of Harp's operational plan was 31st Street. The Garden seats only 20,000, and Crispin's followers in New York numbered in the hundreds of thousands, if not millions. Loudspeakers were installed along Seventh Avenue and 31st Street so that the overflow crowd could hear Crispin's speech. Seventh Avenue was to be closed to vehicular traffic from 28th to 36th Streets, and no cars would be allowed on 31st Street from Seventh to Eighth Avenues. Thousands of people would pack wide Seventh Avenue for eight blocks, and narrow 31st Street as tightly as police barricades would allow.

Opposite the Garden on 31st Street, going from Seventh Avenue to Eighth, are a series of comparatively low buildings, some ancient, some new. An out-of-business cafeteria, one and a half stories, the Capuchin monastery, three stories, a six-story parking garage with walls of open metal filigree. The parking garage is directly across from the 31st Street vehicular entrances and exits of the Garden. Next to the garage is a small open parking lot, then an abandoned building, a bar, a travel agency, a store for rent, an upstairs barbershop with a coffee shop on the first floor, and at the corner of Eighth Avenue, another large restaurant and bar.

Harp, who had somehow managed to obtain the senator's plans, knew that after his speech Crispin planned to leave on foot via the vehicular entrance. He was to walk east on 31st Street, behind police barricades, of course, continuing around to the plaza, where he would give an impromptu talk to the throngs on Seventh Avenue, shaking hands with well-wishers on the way.

For two days a panel truck had been parked on the second level of the garage, backed up to the filigreed wall facing the Garden's vehicular exit. The truck was empty, and that's the way the police would find it when they checked the area. Its floor was cleverly and unnoticeably raised, with the bottom lowered, to provide a concealed lying-down space for Alpha, the marksman. If the plan was in effect, Alpha had been lying in his hideaway for hours. Bravo was scheduled to be at the barricades.

Both gunmen were to use Lugers, with identical cross-hatched, lead-jacketed bullets that would spread on impact, destroying any ballistic markings. Alpha's Luger was fitted with an extended barrel and a telescopic sight for more deadly accuracy.

After dispatching Crispin, Alpha would rush to the roof of the garage. There Charlie and Delta would be waiting with scaling ropes. Working as a team, they would descend from the back of the

garage to the roof of a building facing 30th Street,
then cross two more roofs to an empty store Harp
had rented. Inside the store, they had only to wait
for the limousine, driven by Fox, to get to the
door.

Harp had estimated six and a half minutes for
the entire operation. If Bravo created the confusion they expected him to create, the police would
be concentrating on 31st Street long enough to
allow a clean escape. The back of the parking
garage was, of course, in no way visible from 31st
Street.

It was obvious from his assigned role that Bravo
would be the patsy black. Who were Alpha, Charlie, Delta, and Foxtrot? Whatever his role, Harp
would be somewhere on the scene, in command.

MacInnes and Ron Cohen decided the most
likely place to take Harp would be on the roof. If
he was acting as Alpha the marksman, as a last-
minute substitute, say, for Morris, he would probably exit by that route when he discovered that
Crispin wasn't leaving his bullet-proof limousine
this evening. Police were hidden in an ambulance
parked directly across from the panel truck. If he
got past them, Cohen and MacInnes would tackle
him on the roof, along with, they hoped, Charlie
and Delta, his two fellow mountain climbers. If he
tried to exit via 31st Street, police were waiting
there. If he got past MacInnes and Cohen, police
were hidden in the empty store. Harp was sur-
rounded.

The roof was best, they decided, because it was
likely that Harp might be heading the rescue team,

as either Charlie or Delta.

The black would be easy to pick up. There were not many blacks among Crispin's admirers crowding 31st Street.

Since midafternoon, MacInnes and Cohen had been sitting in a large toolbox in one corner of the rear of the garage roof. Hastily drilled eye holes provided coverage of the entire back edge of the roof. Utilized for open-air parking, the roof had a protective four-foot wall of concrete, extending around the four sides and faced with filigreed metal on the outside.

Surveillance of anything but the roof edge was difficult, because the roof was filled with parked cars. Parkers knew, however, that 31st Street would not be open to traffic again until 11:30 P.M., so there was no movement of cars in or out.

They had talked for a while in whispers. MacInnes was beginning to think he had guessed wrong. The unexplained disappearance of Hank was the flaw that would cause Harp to call it off.

Cohen said, "You haven't been reading the *Times* carefully. There was an item about one Henry Grebs being found on the sidewalk of 81st Street, dead of a heart attack."

Now they had been silent for a long time, uncomfortable in the cramped quarters, bored, yet taut with nervous tension. An edge of MacInnes's former depression settled on him. What the hell was he doing here? Still, it was better than the role he had been playing. Judas to the Prince of Darkness. That was a laugh. Harp, the Prince of Darkness. He and Harp were brothers under the skin. Cold-blooded killers who could strike without warning. Exterminators, Harp exterminating for money and MacInnes through some blundering idea of justice and self-defense but motivated by an ego that was perhaps warped and should not be examined too closely.

And the truth machine? How long could a man go on playing truth and consequences? After tonight the Lie King would return in all his former glory. He could see the headlines. "Lie King Thwarts Crispin Assassination Attempt." Presbyterians and B. F. Skinner believed in predestination, arriving at the theory spiritually in one case and through the mechanics of scientific inquiry in the other. Maybe it was simply his destiny to go on being the truth man.

Be it resolved that the truth shall no longer make you rich, MacInnes. You are rich enough. From this night on you will ply your trade only for the benefit of humanity. You will free the innocent and trap the guilty and never, never, under any circumstances, offer a wild-assed guess.

Crispin's speech continued on and on, too loud, punctuated with static and speaker distortion and interruptions of frantic cheering and applause.

It finally ended. A thunderous roar reverberated up and down the streets, live voices and hands joining with those electronically amplified. The band presumptuously struck up "Hail to the Chief."

Though the parking lot roof was lighted, the

lighting was minimal, sufficient only to find a particular car and drive it down the ramp. The back
edge was in shadows. Cohen and MacInnes
strained to keep the entire length in view. If anything was going to happen, it would happen very
soon.

Somewhere below two sharp cracks resounded,
then two more. Alpha rising from his coffin?

A barely visible figure hoisted himself over the
wall about fifty feet away and immediately
dropped to the blacktop, disappearing into the
shadow made by the wall. Another followed and
was also immediately sucked into the blackness.

Cohen threw the lid up, and they climbed out
silently, lowering the cover slowly without a
sound. They crouched, automatics drawn and
waited.

They could hear the rustle of movement as
someone on rubber soles made his way through
the cars. In seconds he was briefly silhouetted
against the sky near the rear wall.

There was a loud whisper. "Sssst, over here."

The figure moved down the wall.

Crouching, Cohen and MacInnes moved
quickly between the cars until they were in line
with the climbers.

Cohen yelled, "All right men, throw your
weapons over here and lie facedown! You're sur-
rounded!"

There was a flash and a whip-crack of an automatic from the blackness under the wall. A window of the car MacInnes was crouching next to
shattered.

Cohen yelled, "Try to go over the wall and

you're dead. There are five Thompson submachine guns trained on you. We'll cut you in two!''

Three more shots clattered, all followed instantly by metallic clangs as they struck the car next to Cohen.

"Bring up those lights, men!" yelled Cohen.

Where in hell were the lights? They were supposed to follow Alpha within thirty seconds.

Cohen and MacInnes crawled closer. MacInnes fired tentatively at the spot where the last flashes had appeared. His own flash brought a volley that riddled the car a foot above his head.

They crawled closer. Why weren't reinforcements arriving? Surely the goddamned idiots below could hear the firing up on the roof?

The three men had spread out. The flashes were fifteen and twenty feet apart. Obviously they were moving around the wall for a flank attack.

Wait it out. As long as they didn't go over the wall, they couldn't get away. And even if they went over, they couldn't get away. Or could they?

"Watch it," whispered Cohen, "They may be coming at us from the rear."

MacInnes saw a shadow moving on his right and squeezed off a quick shot. There was a shriek of pain and a soft thud.

"You got one," whispered Cohen. "Where in hell are the other two?"

Harp was behind them, looming up out of the shadows.

"All right, coppers, throw your weapons over here and lie facedown!" he yelled, laughing maniacally.

Cohen whirled and fired. Harp was faster.

Cohen patted at his chest as though trying to brush away some mud, then collapsed on his face.

MacInnes fired almost instantaneously with Harp's shot. Harp clutched his belly, dropping to his knees. He crawled toward MacInnes, holding his .45 steady.

"I'm going to kill you with my own bare hands, you fucking shit-faced traitor," he yelled, then unleashed a stream of Liverpudlian obscenity so garbled that is sounded like a foreign language.

MacInnes fired again, tearing away part of Harp's face.

Harp sank to the ground, the .45 still steady. "MacInnes, you son of a bitch, you're going with me."

MacInnes hesitated. He had already killed Harp twice. Did he have to kill him three times? He fired and missed.

One-eyed, Harp was squeezing off a shot with slow deliberation.

The impact knocked MacInnes backward, fiery pain in his chest spreading like a scald through his body. He rolled and felt the cool asphalt against his face.

Vanessa was only a hazy apparition. Through the mist there seemed to be tears on her cheeks. He heard her say, "Kevin, *fight*. The doctor says you're going to die if you don't fight."

It was hard to breathe. The pain was heavy—drug-numbed and frightening. He was hovering on the brink of consciousness, somehow aware that only a small nudge could send him spinning into oblivion.

"Kevin, don't leave me. I need you. Please."
Her voice was tremulous, and the last word was a
small shriek of pain.

In the haze there were two Vanessas. They
blended together to become one, then separated to
become two again.

He fought to breathe.

"Kevin, I *need* you."

"Why?" It was more of a gasp than a word.

"I love you."

Love. An inconstant thing. Ephemeral. But
need, that was something solid. It was worthwhile
for her to *need* him.

"What," he whispered, "can I do?"

She bent over him. "Try. Fight." She kissed
him on the lips gently, barely brushing his flesh, as
though fearful that the pressure of her lips might be
more than the raw wound of his body could bear.

The pain was still a heavy weight in his chest,
but it was less frightening. He was the little train
that could. Puff, puff, puff. He reminded himself
that a man shouldn't joke when he might be dying.
Dying was a very serious business.

She clasped his hand, holding it against her
cheek, then kissing it. Wasn't Morris's blood on it?
No, he had washed it off. But it was a nasty hand
for her to be kissing.

"All right, dammit, I'll try."

Breathe in, exhale. Breathe in, exhale. Breathe
in, exhale. It was easier when you got the hang of
it.

The MS READ-a-thon needs young readers!

Boys and girls between 6 and 14 can join the MS READ-a-thon and help find a cure for Multiple Sclerosis by reading books. And they get two rewards — the enjoyment of reading, and the great feeling that comes from helping others.

Parents and educators: For complete information call your local MS chapter, or call toll-free (800) 243-6000. Or mail the coupon below.

Kids can help, too!

Mail to:
National Multiple Sclerosis Society
205 East 42nd Street
New York, N.Y. 10017

I would like more information about the MS READ-a-thon and how it can work in my area.

MS
Mystery
Sleuth

Name_____
(please print)

Address_____

City_____ State_____ Zip_____

Organization_____

MS-ACE